His new business partner wasn't exactly what he was expecting...

"Where is this Teddy Gamble?" Rhys Delmar asked as he got out of the stagecoach. His fine leather valise was singed by powder burns and shot through, along with its contents, by no less than three bullet holes. "I need to tell the man he'll be required to replace my entire wardrobe."

A lad in the crowd pointed.

Teddy Gamble, attired in fringed buckskin trousers and shirt, and with tightly laced leggings that rose to her knees, had her back to the Frenchman. Rhys looked at the slight form with the masculine clothes and assumed he had discovered the reason for the Gamble Stagecoach Line's shortcomings. Rhys stood and stared. Before he could voice his observations his friend Lucien put them into words.

"N'est-ce pas?" his manservant whispered. "This Monsieur Gamble has the look of an effete, a sissy."

"At best," Rhys said.

On top of the attack on the stage it was too much. Teddy spun around like a hot desert whirlwind.

"At worst," she said, eyes blazing, voice crackling. "I'm a gal who's got as much use for a pair of tinhorn, foreign, starched-shirts as I have for a pair of buzzards."

Rhys's gaze went to the swell of her breasts. "You are a woman!"

He could not have invited more trouble if he had lit a stick of dynamite and stuck it in his pocket.

"Well, thank you for clearing that up."

"Mademoiselle Gamble," he said, with the smooth, deep voice that had weakened many feminine knees. "My apologies. It seems we have gotten off to a bad start."

"You bet your ass we have."

... And that was only the beginning ...

TODAY'S HOTTEST READS
ARE TOMORROW'S SUPERSTARS

VICTORY'S WOMAN (4484, $4.50)
by Gretchen Genet

Andrew—the carefree soldier who sought glory on the battlefield, and returned a shattered man . . . Niall—the legandary frontiersman and a former Shawnee captive, tormented by his past . . . Roger—the troubled youth, who would rise up to claim a shocking legacy . . . and Clarice—the passionate beauty bound by one man, and hopelessly in love with another. Set against the backdrop of the American revolution, three men fight for their heritage—and one woman is destined to change all their lives forever!

FORBIDDEN (4488, $4.99)
by Jo Beverley

While fleeing from her brothers, who are attempting to sell her into a loveless marriage, Serena Riverton accepts a carriage ride from a stranger—who is the handsomest man she has ever seen. Lord Middlethorpe, himself, is actually contemplating marriage to a dull daughter of the aristocracy, when he encounters the breathtaking Serena. She arouses him as no woman ever has. And after a night of thrilling intimacy—a forbidden liaison—Serena must choose between a lady's place and a woman's passion!

WINDS OF DESTINY (4489, $4.99)
by Victoria Thompson

Becky Tate is a half-breed outcast—branded by her Comanche heritage. Then she meets a rugged stranger who awakens her heart to the magic and mystery of passion. Hiding a desperate past, Texas Ranger Clint Masterson has ridden into cattle country to bring peace to a divided land. But a greater battle rages inside him when he dares to desire the beautiful Becky!

WILDEST HEART (4456, $4.99)
by Virginia Brown

Maggie Malone had come to cattle country to forge her future as a healer. Now she was faced by Devon Conrad, an outlaw wounded body and soul by his shadowy past . . . whose eyes blazed with fury even as his burning caress sent her spiraling with desire. They came together in a Texas town about to explode in sin and scandal. Danger was their destiny—and there was nothing they wouldn't dare for love!

Available wherever paperbacks are sold, or order direct from the Publisher. Send cover price plus 50¢ per copy for mailing and handling to Penguin USA, P.O. Box 999, c/o Dept. 17109, Bergenfield, NJ 07621. Residents of New York and Tennessee must include sales tax. DO NOT SEND CASH.

This book is dedicated to the memory of my father, Major Albert Hugh Hudson, who died in Normandy, July 16, 1944, and affectionately to my aunts, Louise Gunnels, Elizabeth Doan, and Mary Veeda.

palms hot, throat filled with a lump, wished she could share his optimism. For her, the thump of her leather boot heels against the bone-dry boards of the sidewalk sounded like the ticking away of a clock.

Her father had hauled in the boards which now echoed the mocking sound of passing time. All the way from California, across the hot, treeless desert, so that Wishbone could have the civilized look of wooden storefronts and the luxury of sidewalks for its citizens.

Without Theodor Gamble's stage line and his initiative, Wishbone would be like any other of the dozens of settlements in the territory, filled with plain, squat adobe huts and dusty canvas tents. Without Theodor Gamble . . . She felt a tightening of the lump in her throat. Theodor Gamble was dead some three months now. Gone with no warning. A hemorrhage somewhere in his head the doctor had said. Nothing would have stopped it. Just as nothing would stop the demise of all her father had left in her hands unless she could stop what was already set in motion.

Deep in thought, she spun into the doorway of Penrod's. She nodded to Milt as she threaded past barrels of briny pickles, a mound of flour in muslin sacks, a brigade of shovels and picks, and the three newest prospectors in town. From the narrow room at the back of the store, the one Milt let out for an office to any who had a need, she detected the pungent aroma of pipe tobacco and heard the reverberation of male voices.

She hesitated a moment, listening until she identified the unexpected one. Another step brought her flush with the open door. Unnoticed by the men inside

One

August 1875

Theodora Gamble's time was running out.

That wasn't true for everyone in Wishbone, Arizona. Certainly not for the two towheaded and barefoot lads who strolled lackadaisically ahead of her on the narrow board sidewalk that fronted the two dozen buildings strutting proudly alongside the main street of Wishbone. Those two were in the midst of a carefree day of mischief and adventure. Certainly it was not true for the three men in city clothes who wobbled out of the First Strike Saloon headed for Penrod's Mercantile. They were new enough in the Arizona Territory to stare at a woman dressed in doeskin trousers, boots and spurs. The trio nevertheless lifted their hats as they would to any pretty lady. For those three, time was only beginning. They would be outfitting for an ambitious run at prospecting in the ore-filled hills above Wishbone.

From the open door of the mercantile store, Milt Penrod's merry whistle lilted out like the sweet song of a morning bird. He sounded like a man who felt he had all the time in the world. Theodora Gamble, she waited beyond the threshold until her eyes confirmed what her ears had told her. Cabe Northrop, whom she had expected to see alone, stood with his back to the door, clouding the room with smoke as he puffed his briar pipe. Northrop had once been a division supervisor for Wells Fargo but now was a special liaison between the heads of the company and the contract lines in Arizona. The man Northrop had been conversing with, a man half his size, a man who should not have been present, sat by the open window. That second man was Parrish Adams.

"What in all of hell is he doing here?" she asked, striding in like she owned the place. Behind her, the door—which she had given a forceful shove—banged shut, punctuating her query.

A square, scarred table, a few chairs, nearly took up the whole of the room. Northrop, nearly wide as the table, took up most of the rest of it. His bulk turned slowly toward her. Equally slowly he pulled the gnawed bit of the pipe from his mouth and frowned. His face was broad like the rest of him, and made to look more so by the flaxen mutton-chop whiskers lining his cheeks. "I asked him," he said, solemn-faced. "He's got an interest in this, Teddy."

"Not in my end of it."

"That's what I'm here to decide," Northrop retorted, florid skin brightening.

With his eyes as icy as her voice had been, Teddy removed her hat and slung it onto a wall peg as she simultaneously hooked the toe of her dust-covered boot under the low rung of a three-legged stool and dragged it from its resting place against the white-washed wall. Teddy Gamble—arms crossed, spine ramrod straight—perched on the rough round of wood that formed its top. Adams, his back to the opposite wall, acknowledged her with a small tip of his head.

Northrop planted his stocky legs wide apart. He allowed her a moment to settle herself as he racked the shank of his pipe on the edge of a tin coffee mug atop the table. The deep-set eyes, usually laughing, usually friendly, bored into her with a threatening look. "Don't go getting too big for your britches, Teddy. You got my letter. You know what this is about."

The letter. Teddy felt the telltale weight of it in the pocket over her heart. The letter warned that Wells Fargo was considering withdrawing the contract her father had won—that would spell the end of the Gamble Stage Line, should that happen.

Her chin snapped up and her cool voice gave no hint of her rising anxiety. "And in my reply I told you that contract stands as agreed."

"We made that contract with your father."

"You made that contract with the Gamble Line, my company," Teddy insisted. She didn't bother to mention that she only owned half. Her half ran the company and Cabe knew it well enough. He knew too that the wording of the freight contract negotiated by her father between the Gamble Stage Line and Wells Fargo clearly bound both parties regardless of who held ownership of the Gamble Line. Unless she failed to fulfill the terms of that contract, Wells Fargo had no legal right to terminate it. She had told Cabe exactly that, in her letter of reply. "A five-year contract with four to run," she hurried on. "And the option to renew. You know that, Cabe. You signed it yourself, you and my father on the kitchen table in his house."

Northrop's wide mouth remained tightly closed as he glanced down at the bowl of his pipe and saw that it had gone out. A minute passed as he pulled a match from a wooden box on the table and struck it on the grainy surface of the office wall. He relit the warm dottle in the pipe.

"Your father was unstoppable, Teddy," he said between slow puffs and draws. "The man didn't live who could back him down." Falling silent again he worked the pipe until it glowed red from the rim and spewed out a plume of white lunt. Through the feathery drifts he again leveled his eyes at her. "But you're not Theodor Gamble, Teddy."

"No. Nobody is," she admitted, shrugging off the bruising impact of his words and the indignation of having to defend herself in front of Parrish Adams. That alone was enough to scorch the hide off a rattler. "But he taught me well," came her measured words. "And he believed in me." She paused and drew a long breath to help hold onto her weakening control. " 'Keep the Gamble Line running, Teddy.' " Her eyes locked with Northrop's. "Those were his last words to me and I aim to do what he wanted."

The look of anger on Northrop's face broke as he hung his head. Teddy hoped she had touched a nerve, one that would sway him her way. Shortly before her father had died he'd invested every cent available to him in new stock and equipment for the Gamble Line. If she lost the line she lost the ranch, too, everything her father had built and been proud of. Legal rights there were, but she had no financial resources left to fight a company like Wells Fargo, should they set themselves against her. The only resource she did have was the memory of the once-strong bond of friendship between Cabe Northrop and her father. She couldn't afford to let Northrop forget about it.

She needed time. She would use anything she had to buy time, even sentiment. Sentiment might not carry her forever but it could secure her a grace period. Given more time, she could prove that the Gamble Line was as dependable as ever. She could fulfill the contract she had, and dare Wells Fargo to refuse her another when it was out. Her muscles tensed as tight as stone, damning the luck that had put her in this spot. Teddy wished for the thousandth time that she hadn't been born female. Had she been Theodor Gamble's son instead of his daughter, Cabe Northrop wouldn't be standing there doubting what she could do. He would know.

Unfortunately she had been born female and he did doubt. She saw the unmistakable signs. In spite of what he'd felt for her father, in spite of his fondness for her, he doubted Teddy Gamble. Skepticism, like a thick swirling cloud of dust, could obscure even the strongest conviction or commitment. Skepticism newly born was what she saw emerging in the deep-set eyes of Cabe Northrop.

She did not flinch before it even though, hidden behind her mask of self-assurance, her emotions whipped and whirled like the troubled winds of an impending storm. All she cared about, all that defined her as Theodora Gamble, all that held her life together hinged on what would be said next. She had pleaded her case as well as could be done in her answering letter—demanded what was rightfully her due, might better state the truth—and now the outcome rode on the decision of one man.

"Be damned." Northrop looked at Teddy, then looked away and began a harried pacing in the cramped room.

Teddy said nothing.

She could only half-blame Cabe for doubting her or for calling her down as he had a few minutes before. He wasn't the only one worried about the troubles that for the past three months had pursued her like a vengeful shadow. Whatever could go wrong had—twice over. She shared her father's name, she shared his dreams. No, she wasn't the indomitable Theodor Gamble as Cabe had so sharply pointed out. Not by a long shot. If she were, trouble or not, no agent of Wells Fargo, not even William Fargo, himself would have spoken to her as Cabe had.

Teddy sighed and, while Northrop shuffled the length of the room solemnly deliberating, cautiously allowed her gaze to settle on the immobile face of Parrish Adams. Throughout her exchange with Northrop he'd kept quiet, though somehow, by a slight move or marginal shifting of his weight, never letting her forget that he shared her humiliation. No more than eight feet from her, he rested, as if ensconced on a throne, in a newly made chair of horn and hide.

The distorted squares of light that spread from the uncovered window did not fall fully upon him but she could tell that he sat erect, arms casually linked over his chest. Eventually he moved a degree to the right, meeting her stare head-on. His face, like hers, was little more than a mask over feelings that must have been as intense as her own.

He was sizing her up anew, she guessed. She could imagine the legions of tenebrous thoughts at play in that deep, shrewd mind, but he was working hard at showing nothing that would reveal the nature of them or give away any emotion concerning what he'd witnessed.

He did not, however, successfully hide everything from her. A gleam from his eyes shone out in the dimness of the room and a twitch, quickly stilled, at one corner of his mouth hinted a brooding pleasure at her dilemma.

Teddy fumed within as the meaning of the gesture registered with her. She knew why he was there. What she didn't know was how successful he'd been in undermining her position with Northrop.

She was about to find out. A heavy sigh emanated from the portly Northrop, forewarning that he had come to a conclusion on the business at hand.

Two

"You'll have to prove yourself, Teddy," Northrop said, breaking the weighty silence. "It ain't usual for a woman to be responsible for the kind of shipments carried in these parts." He wiped his brow and the slick pate of his bald head, with a rumpled square of cambric pulled from his coat pocket. The gesture was a nervous one since sweat didn't last long enough to trickle down the skin in the dry desert air. Still Northrop mopped as if he must stop a flood. Giving Teddy Gamble a warning was a distasteful duty. He liked the girl, he'd watched her grow up. Her father had been a friend of long standing—a man whose word was as honorable as any in the good book.

"The Gamble Line hasn't lost a shipment yet," Teddy retorted. "Or had a delay worse than what a broken axle might have caused." She regretted the lingering note of hostility in her voice. She ought to show gratitude, or be pouring out her thanks. But seeing Adams from the corner of her eye was enough to keep the rancor churning inside her.

Northrop folded the wilted handkerchief and stuffed it into the pocket from which it had come. A moment lapsed as he seemed to weigh her words. "Not yet," he said, recalling the incidents that had prompted him to journey to Wishbone. Admittedly, Teddy was right. Only, he had to remember that what had happened to date was not the whole of the issue. New mines had opened north of Wishbone, and the Gamble Line had the lucrative job of hauling dust and bullion to the agency office in Yuma. Teddy was counting on the new revenue to make up the debt her company carried. His superiors at Wells Fargo were concerned about making up the huge losses, should she fail to deliver the shipments. His job was to head off problems. "But you've had troubles since you took over." His voice got stronger as he thought of the charge Wells Fargo had given him. He was to assess the situation and find a way to break the Gamble contract if he felt conditions warranted it.

"A few," Teddy agreed.

"Four attacks in a scant three weeks, make for worry, Teddy. You can't blame us for wanting to be sure a good record's not about to change," he said stiffly. Like her or not he had to think of the company first, where business was concerned. Teddy needed to understand that he'd cut her no slack because she was female and neither would the holdup men. He wanted her to succeed. He knew the gravity of her need to keep the Gamble Line running. He also knew that the risk he was taking for the sake of his old friend's daughter could cost him dearly if he proved wrong.

Teddy gritted her teeth and shot Northrop a hard look. "I don't blame you."

The glance she gave Parrish Adams said differently. She blamed him plenty. A month after her father's death he'd shown up in Wishbone and offered to buy her out so he could add the Gamble Line's mail and express contracts to his own fledgling line. He hadn't taken her refusal to sell with anything resembling grace. Afterwards the holdup attempts had come regularly. While her skilled drivers and shotgun messengers hadn't lost an express box yet, one driver had been winged and everyone making the runs was nervous.

Teddy couldn't prove Parrish Adams had any connection to the failed holdups. But she was willing to bet her boots that he, at the very least, cheered on whoever was giving her grief. She took a little comfort in knowing that Cabe Northrop was wise enough not to have been swayed by what must have been a splendid statement of Adams's ability to do a better job with the routes out of Wishbone.

"Glad to hear you've got no hard feelings, Teddy," Northrop said, pulling a pair of thick-lensed glasses from a satchel and hooking them on his nose and ears. "You keep those deliveries on schedule and the contract is yours as long as you want it. That's fair, ain't it?"

"It'll do," Teddy said. "I don't expect any more consideration from Wells Fargo than my father did. Or any less," she added loud and clear. "The Gamble Line will run like it always has—without a shipment lost."

Northrop made several notations in a journal, blotted the page, then tucked it in the satchel. He turned to Adams. "Mr. Adams, Wells Fargo appreciates your offer to assume the Gamble Line's contracts but you've heard Miss Gamble's assurances that her company will continue to meet its commitments."

Adams cleared his throat. "I'm sure Miss Gamble has every intention of doing as she has indicated," he remarked to Northrop. His smile was smooth and easy, his manners polished and polite, his voice had the sound of gravel crunched underfoot. "Nevertheless, I want you to know my offer still stands should things change." His quick nod to Teddy had an air of self-assurance. "Miss Gamble may feel differently once she's been at this business a little longer and experienced more of the uncertainties and hardships in a man's work. You remember, Mr. Northrop, that I am prepared, at a moment's notice, to extend the routes of Adams Overland to include this area."

"I'll relay that information to my superiors," Northrop said rising. Glad to be finished with his unpleasant chore, he stuck out an arm and shook Parrish Adams's hand. "Good day, Mr. Adams." He cut short the hug he had for Teddy when he found her shoulders tight and resistant. "A word of advice, Teddy." With his broad back turned to Adams he spoke softly. "Get your Uncle Zack back here to help run the line. What happens won't be up to me the next time there are questions raised about your capabilities."

Teddy opened her mouth to retort that Zachary Gamble's help would just about equal that she'd received from the holdup gang. Instead she said, "I'll think about that, Cabe." Few people knew that her Uncle Zack's decision to leave Wishbone hadn't been entirely voluntary. She preferred to leave it that way.

"You do. And you tell your grandmother I'm sorry

I missed one of those delightful suppers of hers," he stated hurriedly. "I'll be expecting an invitation next time I'm in Wishbone."

"You'll get it." Teddy told Northrop good-bye but didn't follow him out of the smoky confines of the office. She had a few things she wanted to say to Parrish Adams now that she'd been granted something of a reprieve. She wanted to let him know she wasn't so foolish as not to be looking for whoever was behind the calamities that had befallen the Gamble Line. He must have sensed her wishes because he too delayed after Northrop was gone.

"I shoot sidewinders," she said.

"Are you threatening me, Miss Gamble?"

Adams shifted so that the light fell on his face. A smile came slowly to his thin lips, rounding lean cheeks smooth from a recent barbershop steam and shave. Had Teddy been able to find any inkling of honesty in his dark eyes she'd have called him a handsome man. He had all else it took—thick black hair spattered just so with gray, a precisely trimmed and exquisitely waxed mustache, a firm square jaw, a form fit and trim inside a starched shirt and collar and a suit miraculously unwrinkled even in the heat of midday. But Teddy found an insidious look to the man that negated any attractiveness he had. She couldn't see past it to find anything likable about Adams, even if she had nothing but instinct to back up her opinion.

"I am telling you how I deal with snakes," she said matter-of-factly. "I kick over every rock and when I see a sidewinder I shoot him."

Adams stood, casting an elongated shadow in the grid of amber light from the room's sole window. "I can see how that might work for a while, Miss Gamble. For a while. Eventually though there will be a sidewinder you don't see. And that one will get his way." He moved menacingly toward her. "I know I always do. Always. You keep that in mind—when running a business you're not cut out for, gets too burdensome for you." A strange twist of his lips contorted his smile. "And you remember that I can afford to wait. Unlike you I don't have to prove my ability to anyone. Adams Overland has never been held up." Slowly, he looped his thumbs into the pockets of a plum silk vest, starting the heavy gold links of a watch chain swaying against the rich fabric. "So, Miss Gamble, all I have to do is sit back and wait for you to fail. And you will fail. And I will get those contracts, eventually."

Teddy had meant to say more, to tell him she intended to find the men responsible for the holdups and who they worked for. As the damning words formed in her mind, she noted that Adams looked exactly like a hungry coyote poised and waiting for a wounded prey to give up the fight. If she guessed right, the man wanted to rattle her, and force her to say or do something she would regret. She would not give him the satisfaction—not if she had to chew her tongue off. And she would have to, if she didn't get away from the man quickly.

Rising briskly she snatched her hat from the peg that held it, then plopped it on her head. "No, Mr. Adams, you will be a disappointed man. You see I never," she said methodically, "turn my back on a sidewinder. Those I can't see I can always smell."

"Time will tell," came his reply as she stormed out of the office and across the clean swept plank floor of the Mercantile Company without bothering to acknowledge Milt Penrod. He stood conveniently close to the office door dusting a row of canned goods with a folded corner of his white apron.

Outside, Teddy threw her hands toward the heavens and muttered a curse. Above her a pale wafer moon hung in the daylight sky. Last night, as she stood outside the ranch house unable to sleep, that same moon had been red as blood and laced over with dark, moving shadows—a devil moon. All her life her grandmother, Felicity Gamble, had told her such an occurrence bode change for those who looked on it. Sometimes good. Sometimes bad. Last night Teddy had looked hard. Today Cabe had changed his mind about putting her out of business. Now if the holdups would stop.

Distracted, she would have whisked by Horace Roper, her right-hand man in the company, had he not swiftly caught her by the arm.

"Dang, Teddy." He let go of her then turned his head and spat tobacco juice in the dust. "I saw Cabe Northrop runnin' for the stage like he had a war party after him. That skunk ain't pulled our contract, has he?"

"No, Rope." Teddy slowed her feet and forgot the foolishness about the moon. She fell in beside the broad-shouldered man as they walked down the street toward the stage stop. Horace Roper's face was like lined leather, and his eyes had the soft glow of old copper coins. Teddy loved that weathered face, appreciated the look of worry and affection in the kind eyes. In the same way as her father had done, Rope gave her a feeling of comfort and strength. She respected the tough old codger. She would be the first to admit that as company manager he was the major asset of the Gamble Line. Still she couldn't dredge up a smile for him as she relayed what had happened in the meeting with Northrop. "Cabe wants me to call Zack in to help run the company," she said.

"Hell take that long polecat." Rope shook his head then spat again. To his mind Zack Gamble had been an open wound the whole time he'd been a part of the Gamble Line. He for one wouldn't welcome the scoundrel back. "Shows how well he knows Zack Gamble." They walked a few paces more before Rope cocked a bristly brow and asked, "Is the contract ridin' on Zack comin' back?"

"No," she said. "Wells Fargo is honoring the contract as long as we deliver safe and on time."

"Well maybe Northrop ain't quite a skunk," Rope relented.

"Maybe not," Teddy agreed. "But I'd insult a skunk if I called Parrish Adams one."

"He was there?"

Teddy bobbed her head.

"Adams is a slick one that's for sure." Rope stepped up on the board sidewalk where the freight had been unloaded from the last stage. "Don't figure that a man could come into a town and in six months just about run it."

"It figures if you buy the sheriff." Teddy picked up a box and hoisted it on the back of a buckboard for deliveries around town. Rope hurriedly tossed the heavier cartons in beside it.

"Watch what you say, Teddy. Len Blalock ain't much pinned behind a badge but he's the only law in Wishbone. We got to depend on him with these hold-ups we've been havin'."

"The thing is, Rope, Adams could tell Len Blalock to pin that badge on his butt and Len would do it. He's no good to us." Teddy waved the buckboard driver off and pushed open the door of the small building that was the Gamble Line's headquarters. "Besides, I don't like having to watch what I say. I want a sheriff who stands for law and order, not one who clears it with Parrish Adams before he spits."

"Adams might pull out, now that he's seen he can't grab all he wants in Wishbone. He thought you'd leap like a jack rabbit at his offer to buy you out. He didn't expect a woman like . . ."

Rope trailed off, uncertain exactly how to proceed. Like what? The question hung uncomfortably heavy in his mind. Teddy Gamble was a woman sure as the sun came up every morning. The alluring swells and curves of her figure left no doubt of her sex. On the other hand she might as well have been a man for all the use she made of those lovely curves. He couldn't remember Teddy ever sporting a pretty dress or ever testing a man with those soft green eyes of hers. Just for a moment he wondered if Teddy ever thought about being female.

"Like me?" Teddy supplied an answer. "A woman with something besides ruffles and lace in her head?"

"I reckon," Rope conceded. "Anyhow he's learned there's at least one thing in Wishbone that ain't his for the takin'."

"I hope you're right," Teddy mumbled to herself.

Three

Rhys Delmar, having invested the whole of an afternoon in an endeavor of monumental importance to him, did not like the look on the face of the man who sat at cards with him. That ghostly pallor suggested either desperation or ill health. Either was likely to spoil his evening.

"Brandy perhaps, Monsieur Gamble?"

Rhys signaled for his man, Lucien, to bring the brandy. But before the servant lifted the silver serving tray with the crystal decanter and sparkling glasses, Zachary Gamble waved him back.

"Later, maybe," he said, his flat American drawl rolling out the words slower than usual. Never one to turn down a free drink, Zack Gamble for once could not abide the thought of consuming spirits of any kind. Damned English food. A man more accustomed to buffalo steaks and hardtack biscuits couldn't stomach such rich victuals without paying for his indulgence. He was paying royally now. He had a case of indigestion that was ripping into him like he'd swallowed a claw hammer.

"As you wish, *monsieur*. A smoke, perhaps?"

Zachary Gamble gave his head a firm shake. Acknowledging his refusal, Rhys opened a square wooden humidor with a lid of inlaid ivory and silver. Lucien had previously laid it upon the table. He removed a long slender cigar and with measured movement clipped the head with the blade of a silver cutter. By that time Lucien was at his side with a flaming match.

When the cigar was lit and Rhys had enjoyed several deep draws of the excellent tobacco, he opted for a glass of the brandy to accompany it. A flick of his hand motioned Lucien to serve him.

Lucien Bourget, for the third time, shuffled from his watchful post beside the rich maroon and gold silk window coverings. Dragging a leg lamed at a time when he had been waylaid by thugs, he moved slowly on the thick Persian carpet to the nearby drink table. There he poured generously from the lead glass decanter, savoring the smell of the fine brandy as it swirled like molten gold into the glass.

He would be equally generous with himself after his master retired. He had a feeling there would be cause to celebrate. The young master was doing well this evening. Success was welcome after a few lean weeks at the tables had left them with a purse so thin he had wondered how they would pay the rent on the rather sumptuous suite of rooms they had taken in London.

An imperceptible grin—no good servant could show his emotions in the midst of duty—flickered upon the dry line of Lucien's mouth. The matter of the rent, at least, was no longer of concern should the master lose or win. A week earlier, they had vacated the apartment in question. The rent on the present one, he was certain the master paid with regularity.

Rhys, without a nod or a backwards glance at Lucien, took the glass from the manservant's hand. Quietly he sipped his brandy, assessed his cards, and found both pleasing. The American, Monsieur Gamble, had won heavily the night before, from him and from the four others who made up the game. The man was skilled with the cards, artful even, but not as skilled as he was himself. Monsieur Gamble and those other gentlemen had not realized that Rhys had deliberately downplayed his talent at the game, nor had the vociferous American been wise enough to guess that tonight's solitary match had been planned to divest him of his earlier winnings.

Rhys Delmar's long deft fingers absently stroked the mounting stack of signed marks that had already slipped from Monsieur Gamble's side of the table to his own. He did not need to sum them up to know the total was close to ten thousand pounds. He had kept a running count in his head as the game progressed. Unless his information was wrong, which was unlikely—since he discreetly ferreted out an opponent's ability to pay before he sat down to play—there could not be much more remaining for the American to wager.

Zack Gamble looked at his cards and saw a dizzying blur of lines and numbers. Trying to focus his eyes, he blinked his heavy lids and took a ponderous breath, which shuddered painfully from his chest as he exhaled. His already-wan face blanched even whiter.

"How 'bout opening that window, you there." Zack

loosely waved an arm at Lucien. "A man could suffocate in one of these damned smoking rooms."

"You would like for me to put out my cigar, Monsieur Gamble?"

"Damned right I would," Zack grumbled. "If a man wants to smoke he ought to go to the out-of-doors."

Rhys hurriedly extinguished the fuming cigar he held between his fingers. "A thousand pardons, *monsieur*," he said. "Had I known . . ."

"Aw hell!" Regaining a bit of color in his cheeks, as fresh cool air rustled through the silk curtains and swept into the room, Zack waved his hand, cards and all, at Rhys. He didn't know what had gotten into him. Any other time he would have been smoking himself. He was fond of a good cigar, ordinarily. "Don't mind me," he apologized for his abruptness. "A man ought to smoke where he wants to, I reckon. After all it is your house."

"And you are a guest in my house, *monsieur*." His house. Hardly, Rhys thought. Borrowed rooms belonging to the Countess Clemenceau, a French "refugee" in London like himself. The countess was an aging confection of a woman with whom he had made a mutually beneficial agreement—one which he was not proud of, but one of necessity. The countess had youthful passions despite her advancing years. She liked a hot-blooded young man to share her bed. For his services he got splendid accommodations and the introductions which had gained him a long-awaited invitation to last night's gaming.

Still, there was a need to proceed slowly. He had a reputation to disprove. Knowledge of his propensity to win had preceded him from Paris to London. On arrival, he had found himself shut out of gaming clubs, unwelcome in the card rooms of the wealthy gentry who liked a bit of sport to their games. A time of sacrifice was required, a period of losing rounds at the tables until these English concluded that his reputed skill was naught but the usual exaggeration of the French. Once they dropped their guard he would find himself among the first included when the stakes were especially high. He smiled softly as he thought of the moment, the thrill of once more playing to win.

He needed the American's money for that time and he knew that the English, who held such low regard for their colonial cousins, would not hold such a win against him.

"You are ready to begin, *monsieur?*" he asked.

Zack Gamble leveled bleary eyes on the handsome Frenchman, and gripped the velvet-covered arms of his chair. "Zack! By damn, call me Zack! I've been mon-shured 'til I'm choking on it."

Rhys laughed. "As you wish, Zack," he said in polite compliance. He liked this American who had no decorum and no manners, possibly because his own were assumed, a mimicry of those of the privileged sons of the noblemen he'd worked for as a lad. Debauched, some of them, but proud and proper when need be. Thanks to his gift of mimicry he now moved among them. His manners were as perfect as those of the best of them—the nuances of his speech, whether in English or his native French, as refined as those of the best educated among them.

"Zack," his companion echoed, pushing up straight

in his chair, feeling more himself again. "Now how about a hand that will let me win back a pound or two of my own money."

The brief exuberance Zack Gamble felt was not enough to sustain the concentration necessary to win at a game of chance. In under an hour the American's pockets were empty as rain-spent clouds and he'd written marks for every pound and gold eagle in the cashbox hidden in his room. When he paid up he wouldn't have much more left than the price of a good meal.

Weary, feeling as thick-headed as if he'd drowned in drink, Zack reflected on the circumstance he was in, while Rhys Delmar excused himself from the table for a few minutes. The odd thing was he didn't much care. For Zack, money had always come and gone with remarkable ease. Plenty of times he'd been down to wagering his pearl-handled Colt revolver, once even his boots. He'd never stayed busted long, except once. That time he'd been down and out so long he'd done the unpardonable, wagered a few shares of the company on a hand.

Damn! He'd been sure of himself with that hand. Sure he couldn't lose. Self-assurance had not carried him. He had lost and it had cost him more than ten percent of the Gamble Stage Line. It had cost him family. Hell! He blamed Theodor. High and mighty Theodor. Anointed by their father, his mother's favorite. High and mighty, unspotted Theodor Gamble. Damn him! Damn him to hell! He missed him, and Teddy. And his mother. And he was tired, tired as if he had the whole world strapped on his back and he'd been walking with it all day.

Cain and Abel his mother had called them. Brother fighting brother. He'd whipped Theodor that time, the only time, the only way he was capable of whipping him, with his fists. Theodor had taken a close look at the company books after that fight. He'd quickly found that his younger brother had been siphoning money out of the business to support his gambling weakness. Enraged, Theodor had wanted him out of the company, wanted to buy him out, but he'd refused to sell.

"I'll make you a promise, dear brother," Zack had sworn. *"You'll never see me again and you'll never get these shares while I'm living."* He'd ridden away from Wishbone a day later, hating his brother, knowing Theodor had been right. He'd never admitted it though, didn't think he ever would. Let Theodor worry about him, wonder about what he would do with his remaining shares of the company. Let Theodor know that he might toss his only brother out of the family but he wouldn't toss him out of the Gamble Line. Not before Zack Gamble was ready to go.

Zack moaned, wished he felt up to having a drink. He'd been like the young Frenchman once, so cocky and sure of himself, so aware the real game among a table of players was in the minds and not in the cards. Twenty years ago he had been Rhys Delmar, not as handsome, not as polished, but as daring and devil-may-care as they came. And now . . . A pain shot down his left arm, a torturing spray of needles inside the trembling muscles. For a moment, until it eased, he lost his train of thought.

A person's whole world, his whole life could be dealt away in a game of cards. He wondered if Rhys

Delmar knew that yet. Zack shook himself. Maybe he did have the whole world strapped on his back. Maybe it had been there the five endless years since he'd ridden out of Arizona. Maybe it was time to let it go. That thought gave him the first easy feeling he'd had since he'd arrived in London four months back. Zack was grinning when Rhys Delmar returned to the table.

"Another hand, Rhys," he said insistently.

"Mons . . . Zack," Rhys said, trying to dissuade the American. Zack Gamble sounded more the man he'd met the night before, but his face had paled to ashen and his eyes had the pained look of a man in need of a long rest. "To wager with a man for more than he can afford to lose is not my way."

"I'm not busted yet," Zack said loudly. With a resolute look deep in his fevered eyes he tugged at his coat. His fingers went fumbling into all the pockets until at last, from one sewn into the lining, he extracted a thin leather sheath. Worn, contoured like the chest wall it had rested upon for so long, the sheath yielded a packet of yellowed papers which Zack spread upon the table. "I own forty percent of the Gamble Stage Line. Look here," he said, heavily drumming a finger on the documents. "The finest express outfit in the whole of Arizona."

"Zack," Rhys said indulgently. "An express company in the wilderness. What is that to me?"

"About four times as much as you've taken off me tonight. Cash if you want it that way. I can make the arrangements tomorrow with my brother's agent here. By damn, my brother will give top dollar. He wants those shares bad."

Rhys shook his head, feeling a shame he rarely felt when he had won so much. He wasn't about to compound it by leaving the American a complete pauper. "I'll come by your rooms tomorrow afternoon to redeem the marks," he said. "If you trade for cash with your brother's agent then we will play again at a later date."

Zack angrily scrubbed his chair back from the table, planted his palms on the card-strewn surface as he leaned over it and into the face of Rhys Delmar. "You owe me another chance, Frenchman. You picked me clean as a buzzard picks bones. You owe me a chance to win back what I lost. One hand," Zack demanded and felt no remorse that he had lied. His brother had no agent in London. Collecting from Theodor Gamble would take time, but then Zack did not intend to lose.

"As you wish," Rhys said. He had seen that look before, a man's refusal to admit defeat until it bit his head off. Regretfully, he pushed a fresh deck of cards to Zack. He would play the hand but it would be of no account. He had no desire for what the man offered and no desire to ruin Zack Gamble. He also had no desire to relinquish any of his winnings to salve the man's pride. He would play the hand. For now he would give the man what he wanted, then he would be rid of him. Otherwise he was faced with calling someone to remove the stubborn American from the countess's apartment. Tomorrow, when the man was calmer, and had realized how foolhardy he had been, he would be happy to pay his marks and take back his express company papers.

The clock did not move a quarter hour before Zack

Gamble threw up his hands acknowledging his loss. Slowly, with every exertion paining him, he struggled to his feet, slid the worn leather sheath from his pocket and slapped it down on the center of the table. Zack called for a pen and ink, which Lucien quickly provided. Despite Rhys's urging that he wait until the morrow to transfer title, Zack insisted that one of the house servants be called and that he and Lucien witness the transfer.

Begrudgingly, Rhys did as the man asked, knowing it would be all the more of a nuisance to find witnesses for the undoing of the deed. Annoyed, but glad to see the evening at an end without a worse mishap, Rhys pocketed the sheath and the marks so that he would not forget to have them with him when he called upon the American the following afternoon.

"Bring your marks by at two," he said to Rhys, oddly composed for a man who had gambled away the last of his possessions. "I'll have your winnings for you then."

Rhys insisted on having Lucien call a cab for the man. And Rhys saw him to the door as it waited outside.

He was unaware, however, that Zack Gamble was laughing as he left the apartment, laughing in spite of the pain that spread like venom to his shoulder and arm, laughing in spite of the leadenness of his feet and the difficulty of drawing each breath. Let the Frenchman find Theodor if he wanted to collect. Let Theodor find him in hell if he did not like what had become of his brother's share of the company. What did he care? His promise was kept. He would never get back to Wishbone.

But Theodor, high and mighty Theodor, would wish he had.

Four

The black satin eye mask the countess found essential for sleep had slipped out of place on one side, exposing a puffed bluish lid and the ever-deepening series of lines at the corner of her closed eye. Hers had been an elegant face once and even now with the right application of powder and rouge it was enough to turn a head. Her figure, once the talk of Paris salons, had grown rounded and overripe to the point that even the tightest cinching of corset could not restore the wasplike waist she had once proudly displayed. But with characteristic good nature she dismissed her added girth and was known to chirp, "the more to hold, *cher ami*," to her young men.

Rhys cast a glance at the slumbering countess as a thump outside the door awakened him. He saw that in spite of the displacement of her mask, the countess slept deeply, snoring softly as he quietly stirred from the bed, pushing layer upon layer of silk covers off him as he swung his long legs to the floor and reached for his linen dressing gown. Raking a disarray of black curls from his forehead, he hastened—barefooted—to the door to answer the unmistakable knock of Lucien Bourget.

"Hurry," came Lucien's agitated whisper. "I've brought her inside. Hurry! She's calling for you."

To see Lucien ruffled was enough to jolt him completely awake. "Who?" he demanded. "Why?"

"There'll be trouble from this," Lucien babbled as he broke into a shuffling run toward the drawing room. "She'll not last I think."

Totally baffled, Rhys also ran for the drawing room. Muffled moans, and the soft mouthing of his name, drew his chilled feet toward the room. He was unprepared for what awaited him, the crumpled figure, the cries of pain, the smell of blood.

"Jenny!" he cried. "Jenny!"

Jenny lay upon the couch. Her face was tormented, her eyes glazed with pain. Rhys hastened to her and knelt at her side, cuddling her in his arms, finding the front of her black woolen cloak wet through with warm blood.

"Jenny, what has happened to you?"

The woman trembled and gasped a breath as she clung to him. "Done you a bad turn," she whispered. "Should have come to you first—Took it upon myself to right things—For Mariette—"

"Get a physician!" Rhys shouted to Lucien. "And be fast about it!"

Lucien fled the room. His uneven gait beat a loud retreat on the marble tiles of hallway. In the moments since he had found Jenny and brought her inside, he had completely forgotten the well-dressed man he had seen across the street. The red-haired man had tucked a scrap of something white in his pockets and walked swiftly away, as Lucien swept Jenny into his arms.

Rhys bent his head to Jenny's face and kissed her cool cheeks, her forehead.

"Get away, lad," she whispered, "—not safe. Leave now. He'll do you the harm he's done me." Her voice faded so that Rhys could scarcely hear it. "Get away from—"

"Who, Jenny? Who hurt you?" Rhys demanded, too distraught to note Jenny's warning of a danger to him. He held her closer, felt her cringe with added pain, and, wishing to spare her more, lowered her gently to the couch's soft cushions. "Tell me."

Jenny breathed a gurgling breath as a blood-streaked hand clutched a length of gold chain circling her neck. "Mariette's," she said, pulling the chain and locket free and pressing it into his hand.

Rhys knew the locket. His mother had worn it through all the time that filled his memory of her. He thought she wore it still, in death. But there it was, stained scarlet with Jenny's blood. Silently, he took it from the trembling hand and held it in his open palm feeling the warmth of Jenny's body fade from the intricately filigreed gold even as the strength faded from the woman beside him. He supposed his mother had given Jenny the locket before she died. Jenny had been as close as a sister to his mother, her dearest friend.

"Letter," she mumbled. "Alain has—"

"Alain should be here with his mother," he said, gently cradling her in his arms once more. "I'll send Lucien for him when he brings the physician."

Jenny gave a tiny cry. "Alain," she whispered. "Tell Alain I lov- . . ."

He felt a shock run through her, a frisson of movement gathering all that remained of life in Jenny Perrault. He felt the fluttering of it leaving her, like a bird taking flight in the dark of a still night. He felt helpless and small as he witnessed that transition, as he felt the endless emptiness of her body when life was gone from it.

Rhys slumped to his knees and stared at the shell of Jenny Perrault. What had brought her here? What had brought dear Jenny all the way from the south of France? She'd never left her homeland before, he was certain of that. Not even to see Alain. Why now? Had she been trying to warn him of something? Or had she been babbling in delirium? Rhys was so heavyhearted he could barely move. But he explored the pockets of Jenny's cloak. She'd spoken of a letter. He wanted to find it and deliver it to Alain. It seemed so little to do for one who had meant so much to him and his mother. The letter must have been of tremendous importance for Jenny to have spoken of it in her dying words.

His search went unrewarded. If Jenny had carried a letter for Alain it was not with her now. Rhys rocked back on his heels, squeezed his eyes shut and said a prayer of peace for Jenny's soul.

Poor dear Jenny. Dead. What had happened to her? Reason returning, he probed beneath her cloak to discover that the wound which had robbed her of life had been made by a knife. Whose? And why? Who would harm a gentle old woman like Jenny Perrault? No thief would have imagined she carried more than a ha'penny in her pockets.

Hands trembling, questions racking his mind, Rhys smoothed the bloodlessly transparent eyelids over her fixed gray orbs. He turned a fold of her dark, worn cloak over her blanched, lifeless face and left her.

He'd loved Jenny almost as much as he'd loved his mother. Jenny's devoted care had sustained Mariette Delmar through long years of illness and suffering. The last year would have been unbearable but for Jenny. She'd seen that the money he sent obtained the best doctors and treatment for his mother, though finally her weak heart had simply given in to the illness. She'd died less than two months before. The burial cost had taken the last of his resources. He'd left for London shortly afterwards, wanting a change of scene, hoping to find peace in a new place.

What was he to tell Alain? Then the next disturbance came. He was dressed by then, or as close as he would get that day. The countess's plump bare arm was thrown above her head on the down-filled pillow. She continued her soft snoring, in deep sleep, until the insistent, angry rapping at the bedroom door awakened her, abruptly. Confused, she clumsily tore the satin mask from her eyes and unwillingly greeted the morning.

"That man of yours, *cher ami!*" she cried to her young lover. "Stop him before he cracks my head with his pounding!"

Rhys hurried to the door. What had brought about Lucien's insistent pounding he could not guess. The physician must already have discovered he had arrived too late to be of help to Jenny.

"Lucien, what . . ." he started to say, as he flung open the heavy door.

Lucien was accompanied by a pair of constables who stood ready to apply their shoulders to the door. With them was a stranger, an agitated wreck of a man. Rhys had never before seen him.

" 'E's the one!" The man aimed a filthy finger at Rhys. "Put 'is blade in the wench then climbed in 'at window 'ere!" Screeching his accusation he pushed past Rhys and pointed at the bank of Japanese orange velvet draperies covering the bedroom window which overlooked the street. " 'E killed 'er! No doubt about it!"

Rhys, temper flaring, grabbed the stranger by the collar and thrust him hard against the hallway's paneled wall. "Tell the truth!" he shouted. "I've never seen you and you've never seen me."

The constables, each grabbing hold of an arm, voiced warnings as they forcefully pulled Rhys clear of the man. "Your name, sir?" one of them queried.

"Rhys Delmar," he answered, shaking himself loose of their combined grasps. "Marc André Rhys Delmar. Jenny was dear to me. I'd never have hurt her."

" 'E did it!" the stranger repeated.

Rhys had never thought himself capable of taking a life, but as he looked at the man who had invaded his apartment, the man who accused him of murdering the last person he loved, he reconsidered what he might do, if pushed further.

"Be certain, man," one of the constables warned.

" 'E's the one," the man hissed through the gap of missing teeth. " 'Im!"

Fighting his rage, Rhys looked at the lying beggar and was gratified to see the bloke shudder.

"Who is this man?" he asked of the constables. "Who is he to accuse me? He must have done it himself."

"And then run lookin' fer a constable?" The stranger laughed warily. "Ye'r full of it," he said.

Rhys turned his back on the man lest he worsen his cause by attacking him again. "I was in my bed when my man brought Jenny in. I was sleeping," he explained to the constables. "Ask him."

"Was he in his bed, man?" the constable demanded of Lucien. "Did you see him there?"

Lucien Bourget had seen no such thing. But he was as sure of the master's innocence as he was of his own. Besides that, he owed Rhys Delmar his very life if the truth be told. "Sound asleep. I woke him, sir," Lucien insisted.

" 'E's lyin'. 'E's in it too!"

The constables looked uncertainly at the stranger, then at Rhys. Just as Rhys thought he'd weighted the case to his favor, one of the constables spotted the countess peering through the bedroom door. Tangled yellow hair swinging to her shoulders, quivering inside her russet silk robe, she'd heard enough to feel the damaging sting of a scandal.

Face reddening, the oldest of the constables approached the countess. "Madam, can you account for this man? 'As he been out this morning? Think hard."

The countess looked apologetically at her lover. He was the handsomest of the young men she had befriended and the most adept at lovemaking. There was aristocratic blood in those veins—even if it had been fostered on the wrong side of the blanket. She had an eye for good breeding. Even now, her heart fluttered at the sight of the virile Rhys Delmar. She had held those broad muscled shoulders, felt the power in the lean hips, admired the line of the fine high-bridged nose, and looked with wonder into those lazy blue eyes. A hand went to her breast as she recalled the smoke and fire she had seen in those eyes.

A pity. She had begun to grow fond of him, but not so fond that she would willingly jeopardize herself. "I-I can't say where he was," she stammered. "I've only just awakened myself."

She might as well have put a noose around his neck, he thought. The constable's countenance changed. The stranger's nervous toothless grin became a satisfied smirk. Rhys took a long pensive breath. He was as good as hanged. He had not a clue why, nor did he care to stay around and find one. As if he'd burst forth from a cannon's barrel he gave a shout and sped into the countess's bedroom, gave her a mighty shove which sent her tumbling atop the bed she had so recently left. Before the constables could follow he barred the door.

The countess, tangled in the twisted bed coverings, screamed, far louder than she had when he'd pleasured her a few short hours earlier.

"Stay put!" he shouted at her as he made a dash

for the window. He reached it half a step ahead of the shattering water pitcher the countess had flung at him. A glance back caught her crouching on the bed, mouth agape, eyes straining, beginning to believe she'd been bedded by a murderer. He had half a mind to go to her and commit such a crime as she'd as good as convicted him of, but there was no time.

Instead he blew her a kiss as he ripped apart the silk draperies, tore the window latch from its anchoring hook, and recklessly flung the sashes open.

He was a street away by the time the constables broke into the bedroom and assured themselves that the hysterical countess had not been murderously assaulted like poor Jenny. He was another street away before he broke his run and cautiously looked back the way he'd come—to confirm that he was not yet discovered.

For an hour Rhys Delmar wandered about trying to decide the best way to get himself out of the predicament he was in. At the end of that hour he was no closer to a solution. Long past noon, none had occurred to him, not until the cry of a news vendor on the street called out his name.

" 'Orrible murder!" the thin grimy waif shouted, waving his papers high so that no passerby would be tempted to overlook him. "Frenchman sought!"

Rhys grabbed a paper, paying the boy with the only coin in his pocket. He read the account of what had befallen him that morning, including his accuser's damning statement, and the countess's contradiction of Lucien's confirmation that he had been asleep at the time Jenny was stabbed outside the countess's

DEVIL MOON

house. He was alleged to have fooled the servant, stabbed the woman, climbed in the window, slipped into the bed and pretended to be asleep when the servant had come for him.

Swearing, he flung the paper to the paving stones. No one had bothered to question the absurdity of his wanting Jenny dead. Sweet, loving Jenny who had been his mother's companion since the day he'd been born. Alone, afraid to lift his head lest he be recognized, he slunk into the space between two buildings.

He wanted to find Alain and explain to him what had happened. He wanted to find the person who had killed Jenny. But not now. Now he had to leave England or he'd find nothing but the certainty of the gallows. He could do neither Jenny nor Alain any good by swinging from a rope.

He would come back, once he'd made some sense of what had happened, once he had the means to defend himself. He'd write to Alain as soon as it seemed safe to do so.

In the meantime, still confounded by it all, Rhys shoved his hands into his pockets, empty except for the worn leather sheath and Zack Gamble's marks from the night before. What a time to find himself short of funds. Every constable in the city would be out scouring the streets for him. He had to get away soon. For an escape he needed money.

Lost in his troubled thoughts he had changed his direction without being aware of it. When he glanced up and saw where his steps had taken him, a dim ray of hope shone in his mind. Getting money might prove the least of his worries.

* * *

Lemuel Snead, the landlord who discovered the cold body of Zachary Gamble also found the locked cashbox beneath a letter addressed to one Rhys Delmar. The letter he tossed aside; Snead neither read nor wrote. The cashbox caught his eyes. He was an honest man but a curious one. As it was to be his place to see to the disposal of his guest's remains, his conscience took no offense at prying the lock off the box belonging to Zack Gamble.

His good character did not withstand the force of what he found within, money, gold and notes, enough to equal what he profited in a decade, maybe two, operating a tavern and letting out rooms to travelers.

He glanced about, then gave his sudden decision no more thought. He deserved it, he told himself, just compensation for the shock of coming unsuspecting upon a dead man. The American's bill had been paid in full but there were expenses yet to come. He would order a suitable box for the burial, even a headstone. No—A wooden cross would do. He scarcely knew the man after all.

But the money, he deserved it, no doubt of that, he reiterated as he stuffed his pockets with the loot. Door open behind him, Snead cast open a window and tossed the splintered cashbox onto the pile of refuse festering behind the tavern. He had not yet covered the departed Zachary Gamble when he was surprised at his work of sorting through the American's clothing.

"Dieu m'en garde! Monsieur Gamble!" Rhys swore as he saw the stiff, lifeless body of Zachary Gamble stretched upon the narrow bed in his room.

Rhys was only marginally conscious of Snead, who in his shock at being discovered, dropped the woolen frock coat he'd been holding.

"I found him so just now," Snead explained, a trace of his conscience exerting itself. "Died in his sleep, it seems."

But Rhys did not hear what the man said. He was thinking that he was surrounded by death this day, Jenny's, the American's, the inevitably of his own if he did not get away from London. He turned to Snead, face drawn, voice rasping as he spoke. "He was to have something for me," he ventured.

"Your name, sir?"

"Delmar," Rhys offered cautiously, hoping the man had not had time to read the day's news. "Rhys Delmar."

Snead was too nervous to be suspicious of anyone but himself. He remembered the letter that had been with the cashbox and quickly handed it to the Frenchman. "This be it?" he asked.

Seeing his name scrawled upon the paper, Rhys hurriedly broke the sealing wax loose and tore into it, hoping it contained the name of the agent Zack had mentioned. It did not. Instead he found documents of passage inside, confirmation that a cabin aboard the vessel *Lady Jane* awaited Zachary Gamble at tomorrow's sailing. The rest was a note, cryptic, badly written, a suggestion that Rhys Delmar sail aboard the *Lady Jane,* journey to Arizona and look up Theodor

Gamble if he wished to redeem the shares he held. It was Zachary Gamble's last act of defiance to a brother he both loved and hated.

"Mon Dieu!" Rhys swore softly as he added the documents to those already in his pocket. Snead recoiled, thinking he heard a threat from the Frenchman. "He owed me money," he said to Snead.

It was not to Snead's credit that he adapted quickly to dishonesty. "He owes me, too," the landlord lied boldly. "If you be a friend of his perhaps you'll be assuming his burial costs."

"That I will not," Rhys said, seeing his best means of escape from hostile London as dead as Zachary Gamble. Regretting the offering of his name to Snead he spun on his heels, not noticing in his retreat the scrap of paper that floated from his pocket.

He approached the street with care, looking left and right, pulling the brim of his hat low on his forehead. He was aware that much of his apprehension to cross the street stemmed from fear. It was unlikely that any of the constables on duty at those streets would recognize him. Surely none would purposely look for him at the tavern where Monsieur Gamble had taken rooms.

With that thought at the forefront of his mind he was stopped in midstride by the unanticipated lowvoiced calling of his name.

"Monsieur Rhys." The voice came from behind him. "Walk on," the man said. "Only listen."

"Lucien," Rhys whispered. "Do you know me so well?"

"Oui," Lucien admitted and in fact he did. Rhys

Delmar was as much friend as master. Guessing the thoughts of a friend in trouble was not so difficult. "It was a clear deduction that you would claim your money from Monsieur Gamble, as you left the countess's apartment without a farthing."

"He cheated me," Rhys told him. "He managed to die before he paid his marks."

"Tant pis!" Lucien exclaimed. "The countess has claimed the sum you left in her house. And she had cast me out. What more can befall us?"

"I cannot ask you to share this, Lucien," Rhys told his servant as they found a deserted spot behind a shop. "If the authorities have released you go your own way."

"You might have done that when you came upon me robbed and beaten nigh to death in Paris. You did not," Lucien reminded as he faced the young man who had befriended and cared for him when he was at his worst, the man who had given him work when his previous master had said he had no use for a crippled servant. "And now," Lucien said, brooking no refusal. "Where we go, we go together."

"Have you any money?"

"Enough to buy our way out of London," Lucien replied. "And I have your belongings. The countess was anxious to be rid of them."

"And I am anxious to forget the countess," Rhys said abruptly. Her betrayal had been salt in a fresh wound. "Be discreet," he said. "Book a passage, for yourself only, on the *Lady Jane.* She sails tomorrow."

"And you?"

"Taken care of. I will be on board."

"Until then luck be with you," Lucien said as he took his leave.

Rhys watched Lucien limp away, wishing the man had said good luck. He'd had his fill of the other kind.

Five

The driver's blood-curdling yell produced one of equal volume from an ordinarily imperturbable Lucien Bourget.

"On the floor!" the shotgun messenger shouted to the passengers. The deafening report of his rifle, the sound of bullets whizzing past the uncovered windows of the coach, the unmistakable *whump, whump* of slugs lodging in wood made the order unnecessary.

Rhys shoved Justine Blalock, the pretty young lady who shared the Concord coach's spartan interior, to semisafety in the lower part of the compartment, with Lucien. The cramped space would not accommodate another. The best Rhys could do to remove himself as a target was to attempt to flatten himself on the short stretch of the leather-covered bench above the crouching pair. The driver had whipped the team to a bone-juggling pace. Rhys could not hope to stay put long. By bracing his feet solidly against one side wall of the bouncing coach, and firmly gripping the swaying loop of cord that held back the hide curtains, he managed to avoid tumbling onto the heads of Lucien and Justine until the brakes locked and the coach skittered to a rocking halt.

"Ruby's hit!" the driver shouted.

Upside down in the laps of Justine and Lucien, Rhys apologized to the lady as he hurriedly righted himself, and courteously helped Justine get her crushed straw bonnet out of her face. A moment later, with a protesting Justine clutching his sleeve, he flung open the coach door, almost hitting the snorting nose of a skittish horse prancing alongside the waylaid Gamble Line stage.

"Hold it! Don't git out 'til I tell you," shouted the rider. He held a cocked pistol in his outstretched arm, and wore a bandana mask. He reined his nervous horse to a standstill. Dark, anxious eyes assayed Rhys Delmar, noting his expensive clothes. "Be a shame to mess up that purty suit."

The bandit confronting Rhys had two partners. Their faces were also obscured by colored kerchiefs tied tight across the jaws. One spurred his horse nearer the driver's box and aimed his gun at the man's head. The shotgun man, one Strong Bill Ash because of his size, had felt the stock of his rifle explode in his grip when it was hit by a bullet. Strong Bill held his bloody, useless hands in the air.

"Throw down that Wells Fargo box," demanded the man taking aim, unquestionably the one in charge.

"Git it yourself," the driver bellowed at him. "Lemme down to see about Ruby." Tom Cribbet's worried eyes went to one of the lead horses as he tied down the reins. The animal, a sturdy roan mare, stood trembling in the traces as she bled heavily from a gunshot wound to the shoulder.

"Don't trouble yourself," the bandit growled, slowly redirecting his weapon. While the driver sat, mouth wide open, momentarily frozen in disbelief, the man leveled his gun at the mare's head and fired. The animal wheezed once, stumbled, then fell to the ground dead.

The act was too much for the driver. With a whoop of rage he recklessly launched himself from the seat. Before the bandit could aim and fire, the driver's shoulder hit, knocking him from the saddle and carrying both men to the ground. Knotted together they landed in the hardscrabble beneath the thrashing legs of the saddle horse. For a minute or two the pair struggled, but the driver was at a disadvantage having landed hard beneath the weight of his adversary. The bandit, barely scathed, had not lost his gun in the fall. He got an elbow free, then the whole of his arm. Using his weapon like a club, he struck the brave driver in the center of his sun-browned forehead, splitting the toughened skin, knocking Tom Cribbet unconscious.

Justine Blalock had held on when she saw the horse shot, but the sight of the unconscious driver was unbearable. She screamed, a long piercing wail of terror. It ended only when the bandit who had been unseated lurched to his feet and ordered Rhys to step down from the coach. With the mounted bandit's gun trained on him, Rhys had no sensible choice but to comply. With his back against the coach, and the steel barrel of one gun almost at his skull, he stood as still as he was told.

The man on foot grabbed Justine's arm and snatched her out of the coach. She screamed again, louder and longer and shriller than before.

"Shut up!" the man told her. "Shut up or I'll—"

He didn't need to continue. Justine choked off her scream and found her voice. "My daddy will hang you for this," she cried, attempting to jerk her arm free of the bandit's clamplike hold.

The man jerked her against his chest. "Your daddy and what army, little girl?"

"He won't need an army!" Justine spat back. "He's sheriff in Wishbone. He'll hunt you—"

The man slung her arm free and pushed her with such force that her back struck the wheel rim painfully hard. Justine cried out.

Cursing, the bandit kept his gun pointed at her. "Who is he?"

"My daddy is Sheriff Len Blalock," she said proudly, righting her misshapen bonnet.

"Shit!" The bandit backed away, grappling for his horse's reins. Finding them, he led the animal close and mounted. "Git going," he said to his partners.

"The strong box—" the third man began uncertainly, his voice and eyes years younger than either of the other's.

"Forget it." Tugging on the reins he backed his horse a dozen paces then whirled the animal around and galloped off into the cover of scrub and rock near the road.

One bandit spurred his horse and followed immediately. The third, the one who had held his gun to Rhys's head was slow to follow. He was slow enough that when he urged his mount to a gallop, Rhys had already scooped a fist-sized rock from the ground and hurled it at the man. The hollow sound of it striking the base of the bandit's neck brought a gasp from Justine. The stunned rider hit the ground hard. His horse whinnied and loped off without him.

"I will be damned," said Strong Bill as he tied strips of his handkerchief around his injured hands. He wouldn't have given two bits' worth of credence to his French passenger if he hadn't seen what he did. Usually his kind, those overly refined gents who came West in their high-class clothes, dropped in a dead faint the first time they faced a threat.

"Boyhood games." Rhys shrugged. "I regret it was not the other one I hit."

Justine, breathing hard, laid a hand on Rhys's arm and felt the powerful muscle beneath his sleeve. "You are remarkably brave," she said softly.

"No, *mademoiselle,* if anyone is brave it is you." Rhys took her hand and held it a moment. "Lucien," he said. "See what aid you can give that man."

"I'll help," Justine offered as Lucien retrieved a canteen from the driver's box.

With Justine's assistance Lucien worked to revive the downed driver while Rhys bound the prostrate bandit. When the driver was clearheaded enough to stand and walk, Rhys helped unharness Ruby from the traces. He saw a tear streak the driver's stoic face, and a sob shake the rangy torso. All the while Rhys Delmar wondered what refuge he was likely to find in this brutal, spare land that seemed made of nothing but cactus and sand and trouble.

He was in an advanced state of indignation when the coach rolled into Wishbone with an injured driver and messenger, short one horse and carrying a complaining bandit strapped to the luggage rack. The harrowing experience on the poorly protected stage capped the impossibility of convincing the Gamble Line's agent in Phoenix that Rhys Delmar owned almost half the company.

"Take it up with Teddy," the burly, short-tempered agent had told him. "But right here, right now, if you want passage on the Gamble Line stage to Wishbone you'll pay for a ticket and so will your 'manservant.' "

Rhys had been forced to borrow the cost of the two passages from Lucien, in addition to the money for transportation from the port of Boston across the American continent.

Teddy. Zachary Gamble's brother, he supposed, returning his thoughts to the present. Teddy. Some vulgar corruption of Theodor. Teddy Gamble, who ran the stage line badly if Rhys's trip had been typical. Passengers had to furnish their own refreshments and provisions or eat the plain fare dished out by the poor cooks at the way stations. From Strong Bill's words he learned this was not the first attack the line had suffered. Why had Theodor not hired more guards, hired mounted riders to accompany the stage? Teddy. Probably no brighter than his brother Zack Gamble.

Rhys climbed out of the coach. As his feet hit the

powder-dry street of Wishbone he noticed that his best shoes were caked with dust. His good silk cravat was now a bandage around Cribbet's head. His finest bowler hat was no longer in the coach—it had been lost in the confusion of the holdup. And somewhere along the line his most expensive custom-tailored suit had sustained an irreparable rip in the sleeve.

"Look at this ruin, Lucien." Rhys brushed a cloud of dust from his shoulders, then gave up when he saw he was only rearranging the embedded dirt. He stomped his feet to clean his shoes but found the dust there stubborn as dried flour dough. "I am undone by this Gamble Stage Line," he grumbled to the servant. "I tell you, Lucien, this damnable land and this company need civilizing."

"I could not agree more, *monsieur*," Lucien said as he helped Justine Blalock out of the coach. The attack had nearly been his undoing. All along the route from Missouri he had expected an attack of Indians, vicious savages with scalping knives and deadly arrows. That of the bandits came close to fulfilling his dire expectations.

Justine, almost as shaken as Lucien, spoke softly to Rhys. "I'll tell my father what you did," she said. "Once he's gotten over being furious that I decided not to stay another term at school he'll want to thank you."

Rhys put aside his bad temper long enough to recall the charm that came so easily when he was with a woman. "He could not be furious with you more than a moment, Mademoiselle Justine," he told her as he took her small hand in his and lifted it to his lips.

Her face flushed, her hand hanging in midair for a few seconds after Rhys released it, Justine smiled adoringly at him, said a quick good-bye to both men, then fled across the street and into the office of Wishbone's law officer. On her heels, Strong Bill none-too-gently nudged the stunned prisoner in the same direction.

Cribbet threw down Rhys's valise then climbed down to attend the horses. Rhys saw, to his dismay, that the fine leather casing of his valise was singed by powder burns and shot through, along with its contents, by no less than three bullet holes.

His mood changed swiftly. He gave the bag a vicious kick. "This Gamble Stage Line is evidently run by a half-wit," he grumbled. "Where is this Teddy Gamble?" he begged of a youngster who was scrambling up the coach to unload the remaining cargo. "I need to tell the man he'll be required to replace my entire wardrobe. As part owner of the Gamble Stage Line, I—"

The lad nudged his arm. "Right there," he whispered. "That's Teddy Gamble."

Teddy's back was turned to the passengers, as she listened to Cribbet's account of the holdup and checked the condition of the worn-out coach team. Teddy also listened, with forced reserve, to the Frenchman's entire tirade. Her daddy's policy had been that the customer was right. Teddy followed the same philosophy and she was prepared to soothe and reassure the whimsical, overwrought traveler as soon as he calmed down. But his unfinished last statement sent a shocking jolt through her whole body. Her head snapped up and her spine went rigidly straight.

Teddy Gamble, attired in fringed buckskin trousers and shirt, and with tightly laced leggings that rose to her knees, had her back to him. Rhys looked at the slight form with the masculine clothes and feminine curves and assumed he had discovered the reason for the Gamble Line's shortcomings. No man with that build was much of a man. He stood and stared. Before he could voice his observations Lucien put them into words.

"N'est-ce pas?" the manservant whispered. "This Monsieur Gamble has the look of an effete, a sissy."

"At best," Rhys said, moderating his voice too late.

On top of her morning's experience with Adams and Cabe Northrop and another attack on a stage it was too much. Teddy spun around like a hot desert whirlwind. She had a short staff in her hand that she had been using to unfasten the hard-to-reach harness from the traces.

"At worst," she said, eyes blazing, voice crackling. "I'm a gal who's got as much use for a pair of tinhorn, foreign, starched-shirts as I have for a pair of buzzards."

Lucien fell back as the staff she wielded thumped his master's chest.

Rhys's gaze went to the swell of her breasts. "You are a woman!" he stammered.

He could not have invited more trouble if he had lit the fuse on a stick of dynamite and tucked it in his pocket.

"Well, thank you for clearing that up."

The swinging staff telegraphed her anger as the hook on the end of it again thumped Rhys's chest. Before it gouged his midnight-blue brocade vest he caught hold of it. Aside from the countess, Rhys had never confronted a woman ready to do him harm. A man with his good looks and charm might go a lifetime without such an experience.

Chagrined, anxious to make amends, he gave a cavalier bow to Teddy Gamble. As his eyes swept over her, he saw a glint of silver at her throat, a necklace set with pretty blue-green stones. On her wrist she wore a bracelet of similar design. A belt of black leather and stamped silver medallions cinched her waist. Rhys gave her his best smile and decided all was not lost. The jewelry she wore with her strange garments was his clue. Teddy Gamble might wear the trousers of a man but she was not without a woman's vanity. "Madam—moiselle Gamble," he said, with the smooth, deep voice that had weakened many feminine knees. "My apologies. It seems we have gotten off to a bad start."

Teddy gave him a look so hot he felt it singe his skin. Snatching the staff out of his grasp she stretched herself up to a tall five feet four inches.

"You bet your ass we have!"

Six

Inside the Brass Bell Saloon, Teddy led to a corner table, kicked back a chair and sat.

"Marc André Rhys Delmar at your service, *mademoiselle.*" Smiling to full effect Rhys slid into a second chair and squared himself across the scarred bar table from Teddy Gamble. Her expression was that of a caged cat, one of pent-up energy and barely held-back anger. He stared at her because it was impossible to do otherwise. She was like no woman he'd ever seen. Her face was finely boned. And her hands had tanned a honey-brown from the sun. They were nearly the same color as the fringed buckskin shirt and trousers she wore. Her eyes, all banked with angry fire, were the most striking he'd ever encountered, a glowing green color as remarkable as the stones she wore.

"It's plain Teddy, here," she said. "I don't need any *mademoiselle* or mouthful of names to know who I am."

With a whisk of her hand, she pushed the dusty hat from her head and sailed it into the seat of an empty chair at the table. Rhys had been prepared for a cropped head of straggly hair but was surprised to discover that Teddy Gamble had an abundance of shining tawny locks which had been gathered in a braid and pinned beneath her hat. With some relief he concluded he'd been right to suspect that the woman had at least a tiny element of femininity to her.

"A thousand pardons, *mademoi*—Teddy," he said. "I only intended politeness."

"Well don't tangle yourself up in it," Teddy snapped. "Just spit out why it is you think you're part owner of the Gamble Line."

Rhys flashed another smile. "It is not what I think. It is what is true." He fished in his inside coat pocket for the leather packet in which he'd placed the papers given him by Zachary Gamble. "Monsieur Zachary Gamble wagered his share of the company in a game of cards." With—for Teddy—agonizing slowness, he spread the papers on the table for her to view. "He lost."

Teddy's heart faltered a beat. Her Uncle Zack's exaggerated penmanship was unmistakable. He'd signed his interest in the company over to the Frenchman as a pledge against a gambling loss. And evidently her Uncle Zack had either been unable or unwilling to ante up the cash to buy that interest back.

But be that as it may, Teddy wasn't about to accept the fancy man's claim without a challenge. "Uncle Zack will have to tell me himself that he surrendered his interest to you," she said coldly. "For all I know you robbed him and forged that signature."

Rhys blanched white. He came halfway out of his chair, then thought better of his action and eased himself down again. *"Mademoi—"* He paused, blew out a long breath then spoke with deliberate slowness to Teddy. "If Monsieur Gamble could tell anyone anything I would not have come halfway across the world to redeem these documents."

"What do you mean?" Teddy hissed.

"Your uncle is dead."

"How?" A chill of suspicion ran up her backbone and ended in the cold stare she gave Rhys. "Did you—"

Rhys shook his head. "He died in his sleep before he could make good his pledge. I'm surprised the authorities haven't notified you—his family."

"I'm his family." Teddy felt the sickness that had been threatening all day settle hard in her stomach. The only imaginable thing worse than having Uncle Zack return and put his stamp of ruin on the business was having this Frenchman here in his stead. A wave of guilt hit her right behind that notion. She was Zack's family, she and her grandmother, his only living blood kin, and she hadn't been able to foster a charitable thought about him. And dammit! She had loved him. The troublemaking old fool!

Tears started to well in her eyes but she'd be horse-whipped before she'd let Marc André Rhys Delmar see them. Mumbling a string of swearwords, Teddy pushed away from the table. She stood.

"Mademoi—Teddy!" Rhys called after her as she fled the saloon. Seeing that his raised voice had brought all eyes his way, he made a polite nod to no one in particular, grabbed his papers, stuffed them in his pocket and rushed out. He caught her just outside the swinging doors. "Our business—" he began.

Teddy shoved him aside. "Give a body time to

grieve, won't you?" A moment later she'd swung astride a horse, a big rangy spotted animal that looked to Rhys more suited to the plow than the saddle. The horse's hooves kicked up dust that settled in with the other stains on his best suit as she galloped out of town.

Lucien was at Rhys's elbow when he turned around. "Our accommodations, *monsieur?*"

Rhys sighed and looked into the distance at the sinking sun and the showcase of amber and red light in the evening sky. Teddy Gamble, who'd proved as inhospitable as the desert, was already out of sight. Fortunately though, at the far edge of town, he spotted a sign for the Gamble Line's stable. He nodded toward it. "We'll see if there's an empty stall," he told Lucien.

"Git up, mister!" Horace Roper stabbed the tines of a pitchfork into the hay, six inches from Rhys's face. "We don't cotton to skinflints 'round here."

Sending straw flying in every direction, Rhys bolted to his feet. Lucien stood backed into the corner of the stall trembling like a leaf in a gale and muttering incoherent words in his native tongue. The man wielding the pitchfork had pulled it free of the ground and held it like an Indian spear.

"You misunderstand—" Rhys protested. "I am—"

"Trespassin'." Rope supplied. "Now get out of here, the both of you, before I give you something to remember."

"Hold up, Rope." A familiar voice came from the

door of the stable but Rhys was hesitant to turn about and put a face to it. The man called Rope was still threatening to put holes in him. "This here's the man that brought down that bandit on yesterday's run."

Rope gave the straw-littered Rhys Delmar a scrutinizing look. "This dandy?"

Strong Bill, hands swathed with strips of clean bandage, had reached the stall. "I'll allow he don't look like he could chunk a rock and knock a fellow out of the saddle, but that's what he done."

Rope tossed the pitchfork into a pile of hay. "Sorry," he said and offered a hand to Rhys. "Reckon I owe you thanks and reckon you owe me a reason you're sleepin' in one of my stalls."

"Reckon he thinks he's entitled." Teddy led the big spotted horse into the stable and looped a rein around a post. "He claims he's part owner of the Gamble Line."

"The hell you say!" The hand Rope had offered swung back to his side as the challenge rose in his voice.

"I'm sorry to say part of his story has proved out," Teddy added. "A letter came in today's mail sack, a notification from London authorities that Uncle Zack died back in June, more than a month ago."

"What's the other part?" Rope inquired.

"That before he passed on Uncle Zack managed to do us in by wagering his share of the company in a card game and losing."

"To him?"

"So he says."

"So the documents Monsieur Gamble gave me say,"

Rhys insisted. "They are properly witnessed." He motioned to his companion. "Lucien can prove his signature and—"

Teddy gave the other man a hostile look. "We'll need to verify that other one," she insisted. "And until we do you own nothing but paper. Understand?"

"No." Rhys brushed straw from his trousers. "As I see it I am the one put out here. I want none of the Gamble Line, only the cash that is its value. Had Monsieur Gamble not died he'd have settled his marks and bought back his share of the company the day following our game." He didn't bother to add he had had his doubts. "As it is I've had to come to you. And, I assure you, I am most anxious to conclude our business so that I can leave this uncivilized place."

"You can leave any time you like," Teddy shot back. "But I'm not making good any of Zack's marks." She huffed out a breath so hard the force of it lifted the fringe of tawny brown hair from her forehead. "And if you want cash for that paper you're carrying, you'll have a long wait 'cause I'm not parting with a penny until I know every claim you're making is legit."

"That could take months. A year even," Rhys protested.

"At least," Teddy returned. "But you won't get a dime or a dollar until I get someone trustworthy in London to track down that other witness and verify what you're saying. Until I do I'm doing nothing on this end."

Rope nodded to Strong Bill and the two of them

ambled off toward the feed room, close enough to hear, but out of the way of Teddy's temper.

"But *mademoi*—I'm afraid I can't wait that long," Rhys insisted. Especially now, he did not want anyone asking questions about him in London. "My need is immediate," he said.

Teddy rubbed a hand across the warm flank of her saddle horse. She had a slim hope that the Frenchman's story and the letter were a hoax, but knew her uncle Zack too well to count on that contingency. Her uncle had had a weak heart and a weaker head. This was just the kind of mess he'd leave behind if he'd truly passed on. So in the event the worst was true, and the Frenchman was her partner in the Gamble Line she couldn't afford to antagonize him too much.

She couldn't, however, resist antagonizing him some. Marc André Rhys Delmar had brought her trouble on top of trouble. For a moment, as she breathed out a sigh of resignation, she considered that if all that had happened in this one day wasn't so ridiculously unbelievable she'd haul off and bawl. Instead she stared hard and accusingly at the Frenchman, then hastily looked away. Damned if she liked the way he'd met her stare. Those blue eyes of his had made her feel as if the blood flow had changed direction in her veins.

"If you're short of cash," she said coolly, "we can use some help in the stables. You can give Rope a hand. The job includes a meal and you can keep the stall. The same goes for your friend."

"I am Monsieur Delmar's valet, *mademoiselle*," Lucien said nobly.

"Valet?" Teddy laughed. "Well, hell, I reckon you can hold his coat while he pitches hay."

Brushing briskly at the straw on his sleeves, Rhys stepped toward Teddy. "You've no call to insult my man," he said.

Teddy stopped short and shrugged her shoulders. "Never intended to," she said. "I was insulting you."

Rhys, bristling, started after her as she stalked off. Lucien held him back until she was out the door. "Monsieur Rhys," he began in all earnestness, "do you suppose there are many like her in Arizona?"

"Assuredly not," Rhys said. "God would have shattered the mold once he saw his mistake."

A few steps ahead of Teddy, Rope strolled out of the stable. Propped against a hitching rail he rolled a smoke and waited. He heard her cursing as she emerged from the barn. The rhythm of her brisk footsteps broke as she kicked a good-sized rock out of her path.

"Mind how you rile that Frenchman, Teddy," Rope said quietly. The tiny flare of his cigarette beamed through the darkness. "The fellow might have a sharper mind than you credit."

Teddy stopped and lifted her eyes to the heavens. She wasn't in the mood for advice, good or otherwise. "I'm just stalling him 'til I've got the cash to settle up with him." She sighed heavily and with slower steps, strolled in Rope's direction. "You're forgetting,

Pa put the last of our capital on those three new coaches he bought a month before he died."

"Uh-huh." Rope drew a long puff off his cigarette. "Meanwhile you got that Frenchman raw-nerved as a fresh-broke horse."

Teddy groaned loudly. "Don't know why that fellow ought to feel any better about this situation than I do."

"I reckon if you'd settle down a mite you would," Rope said. "Ain't you forgettin' there's somebody around here with the cash to cover his claim?"

"Hell!" The clouds in Teddy's mind parted and the light came through in a flash. "Adams!" She kicked hard at the hitching rail. "I hadn't even thought of him."

"Well think. 'Cause Adams is sure to hear about this by mornin' and he'll be a lot nicer to the Frenchman than you've been."

"Hell!" She grimaced. "Adams will probably kiss him." Angrily she jabbed a finger at Rope. "And don't go saying that's what I ought to do."

"I'm only sayin' you ought to use a little more sweetenin' and a lot less salt on that fella. You gotta give him some reason not to jump at what Adams is sure to offer. Better yet, take him out to the ranch. Keep him out of Adams's reach if you can."

Groaning again, Teddy agreed. Rope was right. Parrish Adams was evidently stuffed with money right up to his beady eyes. He'd bought out every rancher in the area who would turn his spread loose. No, Adams wouldn't have to search for a way to cover Delmar's shares.

She gritted her teeth and felt knots of anger tighten

in her chest. Thanks to Uncle Zack she had to be nice to the Frenchman, even though it galled her. Adams would turn the world over to get forty percent of the Gamble Line. He'd rooted up half of the globe trying to get the ten percent Zack had wagered and lost before leaving Wishbone. Rope owned that ten percent now, but it had been sheer luck that he'd found the gambler Zack had lost it to at a time when the man was down and out.

She'd heard Adams was still looking for the man. When he heard about Delmar he'd be foaming at the mouth thinking he might be close to getting his hands on fifty percent of her company. No telling what he would pay. She felt her breath coming fast. The devil take Adams. He was going to be disappointed. She was going to see that he never even got as much as a ticket on the Gamble Line. She could count on Rope to stand with her against anything. But the Frenchman . . .

A string of curses ran through her mind. She'd do what she had to.

"Take him out to the ranch," she said. "Him and that valet of his. Tell him we'll talk over breakfast in the morning."

Seven

In the bedroom of a London house, a servant offered the stout Englishman Avery Knox a breakfast tray. The master shoved it back into the servant's hands. Caught by surprise, the servant fumbled his hold on the heavy tray. He sloshed a few drops of coffee onto the tumbled bedclothes about his master's feet.

"Blast!" Knox swore and jerked his feet away from the scalding spill. The flustered servant quickly set aside the overburdened tray, and haphazardly blotted the stains with a napkin.

"Do that later," Avery Knox snapped at the inept man, recalling silently what he endured in the name of economy. In recent months he'd had to let the best of the servants go and did not like the change it had made in his lifestyle. But for a while longer he would have to be conservative and put up with clumsy, lazy fools such as Meigs. "Get Seward in here," he demanded. "I want to see him."

"Very well, sir." The servant started out of the room so hastily that he caught his foot on a throw rug and nearly lost his balance.

A curse erupted from Knox before the man had

regained his footing. "Meigs!" he shouted after the man. "Take that tray with you!" As Meigs turned back, Knox shrugged deeper down into the bedclothes. "Must I tell you everything?" he asked.

"No, sir." In a hurry to comply and escape his master's foul mood, Meigs snatched up the tray and raced out the open door.

A few minutes later a stockily built man with full, flaming red whiskers stepped in. Being a cautious sort, Derby Seward glanced around as he entered, to assure himself that he and Knox were alone. They were. The room was scantily furnished, though Seward's memory and the marks on the carpet recalled that there had once been a large chest and a long settee in addition to the half tester bed and the chairs and small table that remained.

A desperate man was a vulnerable man, Seward thought to himself as he shut and latched the door behind him. And Knox was at the point of desperation if he had begun to sell his furnishings in order to meet his pressing financial commitments.

"You wanted me?" Seward asked nonchalantly, determined that he would not be put off, even if Knox had to sell the garments from his back.

"Like I want the pox," said the other irritably. "But I have need of you."

"State your business." Seward stroked his thick whiskers as he strode nearer the bed. They were his pride, recompense for the bald pate that had emerged so early in life and spoiled his looks.

"The same as before." Knox, still in his nightshirt,

stuffed a fat feather pillow behind his back. "The Frenchman and the letter."

"Delmar's left," Seward reminded. "And with a noose awaiting him, he's not likely to set foot in London again. As for the letter," he continued. "The Perrault woman did not have it with her. We can assume with confidence that Delmar never received it and is none the wiser to its contents."

"Unless the Perrault woman lived long enough to tell him," Knox pointed out.

"Impossible!" Seward said hotly. "The woman died in his doorway. A servant dragged her inside. Couldn't have mouthed a word to anyone."

"So you've said," replied Knox. "But after thinking it over I've decided too much is at risk to leave anything to chance."

Seward shrugged. "It'll be a cold trail to follow now."

"Whose fault is that?" Knox retorted. "If you'd done what I wanted—"

"I did what you asked." Seward nudged a chair nearer the bed and sat, throwing his weight against the slatted back as he rested his right ankle above the cap of his left knee. Mocking Knox's aristocratic accent he repeated the orders Knox had given him. "Get him locked up. I leave it to you to find a way to make him guilty of a crime. Just make certain Delmar cannot comply with the terms of the will. And be quick about it, man."

"You were too quick," Knox complained, shifting his bulk into a more comfortable position. "The man is accused but he cannot be tried and hung if he cannot be found. Humph! Better you had used your head and put that knife through Delmar's heart."

"You said—"

"I bloody well know what I said!" Knox bellowed. "No need to drive it in." His booming voice fell. He knew he had no one but himself to blame for his situation but that fact made him no more willing to accept responsibility for his rash actions. Rather, he saw himself as a victim of circumstance, a man put upon by others. Or, more correctly, by one man. With eyes narrowed, Knox mumbled—more for his ears than for Seward's—"Bloody, backstabbing bastard."

"You refer to your uncle, I presume."

Knox's eyes lifted. "You presume correctly. Mad as a hatter too, Lord Andrew Knox. Kept his bloody secret for thirty years. Foisted it on me after he was gone. A nasty trick from the grave." Knox laced his fingers together and rested them on his round belly. "I never liked him, you know."

"So you've said." Seward nodded. Knox had an irritating way of snorting a breath between his briskly spoken sentences. For Seward, that habit, and the fact that he had listened to the story several times, had quickly begun to grate at his nerves.

"Hated him, in fact," Knox continued, oblivious to all but his own need to be heard. "Treated my father like a servant. Drove him to an early death." He snorted. "Stayed at me like a hound to a fox."

"A regular viper," Seward concurred.

"Worse," Knox insisted. "A miser. Carped at me for thirty years. 'Mind your step, boy, or I'll leave the lot of what's mine to the church.'" He looked directly at Seward. "I believed him I can tell you. He never parted with a tuppence if he could avoid it. Sat on his estate and watched his fortune grow. Let me think I was his heir. Never said a word about—"

"A wife and son," Seward supplied, ready to bring the tedious recounting to an end.

Staring straight ahead, Knox unlaced his fingers and began rubbing the satin edge of the velvet coverlet between the fat pads of his thumb and fingers. "Kept his bloody secret for thirty years," he mumbled. "Never a peep about it. 'Course I'd heard stories from the servants of the old man's liaison with a French kitchen maid," he said. "Bred her then turned on her. Nearly beat her to death with his fists before she ran off and dropped the brat." Knox shook his head bringing himself out of a daze. "Who'd have guessed he married the wench before she took off. Or that he never bothered to divorce the chit once she was gone."

He did not wait for an answer but instead stuck out a big hand and reached out for the bell pull. He was ready for coffee now. And Meigs could bring the rum. He was feeling poorly. Thought he might keep to his bed today.

Seward had gotten drawn into the tale in spite of himself. "Too much pride as I see it," he said. "Lord Andrew Knox wouldn't let it be known that an earl had wed a kitchen maid and could not hold her." His fingers stroked briskly through his beard. "But he left you an out, were you of a mind to take it."

Knox nodded. His small eyes had narrowed so that they almost disappeared into his round fleshy face. The terms of his uncle's will left his title and all but a pittance of his fortune to the son he'd never acknowledged, Marc André Rhys Delmar. Avery Knox, who had always thought of himself as his uncle's heir, would inherit only if the son should be found in prison or be deceased. His uncle's solicitors had already established that Delmar was living but as yet had failed to locate him. Meanwhile time dragged on and Knox's purse got thinner.

To worsen matters, since the Perrault woman's murder he had been told by his uncle's solicitors that the estate could not be settled until Rhys Delmar was either convicted or cleared.

"I tell you I believe he wanted me to destroy Delmar," Knox said slowly. "Wanted me to even the score with the wench for running off like she did. For making a fool of him." He coughed to clear his throat then turned glazed eyes to Seward. "He always thought of me as a son. Said so." With that pronouncement the small eyes brightened. "I mean to do it," he continued. "See Delmar dead. It's what my uncle meant me to do. No doubt of it. The old man wants me to pay tribute to him before the title and fortune pass to me." He turned the now-wide eyes on Seward. "Mad as a hatter, he was."

A family complaint, Seward thought. But what did he care? He'd bargained for a share of the old man's fortune when it fell into Avery Knox's hands. What he had to do to get it was of no consequence to him. "I'll need more money to find him," he said.

Knox made a mental count of what he had left from his father's small estate. Not much. He'd spent as if there was no limit to it. He'd seen no need to be prudent. He was Andrew Knox's heir, destined to receive a fortune he could scarce spend his way through in a lifetime. But until that fortune was in his hands he had precious little left to live on. Still, he would invest it in finding Delmar. His uncle's wish was becoming clear to him. Andrew Knox had always put his nephew to the test—had always demanded more than seemed possible. He'd left his title and estate as a prize.

Avery Knox had to earn it, prove he was up to the measure. Well, he was. He'd misunderstood before. Only tried to keep Delmar from knowing about the will, only tried to send him to prison. But he'd make no mistake this time. He'd do Delmar in. By Seward's hand, of course. He would not soil his own. "I've a little left," he said. "Find him. Kill him."

Derby Seward smiled.

The Countess Clemenceau prided herself that she was acquainted with everyone of note in London, but she did not recognize the gentleman with the flame-colored whiskers. Had his carriage not borne the crest of the Duke of Mitford she'd not have received the man. But now that he was in her drawing room and the tea had been brought she was beginning to believe she had made the right decision.

Curiosity, of course, had decided her against all else. The duke, to date, had declined all invitations to her parties. And now, here was his solicitor to see her.

"This is a matter of some delicacy, Countess," Derby Seward said, borrowing again the inflections of speech from the more educated Avery Knox. "He begs your indulgence."

"My pleasure is to oblige the duke in any way he wishes," the countess replied. Already she could imagine the coup of having him in attendance at her next gathering. One favor for another, as she saw it.

"The duke will be pleased." Seward began with a cheerful note then turned serious as he continued. "He wishes to inquire after an . . . acquaintance of yours. A Frenchman."

Her face flushed beneath the powder and rouge. She had been made a laughingstock because of Rhys Delmar. Any reference to the man was not tolerated in her presence. Had Seward not been the duke's representative, she'd have him shown out. Instead she looked about quickly to be certain no servant was within earshot. "I scarcely knew him, Mr. Seward," she began. "But—"

Seward made a dismissive gesture. "That is understood, Countess. The duke only hoped you might recall some tidbit of information which slipped your mind when you spoke with the authorities. You are his last hope, you see. The Frenchman owes him a gaming debt." He paused to allow her a moment to absorb what he had said. "As a matter of principle he never leaves a debt uncollected."

"The duke is wise." She took a deep breath seeing a ray of hope that her embarrassment might be turned to a triumph if only she could think of something of importance to tell the duke's solicitor. Unfortunately, try as she might, she could think of nothing. "But I am at a loss," she said.

"The name of a companion, perhaps. A destination he might have mentioned before—" He left his sentence unfinished, purposely reminding the countess of the circumstance of Rhys Delmar's departure from her house.

She reached nervously for her tea. "He never spoke of leaving," she said apologetically. "And he had no companions I was aware of." As she sipped her brow furrowed, showing the deep lines she had so carefully sought to conceal. She must think of something to tell Seward. She must help the Duke of Mitford. She needed him at her table. The scandal of a murdered woman in her house had nearly ruined her. Almost painfully she probed her mind for anything she might offer the solicitor. "There was a servant," she said at last. "Devoted to the Frenchman." She would not speak Rhys Delmar's name. If she did she would be beset by the shame of the scandal and the agony of missing him. For all the disaster he'd brought her, she missed him. "Bouchet—No. Bourget," she said at last. "Lucien Bourget." She looked hopefully at Seward, wanting him to acknowledge that what she'd remembered would be useful. "The man is lame. He should not be so hard to find."

"Not at all," Seward said, rising though he had not touched his tea. "You have the duke's gratitude, Countess."

Visualizing herself fully reinstated in society, the countess rose and called for her butler. "Perhaps he will tell me so himself," she said.

Seward nodded. "You may depend upon it."

Her happiness had the effect of stirring her memory

even further. She clasped her hands together, looking pleased as a child with a bit of cake. "I have recalled something else," she said. "I lent a room to the Frenchman the night before he left. He entertained an American at cards, only the one gentleman."

Seward had been about to follow the butler to the door, but turned back. "You remember his name?"

"Oui," the countess said proudly. "The coincidence of it. The gaming. The cards. He was called Gamble."

"Gamble," Seward repeated, one hand absently stroking his red whiskers. "An American you say."

"Oui," the countess confirmed, quite proud of herself. "And beyond his means. He backed his marks with papers from a stage company in some unheard-of place. Rhys was afraid the American would not be able to pay them off."

"They were worth a large sum?"

"Quite," she said. "He'd not have let it go uncollected."

"You've been helpful, *madame,*" Seward said, sure she was right. A gambler did not walk away from his winnings.

"About the duke," the countess ventured.

"He will call on you," Seward said as the butler led him out. *But do not hold your breath.* He laughed as the door closed behind him. The countess would wear herself out preparing for the duke's visit. But then most people were gullible fools. Those that were not could be had for the right price. A few coins in a palm and one might get most anything, even a lift in a duke's carriage if the duke was elsewhere.

A street away, Seward hailed a cab. The trail was

not so cold as he had feared. He would find the American first. He would be easier to trace, since he was likely to be in one of the inns favored by colonials. From Mr. Gamble he was certain to get a clue to Delmar's whereabouts. Seward was no stranger to the gaming tables. He knew that a man was apt to talk of anything over a hand of cards, even of where he might go next.

Eight

Rhys had not expected this. At the invitation of Horace Roper, Rhys approached the main house at the Gamble ranch. The frame structure resembled those he had seen in the East, a two-story building with a turret and wrap of porches, a rose garden and a picket fence in front. Inside he found gleaming walnut paneling and a handsome staircase descending into the front hall.

Rope led him into a parlor which opened off the hall, a room which had wisely been decorated in shades of cool blue. A pattern of forget-me-nots lined the pleasing wallpaper. Soft blue velvet covered the settee and chairs. The room was charming, tasteful, a departure from the austere adobe bunkhouse where he and Lucien had spent the night.

The house and parlor were not, however, the greatest surprise he received at the Gamble ranch. That credit belonged to the woman he observed descending the staircase. Her hair was carefully coiffed, her carriage straight, her countenance serene. His eyes followed as her gliding steps brought her to the last tread and her hand slid from the banister. She wore a dress of black silk, simply but beautifully cut. She was all elegance and grace, so different from Teddy Gamble that Rhys could hardly believe they shared the same bloodline.

"Madame Gamble." He rose as she entered the parlor and introduced himself before Rope had a chance to do it for him. She offered him her hand. He took it and pressed his lips to the back of it. She was Felicity Gamble, Zack Gamble's mother, Teddy's grandmother. She was in mourning for her sons, one of whom she had not seen in many years. "I regret to have arrived with bad tidings," he said sincerely. "I offer my sympathy and hope you can forgive my need to come here and—"

Her soft smile stopped him. "I understood my son Zachary, Mr. Delmar," she said quietly. "He had an unwitting way of entangling others in his life and ours. I can hardly blame you for his actions."

Teddy, in buckskin and boots, had come in behind Felicity. "Ha! Could have said no to a card game with an ailing man," she mumbled.

"Teddy!"

"All right, Grandmother." Teddy gave the older woman a quick, conciliatory kiss on the cheek. "Best manners in the house, I know."

"See that you remember it." Felicity gave her granddaughter a stern look. "Mr. Delmar is our guest." She turned to Rhys then. "We would like you to join us for breakfast, Mr. Delmar."

Rhys made a slight bow. "I am delighted to do so," he said, smiling inwardly, feeling, at last, that he had an ally. Making a courtly display of his manners, he escorted the older woman to the dining room across the hallway. Rope and Teddy followed, pausing for a moment to speak privately while Rhys assisted Felicity into her chair. He'd have done the same for Teddy a moment later but she brushed him off. "Don't need any help," she said tersely.

"Teddy has an aversion to social graces, you may have noticed," Felicity commented as she gracefully unfolded a crisply starched square of linen and placed it in her lap.

"She is—" Rhys looked at Teddy and deliberated for a moment. Untamed, he thought, like one of the wild, spirited mustangs he'd seen from the window of a train during his long journey. One in particular, a splashy golden steed, had seemed to delight in racing the engine, or the wind. Teddy had that same wildness, that same air of challenge about her. "Original," he remarked, pleased to note that his comment made Teddy squirm.

"I see you are not without tact, Mr. Delmar." A hint of a smile turned up the corners of Felicity Gamble's lips. "You'll find yourself in the minority at the Gamble ranch."

"If you two are through discussing my character maybe we can have breakfast," Teddy said curtly. "Rope's got to get into town to see the first run out."

"And we do have a little business to talk over," Rope said, aligning himself with Teddy but clearly deferring to Felicity's wish for civility at her table.

Felicity, still smiling faintly, motioned for a servant to bring the food. "Maude is part of the family," she explained, as a plain-faced woman in a blue gingham dress and white apron dished helpings of eggs and sausages from a crockery platter. "This house couldn't run without her."

"Not if anyone wanted to eat," Maude said good-naturedly. She was nearly the same age as Felicity but Maude moved with a youthful energy born of fresh air and simple living, breezing around the table and serving everyone in a few short minutes, then repeating the circuit and handing round a basket of steaming biscuits. "Mrs. Gamble's cooking is too fancy for the ranch hands," she said. "And Teddy wouldn't know flour from grist."

"Thankfully," Teddy retorted. Her brief glance at Maude unexpectedly caught Rhys's eyes on her.

The others were busy buttering biscuits and stirring cream into the coffee Maude had poured. Rhys did not bother to pull his gaze away, even though Teddy's face looked as if it ached to scowl back at him. She hadn't put up her hair today. It was combed back and tied at her nape with a strip of beaded buckskin—the sort of adornment he imagined an Indian woman might wear. Her hair was pretty, nearly down to her waist, the whole skein of it was glistening like honey pouring out of a jar.

He kept staring, realizing, at length, that Teddy Gamble fascinated him. She *was* original, quite a change of pace from the women of his experience. He was accustomed to faces masked with powder, paint and guile. Hers was scrubbed clean as that of a child who had just walked away from the washbowl. She seemed to wear her feelings up front—no pretense about her at all. He found the trait commendable, even if the feelings she had for him were mostly unfriendly.

What's more, she seemed less forbidding in her grandmother's house, where she was surrounded by fine polished furniture and delicate lace curtains. Yesterday at the scarred table in the saloon she'd seemed so much a spitfire he hadn't known how to react to her. But here, at a table covered with snowy linen and set with porcelain china, Teddy was the one who looked out of place and acted out of sorts.

Made her even prettier, he decided. And easier to read. He considered himself a master at reading people. With Teddy there was agitation, and display of her formidable temper. He suspected it was even shorter than usual today. If he did not miss his guess there was something afoot here. He thought of the invitation Rope had extended for him and Lucien to move into quarters at the ranch's bunkhouse. Not given out of charity. Oh no, not from Teddy Gamble. When *she* pretended to be nice she had something up her sleeve.

An idea came to him all at once. This *was* a contest, the same as a game of chance. Teddy's brashness, her refusal to accept the legitimacy of his claim was a bluff. She was stalling. But for what reason? He considered, uneasily, that perhaps his share of the Gamble Line was not as valuable as Zack Gamble had represented it. Or perhaps it was worth much more and Teddy did not want to ante up so much. Or maybe she did not want to ante up anything at all. Maybe she was stalling until she could find a way to cut him out of what was rightfully his.

Oddly, he felt himself almost immediately restored in body and mind, though the trip west had been physically grueling, and his head had never been at rest over what he had left behind in London. Almost as quickly, Rhys understood what had energized him. Teddy Gamble had issued a challenge, whether she had meant to or not. No matter. She had made a mistake. Rhys Delmar had never been bluffed out of a hand, nor had he ever walked away from a challenge. Indeed, only once had he ever run from trouble.

"Do you find our food unpalatable, Mr. Delmar?" Felicity's question broke his train of thought.

He realized he'd not even picked up his knife and fork. Smiling, he did so at once and took a bite of flavorful sausage, finding he was suddenly ravenous. "Excellent," he insisted before taking another mouthful. "How fortunate you are to have Maude."

Grinning, her cheeks a candy red, Maude made her way to the kitchen. A few minutes later she was back with a fresh jar of prickly pear jelly and was insisting that Rhys try it with his biscuits. He did, and swore it was easily the best treat he'd had since leaving France. He had not forgotten Jenny, nor his vow to avenge her. But for now he must make the most of life in the Arizona desert. And Teddy Gamble was about to learn that Rhys Delmar would play the fool for no one.

Teddy thought Rhys looked exactly like a fox at the coop. What's more she had the distinct feeling the coop was hers and that she was powerless to save her prized hens from the likes of Rhys Delmar. Briefly she closed her eyes and asked the powers above what she had done to deserve so much adversity in so short a period of time. The powers, however, did not answer. Teddy was left with the uncomfortable task of figuring it out and combating it on her own.

As for Delmar, he troubled her more than a little bit by looking so at ease and confident in her grandmother's house. She'd preferred keeping him confused and defensive. A man was easier to handle when he was like that. But here he sat, cocksure and smiling with her grandmother and Maude fawning all over him. If she dared she'd give both of them a tongue-lashing for making such a fuss over him. Didn't they realize that the scoundrel was threatening to take their livelihood? Uncle Zack, at least, had been an easy partner—not bothering himself with how the Gamble Line was run as long as the company periodically sent him money.

Well. She sighed and pushed her plate aside. Her usually hearty appetite had departed, and her breakfast was mostly uneaten. She and Rope had concocted a plan for keeping Mr. Delmar and his claims at bay until they were better prepared to settle with him—or could find a way of sending him packing empty-handed.

"Mr. Delmar," she said resolutely.

"Rhys." Smiling slyly he cut her short. "This is an informal land I have learned. You are plain Teddy. I am Rhys."

The day before, she had made fun of the string of names he'd used to introduce himself. Today he was taunting her with her own words. Teddy's temper flared but she dampered the heat. Flying into a rage wasn't going to accomplish what she and Rope wanted to accomplish.

"All right, Rhys," she said, giving a flat pronunciation to his name. "Rope and I have come up with what we think is a fair arrangement until we get an answer on the validity of your claim."

"Something other than cleaning stalls?"

The words annoyed her, the tone raised an alarm. Not trusting herself to speak and knowing Rope had an I-told-you-so-look on his face, Teddy locked her tense fingers around the handle of her coffee cup and raised it to her lips. She wondered what had happened in the past twelve hours to give the Frenchman all that brass. For a few seconds she wondered if he was even the same man she'd backed down at their last encounter. This Rhys Delmar looked larger and—dammit—virile as a stud horse.

She could see him quite clearly over the rim of her cup. She noted the sardonic smile, and the peculiar gleam in the pale eyes. An apprehensive shiver came unexpectedly. The way his eyes shone, and the way he was looking at her gave her a perverse and puzzling mix of aversion and excitement. Men around Wishbone had long ago given up thinking of Teddy as an available woman. She was one of the boys to them. So it had been a stretch of time since a man had looked at her in a predatory way, as if he noticed her curves, wanted to see them uncovered, wanted her.

Teddy felt more heat building inside her—not her temper but something wilder, something unfamiliar. She was, abruptly, too acutely aware of the man. Her vision was made keener by the strange heat. She saw what she had refused to notice before, the luster of his black hair, the enticing way the overlong locks curled over his crisp collar. He had a way of giving a half smile. When he did, she felt the power of it like the flame of a match to tinder. She put down her cup. Her hand slid to her throat where she felt her wide silver and turquoise necklace growing hot as a branding iron against her skin.

He followed the involuntary movement with pale eyes that glittered wickedly from beneath thick black lashes. His gaze was like an assault nearly taking her breath. She willed herself to glare back. As their eyes met she came to the disturbing realization that he was fully conscious of the way he was unnerving her.

Indignant, she broke her gaze away and inhaled sharply. Once, she'd been near enough to a lightning strike to feel the jarring current of it hit the ground. The same sort of electric jolt coursed through her as the thought dawned that Rhys Delmar was not the witless, dandified half-man she'd assumed he was.

He was dangerous, definitely dangerous.

"Teddy? You were saying?" As if to prove her the witless one, to make her wonder if she had imagined what she felt and sensed, his expression, when he called to her, was innocently benign.

"Forget that," Teddy said, not about to offer an apology for her hasty words of the night before, but anxious to keep her unwanted partner away from Parrish Adams. "Rope and I feel that the only fair thing under the circumstances is to put you up at the ranch until this is settled. You and your—uh, valet can keep the room at the back of the bunkhouse and take your meals with the hands. No need for you to sleep in the stable or pay for lodging in town."

"An interesting change of heart," Rhys commented. Now he was sure she was stalling. She wanted to keep him close enough to keep a watch on him. Or did she want to keep him away from something? The stage line maybe? "I'll think it over," he told her.

"Think it over? Now look here—" Teddy started.

"You think it over and let us know," Rope interrupted, seeing that Teddy was about two steps from snapping the hold on her temper. "Teddy hasn't thought to say it but I'm the third partner in this company. I, for one, am willin' to give you a fair shake."

"Shake?"

"Deal," Rope explained. "But anybody can understand that when a stranger shows up claimin' part of what you've worked and scraped for, you want to make sure he's not tryin' to pull wool."

"Anyway," Teddy chirped in. "I've already sent a letter off requesting that witness in London to give us a statement. Don't reckon there's any doubt what that man of yours will say."

"None," Rhys replied, giving the half smile. He wasn't happy to know that Teddy's inquiry was already on the way, but he would not let her know that. He'd been prepared to suggest that a friend of his get the deposition, someone who could do it quietly to ensure the authorities searching for him did not hear of it. But Teddy had preempted that possibility. He said a silent touché to her. She had raised the odds. Did she know that?

Teddy felt a flash of fire inside as he gave the quick

smile and the long look. She scowled but tried to keep her voice even. "Unless there's trouble finding that witness, it shouldn't take more than a few months to hear back. If what you say is on the level we can pay you what your share is worth at that time."

Rhys shrugged indifferently, but his eyes sparkled wickedly. Let her worry. It would do her good. "Who is to say?" he asked, as if he had not a care in the world. "By then I may have come to like this land and running a stage company. I may want to keep my shares."

"Keep?" Teddy's voice rose. "And where do you get the idea you'll be running anything? Look here—"

"Simmer down, Teddy," Rope's cooler voice drowned Teddy's out. "Nothing will be running if we don't get into town."

Teddy rose quickly, nearly choking on her temper as she saw Felicity Gamble's frown.

"Don't concern yourself about me," Rhys called after her, noting the quick rhythm of her hips as she stalked off—the way the buckskin fringe of her shirt danced around her squared shoulders. "I shall be perfectly content in the company of two charming ladies."

Nine

"If you two don't take the prize." Parrish Adams addressed the dusty riders who had come into his Diamond Saloon and ordered a couple of whiskeys.

The older and stockier of the two shrugged. The younger man looked sheepishly at Adams and said, "We didn't know—"

"Not here, Pete," Adams interrupted. "You and Boyd come on in the office to talk."

As he walked toward a doorway beneath the stairs that led to rooms on the second floor, Adams cautiously cast a glance around the saloon. The Diamond, with its gilt-framed mirrors and mahogany bar and genuine oil paintings on the scarlet papered walls, was a real showplace for Wishbone. Despite its attractiveness the saloon was usually short on patrons before noon. This morning was no exception. Only one other man stood at the bar and he had his head hung over the beer he was trying to make last. The few other men who had ventured in this early, occupied tables. Most of them were engaged in a poker game. The girls Adams employed didn't come down until afternoon, when there was enough business to make it worth their while.

"Sorry, boss," Pete Smith apologized. "Wasn't thinkin'."

Adams closed the door behind him. "Which is usually the case," he said testily. "Like it was yesterday when you held up that stage."

"Nobody told us that girl of Len Blalock's was gonna be on it," the other man, the one called Boyd, countered in defense of his brother. "I was funnin' with her a little and when she told us who she was it got us rattled."

"So damn rattled you rode off without the strongbox, not to mention leaving Luther behind." Adams motioned them into chairs while he perched on the corner of his big walnut desk. He was angry enough to shoot the two of them. He had not anticipated such a show of resistance from Teddy Gamble or that her drivers and guards would take such risks to defend their cargo. Most of all he had not anticipated that Boyd and Pete Smith and Joe Luther would be the most inept road agents ever to stop a stage.

Having to use them at all irked him, not because he minded going around the law, but because he preferred outsmarting his enemies to outgunning them. Men who depended solely on gunplay to get what they wanted were liable to have short lives. Adams's many and lofty ambitions included longevity. What was the point of getting what you wanted if you weren't around to enjoy it? Or if the weakest link in the chain, a man like Joe Luther, could bring all your carefully executed plans to quick disaster?

"We couldn't help Luther," Boyd said. The heel of his boot made an agitated tap-tap on the floor. "He was flat out and that driver had found his gun by then."

With fire in his dark eyes Adams leaned toward Boyd Smith. "So you rode off and left him to be taken to prison and put all of us in jeopardy if he talks."

"Luther won't say nothin'," Pete piped in. "He knows you'll get him out. Besides, wouldn't be no use confessin' to Sheriff Blalock."

That was true but it missed the point as Adams saw it. He didn't like failure. So far, these three hadn't given him much else. A sneering smile showed both his distaste for his companions and his disgust for their actions. Adams fingered a waxed coil of his mustache, pausing briefly as he cut his eyes toward the back door of his office, where he thought he saw a shadow pass along the threshold. "I may not get him out," he threatened. "I may let him board in that jail until he smartens up."

"Aw, don't do that, boss. Luther's all right," Pete insisted.

"He's an idiot," Adams said coldly. "Getting himself knocked off a horse by some foreigner who didn't even have a gun." The irritation in his voice manifested itself in the tightening muscles of his lean face. "But maybe getting his head cracked with a rock did him some good."

"Couldn't have hurt him any," Boyd said, wanting to make clear that he shared the boss's sentiments about Luther.

"Naw," Pete agreed, laughing.

Adams took advantage of Pete's noisy hee-haw, to slide quietly off the desk and reach for the knob of the back door. Before either of the men with him realized what he was doing, Adams had twisted the brass knob and jerked the door inward. A woman in a daringly cut red dress came stumbling into the office behind it.

"Eavesdropping is terribly common, my dear," Adams said coldly. "Like you."

If she was offended she didn't show it. She gave a coy smile and carefully smoothed her platinum curls, as she looked Adams in the eye. "I suit you," she said.

"For the time being," Adams retorted, reaching around her to close the door she'd been leaning against. He took another moment to select a cigar from the teakwood humidor on the cabinet behind his desk. He trimmed and lit it and puffed, making it insultingly plain that he did not intend to offer smokes to the Smith brothers. Not that either of them minded, with the pretty blonde preening and smiling in front of them. But Adams soon deprived them of that pleasure too.

"You two get out on the street and learn what you can about that foreigner who downed Luther," he said irritably. "Then get over to the jail and tell Luther not to worry." Boyd was on his feet, Pete at the door when another order came. "And tell the sheriff I want to see him immediately."

When they were gone he grabbed the woman and pulled her to him but when she lifted her face for the expected kiss he roughly twisted her arm behind her back and snarled at her. "Don't do that again, Norine," he warned. "Having my wife spying on me makes me look like a fool."

DEVIL MOON

The pain of his manhandling excited Norine. She purred with pleasure as she slowly and sweetly answered him. "I wasn't spying, darling. I came to tell you something important and didn't want to interrupt at the wrong moment."

Adams let go of her arm. "What is it?"

Freed, Norine wrapped herself around him, pressing against all the places she knew were sensitive to her charms. "That detective you hired," she said breathlessly. "He sent a letter."

Clearly moved by his wife's antics, Adams, nevertheless, kept his hands at his sides. "Don't take all day to tell me, Norine."

She stepped back, putting distance between them as she smiled up at her husband's intent face. "He found that gambler you wanted him to find, the one who won part of the Gamble Line off old Zack Gamble."

"And—"

She sighed. "The man already sold out to somebody else."

A jerk shook Adams's lean frame. "Who?" he demanded.

Norine stretched, curling her spine backwards and thrusting her nearly exposed breasts even further out of the tight red bodice. An unconscious malice lay behind her action. She liked her husband's full attention at all times, no matter how pressing a distraction might come along. When she was sure he was completely focused on her, with both mind and body, she told him what he wanted to know. "Horace Roper bought it off him about a month ago."

Adams clinched his fists and sucked in a breath

that didn't come out for several long and painful seconds. In the interim his face turned red as flame. He looked as if he would explode. "For that bitch," he said at last.

"For himself, apparently," Norine continued, wiggling a step closer. "Ten percent of the company is registered in Roper's name. The other forty still belongs to old Zack."

Adams, outraged, made the unsettling move of turning his back on Norine. "She thinks she's outsmarted me," he said. His voice was low and held a threatening note.

"No, darling," came with strained sweetness from Norine. "Teddy Gamble doesn't know you're behind the attacks on the Gamble Line. How could she?"

Adams turned. Sometimes, often, Norine tried his patience. "She knows. She can't prove it's me but she knows. If you'd heard her yesterday after Northrop left our meeting you wouldn't doubt what I'm telling you."

"So what?" Norine lifted her dainty ring-clad hands. She stretched them out and slid them down her husband's hard chest. "It's only a matter of time before she's out of business, and it won't matter who has the shares."

Adams caught her marauding hands and held them tightly between their two bodies. "It matters because I could have enjoyed taking down the Gamble Line from the inside out. Not to mention the great waste of destroying something that will eventually belong to me. I wanted that ten percent," he said hotly. "With an interest in the company, even a small one, I'd have been well on the way to getting full control. I'd have known about everything—assets, schedules, deals with the miners. Now, my dear, everything must continue to be done the hard way."

"Nothing wrong with the hard way," Norine said suggestively. "It always turns out right for me. Besides," she went on, delighted with the harsh glare Adams gave her, "you'll win." She inevitably found Parrish Adams most exciting when he was angry. At the moment he was seething and she intended to take advantage of his fury. With little resistance from him she tugged their hands down to groin level and began slowly stroking her husband.

"You're damned right, I'll win," he growled at her, though he made no effort to stop her assault. "I'm taking over this territory." He began to rock against her. "From here to California. And when I do, nothing will move in or out unless Parrish Adams gets a cut. No ore, no payrolls, no supplies, nobody. I'm building an empire here and no chit who can't make up her mind if she's a rooster or a hen is going to stop me."

"I know what I am," Norine purred. Her hands had unfastened his trousers and closed around his hardness, making brisk strokes that had begun to take effect.

A throaty groan emanated from his throat as he jerked free of her, whirled her around, threw her face down over his desk and snatched her billowing silk skirts up over her head. "You're a whore," he said, and drove into her.

* * *

The room smelled of perfume and sex. Norine, purring like a satisfied cat, lay across the desk as he'd left her. Adams had adjusted his clothes and was washing his hands when a knock came at the door that opened to the saloon. Cursing, he pulled his wife's wrinkled skirt over her naked bottom and pulled her to her feet. "Get out," he said.

"Adams? You there?" Len Blalock's hesitant voice came behind the sound of Norine's scurrying footsteps.

"Come on in," Adams replied to the sheriff as he ran his hands over his tousled hair and smoothed it to his head. Coatless but presentable, he was in the leather chair behind his desk when the lawman stepped in.

A silver star shone from the gray serge vest Len Blalock wore over his white shirt. His face was wide, his skin weathered. The combination of sun and worry made him look older than his forty-seven years. He was a heavily built man but much of his weight had turned from muscle to fat with the years. A good portion of it had settled around his middle where it all but obscured his gunbelt. He hadn't, though, quite lost all the instincts that had once made him a good lawman. He caught the faint essence of Norine's perfume and looked for her. "Thought I heard your wife," he said.

"You didn't," Adams retorted. "Have a seat." While the sheriff pulled up a chair Adams relit his cigar. He puffed heavily, filling the room with pungent smoke and quickly ridding it of telltale odors. He did offer a cigar to the sheriff but the lawman declined, citing a breakfast that had not set well with him.

Len Blalock was the kind of lawman Adams liked, a man who had been at his job a decade or more and come to the conclusion that the price of honesty and keeping order had been too high. Adams had observed those traits in Sheriff Blalock when he'd come to Wishbone and opened the Diamond Saloon. He'd made a point of doing the sheriff a few favors, had helped him settle a debt on his house and loaned him money for his daughter's schooling. And then he'd owned him. All of that had taken place just far enough back for the sheriff now to start having second thoughts about selling out. "Been avoiding me?" Adams asked the man.

"No. Being careful, that's all," the sheriff said too quickly to be convincing. "Got your man locked up. Didn't want anybody making a connection before he goes to trial."

Since yesterday Blalock had worried himself sick wondering what would happen when Joe Luther did go to trial. He was fairly certain Luther would be convicted. All those witnesses on the stage, including his daughter, had seen his face. Once he was convicted and looking at prison, what was to keep Luther from revealing who he worked for or that Len Blalock had played a role in the attacks on the Gamble Line?

Feeling dry-mouthed, the sheriff waited for enlightenment from Adams, hoping against hope that the man had a solution that would spare them both being named conspirators to the crime. At the same time he was wishing he'd never met Adams. And he was acknowledging to himself that, much as he wanted to, he'd never dare break with him.

His efforts to hide his feelings from Adams had his stomach feeling full of rocks. His head felt as if it were split. Seeing Justine and Joe Luther in his office yesterday at the same time had brought home to him an inkling of what he had bargained away. He hadn't thought of his association with Adams as selling out until then. He'd realized how close Justine had come to being mauled and killed by men he'd been helping protect.

The trouble was, he couldn't see any way out of the predicament now. He'd agreed to look the other way while Adams harassed the Gamble Line until Teddy Gamble was willing to sell out or had lost her Wells Fargo contracts. In return Adams had promised there would be no killing. Now he doubted if Adams would keep his word.

He was ashamed of what he'd become—for the promise of a few dollars—but afraid to buck Adams. He put a hand to his brow as if to still his throbbing head. He'd been a fool to throw his hat in with the businessman, but he'd be a bigger one to try and get it back.

Adams, black brows drawn together, sat and watched Len Blalock stew. He could as good as guess what was going on in the sheriff's mind. Smiling perversely, he rocked back in his chair and laced his fingers together behind his neck. "Don't worry about Luther," he said. "He's not going to trial."

The sheriff shook his aching head. "Don't see how

even you can prevent a trial—unless you've got the circuit judge in your pocket."

"Not yet," Adams retorted.

"Then how—"

"Luther's going to escape. You see to it."

"Me? Let a prisoner escape." Momentarily disbelieving what he'd heard, the sheriff stared at the still smiling Adams.

"Either that or shoot him. Makes no difference to me. But Luther doesn't go to trial."

Some of the courage he'd once possessed filled Len Blalock. "I've got to draw the line here, Adams," he said. "I've got a reputation for running a tight jail." He pushed out of the chair and stood, legs wide apart, before Adams's desk. "And I don't shoot down an unarmed man."

Adams was unmoved by the sheriff's protests. "You'll find a way," he insisted. "Incidentally wasn't that your daughter who came in on yesterday's stage?"

Uneasily, the sheriff nodded. Justine was the love of his life. He'd been both father and mother to her since his wife had died ten years back.

"Pretty girl." Adams's face had a feral look that gave even the hardened sheriff a chill. "Too bad she didn't stay in the East where it's safer."

Defeated by the implied threat, Blalock dropped his head. He'd compromised all he'd once believed in, to provide for Justine, to get her out of Wishbone and in a place where she'd rub shoulders with finer people, maybe find a husband who'd give her the better life she deserved. Justine, though, had ideas of her own. She'd left her expensive school and come home unannounced, stating she'd missed her pa too much to stay away. He cringed at the thought of her ever finding out what he'd done.

Grimly he nodded to Adams. "I'll see that Luther gets away tonight."

Ten

The stock saddle with the high pommel and the flat-topped horn took some getting used to. But the dun gelding Rhys had borrowed from Felicity Gamble had a smooth gait and an easy mouth. Half a mile from the ranch, Rhys had abandoned the posting style he was accustomed to and adapted to moving his body with the horse.

Even so, he would not have been mistaken for a cowboy, not in the closefitting knee-high riding boots and snug buff-colored trousers topped by a superbly tailored black jacket. Had there been any doubt left, the black silk ascot Lucien had expertly tied inside his starched collar would have removed it.

Lucien, outfitted in a hammertail frock coat and bowler hat looked even more the odd fellow. Unaccustomed to riding, he had adjusted to neither horse nor saddle. Staying astride his mount had proved to be a struggle, made all the more difficult because of his lameness. After the first few minutes he had abandoned the stirrups due to the discomfort they gave him, and put all his concentration into gripping the leather-clad horn. As a result he bounced loosely around the worn seat of the saddle and would surely have fallen to the ground had not the curve of the cantle served as a buffer to his slipping and sliding. Thankfully, too, the old mare he rode was slow and patient with her inexperienced rider.

Patience, however, quickly deserted Lucien. "I tell you, Monsieur Rhys, I belong in the city, where there are cabs and drivers to be had. This place—" In a moment of despair he threw up his hands and nearly tilted himself off the horse. "This animal," he said, abruptly seizing the horn and righting himself, "I cannot abide."

"I should have insisted you stay behind," Rhys said, realizing that somewhere along the journey from London to Wishbone, Arizona, Lucien had ceased being the preemptive caregiving servant and had become an anxious and apprehensive friend. That being the case, he felt duty bound to make a change in the association they had. "But now that we are here," he said, "and because I do not think you would undertake the return journey alone, I feel I must make amends for having imposed my troubles on you."

"There is no imposition, *monsieur.*"

Rhys did not know how his words would be received, but he felt compelled to speak his mind. The open country of Arizona, the great sweeps of desert and towering bare-faced mountains made a man aware he need only have the limits he chose for himself. Rhys had begun to question the ones he had, more often than not, chosen by default. Of more concern was the worry that he had chosen for Lucien, too. He did not know how, or even if he might rectify what was amiss in his life, but he knew wholeheartedly that

Lucien must have the chance to pick his own way. Here and now, he was convinced, was the place to begin. "I think it is only right that I dismiss you from your duties," he announced.

Lucien paled. "You are dismissing me? *Monsieur!*" Lucien sputtered. "What am I to do?"

"I am dismissing you from service only," Rhys explained. "You are free to stay with me if you wish, but as an equal, not as servant to his master."

"Monsieur!"

"Lucien, I insist," Rhys said. "Be your own man. You have the wit, find the will. Both of us know you are nearly as adept at the tables as I am. Find a game. You could make a decent living. Better yet open an establishment of some kind. Here or elsewhere. Put your talents to use. I've no doubt you can do better for yourself than I have done for you."

A few minutes later, having recovered from his shock, Lucien, who had begun to find the prospect of freedom intriguing, put a question to Rhys. "And you, *monsieur*, what will you do? Surely you do not wish to stay here longer than is necessary."

Rhys smiled. Old habits held fast. "You forget yourself, Lucien," he said. "I am Rhys to you now."

The former servant looked uncertain then broke into a big grin. "As you wish," he said.

"I stay as long as I must," Rhys continued. "I mean to get what is mine." He got a devilish gleam in his eye. Lucien had seen it when Rhys knew the table was rich and the players overrated. "And not to be toyed with in the process," he added. The smile he gave then was off-center and Lucien knew he was thinking of

Teddy Gamble. "I mean to return to London with my pockets full." He straightened in the saddle as he spoke. "That dimwit who gave evidence against me was paid by someone. He might forget his lies for more gold. Whether he does or not, I am curious to know what act of mine has made an enemy who would take such pain to ruin me." The smile was gone now. His eyes had grown shadowed, his expression grave. "I have had long nights to think on it," he pronounced grimly. "What happened was planned long in advance. What's more, Jenny knew why she was killed. She wanted to tell me but lacked the strength to say the words."

"Then you did not mean it when you told Mademoiselle Gamble you might keep your shares of the stage line?"

A silence ensued as Rhys considered the question. He had not meant it when he said it, but, having put it to voice he had found the prospect of an entirely different life held some appeal, as did Teddy Gamble. Should he find the wagering high in the local saloons he might bankroll his defense in London solely with his winnings. After all, a stage company, if well run, would be worth more in the future than now. To Lucien he said, "My friend, when one is wishing there is the whole world at hand."

An hour later the pair rode into town and attracted more than a few stares when they paused in the middle of the street to flip a coin. "There are two saloons, Lucien. One for you. One for me. Take your pick."

Lucien looked about and decided the plainer front of the Brass Bell held more appeal for his simple tastes. "Heads," Lucien called.

Rhys tossed the coin. "Heads," he said. "The beginning of your lucky streak," Rhys told him.

They left the horses at a hitching rail, agreeing to meet again at nightfall, the size of their winnings determining whether they would return to the ranch or find more comfortable lodgings in town. Rhys watched Lucien limp away, then, with what he swore was the last loan he would take from his former servant weighty in his pocket, turned down the board sidewalk toward the Diamond Saloon.

He did not get far.

"Mister! Delmar!" The summons came from the open doorway of an office that appeared to be a small and dark cubicle.

Hearing the clank of spurs and the stomp of boots coming his way, Rhys stopped and turned. The man who had spoken to him wore a badge on his chest. For one damnable minute Rhys wondered if he'd already been traced and was about to be arrested, but then remembered that the young woman on the stage had said her father was the law officer in Wishbone.

"Sheriff Blalock?" he ventured.

"Right. Been looking for you," the man said. His face showed the strain of a demanding day. Len Blalock pushed back his hat, revealing a line of white skin on his forehead that the sun had failed to reach. "Come on in the office," he said. "Want to say a few words to you."

Still not entirely certain if he was to be commended

or arrested, Rhys followed the sheriff. The room was larger than it had looked from the street, narrow up front and widening to a T in back where a pair of cells had been set into thick adobe walls. One was empty. The other housed the prisoner he was responsible for capturing. The man was stretched out on a bare cot and had crisscrossing strips of white bandage around his head. The look the man gave Rhys made it entirely clear what he would do if there were no bars between them.

Rhys turned his back to the man and sat near a cold pot-bellied stove close to the sheriff's desk. "Is there something I can do for you, Sheriff Blalock?" he asked.

"You can let me thank you," the sheriff replied solemnly. "My daughter tells me you were quite a hero during that holdup yesterday."

"I did nothing," Rhys insisted. "If the truth be told, your daughter is the one who spared us whatever those bandits intended to do. She but spoke your name and they flew."

The man in the cell snorted but Rhys attributed the sheriff's sudden stiffening to a lawman's alertness.

"She's a brave girl," Len Blalock said. "Foolish but brave. I sent her off to school in Philadelphia." He gave a mirthless burst of laughter. "I wanted her to stay there, get a good start in life."

"Perhaps she'll go back," Rhys offered, for clearly the man was grieved that his daughter had not valued the chance he'd given her.

"Maybe," Len Blalock said. "Anyway, just wanted to let you know I owe you for helping Justine. You need anything in Wishbone you let me know," he declared firmly. "By the way," he added as Rhys was about to leave. "What is it that brings you to our town?"

"Business," Rhys said without hesitation.

"Business? I had you figured for a gambling man."

"My business started at the tables," Rhys explained. "I met a man called Zack Gamble."

"So Zack wound up clear out of the country," Blalock said, knowing Adams would be glad to learn of the prodigal Gamble's whereabouts. "How is the that old card stripper?"

"Dead," Rhys said. "Which is why I come to be here." He explained how Zack's departure had left him holding marks and the unwanted shares of the Gamble Line and how, though it was an inconvenience of great magnitude, he had come to collect from the other partner.

"Well, I'll be damned!" Len Blalock felt like a man reprieved. This was what Adams had been wanting, a way to get a death grip on the Gamble Line without depending on the likes of Luther and the Smith brothers. Men like those three were a risk because there was always one who would sell out if the price and the time were right. The Frenchman, though, would be an easy mark for a man like Adams. The proper persuasion and he could buy the man out. With what had once been Zack Gamble's share of the company he'd have his hooks so deep into Teddy Gamble that she would be forced to sell out to him. Maybe, too, Adams would be grateful enough to reward him for finding out about Delmar. Maybe he would be able to take Justine and leave Wishbone for good.

All this he thought with some pangs of conscience. Teddy was a few years older than Justine but the girls had been friends growing up. He'd had his differences with Ted Gamble but—

He swallowed his pride and his guilt one more time. He had to think of himself now, and of Justine. Nobody else mattered.

Eleven

The smell of whiskey and tobacco—the soft glow of the gilt frames of provocative paintings and of gleaming mirrors—all were a pleasant change from the stale air and faded wanted posters papering the sheriff's office. Rhys paused inside a pair of bright red swinging doors long enough to take an appreciative glance at the plush interior of the Diamond Saloon.

A faro game was running in a back corner. A round of poker had started up nearby. A puffy-eyed saloon girl with hennaed hair sat on the carpeted stairs. Her bored expression vanished when she saw Rhys. The fine clothes, the well-groomed look indicated a fat bankroll she might tap into. She got up, gave herself a shake. As he started toward the bar she started toward him.

"You're that Frenchman that came in on the stage yesterday, ain't you?" she said, sidling up close enough to rub shoulders and give him the benefit of her strategically dabbed-on perfume as he reached for the beer he'd ordered.

"Oui, mademoiselle," he said with a smile and a nod intended to convey politeness but not interest.

"You're the one that beaned that holdup man, ain't you?" asked the girl, unwilling to be ignored.

"Oui," he said, this time looking her way.

"I'm Honor." She giggled. "Don't have any, just called that." Having made the eye contact she wanted, Honor took the liberty of placing her hand on Rhys's arm. "I'd be pleased to share a beer with you . . ."

"Rhys," he said. "Rhys Delmar." He slid a coin to the bartender. "A beer for Honor, if you please."

The girl smiled like she'd won a prize then cupped her hands to her mouth and gave a shout. "Sally!" Honor looked toward the gallery railing onto which opened half a dozen red doors. "Maisie!" she called. "Come on down here!"

Two girls peeped out from doorways above, one who looked young enough to be in school, one marginally past her prime. The dresses they wore were replicas of the red and black satin Honor had on. The ruffled skirts had been scandalously shortened almost to the knee and the bodices were skimpy satin covered corselets held up mostly by imagination.

"Mesdemoiselles," Rhys made a sweeping bow and ordered beers for Sally and Maisie. He knew he was getting the newcomer's treatment, that the girls were testing him for generosity and that soon one of them would suggest a tryst upstairs. He had been in enough bordellos and taverns to know the way of things and to know that a man had to be careful how he extricated himself from the clutches of sporting women. They had long memories.

"You gonna be in Wishbone a while, honey," Honor

spoke silkily. "We don't get many gents with class. Not nearly enough."

"I'll be around a while," Rhys told her. "Long enough to get to know all of you better." He winked and got a round of giggles from the girls. "We'll take care of that sometime when I don't have my mind on the cards."

"It's not your mind we're interested in," Maisie told him. For one who appeared so young, the slender, dark-haired girl, had a boldness that indicated she'd had years of practice at her trade. Smiling an invitation at him, she reached a slim hand to the black locks that hung in curls over his collar. "You're a handsome one, I'll say that for you."

"I ain't never seen eyes that purty, not even on a woman," Sally, a blonde by choice, chimed in. She nudged Maisie away and stepped up close, past the line of propriety. With a hand to his chin she turned his head slightly to the left and then to the right. "Bein' pale blue like that, they kinda make me think of moonlight on a warm night."

"Ummm," Maisie said over her shoulder. "They kinda make me wanta melt."

Taking Sally's and Maisie's hands in his Rhys lifted them and touched his lips to the backs of each. *"Merci,"* he said, "you are sweet, both of you."

A touch of jealousy set in with Honor who, after watching the exchange of compliments, had decided that *she* found Rhys Delmar first and didn't want to share him after all. "Leave him be," she said, shooing the other girls away. "It's poker he's after today. You heard him." Grumbling and reluctant, but conceding to a code of finders-keepers the girls had among them, Sally and Maisie left to ply their art on a couple of ranch hands who had come in after Rhys. Honor, anxious to ingratiate herself with the man she had decided might be worth her time even if he was penniless, caught him by the hand and led him toward a table of four men who had just broken out a fresh deck. "These boys keep a game going night and day," she told Rhys. "And they're always lookin' for another player to bring some money in since all they do is swap theirs back and forth. Reckon you can hold your own with them."

"I can only try," Rhys said, grateful for the girl's intervention as she introduced him around and let the foursome know he was looking for a game. Like Honor had said, they welcomed any addition to the pot. One of them pulled a fifth chair to the table and Rhys sat down. He found the men a friendly bunch, not much challenge to his ability but good enough to make for an interesting game.

Eventually Honor got tired of teetering at the back of his chair and left to socialize with other customers of the Diamond. A few hours later Rhys had pocketed a good share of the pot and was wondering how Lucien had fared. He'd also come to the conclusion that he was not likely to come by a fortune at the tables in Wishbone, not if these men were indicative of the lot he'd find willing to be dealt a hand. For unlike the wealthy and jaded men he had matched his luck with in Europe, these men were drifters and ranch hands with only a few dollars in their pockets. The stakes were hardly high enough to make the hours spent with them worthwhile.

"I'm foldin'," one of the players said. He'd identified himself as Spud, a part-time trail cook who spent half his time at the tables trying to stretch his pay. He'd pared it down today.

"Me too," another said, dropping his cards to the tabletop. He was a cowboy who had gotten too old for the range and, like Spud, had turned to poker-playing to fill the time. He was called Lucas, one of the few Arizonans Rhys had met without an inexplicable nickname.

Rhys bade them farewell, then sat alone at the table and tallied his winnings as the other players left for beers and a stretch. The amount was even more disappointing than he'd first thought. He could provide for meals and more comforts in a room, than he'd found in the bunkhouse at the Gamble ranch. But at this rate, unless he devoted years to the endeavor he would scarcely win enough to pay his passage back to London.

Disappointed, he was debating the wisdom of temporarily moving on to a larger town, where the stakes might be higher, when he saw Honor wending her way toward him. For no discernible reason he began comparing the red-haired girl to Teddy Gamble, pitting Honor's provocative smile against Teddy's acid grin, the exaggerated sway of Honor's full hips against Teddy's purposeful stride. They were nothing alike, one so accommodating a man could lead her anywhere, the other so antagonistic a man had better watch his step.

From the back of his mind emerged the thought that Teddy Gamble would be happy to see him leave Wishbone, even temporarily, happy to have him out of her way. He could almost hear her shouting "good riddance" after him. She was a spitfire, that one, and, he admitted, the first woman he'd ever met who evidently wanted to shoot him on sight.

A faint smile briefly twisted his mouth. How could he walk away from a woman like that? He didn't see how he could, not if he wanted to keep what was left of his bruised and battered pride. Teddy Gamble was a woman who needed taming. And he was the man to do it. He laughed softly to himself. Turning all that shrewish fervor to *amour* had an irresistible appeal. He made a wager with himself that by the time they came to terms on the business regarding the stage line, he'd have her bedded and begging him to stay. That she-cat might think she would get the best of him—and maybe she would, but it wouldn't be what she expected. The faint smile deepened, giving Honor a lift of spirit that would have been dashed had she known his thoughts were on another woman.

"Thought you'd like another beer," she said sweetly, easing into one of the vacant chairs and sliding a foam-capped glass toward him. "You've been at it for hours."

"Merci, my *chérie,"* he said. "I am thirsty."

"I like that French talk," Honor said. "Most of these cowboys got dirty mouths when they talk to us girls. Your way is real refreshin'." She'd slid close to him and laid her hand over the one he rested atop the table, but abruptly her bubbly smile vanished and she pulled her hand away. Hastily she got to her feet.

"Honor?" Rhys was mystified.

" 'Scuse me," she said, shoving a chair out of her way.

Rhys turned about, wondering what had gotten into the girl. He saw her red skirt and petticoats swish from side to side as she hurried toward a doorway at the rear of the room. A dark-haired man waited a few steps inside. When Honor was through the door, he shut it behind her. The Diamond's boss, he assumed, hoping he hadn't gotten the girl in trouble by distracting her from her moneymaking activities. He would do what he could to rectify the matter. He owed the girl. She'd gotten him in the poker game and, if not well-fixed, he was better set than when he'd come in.

He'd give her a tip. She deserved that and it ought to ease things with her boss.

As it turned out, the latter was not necessary. Honor came strutting back after a few minutes and she was smiling bigger than ever. "Miss me?" she asked.

"Like the sunshine," Rhys told her. He looked toward the office she'd left. The dark-haired man stood in the doorway leaning against the jamb. "Is anything wrong?"

"Not a thing," she said. "Mr. Adams—he's our boss—wanted to talk to me for a few minutes. Said I was one of his best girls. 'Course I knew that." She laughed. "Had enough of those trail riders tell me so. Anyhow, Mr. Adams noticed you playin' cards and how good you were at it. He said a man that can play like you do deserves a good cigar." Very slowly she reached two fingers into the V between her breasts and pulled out a long hand-wrapped cigar. "He sent you one of his special-made ones," she said.

Rhys glanced behind him and nodded his thanks to the dark-haired man standing there. "This Adams owns the Diamond?" Rhys asked Honor.

"He owns the Diamond and lots of things. Lots of people, too."

"People?" Rhys pinched the end off the cigar and got a match from his pocket. He lit the cigar and puffed deeply on it, enjoying the fineness and quality.

Honor made a nervous glance at the closed door of the office. "I didn't mean that," she said softly. "A lot of people work for Mr. Adams, that's all I meant."

"Speaking of work," Rhys said. "Would Adams mind if you took off long enough to lunch with me?"

"Well, I—" She made another nervous glance at the office door.

"I'll pay for your time, if that is what bothers you," Rhys assured her. "But lunch and a pretty smile is all I want."

Honor gave the smile immediately, the first genuine one he'd seen on her face. "You don't mind if we order something up to my room, do you?" The girl clutched his arm possessively while making certain both Maisie and Sally saw that she had latched onto the Frenchman. "It would make the other girls real envious if they thought—"

He leaned in close and kissed her cheek, not displeased to have made a friend of the girl. She could be useful to him and clearly it had been a long time since a man had wanted anything other than sex from her. He liked Honor but did not feel a strong physical desire for her. Maybe because he sensed she needed a friend as much as he did—maybe because his intimate thoughts were of someone else. Whatever the reason, he felt no disrespect for Honor because of her occupation. She made her way the best she could just as he had always done.

Taking Honor's hand in his he drew her to her feet. "Let them put their imaginations to the test then."

Honor giggled and proudly led Rhys through the center of the saloon and toward the stairs. "We're gonna have ourselves a fine time," she said loudly.

Twelve

"How the hell did he get into town?" Outside the Diamond, restrained by Rope, Teddy Gamble was fighting mad.

"Sweet-talked your grandmother into loaning him a horse, would be my guess. Womenfolk always take a shine to a fella like that. Want to get all accommodatin'."

"I feel like accommodatin' him with an axe handle." Peering through the beveled glass window of the Diamond's front, Teddy saw Rhys wrap his arm around a saloon girl's waist and start up the stairs. "I knew I should have told Felicity how important it was to make sure he stayed at the ranch." Her hot breath made a small circle of mist on the glass before she lifted her head. "Dammit if he doesn't have a knack for winding up where he doesn't belong." Stepping back, sighing like she was letting out all the woes of the world, Teddy squared her shoulders and looked angrily at Rope. "Are you going in there to get him or am I?"

"Neither one of us is going in to get him," Rope said. He hitched up the gunbelt that had taken to slipping below what had, in recent years, become a slightly barreled belly. "The man's got a right to take a tumble if he wants to."

"Not with one of Adams's tarts he doesn't," Teddy retorted and headed toward the Diamond's bright red doors only to find her path blocked by Rope. His thatched brows twitched once, then quickly lifted. "If he starts bragging to the girl that he's a partner in the Gamble Line, Adams will know it before that Frenchman gets his britches back on."

Rope, who had a mountain of patience and needed it with Teddy, shook his head. "I don't reckon he's goin' up there to talk, Teddy."

"Sure he is," she snapped back. "Bragging and rutting go hand in hand."

Rope rubbed his grizzled chin and looked puzzled. "How would you know?"

"I heard! Dammit, Rope!" Teddy stamped her foot. "How can you stand there and do nothing with Delmar as good as sold out to Adams?"

"Well, it ain't easy, I'll admit," he said slowly. "But just suppose Adams don't know what the Frenchman's got. You and me go bustin' in there and Adams won't rest 'til he finds out why."

Teddy found it hard to disagree with his rationale, but tried. "So you think we should wait out here, hoping Delmar hasn't said and won't say anything—and that as soon as he finishes humping that tart he'll trot out grinning?"

Rope had half a mind to take Teddy over his knee and tan her hide for talking worse than a trail hand, but figured it wouldn't do any good, not if all the switchings Felicity had inflicted on her hadn't succeeded in giving her ladylike ways. "Any waitin' we do," he said, "will be at the office. So get off your high horse and come on. Since we obviously didn't succeed in keeping the Frenchman out of town we've got to make another plan for dealin' with him."

"Assuming he hasn't already dealt with Adams," came her impudent reply. She glanced up at the second floor of the Diamond and saw a red curtain draw closed across one of the upper room windows. She needed no more than instinct to tell her that Rhys Delmar and the saloon girl sought privacy behind it. Totally discomfited she concluded he was up there behaving like a man with no worries. She found new ones almost hourly heaped on her head. As if to confirm her assessment she spotted the sheriff moving at a fast pace down the walk toward them. "Hell!" she said. "Here comes Len Blalock running to Adams to pick up his orders for the day."

"Watch your mouth, Teddy, we got trouble enough," Rope warned.

The sheriff, about a hundred yards away, popped open his pocket watch and checked the time. He'd planned on getting to the Diamond right after Delmar had left his office. But Blalock had been delayed by trouble with a couple of drunks engaged in a fistfight at the Brass Bell. About the time he and his deputy had those two incarcerated, Justine had come in and reminded him of his promise to join her for lunch at Sprayberry's boarding house. He'd just gotten away, but he didn't suppose there had been any harm done by letting Adams wait. The man was too damned demanding anyway.

Len Blalock's dark mood wasn't made any better by catching sight of Teddy and Rope outside the Diamond. They were sure to give him grief about his lack of success at finding the men who had been attacking the Gamble stages. He halfheartedly hoped they would want to avoid him as he did them and would have crossed the street before he reached the saloon. But as he got closer he saw that Teddy was standing there like her boots were nailed to the sidewalk. Putting up a stalwart front, he kept walking, giving a curt nod to the pair as he sought to pass. "Afternoon, Teddy. Rope."

"Afternoon, Sheriff," Teddy said, swiftly forgetting Rope's warning to rein herself in. "You catch those other road agents yet?"

Reluctantly, he halted. "Not yet, but I will," he said matter-of-factly.

"Like you caught all those others?" Teddy didn't wait for an answer, and didn't actually expect one. "Let me see, how many have you brought in." With a studied look she counted on her fingers. "One . . . One, isn't it? One a passenger turned over to you. Looks like, at the least, you *could* get a lead from the one you've got in jail."

"He won't talk," the sheriff countered, uneasily shifting his weight from one foot to the other.

"Is that it?" she taunted. "Or is it that you're not listening?"

The blood drained from the sheriff's face as, for a moment, he stood tightening and releasing his big, scarred fists. "I'm gonna pretend I don't know what you mean by that," he said at last.

"It ought to be easy." Teddy glared at him. "You've had plenty of practice pretending to be a sheriff."

One hand raised, he made a step toward her. "I've had about enough of you, Teddy."

"Yeah! Well—" A jerk on her arm stopped Teddy from shortening the distance between them.

"She's done," Rope said. He dragged the protesting Teddy down the street, holding onto her until he felt the tight muscles in her arm relax.

"Thanks a lot for backing me up," she said grumpily.

Rope shook his head in consternation. "One day I expect to see a fuse sprout out of your scalp."

Teddy craned her neck to confirm that Len Blalock had been about to enter the Diamond, saw she was right, then looked back at Rope. "What's that supposed to mean?"

"It means you're a hothead, Teddy. That you don't know the difference between when to play a card and when to hold it."

"Maybe you're right," she said, her temper cooling off as quickly as it had flared. "Sorry, Rope. I didn't mean to stir up any more trouble. Really."

"That's all right," he mumbled, momentarily forgetting that the time to be suspicious of Teddy was when she was too agreeable.

A second later she'd left his side, hopped off the sidewalk and started briskly across the street.

"Hold it! What in tarnation are you up to, Teddy?"

"Nothing." She pointed at Penrod's Mercantile. "I told Felicity I'd pick up some things, thread and such, for her." Smiling, she waved away his deepening concern. "Stop your worrying and go on," she insisted. "I'll catch up in a few minutes." With that, she continued in a beeline across the dusty street toward Penrod's. She glanced back just once to make sure Rope had bought her story and was continuing to the office.

When she saw him round the corner, she spun about in her tracks and headed back the way she had come before the dust had drifted off behind her. She quickly crossed the sidewalk and ducked into the narrow, shadowed alley that ran alongside the Diamond. Stepping lightly, she started up the weathered treads of an outdoor staircase that led to the narrow stretch of porch on the second floor and on to the window of the room where she'd seen the curtain drawn.

The sash was up. The room was quiet. Except for the rhythmic squeak of bedsprings and an occasional feminine squeal. Teddy grimaced and eased the curtain aside only to find the unexpected. Rhys Delmar, coatless but otherwise fully clothed, had one booted foot on the edge of the bed and was jostling the mattress up and down. On the foot of the bed enjoying the bouncing ride and clothed as fully as she'd been when she'd led Rhys from the barroom, sat the red-haired saloon girl. She was responsible for the squeals.

"Your reputation is spared, *chérie,*" Rhys said cheerily to the laughing girl, then whirled about, having gotten a startling surprise from a glimpse of the mirror. "Yours, my dear," he looked toward the window where Teddy was half hidden behind the red curtain, "I fear will suffer from being named a Peeping Tom."

"Looks like I missed the good part," Teddy retorted, feeling her ever-ready temper starting to simmer.

Motioning to Honor to stay put, Rhys eased away from the bed and walked a few steps toward the window. "No, Teddy." He spoke her name so softly, so enticingly that, in spite of her anger she felt an unanticipated shiver of response sweep her. She disguised her chagrin with a frown as he drew near. And she left the obedient but curious Honor to stare in disbelief at Rhys's familiarity with Teddy. When he was close enough that only Teddy could hear him, though Honor was holding her breath to catch the words, he whispered, "I'm saving the good part for you."

"Assuming there is a good part," Teddy came back. "Something that's not worn down to a nub from overuse."

"Curious?" The corners of his sensual lips turned up in a taunting grin.

Teddy felt her face and ears burning but wasn't about to be outdone. She put her hands on her hips and gave her hat-clad head a toss. "Not a bit," she said. "But if I cared, I'd ask why you were jiggling that bed with your foot instead of tossing in it with that redhead. Seems like a waste of good money to me."

He stood framed in the window with the sunlight washing over his face highlighting the fine strong lines of it, setting his pale, unsettling eyes aglow. She had tried so hard to view Rhys Delmar as an adversary, someone to be outwitted and weeded out of her life. Now she could not stop herself from seeing the man.

She could understand why the saloon girl had stuck to him like a burr. He was all polish and charm right down to his dandified clothes. His vest of ice blue silk, like his eyes, shimmered blindingly in the sunlight. Buff riding breeches hugged his sinewy legs, and there was, Teddy could see, nothing about him worn to a nub. As she looked up, her thoughts were all too clear. She saw that his face had the detached and amused look that had so infuriated her at breakfast.

"I'm happy you've taken such a personal interest in my welfare," he said smoothly.

She removed her hat, gave the dusty crown a thump, then repositioned it on her head. "I'm interested in the part of your welfare that's related to my welfare," she said, looking past him. The saloon girl had wiggled down to a corner of the bed, where she sat perched like a hungry bird leaning forward and seriously straining her tightly laced corselet as she tried harder to hear what was being said at the window. The girl had looks, Teddy conceded, and didn't mind showing her assets. She was also probably a direct pipeline to Parrish Adams, which annoyed Teddy no end. "If you can tear yourself away from that trussed-up trollop," she said caustically, "come on out here. I've got a business to run and I've decided that as long as you're claiming to own part of it you ought to be pitching in."

"Hay?"

"No. Hell." Her eyes flashed. "Not hay. You can do what I do provided you can keep up."

Rhys smiled, turned to Honor and made a gallant bow. *"Chérie,"* he said. "Your pardon, please. I must leave."

"What about the lunch we ordered?" Honor protested, but not too loudly. She knew about Teddy Gamble's temper and the Colt the other woman sometimes wore strapped to her side.

Rhys flipped her twenty dollars. "Enjoy it and have yourself a deserved rest, on me," he said.

Honor blew him a kiss. "I'll see you later—darlin'."

Rhys nodded, grabbed his coat from the back of a nearby chair and lightly swung through the window.

"Did you tell that gal why you're in Wishbone?" Teddy demanded as they traversed the weathered planks of the upper porch.

Rhys stepped to one side and allowed Teddy to start down the roughly made stairs before him. "Are you asking if I told Honor that I am here to redeem my shares of the Gamble Line?"

Teddy's frown cut lines in her forehead. "That's what I mean. Did you?"

"No, our conversation ran along a more personal line."

"I'll bet." Teddy retorted. "Did you tell anyone else?"

She had aroused his curiosity with her questions. Evidently she wanted the situation kept quiet. But why should acknowledging his involvement in the company be a cause of concern? He supposed he'd need to find out. He also supposed, quite correctly, that she wasn't going to like what he told her next. "Only the sheriff," he said.

She drew up short and he nearly bumped into her. "Well, hell! Might as well have taken the headlines in the *Wishbone Gazette.*" Scowling, she started walking again.

Rhys followed. "Do you always speak in that way?"

She tossed her head back and made a face at him. "Like what? You mean do I always cuss? Hell, yes, I do. My father believed in speaking his mind and I do too. You don't have many misunderstandings when you speak your mind."

"I recall that your uncle Zack spoke his mind," Rhys said. "Were they much alike, your father and Zack?"

"Like opposite sides of the same coin," Teddy replied, then paused, getting an unbidden image of her father and Uncle Zack the last time they had been together, each man red-faced with anger and shouting accusations at the other. She'd feared there would be bloodshed before they were done, but Zack had ridden out of their lives. Felicity had been heartbroken over the rift. Her father hadn't been fit company for months afterwards. Zack and Theodor Gamble had been a paradox, any strength in one countered by a weakness in the other. "Both were blunt and stubborn and ambitious," she continued as if there had been no lapse in her reply. "The difference was, my father used those traits to build things. Things that would last. Uncle Zack's plans never got past the talking stage. The two didn't get along."

The tip of her tongue showed as she moistened her lips, a nervous but girlish gesture that made Rhys aware that Teddy Gamble knew what hurt and pain were about. He stopped himself from speaking up and saying everything would be all right. That was preemptive and even if she did have a vulnerable side to her that made him want to nestle her in his arms, she was also a woman who would run right over anyone who got in her way.

Thirteen

Parrish Adams rolled out across his desk a well-used map of the Arizona territory and ran his lean finger across a section he had outlined in red. The irregularly shaped area stretched from Yuma up to Wickenburg and swung south past Tucson and toward the border. *His territory.* Or soon it would be. He might not hold deeds to all of it, but he would control all freight and passengers that moved across it. When he did, he would control access to the rail lines that were scheduled to be built across southern Arizona.

He would be the most powerful man in the territory. And the richest. That alone, though, was not enough. He wanted to be admired and respected. He wanted his name mentioned in the same breath with those of men like Bill Cody and George Custer. That was the only reason he'd shown any restraint in bringing about the demise of the Gamble Line. He'd managed to get where he was by being smart, and not allowing too much tarnish to attach to his name. Theodor Gamble's friends still kept an eye out for Teddy. He couldn't allow the trouble she was having to be traced to him. As a safeguard, he'd only sent men whose loyalty he could count on to make attacks on the stage, damned incompetents that they were.

Frowning, Adams rolled the map and angrily slid it into a lower desk drawer. The time had come for sterner measures. Luther's capture had shown that he was only trading one risk for another by using men who were known to work, at times, for him. Loyal or not, there was the chance that someone would make the connection. Should Teddy Gamble get killed in one of the holdups—the thought appealed to him but the complication of such an event did not—Adams couldn't afford having the killers traced to him.

His expression clouded as he thought of Teddy. Damn her! She was trouble. She had him way behind schedule. He'd thought that a few holdups would scare her into selling out. But she was too stubborn for her own good. Making sure both doors were locked, he went to the safe concealed behind a wall panel. As was his custom he made a check of the contents when the door swung open, found it met his satisfaction, then removed a bag of gold coins. He locked the safe then poured the coins into his hand and counted them. His backup plan for acquiring the Gamble Line would not come cheap.

The gold coins warmed in his hands before he returned them to the leather bag. Five hundred dollars. Enough to tempt Taviz and his gang of bandidos out of the hills if they knew more was waiting for them. Taviz was Mexican, as were two of his gang. The other was a half-breed Apache who collected scalps. The four of them and their women lived up in the hills like a pack of animals.

Adams tossed the bag of gold in the air and caught it. He smiled to himself. Boyd could start off tomorrow to find Taviz. The money would bring him running, that and knowing he'd get to take a few Wells Fargo strongboxes. Taviz hated Wells Fargo. One of their agents had sent the Mexican to prison for several years. Since his escape he took his revenge on the company whenever the opportunity arose. Adams had used him a time or two before, when he needed help acquiring a piece of property from a reluctant seller, but there was no one alive who could say the Mexican was in his employ.

Yes. Adams laughed briefly. Taviz would enjoy this job. Short of killing Teddy, Adams meant to give him free rein to do whatever was necessary to bring the Gamble Line to a halt. When they were done, Wells Fargo would be pulling their contract from Teddy and she would be begging him to buy her out. But he wouldn't have to then. All he'd need to do was pick up the pieces.

With the gold tucked in his pocket, Adams crossed to the saloon door and turned a brass key in the lock. Teddy Gamble had no business trying to run a stage company. But she had let her last chance for a buyout pass, and she had stood in his way far too long. Too bad she had never learned what a woman *was* good for, but maybe Taviz would teach her that. Adams pushed the door open and looked out in the saloon for someone to fetch Boyd. He was smiling, thinking just maybe he might get the chance to teach Teddy that lesson himself.

"Have one on the house, Sheriff," he said, surprised to find that Blalock had stopped at the bar for a shot of whiskey. Usually the man was conscientious about not drinking on duty.

"Thanks," the sheriff said, picking up his glass after Harley the bartender refilled it. While Adams barked an order to the old man who swept up the place, the sheriff ambled toward him, hoping Harley wouldn't think to mention how long he had been standing at the bar or how many shots of whiskey he'd already had. He'd been trying, unsuccessfully, to dull the sting of Teddy's words. He had only succeeded in making himself feel worse, but maybe being a little drunk would make the meeting with Adams more bearable. "I've got some news for you," he said, trying to keep the distaste out of his voice.

Adams shut the door behind him. "About Luther?"

"No," Blalock said, "about that stranger that came in on the stage. Justine kind of took a shine to him after that—experience yesterday. So I made a point of looking him up to thank him for what he did for her." The irony of what the sheriff said didn't seem to have registered with him but it did with Adams. He listened in stone-faced silence as Len Blalock continued. "Like I usually do of any stranger, I asked him what his business was in Wishbone."

"He's a gambler," Adams said impatiently. He wasn't interested in a rundown on the stranger. Gamblers came and went in Wishbone. He expected this one would too. "As good a one as I've seen," he continued. "He was in here all morning. Right now he's upstairs with one of my girls."

"You'll be glad of that," Blalock said. "He's got something you want."

"I doubt that," Adams came back, beginning to wonder if Blalock wasn't getting soft in the head.

The sheriff gulped down the shot of whiskey he'd been holding, then looked Adams straight in the eye. Having had time to think about it, he had come to the conclusion that Adams's buying into the Gamble Line was the best solution for everyone, except maybe Teddy. She would be ruined for sure, but there would be no more holdups and he wouldn't find himself in the position of turning his head to the law anymore. Wanting his words to have all the meaning with Adams that they had for him, he spoke slowly and carefully. "He's got Zack Gamble's shares of the stage line."

Adams's dark eyes widened. "You're lying."

"I swear." Blalock squeezed the tiny shot glass inside his fist, then fearing that in his anguish he would break it, set it aside. "He told me himself. He won them off Zack in a card game over in London. Then Zack up and died before he could cash in with him. He's here to collect the money from Teddy."

The news was too good to be believed and Adams's skepticism slow to leave. "You're sure about this?"

"As sure as I'm wearing this badge." Blalock's weathered hand brushed over the silver star pinned to his vest. "Don't reckon he'd be too particular about who bought back those shares."

Adams had started to pace the carpeted floor, his

mind playing out scenarios of just how gratifying it would be to announce to Teddy that he was her newest partner. Seeing her face when he told her, watching her squirm when she knew she was licked, would be worth any price he had to pay. That the Frenchman was, at this very minute, upstairs in his saloon seemed a confirmation that this was meant to be. But then he'd always been lucky.

Adams's pleasure over the prospect of getting exactly what he wanted did not dim his wits. The Frenchman had been in the Diamond for hours, which meant the sheriff had found out about the shares early in the morning. He smiled cruelly. "I suppose there's a reason you took your time telling me about this."

The sheriff nodded nervously. He sometimes suspected Adams could read his mind. And if he could he would know that the main reason he hadn't come at once was that Adams made him feel like a two-bit errand boy. And because, in a sense, that's what he was. "H-had to wrestle a couple of drunks out of the Brass Bell," he stammered. "Then Jus—"

"Never mind," Adams interrupted. "Unless Honor is more talented than I think she is, that Frenchman will be through with her by now." He laughed, and smoothing his slicked-down hair, started out of the office through the back and private door. "I reckon he'll be feeling real agreeable, too."

He took the steep steps briskly with Blalock struggling to keep up. Honor's gleaming red door was the only one closed. It was three rooms down from the stairwell.

Adams didn't bother to knock.

"Get out! Oh—" Honor, who had been flopped back on the pillows of her tousled bed enjoying the sumptuous lunch Rhys had ordered, jumped to her feet when she saw who had thrown open the door to her room. "Sorry, Mr. Adams," she mumbled, anxiously patting down her rumpled skirt as she twisted about, looking for the shoes she had kicked off.

"Where's the Frenchman?" Adams demanded.

"He left."

Adams shot an accusing glance at Len Blalock who had hoped to have the pleasure of introducing Adams to the Frenchman. "I can see that." His anger showed in every step, as Adams strode into the room. "How long has he been gone?"

Honor, using a toe to drag a high-heeled slipper out from under the bed, kept her eyes cast down. "A quarter hour. Maybe not that long," came her weak reply as she nervously brushed a breadcrumb off one of the ribbons adorning her corselet. Adams didn't tolerate the girls lingering upstairs after an "appointment." "He—Somebody came for him."

"Who?"

"That Teddy Gamble," Honor said, deciding to take the role of a spurned woman. "Poked her head in the window and crooked her finger and he went off with her." She worked one stocking-clad foot into the slipper she had managed to retrieve, giving her a decidedly unbalanced stance. "I made him pay for his time, mind you." Feeling bolder at last, she lifted her head and thrust her hands on her uneven hips. "But it made me danged mad anyway, I can tell you."

Adams, whose sour expression hadn't changed since

he'd entered the girl's room, spotted the tattered corner of a dime novel protruding from beneath the nest of pillows where Honor had been reclining. On one side of the bed was a nearly empty luncheon tray. Her missing shoe was across the room against the washstand. She had obviously kicked it off when she crawled onto her bed.

"I can tell you've been suffering." Adams turned his back. Not seeing his harsh face only made Honor's fear of him stronger. "Might make you feel better to get downstairs and do what you're paid for," he said.

"Yes, sir." She hobbled across to the washstand and retrieved her other shoe and hastily put it on. She tried to speak up, to offer an apology to Adams for all the wrongs he'd made her feel, but the words died on her lips and, dry-mouthed, she hurried out hoping their would be no retribution.

Len Blalock fared less well. Left alone with Adams he felt much as the girl had.

"I cannot abide anyone in my employ not doing what is expected of them." Adams strolled around Honor's room, poking at various items, lifting a silk scarf on the dresser, looking into the plain pine armoire, at the girl's meager belongings.

"I didn't know he'd tied up with Teddy," Blalock offered. "I'd have come right to you but I had to take in those drunks—" Not acknowledging the sheriff, Adams strolled out of the room with the man following. "Teddy couldn't have the money to buy back those shares," erupted from Blalock, too fast and too desperately to gain the redemption he sought. "She's near broke, I heard."

The lamp had gone out above the narrow back stairs. Blalock heard the steady click of Adams's steps as the man descended ahead of him. He heard, too, the echoing whine in his voice and was sickened by it, but, try as he might, couldn't find within him the nerve to tell Parrish Adams he could no longer do his bidding. Instead he followed like a dog trained to heel at his master's feet, wondering how many detestable things he would have to do before Adams was satisfied.

"You get that Frenchman in an agreeable state of mind and you get him to me," Adams said. "Use Pete and Boyd if you need them."

In the dimly lit back hall, with the shadows playing strangely on his lean face, Adams hardly looked human. Blalock, compelled to face him as he stepped off the last tread, felt a hard twist in his gut, a realization that he hadn't been merely trading favors with Adams. He had sold out to the devil and there was no way to reverse what he had done. He understood now why the girl Honor had been so afraid. Adams was a man without mercy, the sort who took revenge on those who failed him.

Fourteen

"You know Strong Bill and Rope. This fellow is Bullet Lamar, he looks after the stock."

Teddy had assembled the main crew of the Gamble Line for Rhys to meet. She wanted him to know about each man's duties and to understand just what it took to keep a stage line running. All the way from the Diamond to the Gamble office, which was across the street from the stable, she had been telling him about the various runs and schedules. She had also told him that the Gamble Line began with her father's dream to build a premier stage line out of Wishbone. And she spoke of her desire to keep her father's dream alive.

"Bullet," Rhys shook the man's hand, thinking "bull" would have been more descriptive of the stockily built fellow. About Rhys's height, Bullet had twice his bulk. His massive arms were as large as many a man's thigh. He looked more Indian than white. He wore his straight black hair long, and it was held close to his head by a beaded leather band tied around his forehead. Like Teddy he wore a heavy silver bracelet set with turquoise stones. At his waist was a silver concha belt threaded onto a thick strip of tanned leather. The inevitable gunbelt rode low beneath it. Bullet's tooled holster was anchored by a strap to his heavy thigh.

Bullet's eyes were black as a night sky and seemed never to blink. He seemed ageless. His stoic face was as impassive as one of the high canyon walls found throughout Arizona.

He was a man of few words and he didn't spare any of them for Rhys, merely nodding when Teddy told his name. She took it upon herself to reveal a little about Bullet as they walked through the dusty street to the stable for a look at the stock and equipment Rhys now owned in part—or would own. "He keeps the horses healthy and he trains them to pull as a team," she explained. Her stride found the same cadence as Rhys's as they entered wide doors of the stable. "We call him Bullet because he's got three slugs in him no doctor could dig out." Bullet, listening to but not looking at Teddy, moved away from the others and slipped into a stall where he began rubbing down a dappled mare whose bulging belly indicated she was soon to deliver a foal. "Fifteen years ago my father found Bullet out on the desert all shot up. He hauled him in to the ranch, looked after him until he got him well, and," she paused, "we haven't been able to get rid of him since." Smiling mischievously she looked at the half-breed who had made himself busy feeling the mare's legs from shoulders to fetlocks. "Isn't that right?"

Bullet, crouched beside the mare, spoke without looking away from the animal. His voice was nearly as overpoweringly big as the man himself, but Rhys thought he detected affection in the gravelly tone. "Tell it your way, Little Bit," he said.

Little Bit. Rhys tried to find the rationale for the term Bullet had used to refer to Teddy. Though not petite she was a small woman, so "little" he understood. "Bit" he did not. A bit was the metal bar which fitted into a horse's mouth. He didn't get a chance to ask what unknown meaning the words also had or how they related to Teddy. The restless mare had begun to snort and whinny and had drawn his attention. The animal was fidgeting in the stall, complaining of her burden to the man who gently stroked her underbelly. A brood mare who acted that way could have a difficult delivery when her time came. He knew more than he had ever wanted to about horses, since he'd spent his early years as a stable hand, tending the hundred head on the French estate where his mother had worked.

A dalliance with the master's youngest daughter had sent him packing before he was sixteen. For the next five years he served as a groom elsewhere. Finally he had gotten proficient enough with cards and other games of chance to decide he could make a better and easier living at the gaming tables. He had been right. His skill and his good looks had brought him out of the stable and into the parlors of the class he had once served.

He nearly laughed aloud as he considered that somehow life had brought him back to the stables. Given the route he'd taken, he was not sure he was any better off than he had been ten years before when he had eagerly departed them.

"Another thing about Bullet," Teddy said, walking toward a row of empty nail kegs that did duty as stools. "He won't talk your ears off, not unless maybe you're a horse." She sat on one of the kegs. "Besides looking after the horses we have, he's the man responsible for buying new stock. He also rides the line and sees that the animals get rotated properly from station to station so no one horse is overworked. Watching how the animals are used saves the horses and saves us money," she said. "Strong Bill—"

The rangy shotgun man, who had propped against a hay bin, spoke up. "I'm chief messenger—" Seeing the confusion on Rhys's face he tried again. "Guard," he said. "I hire and train the men who ride as guards. It's my job to decide when a shipment merits more protection than our usual single man on a run. Until lately the reputation of our marksmen kept us trouble free." He shrugged uneasily. "We haven't lost a payload yet, but we've sure had our share of trouble lately. You've seen some of it." Pausing, he cocked his head to one side and took a long, studied look at Rhys. "You any good with a rifle?"

"I've had more experience with a pistol, but I can usually hit where I aim," Rhys said.

Strong Bill laughed, remembering how accurate Rhys had been aiming a rock at the fleeing holdup man. "Your aim is sharp enough," he said. "I could give you some lessons with my Winchester if you like."

"Whether he likes it or not," Teddy volunteered. "Anybody who's part of the Gamble Line has to be a good shot. If we have to double up on guards we'll need every man we've got."

"Your pardon," Rhys said, rebelling at Teddy's assumption. Since she had decided to give some credence to his claim, she expected him to follow her orders. "I do not need instruction to shoot a rifle. While I am happy to have been of service when required, I have no intention of becoming a stage messenger." He nodded politely to Strong Bill. "Or of tending horses." He nodded to Bullet. "I'm sure these men are excellent at what they do and as they have managed without me in the past will not need me in the future." He turned a steady gaze on Teddy. "I have a way to pass the time until the verification comes from London."

Teddy jumped up. "Do you mean dealing cards or bedding chippies?"

Eyes fiery, face flushed, she looked like a cat ready to pounce. Rhys smiled at her, that maddening half smile that drove Teddy closer to the brink of fury. "Both," he said.

Her flushed face darkened. She turned her wrath on him. "I should have known a no-count dandy wouldn't want to throw his lot in with real men."

With a small bow, Rhys tipped his hat to Teddy, intensifying her anger. "Well, now, if you had said 'real women' we might have had a point of contention."

He felt a little ashamed at the pleasure he got setting her off, but she never spared the nettle when she spoke to him, and, she was terribly pretty when her temper soared. He grinned and gazed into her fiery eyes wondering if Teddy's other passions would be as intense. How very interesting it could be to find out.

"I ought to wipe that grin off your face with a pitchfork," she shouted.

Rhys saw her reaching for the instrument she had threatened to use. But Rope stepped in and stopped her. "Simmer down, Teddy," he said. "Ain't you got something to do anyway?"

"No!" she retorted, set for an all-out row with Rhys and backing off only when she got a good look at Rope's face. He didn't get that cockeyed expression often, but when he did Teddy knew better than to buck him. "Oh, all right," she said, though not graciously. "I'll head back to the office and check over the schedules for next week." She spun around, giving Rhys one last look that showed the depth of her irritation. "No use wasting any more of my breath on this tinhorn," came over her shoulder.

Strong Bill knew Rope well enough to say he also had something to do. Bullet said nothing, but rambled off through the stable and toward the corral in back.

Rope let the dust settle behind the three of them before he spoke up again. "The Gamble Line means a heap to Teddy," he said. "How about you and me have a drink over at the Brass Bell and I'll tell you the reasons why Teddy left off."

"My pleasure," Rhys said. Any help in understanding Teddy's volatile disposition was welcome, and he wanted to see how Lucien had fared at the Brass Bell. "She has a way of giving me need of a drink."

Rope nodded his agreement and reached into his

shirt pocket for his tobacco pouch and cigarette papers. He offered to roll one for Rhys but Rhys declined. "My mama used to say a rhyme about little girls bein' made of sugar and spice and everything nice." As he spoke he sifted tobacco into the waiting paper and, using one hand and the skill born of much practice, quickly rolled the smoke. "Teddy's a girl that shook out with too much spice." Pausing on the wooden sidewalk he tucked the pouch back into his pocket, pulled out a match and drew it across the rough surface of a post that held a tin top over a portion of the walk. "But she ain't half as mean as she acts." Walking on, he cupped his hand over the match, lit up and took a draw off the cigarette. "Well, hell, yes she is—but there's a reason for that too."

Intrigued but not wanting to look half as interested as he was, Rhys merely nodded and looked down the street where the Brass Bell's sun-faded sign hung above the front doors. Wishbone's other saloon was as unassuming as the Diamond was pretentious. A person might walk by its unpainted front without noticing, had there not been the merry tinkle of piano music floating out the open window and doors.

Rhys wondered why Rope preferred the Brass Bell to the better-appointed Diamond as, shoulder to shoulder the two of them, a truly odd pair, continued toward it.

Rope, in his worn denim trousers and red suspenders looped over the shoulders of his buckskin shirt, left a wisp of smoke behind as he went. He hoped, with a few drinks and a lot of honesty, that he could mend any fences Teddy had torn down. But secretly he was worried that the nattily dressed Rhys Delmar might have been insulted one time too many, and might not care why Teddy Gamble was prickly as a cactus spine. He wasn't sure either that he wanted to know how Teddy had gotten Delmar out of that saloon girl's room. Lord, she was a trial to a man. He reckoned if he had a dime for every time he had wanted to take her over his knee they wouldn't have any money trouble.

At least the Frenchman didn't act as if he'd been propositioned by anyone other than the girl. Which was a good thing. Right now all he and Teddy had to offer the man was a promise. He wasn't sure how that would stack up against Adams's hard cash, especially not after how Teddy had got at the Frenchman's throat. But maybe if he got his offer in first, there might be a chance.

Rope pushed open the Brass Bell's doors. The place smelled of sawdust and beer and cheap whiskey, but had its share of customers. A glance confirmed what Rhys had been too preoccupied with Teddy to notice the first time he'd come in. The decor was no match for the Diamond's. The gold, flocked paper on the walls was spattered and stained where careless cowboys had sloshed beer. The worn tables, many with names carved in their scarred tops proved that many customers left their manners at home. But the place was lively and none of the customers looked as if they wished they were somewhere else. He hoped the same was true for Lucien, who was nowhere to be seen. His valet—former valet, he reminded himself—might have felt ill at ease in a rough-and-tumble place like the Brass Bell.

"I'll get a bottle. Find yourself a seat," Rope said and made for the bar.

Fearing Lucien might have found his first day on his own too much to contend with, Rhys first made a round of the saloon but failed to find Lucien. He had either left or sought solace upstairs.

A simple set of steps ran up to a narrow balcony above the saloon. Rhys looked for someone to ask who had gone up recently. A Frenchman who limped would not be hard to remember. Knowing that the bartender probably kept tabs on who the girls entertained Rhys started toward the big red-faced man. As it turned out he did not need to inquire. From a cluster of men in a back corner he heard Lucien's distinctive accent, and surprisingly, the sound of feminine laughter.

The group parted before Rhys reached it. A faro box had been the attraction. Behind it stood Lucien Bourget minus his coat. A fat purse protruded from his breast pocket. He'd evidently had a good day running the game.

"Monsieur!" Lucien waved excitedly to Rhys.

"Lucien." Rhys stood back and shook his head. "You amaze me. In a day you acquire a faro game and—what is this? A friend?"

Standing beside Lucien with a hand possessively on his shoulder was a woman in a bright yellow and black striped dress. Her raven hair, pinned up in a chignon, made a sharp widow's peak which was cut through by a streak of silver. In her youth she had undoubtedly been a ravishing woman. Even now, in what appeared to be her middle years, despite a more plump than fashionable figure, she still caught a man's eyes.

"Monsieur," Lucien spoke excitedly. "This is Carmen. Carmen Bell. The Brass Bell is hers."

"And this is *my* new faro dealer." Carmen bent her head to Lucien's and gave him a kiss on the cheek. Straightening up, she winked at Rhys. "He's got the most skillful hands I ever saw."

"Carmen has kindly given me a room here." For a moment Lucien's eyes were downcast. "Of course I told her that you and I had plans toget—"

"No." Rhys spoke up quickly. "You are free to make plans as you wish."

"Monsieur—" Seeing Rhys's frown he corrected himself. "Rhys. You are certain? I feel I am obligated—"

"You aren't. Stay here with Carmen. Work for her." Seeing that Lucien fairly beamed at his assurances that he was his own man, Rhys continued. "You have been a fine servant and a fine friend but this is right for you now. As for me I too have found I can provide for myself in this town. So, my friend, with no doubt that you will be the best faro dealer in the territory, I wish you well."

Lucien grasped his shoulders and, in the European style, would have embraced him had not Rhys pointed out, that here, a handshake was the proper gesture.

Lucien clasped Rhys's hand and pumped his arm. "I thank you for all you have been to me." The tremor in his voice expressed his emotion even better than his words. *"Monsieur,* should you ever need me again, know that I stand ready to resume my position with you."

"Be happy in your new life, Lucien," Rhys said, knowing instinctively that Carmen had a good heart and would be just the guide Lucien needed to help with the changes in store for him. He took her plump hand and kissed it. "You, *madame,* I congratulate. You will find no finer man than Lucien Bourget."

"Honey, I know that already," Carmen said sweetly. "Why he's got more style than all the cowboys in Arizona territory tied up in one sack." When Rhys freed her hand she locked her arm with Lucien's. "You can bet I'll hold on to him."

Fifteen

From the table he shared with Rope, Rhys watched Lucien climb the stairs with Carmen Bell. Already the woman was having a good effect on his former valet. With Carmen at his side, Lucien's limp was scarcely discernible. Lucien was lucky to have quickly found a job and a woman who appreciated his special talents. Rhys caught himself feeling less fortunate.

Lucien's gain was his loss. Rhys wished his friend well, but he experienced an emptiness inside nearly as severe as he had felt when Jenny had died in his arms. He would miss his companion—miss having someone always at hand to listen to his plans and to make courteous suggestions should he see a flaw in them. But he was convinced that the parting with Lucien was for the best. In Europe a servant had scant hope of ever rising above his station. Here, Lucien had the same opportunity as anyone. He deserved to make what he could of it.

Rope set down a nearly empty glass and wiped his mouth on the back of his hand. "You seem mighty intent on somethin', son," he said, having waited through a few minutes of silence and having observed the clouded look on Rhys's face. "If it's the way Teddy was actin' don't let it get to you. She always stomps and kicks before she settles down and thinks straight. I reckon she's about the feistiest female in the territory. She—"

"You were going to tell me why." Head back, Rhys drained the shot of whiskey from his glass.

Rope swirled the few drops remaining in his. "This is my opinion, mind you," he said, speaking more quietly than before. "And it all started a long time back, ten, maybe twelve years now." He paused and filled his glass. "See, Teddy started out in life as sweet and pretty a little filly as you ever saw. Up until the time her ma died, Teddy wore lace and bows like any other young lady. Her ma saw to that. Had Teddy curtsying and playing piano by the time she could talk. Then Sarah Gamble died and not long after that Teddy's brother—"

"She has a brother?" Rhys thought he had met all of the Gamble clan but remembered no brother or even a mention of one.

"Had," Rope said grimly. "A twin. Timothy was his name. Timmy we called him. They were close those two. Played together. Rode together." He stopped for another drink and a moment of reflection on peaceful days, when it seemed that nothing could go wrong. "Ted Gamble loved both his youngsters but I reckon it's fair to say he favored the boy. More so after Sarah died of a fever and he knew he wouldn't marry again."

Rhys recalled thinking that Teddy was no stranger to tragedy. With Rope's revelation he saw how right he had been. Teddy had lost most of her family. No small wonder she had a testy nature or that she wanted to protect what they had been part of. He wondered how the boy, her brother had died. If he had been anything like his sister he must have been a strong and robust lad. With no hesitation he asked, "What happened to Timothy?"

Rope's bushy brows flicked up nervously. "I'm gettin' to that," he said. " 'Cause him gettin' killed is what changed Teddy." Rope sighed, wondering if he was making a mistake telling a near stranger about the personal side of Teddy. He hesitated a few seconds, figuring he would let a hunch lead him. If he was right, the Frenchman wasn't too bad a man deep down. Otherwise he'd be raising a bigger ruckus than he was, over not getting his money right away. Hoping his hunch wasn't merely wishful thinking, he continued. "It happened, like I said, about a dozen years back. Timmy and Teddy slipped off the ranch on their ponies one day when they had been told to stay close because of the weather. I'd say Timmy was the cause of that. He was a rambunctious youngster, a lot more like his Uncle Zack than anyone cared to say. Well, the two of them got caught in a flash flood and Timmy drowned."

"And Teddy witnessed his death?"

"Near as anybody knows," Rope replied. "She was half drowned herself, then pneumonia set in and it was nip and tuck whether she would make it. Once she got well enough to talk about what happened she refused to. Just kept sayin' it was all her fault for not making Timmy stay at the ranch like they had been told. Always had a notion she was his big sister 'cause she had been born a few minutes before him. Couldn't nobody talk that feelin' out of her or make her see that most likely it was Timmy's stubborn streak that put them in danger. Anyhow, soon as she was up and around she put on her brother's clothes and I don't reckon she's worn a dress since."

He started to pour Rhys another drink.

"No more," Rhys said quickly.

Rope nudged the cork into the bottle. "Now me," he said, "I always figured—Teddy bein' the delicate little thing she was back then—that she got in trouble out there once the water started comin'. Timmy must have lost his life tryin' to save her. Afterwards I think Teddy turned tomboy so she could try to make up for Timmy's death. She knew how much having a son meant to her pa."

Rhys felt a sudden compassion for the young Teddy. He knew what it was like to lose loved ones. And, since Jenny's death, he knew how it felt to believe you were somehow at fault. "Surely her father didn't blame her for the boy's death," he said, wondering if Theodor Gamble had been so devastated by grief that he had failed to reassure and comfort his daughter.

"No," Rope said, "but his heart was broke and he couldn't help showing it. Teddy was all he had left and he wanted her close at hand. The rougher she acted the more he praised her. I reckon in his way he encouraged her to be like she is. Felicity tried to tell him he was wrong but Theodor kept sayin' his Teddy could do what she wanted. Well, pretty soon she could out-ride and out-shoot any boy in Wishbone and I reckon that's still so."

And out-cuss, Rhys suspected. He was intrigued,

however, by a ladylike Teddy Gamble, a pretty young girl in lace and ribbons whose fingers danced over ivory piano keys instead of the ivory handle of a pistol. That Teddy, all grown up, would be something to behold and he hoped he would get the chance. Why, he would be willing to hand over his shares of the Gamble Line for a glimpse of that Teddy, for a chance to hold her in his arms for a night.

But Rhys was not willing to trade his freedom for it—not when that meant allowing Jenny's killer to go free. No, the truth was that while he might bide his time for a few months until it was safe to return to London, he did not have the luxury of a leisurely pursuit of Teddy. That, however, did not preclude a pleasurable pursuit. He might have a shortened timetable but he would make the most of it. Who could say. They had a common bond. Both had known loss. Both wanted the Gamble Line sound and solvent.

On top of that, he didn't trust the girl. How was he to know she had not put Rope up to telling him a sad story to make him more agreeable to whatever terms she might come up with next. Maybe the old wrangler sincerely wanted only his understanding. But there was the possibility that Teddy was shrewd as a fox and had used Rope to lay a false trail. She was an enigma, he thought—not quite sexless in her buckskin and boots, but far removed from the picture Rope had painted in his mind, a vision of Teddy in lace and silk—so lovely.

"She's held up well for all her trouble," he said, carefully gauging Rope's reaction to his reply. "Seems tough as whipcord. Ted Gamble must have been proud to have had a daughter who could take up where he left off."

"He was proud of Teddy," Rope agreed. "Just never let himself see that he was cheatin' her out of what a woman ought to have."

"Which is?"

"A man to love. Children at her knee. Same things he gave to Sarah." Rope sighed. "Ted meant right by Teddy, but he was selfish in his way."

"I'm sure she could have those things if she wanted them enough."

"Yeah. I reckon she'll think about it one day. And I reckon I ought to remember she would put a bullet in me for tellin' all about her if she knew it. Teddy don't like nobody meddlin' in her business but I wanted you to see why she's so all-fired set on savin' the Gamble Line. It's her way of hangin' on to her pa and Timmy." He looked hard at Rhys. "I don't like to think what would happen to Teddy if she couldn't keep it runnin'. "

"It's not my intent to stop the line from running," Rhys said, reading, as he suspected, some deeper purpose in Rope's anxious eyes. Clearly he loved Teddy as much as her father had and would do anything to protect her, even to spinning a heart-wrenching yarn to mislead a new partner. He was convinced Rope was keeping secret as much about Teddy and the stage line as he was telling.

Rhys leisurely uncorked the bottle and took yet another drink. He began to go over a few things in his mind. First they had tried to run him off, then they had tried to keep him secluded on the ranch. They were definitely trying to hide something from him. And he was positive he would be best served by taking a room in town and keeping a watch, from a distance, on Teddy and the stage line.

"Wish you'd reconsider stayin' at the ranch," Rope said. "I think I could persuade Felicity to air out a room in the house—"

Rhys smiled. "Thank you, no," he said. "Lucien has found accommodations for himself here at the Brass Bell and I prefer to stay in town as well. Taking a room here will save me a long ride when I'm in the mood for a late night drink or a game of cards." He noted the concern in Rope's expression as he continued. "I would be grateful, though, if you would return Madame Gamble's saddle horse and the mount she loaned to Lucien."

"Be glad to," Rope mumbled.

"And you may tell Teddy I will contact her in a day or two when I've had time to decide what compensation will be suitable while we wait for confirmation of my claim."

"She won't—" Rope stopped himself. Either he had wasted his breath revealing confidences to the Frenchman, or the man wanted time to think over how what he had revealed weighed into everything. Once more he decided to give Rhys the benefit of the doubt. "I'll tell her," he said.

Rope, on his way out, stopped at the bar and paid for the drinks. A few minutes later Rhys leaned against the polished oak and asked the barkeeper if he knew a rooming house that served meals.

"Sprayberry's," the man said. "Mae Sprayberry's

got the best victuals in Wishbone and you'll find her prices fair. The house is a street back from here, the white one with the picket fence." He wrung out a cloth and swabbed it over the bar where a man had spilled whiskey. "You'll smell the bread baking before you get there."

The same aroma had filled his mother's kitchen on baking day. Fresh and rich, it had always teased his hunger and quickened his pace. It did so now as he eased open the small swinging gate in front of Sprayberry's boarding house. The two-story frame structure with the wide porch on front had a small bell mounted above the front door. Rhys tugged the cord that hung from it. Moments later a silver-haired woman in a calico dress and white apron opened the door. Flour dusted her hands. She had a powdery smudge of it on her chin and cheek.

"Can I help you, stranger."

Rhys gave his most winning smile. "Madame Sprayberry?" She nodded. "I am told you let rooms," he said.

"To a select few guests." She pushed a stray wisp of hair off her forehead streaking it with flour. "I require a reference."

"Madame, I am newly arrived in town."

"You best try elsewhere," the woman said. "I can't take boarders, least of all men, with no one to vouch for them."

"Mr. Delmar is all right, Mae." With bright eyes and sparkling voice Justine Blalock wedged into the door opening with Mae Sprayberry. The sprinkling of flour on her arms and apron indicated she was assisting with the baking. "He's the one I was telling you about. The man on the stage. Papa knows him too."

Reaching over Justine, Mae Sprayberry pushed the door open wide. "Come on in, Mr. Delmar. I do have one room available and I suppose there's no better reference than the sheriff's, and seeing he lives next door I reckon you'll do."

Had he known Len Blalock lived in the small house next door, he might have looked elsewhere. But at this point he saw no way to gracefully withdraw his request for lodgings. He could only hope the nearness of the sheriff's house did not put him under any undue scrutiny from the sheriff or his daughter.

"Hope you don't mind stepping in the kitchen." Mae motioned him along through a well-furnished parlor and wide hall to the back of the house where the kitchen was located. "I've got bread in the oven and Justine and I are kneading dough for the next batch." She went back to the work she had evidently left to answer the door. "I charge three dollars a week in advance. That's for a room and two meals. You get breakfast and dinner. Breakfast is at seven, dinner at six, sharp. There's a pump out back." Her hands moved skillfully on the lumps of dough, pushing, pulling. "You get your own water for washing. I'll make your bed every day for two bits extra or you can do it yourself but I require that beds be made before you leave the house. I don't keep a sloppy establishment."

"I could do that for you," Justine volunteered. "No charge for the service."

Mae gave the girl a questioning look. "Justine's helping out since she got back," she said. "Wants to know how to run a house proper." She patted a lump of dough into a baking pan. "A girl ought to know how."

"Papa and I take most of our meals with Mae," Justine said. "She's good enough to keep a plate warming when he can't get to the table."

"Which is most times," Mae commented. To Rhys she said, "I've got four rooms down. Yours is the last one off the hall. It's got an outside door which you are welcome to use. Just see it's locked when you go out."

"To be sure, *madame*," he said, pleased he would have some measure of privacy in his comings and goings. Smiling still, he peeled three dollars from the roll of bills in his pocket and, at Mae's direction, placed them in her apron pocket. "My valise and trunks are at the stage office," he said. "I'll need to see that they are delivered here." Excusing himself with an exaggerated and courtly bow, he turned to leave. He was hoping that before the day was done he could find a new game, either at the Diamond or the Brass Bell.

Justine blushed as she untied her apron and slipped it off. "I'll see him out," she said to Mae.

"See that you're back by six," Mae called after him. "I don't seat anybody after that."

Rhys looked down at Justine as they walked out together. She was young and pretty—refined, at least by the standards of the other young women he'd met in Wishbone. She was restless, too, a proper girl ready to try her wings. He knew by the way she was looking at him she might make her first fluttering flight in his direction. But he dared not let her. She was the sheriff's daughter and he did not want to come up hard against the law here. Len Blalock was beholden to him at present and he would be wise to keep things that way. He might need an ally should he be traced before he was ready to confront his accusers in London. He'd not have an ally if he seduced Sheriff Blalock's daughter.

At the front steps Justine paused. "I'm glad you're here," she said. "It'll be nice having you close—" The words had slipped out unbidden and her face flushed with color. "Nice seeing you every—Well, nice," she finished.

And dangerous, Rhys thought.

Sixteen

The heat of the day had settled in, that hot dry air that wavered ever a step ahead. Most about town had headed for the coolest spots they knew. Rhys had felt as if he were in a furnace as he sat at a low-stakes game in the Brass Bell, a place he'd decided was best left to Lucien. Finally the heat had gotten the best of him, and seeing that it was near the dinner hour he'd thrown in his hand and left.

He wondered if he would ever get used to the heat. He lifted the new hat he'd bought only minutes before. Running his fingers through his hair to let a little air reach his scalp, he thought about and pitied Mae Sprayberry and Justine Blalock, who worked near hot ovens all day. Even so, his mouth watered for a slice of the fresh bread he expected to find on the table at dinner.

He hadn't yet gotten accustomed to the food he'd been served in America. His palate, he supposed, had gotten used to the rich sauces and delicacies of his native country. But American cuisine, if not as appetizing as that he preferred, was hearty and sustaining. He was beginning to grow accustomed to the flavors. And he was ready for some of it. His hunger was all the more for having passed up lunch for Teddy's benefit.

So with the next meal uppermost in his thoughts he moved along the quiet street. He had reached a point where the walkway narrowed because of a storeroom that had been built out over part of the boardwalk. He noticed the quickening sound of footsteps behind him.

He glanced over his shoulder assuming that anyone in such a hurry would want to pass. He never suspected that wasn't the case. Not until another person stepped from an alley—directly into his path.

"Pardon," he began, stopping when he saw that a kerchief obscured the lower part of the man's face.

Realizing he was in trouble, Rhys spun back slamming his elbow into the chest of a second man who had come up behind him. That man, knocked off balance, gave an angry grunt.

"I'll give you trouble, if that's what you want." Clutching his chest, the man growled out a curse, drew his gun and raised it at Rhys as if to shoot. "Now hold still!"

"Don't shoot him!" the other man hastily shouted at his partner.

Rhys had but a moment to celebrate the second man's cooler head. He used the moment to advantage, as he whirled away from the man with the weapon, then lunged back and drew from beneath his coat the small four-shot revolver he carried. But he was not to get off a shot. The second man had drawn, too, and with the butt of his gun clenched in his fist brought it down broadside on the back of Rhys's head.

The blow would have split his skull except for the cushioning of the hat he wore. As it was, the impact knocked him off his feet and left him so stunned he couldn't see clearly. He was aware of the two men standing over him. Both had kept their faces covered.

The man he had elbowed pulled the hammer back on his gun. "You're in the wrong town, mister," he said.

Expecting to feel a bullet rip through his flesh at any moment, Rhys was only vaguely conscious that the voice was familiar, that both of them were.

"Dammit! Don't kill him I said!" A third voice, coming from inside the alley, from someone he could not see at all, was the one that broke through the webs in his mind and made him aware he'd met all these men before.

Struggling to get up, he tried to put faces with the voices. But he had met so many new people, and heard so many new voices lately, he couldn't make a match. He pushed up on his knees, saw his gun in the dust a few feet away. He tried to gauge his chance of lunging for it and firing at one or more of his attackers. His fuzzy calculations fell apart when the man he had hit, picked up the weapon.

"I ought to shoot him with this little palm-squeezer." The man got a firing grip on the black pearl handle of Rhys's derringer but instead of shooting eased it into a pocket, doubled over and groaned. "Think he cracked my rib."

"I'll see if I can return the favor and let him know he ain't wanted here," the other man said. A swift kick with the hard toe of a boot followed. Rhys groaned and clutched his rib cage. The man who had injured him laughed. "I advise you to get out of town, stranger. We don't need no fancy gamblin' Frenchmen in Wishbone."

Rhys's brain was beginning to work normally again by then. He swung out at the leg that had kicked him, catching a black boot as it swung in for a second strike. Giving a violent twist, Rhys managed to throw the attacker to the ground. Shouting, hoping to draw the attention of someone who might aid him, he flung himself on the downed man, growling a threat as he drew back a fist. Before he'd carried through on the swing, he felt himself jerked upright and then had his arms pinned behind his back. The man he'd brought down came scrambling up, cursing, his big fists flying and pummeling Rhys in the belly, striking his already bruised rib cage half a dozen times then finishing the assault with several ringing blows to his jaw.

"Enough!" the faceless voice from the alleyway pronounced as Rhys's head slumped to his chest.

Rhys moaned. A trickle of blood ran from his lip. He sank to his knees when he was let go, and hung there a few seconds until a solidly planted boot shoved him into the ground. He lay swallowing dust, getting grit in his eyes, as hands roughly groped in his pockets. He tried lamely to defend himself and his property but had the feeling his wild blows were merely striking air.

He was still flat on his face, beneath a hitching rail on the deserted street, long after his attackers had finished with him and hurried off. Too weak to get to his feet, he rolled over on his back and eased an arm over his eyes to shade them from the burning sun. He was waiting for the pain to diminish enough that he could hoist himself up. Eventually enough strength returned for him to catch hold of the hitching rail and pull himself upright.

He wasn't far from Sprayberry's and he dragged himself there. Slow steps carried him through the gate and up the steps to the front door where he collapsed.

Hearing a ruckus, Mae and Justine peeked out a window and saw Mae's newest boarder prostrate on the front porch. Knowing he hadn't had time to get falling down drunk since he had left, Mae forgot caution and hurried out to aid him. An anguished Justine followed in her wake.

"I'm telling you, Justine, even if your father *is* the sheriff, this town is getting worse than Tombstone ever was. A stage robbery every week, citizens beaten senseless on the street."

Mae was a big woman but she needed Justine's help to haul Rhys into the house and to heave him on the bed in the room she'd let to him.

Breathing hard, Justine defended her father. "Papa does his best," she said. "But he's one man."

Mae swung Rhys's long legs up on the bed. "Get his boots off," she ordered. "No sense having my quilt ruined too." She gave the woebegone Justine a sympathetic look. "I know your papa does his best but— Oh! For pity's sake, look what they've done to his face." Gently lifting Rhys's head she placed a fat feather pillow beneath it. "Get some cool water and some cloths, Justine. I'll get his shirt off."

As she stripped off his soiled coat and vest, Mae noted with concern the many bruises starting to darken on the man's face. With gentle fingers she unbuttoned his shirt and eased it from his back and arms. He'd been badly beaten but was beginning to come around.

"Here's the basin and—" Justine sucked in her breath at the sight of the shirtless Rhys Delmar. Once or twice she'd seen the rangy torso of a cowboy splashing himself clean at a water trough. But even with the bruises and scrapes, Rhys's broad and muscled chest, with the sprinkling of dark hair, was much more impressive. She could not take her eyes off him, not until Mae spoke to her.

"Stop lollygagging and bring them over here," she demanded. "Cool compresses ought to stop some of that bruising." She grabbed the basin from Justine and placed it on the bedside table. "I swear I wish I knew who did this to such a fine young man." Making a clucking sound, she hastily soaked a cloth, squeezed it out and laid it on his swollen cheek. "No sense in it. Nobody safe on the streets," she mumbled as she worked.

Justine, once over her shock, joined in placing soaked cloths wherever she saw any sign of an injury. "Will he be all right?" she asked anxiously.

"Right as rain," Mae assured her. "He's not soft as he looks in those fancy duds of his." Mae had seen her share of undressed men, having buried two husbands and raised three sons who got in an occasional scrape. "I'd say the worst thing that happened to him was a bump on the head." Gingerly she ran her fingers over his skull. Almost directly centered on the back of it she found a telltale lump. "Uh-huh," she said. "There it is. Big as a hen's egg."

Rhys was stirring by then, his half-closed eyes flickered and sprung open. Giving a shout, he tried to fling himself off the bed.

Mae put a hand on his chest and gently held him down. "Settle back," she said. "Looks like you've had a high time of it and ought to rest now."

Quickly taking in his surroundings and seeing no one more threatening than a pretty girl and a sensible woman, Rhys did as ordered. "A low time, *madame*," he said raggedly. "And I confess I gave a poor accounting of myself." He breathed heavily, then winced as he realized even that natural act gave pain. "I was waylaid by two men. No. Three," he said, remembering the third who had been hidden in the alley.

"Robbed?" Justine touched him gently on the cheek that wasn't bruised.

Rhys patted his trouser pockets, and discovered, to his dismay, that the majority of his winnings had been removed. "Yes," he said. All he had was a few dollars that he had transferred to an inner pocket. From the feel of it that inner pocket still held a small amount of money, and Zack Gamble's marks.

His sigh turned to a moan as Mae lifted his arm and ran her hand over his battered side. Justine reached across him to touch in the same place but Mae slapped her hand away. "No you don't," the older woman said, snaring the edge of a sheet and pulling it over his bare chest. "You stick to doin' what you can for that handsome face."

Justine's own face turned crimson but she dutifully placed a fresh compress on his cheek.

Rhys closed his eyes. That, at least, didn't hurt. Though everything else did, and he swore he could see stars inside his head. Damned if he wasn't having the worst luck of his life. Money-wise he was nearly as bad off as he had been before he'd sat down to gamble in the Diamond. If he counted the injuries he'd received, which felt limitless, he was worse off. He supposed he should be grateful he'd already paid a week's room and board, but had a feeling he'd have no appetite for tonight's much-anticipated meal.

Someone hadn't wanted him to get comfortable in Wishbone, someone who had been watching his movements and waiting for him when he had left Mae's. He started trying to think who might be responsible, beginning with anyone who might know how much money he had won and want it badly enough to attack him. Somehow he couldn't picture any of the men he'd played cards with, as desperate enough to resort to robbery.

Come to think of it the attackers hadn't talked as if robbery was what they really had on their minds. He'd been warned to get out of town. He reflected on that warning. Why would anyone after his poker winnings want him out of town? Wouldn't it make more sense for him to stay around and win more for them to steal?

Why, indeed, would anyone want him to leave town? Except Teddy. Damn her. Could she be behind this? He didn't like thinking that she was, but he had to consider that she could be. And he had to find out if she was so desperate to be rid of him that she would hire thugs to drive him off.

"I have to go out." He threw the sheet off and started to get up.

Justine gasped. Mae pushed him back down and covered him. "Not tonight, sonny," the older woman said. "You've done all the gallivanting you're going to do before tomorrow."

Rhys conceded and slumped into the soft mattress. The way his head was spinning he wouldn't last two minutes on his feet.

"That suit you, Sheriff?" Boyd Smith's cackling laughter was the only sound in the dusty silence behind Wishbone's jail. "That Frenchman didn't look near so cocky as the other day when we pulled him off a stage."

"Shut up, Boyd." Len Blalock was sickened by what he had just participated in. Beating a man for no reason went against the grain. Adams had a reason though. He wanted the Frenchman softened up—put in an agreeable mood, so the only thing he'd have on his mind was getting quick cash in his pocket and getting out of Wishbone. "You were rougher than you needed to be," he said to Boyd.

"Rougher? Hell!" Pete coughed then winced at the tight pain in his side. Angered by his injury he stiff-armed his brother knocking Boyd back a step. "You never should have let him get a lick in on me."

Boyd shoved back. "I ain't your ma," he said. "Look out for yourself."

DEVIL MOON 173

"Shut up, both of you," Blalock said. "And get out of town. 'Bout midnight have a horse waiting behind the livery."

Pete laughed. One short burst brought him more pain. "You expectin' a jailbreak, Sheriff?"

Blalock's chest swelled and his face turned red. "I'm expectin' a horse to be tied behind that stable. What's to become of him ain't your business." He turned toward the jail's back door. "Now get out of here. And change them clothes before you come riding back into town or that Frenchman will know you by your smell."

When they were gone he took the ring of keys from his belt and unlocked the heavy wooden door. He locked it behind him, like he always did, though this time there wasn't much use in it.

"Pavy? You still here?"

Pavy, the deputy, was more eager than bright but he was good at tending the office and keeping the prisoners fed.

"Waiting for you, Sheriff," the big, raw-boned Pavy replied.

"I'm here now," Blalock said. He sifted through the papers on his desk, though he knew he'd given them a thorough going over early in the morning. "Get on home to that new wife of yours. She'll like having her man home for supper for a change."

"I reckon she'll thank you for letting me have a night free." Pavy's wide face reddened. "Luther's already had his meal. He shouldn't bother you."

"I told you I had a toothache," Luther called out loudly from the back. "I need to see Doc Spivey."

With a troubled look on his face, the sheriff glanced at Luther, then at Pavy. "Go on," he said. "I'll see to him."

"No seein' to do," Pavy said flatly. "Doc Spivey's gone up to Phoenix and ain't nobody else in town who'll work on anybody in the jail. He'll have to wait 'til the doc gets back. I told him that."

"Go on." Blalock ushered Pavy out the door and watched from the window as the deputy's steps took him briskly off toward his house and bride.

At his desk, Blalock sat stiffly in his chair looking around his office at the souvenirs of his job. On the wall hung a gun he'd taken off a killer he'd backed down after the man shot dead the whole Gibson family in '70. There was a plaque the town had presented him after ten years of service. "To the esteemed Sheriff Leonard Blalock for his trustworthy—" He couldn't read any more, not with his conscience blinding him. Not when he wasn't "trustworthy" anymore. Not after today.

Too tense to stay seated, he got up and paced the floor. Up until today the worst he had done was look the other way. Today he'd ordered an innocent man beaten. In a few hours he would let a guilty one go free.

"This tooth is killing me, Sheriff. I need the doc," Luther complained from his cell.

Blalock stared at him. "You can look him up in Phoenix. You won't be around here much longer."

"I need a drink. Somethin' to dull the pain."

"Stop bellyachin'."

Hunched on his cot, Luther shot a murderous look

at the sheriff. He might have to wait a few more hours, but he wasn't leaving Wishbone without a drink.

Seventeen

"Bring the port, Meigs. And a glass for Mr. Seward." Meigs cleared the remains of Sir Avery Knox's dinner from the table in the small dining room while his master and the guest moved to the adjoining parlor, where a fire had been laid.

Knox settled into the large upholstered chair nearest the fire, a chair which, from much use, bore indentions for every round of the big man's contour. While he waited for Meigs to return, he leaned toward the flames and rubbed his fat hands together. In spite of the fleshy padding that overeating gave him, he felt the cold more than most.

Seward drew a lighter chair near the grate and sat as well. Seward had not been invited for dinner—a circumstance which he did not mind overmuch, thinking it likely he got better at the pub down the block. He did not refuse the offer of port. Knox kept a good cellar. He would be stingy, Seward knew, pouring a miserly portion for his guest then indulging himself once he was alone.

"I've got news for you," Seward said.

"Hold it a moment," Knox responded. Meigs had returned with a tray and glasses. He placed it on a table and started to pour. "Easy with it, Meigs," Knox ordered. "We won't drown ourselves in it. We need clear heads."

Seward grinned. Knox held no surprises.

Knox made the chair creak beneath him, as he reached for the glass Meigs offered him. He allowed Seward time to take his, then rushed the servant on his way. "Out with it, man," he said. "Let's hear what's taken a fortnight and every shilling I advanced you to find out."

"Paid," Seward said, "for time and effort spent."

"So be it." Knox was growing impatient, his reserves thinner. He'd not had an invitation of note in months. His friends had learned of his predicament and were distancing themselves from him should he turn out a pauper. His embarrassment was nearly as great as his girth. He had stopped going to his club, hadn't paid his dues either and expected a dunning letter any day. Even Seward looked at him with disdain.

"You've not given me the easiest of assignments," Seward complained. "And I do not work for charity though you've nearly made a liar of me on that." Knox looked grieved, which pleased Seward.

"Tell me of Delmar," the rotund Knox demanded.

"I managed to track the servant," Seward said. "Once the countess put me on to his name. A cripple fellow, extremely loyal to Delmar by all accounts. Seemed to have disappeared after the—incident." He grinned. "But as we both know, a man cannot actually disappear. And a man must eat, as you can attest." He looked accusingly at Knox's middle.

"And sleep," Knox said irritably. "Where is the man? Will he talk?"

"Any man will talk if properly induced. Bourget, though—that's the servant—has sailed to the colonies."

"The colonies?" Knox, fearing he'd spent time and money for naught, was crestfallen.

"I bought a passenger list," Seward continued. "Thought it unlikely Bourget, being a loyal sort, would leave his master in the lurch."

"Delmar couldn't have left. The inspector sent his name and description 'round to every vessel docked. He'd have been turned in."

"A man can change his looks and his name," Seward suggested.

"You think he's sailed to the colonies, too?" Knox said weakly. "Why it's half a world away." He dropped his head into his hands. "I'll never find him in time, if he has. I'll be ruined."

"Take heart," Seward said with an uncharacteristic show of concern. "If you have not found him neither have the magistrates or your uncle's agents. Old Andrew's estate is yet intact and waiting for you."

Knox, dismay evident in his deep-set eyes, looked up. "I have debts, man. I could be in prison before the estate is settled." He got a grim look then, one fired by anger and hatred. "You should have killed him."

"A man alive has yet to die," came Seward's philosophical response. "Consider that if he comes back here he goes to prison and you are spared."

"Did you hear nothing I've said?" Knox barked. "I

need the estate settled posthaste. I cannot wait what might be years for Delmar to reappear." Another more terrible thought occurred to him. Suppose the solicitors found Delmar first and he promised a rich reward should they clear his name. A man with money and wit could circumvent the law. A sound, much like a sob, shook out of his wide chest. "I am ruined."

"Not yet," Seward promised. "I can find Delmar. I know the name he used to flee and I have a good idea where he was bound."

Knox jerked his bent head up. "Damn you, Seward," he said. "Tell me." Seward sat quietly looking into the empty glass he held. Knox himself rose and poured it full. "Tell me, man," he begged.

Seward paused to drink, deliberately antagonizing Knox. Finally he spoke. "I looked for the man Delmar last sat at cards with. A man called Gamble. He had unfortunately died that same night."

"Murdered?"

"Passed on in his sleep," Seward said. "Seems he had a visitor the day after his departure."

"Delmar?"

"As the innkeeper described him, yes," Knox said. "He was disturbed. Said Gamble owed him money. Kept asking if the man had left anything for him. The innkeeper gave him a letter and Delmar went away." Seward grinned, sending his red whiskers into a quiver. "I've a feeling this Snead at the inn pilfered anything of value from Gamble before Delmar got there. He had the look of a man lately come to prosperity."

"What's the bloody point of this story?" Knox

asked irritably, beginning to suspect that like everyone else, Seward was tormenting him.

"The point is, I found the dead man's name on the passenger list of the same ship on which the servant Bourget booked passage. And he sailed."

"What? How could he?"

"That is what I say. How could a dead man rise from his coffin and sail off to the colonies?" He drank of the port. "The answer is that he did not. Mr. Delmar took his place and, if I am not a half-brain, he has found the perfect place to hide. Almost perfect," he amended.

Knox's fear gave way to grim determination. "How soon can you follow?"

"Tomorrow," Seward assured him. Then more lightly he said, "There is the matter of another payment."

"You'll have it." Knox twisted a gold ring off his middle finger, and took a last appreciative look at the glittering diamond he had hoped to hold on to. Then he handed the ring to Seward. "When it's done, get proof that he's dead. I want no doubt remaining."

"Murder's expensive business." Seward turned the ring in his hand. It was a fine piece. He might have it cut down and keep it. "This will do until I'm back," he said.

"You can name your price when you're back," Knox said, too relieved to question what those words might cost him. When Seward was gone, he heaved out a sigh, cursed his uncle, and rang for Meigs. "I'm cold," he said, missing the familiar weight of the ring on his finger. "Put more wood on the fire. And bring another bottle of port."

* * *

Luther was chilled through—not from the cool desert night but from the mild fever the infected tooth was causing. Joe Luther felt bad but not so bad that he resisted making a last dig at Sheriff Blalock as the man gave a shove that hurried him out of the cell.

"Been right nice visitin' with you," Luther said. "Now anytime you want to rob a stage you come on out. You're welcome to ride with us."

"Get moving, Luther." Len Blalock shuffled over to his desk and leaned on the corner of it. He'd turned the lantern down so the office was nearly dark. Even so, he could see the mocking grin on Luther's face. He wanted to hit him right on that swollen jaw. He never suspected that Luther was thinking along the same lines.

"I'm goin'," Luther said, but moved in the opposite direction of the door. "Just wanted to tell you I thought up a story to help you out so you won't look a complete dunce letting a prisoner escape." Luther laughed. "You can tell folks you stepped over to the cell to give me a drop of laudanum for my toothache and that I slugged you and got the keys."

"Don't do me any favors," Blalock retorted.

Luther laughed louder. "Just this one," he said. With that he drew back and punched the sheriff below the right eye. The stout blow knocked Blalock across his desk. While Len Blalock was trying to right himself, Luther grabbed the gun from the sheriff's holster and ran. He kicked open the back door and, keeping to the shadows, sped down the street.

Luther knew where his horse was but didn't go there. He'd been ordered to ride out of the territory and he would, when he was ready. But he wasn't going anywhere until he had a few bottles of whiskey in his saddlebags. He didn't suppose Adams had thought of supplying him with that, or considered that he might like to say good-bye to Maisie. The saloon girl was kind of sweet on him and he liked the way she showed it. Yeah. He liked it and he thought he'd say a so-long to Maisie before he left. No telling how long it would be before he was back in Wishbone or how long it would be before he found another girl that liked him as much.

Using the same rough wooden stairs that Teddy Gamble had climbed earlier in the day, Joe Luther stealthily made his way to the Diamond's upstairs balcony and tiptoed along the uneven boards to Maisie's window. He slipped quietly inside, feeling secure in the darkness as he carefully made his way across the floor.

Cracking the door a few inches he peeped out and waited for Maisie or one of the other girls to come by. He didn't have to wait long. Within a few minutes he heard another door open and shut and then a smiling cowboy strode by hooking his belt and whistling a tune. Honor came along shortly after him.

"Pssst," Joe called. "Honor."

She knew him at once. He'd been one of Maisie's regulars until he'd gotten arrested. "What're you doing out, Joe? Thought you were locked up for good," Honor said gaily.

"Hush up," Joe told her. "I was locked up for good

but now I ain't. So be a good girl and go down and get Maisie for me." He caught her tightly by the wrist before she turned away. "Tell her to bring up two bottles of the best whiskey." To be sure she remembered what he wanted, Joe squeezed Honor's wrist until she whimpered at the pain. "And don't let on to anybody else that I'm up here."

"I won't, Joe." Honor rubbed her chafed, aching wrist, and hurried off. She found Maisie over by the piano wrapped around one of the newly outfitted prospectors in town. The girls always tried to get to the prospectors before they went off in the hills. Most of them didn't have any money again after that.

Maisie didn't disengage from her friend until Honor had whispered her message a second time. "You sure?" Maisie said, her expression crestfallen beneath a layer of powder and rouge. "You aren't funnin', are you?"

"He's up there," Honor assured her. "Waitin' in the dark."

Maisie shivered. "I don't like it. Mr. Adams don't want trouble here."

"Don't you worry about Mr. Adams," Honor said. "I'll see to him. You get those bottles Joe wants and get on up there before he gets tired of waiting."

Harley was reluctant, but Maisie persuaded him she needed two full bottles of whiskey. With one in each hand she hurried up the stairs and to her room.

"Joe," she whispered, easing open the door. She let out a yelp when he jerked her all the way in and threw his arms around her.

"Baby, I been needin' you," he said roughly. "And

this." Stepping back he took one of the bottles from her and popped out the cork. Turning it up, Joe Luther guzzled greedily, letting the strong liquor spill from his mouth and dribble over his chin and soak down his shirt front. He stopped drinking when he needed a breath. "This is cheap stuff," he complained. "I asked for the best."

"It's all Harley would let me have," Maisie said, wishing Joe Luther'd had the good sense to ride off soon as he got loose. Her worried gaze kept darting to the door then to him. "He wanted to know why I needed two bottles."

"What did you tell him?" Still in darkness Joe pulled Maisie over to the bed and down beside him.

"That I had a thirsty customer."

"Baby, you do. And as soon as I dull this toothache that's been drivin' me out of my head I'm gonna drink you up."

"How did you get out of jail?" Maisie asked. "I didn't hear about you being let go."

"You'll hear about it tomorrow." He chugged more from the bottle. "By then I'll be long gone and you'll be missing me." An arm slid around Maisie's shoulders, a hand probed roughly down the front of her dress. "But don't you worry. I'm not going before I give you something to remember me by," he said.

Maisie wiggled over closer to him, hoping what he was going to give her included money. "That's fine, Joe," she said sweetly.

Ten minutes later Joe was half-drunk and half-naked and had divested Maisie of her corselet and skirts. With a bottle in his hand he lay atop her, his passion and his aim not coordinated enough to get him where he wanted to be. Frustrated by one more missed jab in the dark, he swore at Maisie.

"Shit! Give me some help, baby." Light flooded the room at that moment, spilling in from the open door and the lantern Harley held high in front of him. Luther dropped the whiskey bottle and swore. "Dammit! I ain't through," he said, reaching for the gun he'd lost somewhere in the covers.

"Leave it be, Joe." Parrish Adams spoke, his voice sizzling like a hot poker plunged in a bucket of water. "Maisie! Git!"

Maisie scrambled up and out. Modesty was no problem to her as, in the altogether, she bounded past Adams and Harley and into the room next to hers. When she was gone, Harley set the lantern down on the small table by the door and backed out, leaving Adams and Luther alone in the room.

"You lost, Luther?" Adams had a long-barreled revolver in his hand, the nose of it pointed down, his finger resting lightly on the trigger.

"Naw." Luther rolled up to a sitting position and looked around, his lusterless eyes searching for his trousers and boots. "I needed liquor," he said. "Got a toothache."

He found the trousers but they were turned inside out and he was too inebriated to figure how to get them right. After much fumbling he got one pant leg straight and slid his leg into it. Eventually the other pant leg fell into place and he got both feet in. He stood to pull them on, wobbled as he jerked them over his hips.

"I told you to ride out of the territory," Adams said calmly. "I expect a man who works for me to do what I say."

Luther's boots were caught in the tangled covers. He found his gun beneath one of them and picked it up. With it dangling loosely in his hand he turned. "Got a toothache," he mumbled.

He had his right boot in the other hand. He was blind drunk and stumbling around looking for the missing left boot.

Adams shot him dead.

Eighteen

From the small office window Teddy watched the stage roll in right on schedule. Another run with no trouble. She supposed it was too much to hope they had seen the last of the holdup attempts. Whatever was responsible for the bandits backing off, she was grateful. She'd had a telegram from Cabe Northrop saying Wells Fargo was pleased her company had brought in one of the bandits. That had come the day after Joe Luther broke out of jail and got himself killed over at Adams's place.

Real peculiar that the fellow went there when he could have ridden out of town. She had her suspicions that there was more to the story of his breaking out than Len Blalock had told. But the sheriff was sporting a shiner and had lost his gun and keys to Luther. Not for long, though. Blalock had both back within a few hours. And folks around town were spouting off about Adams being a hero and keeping the streets safe for decent people.

Couldn't anybody besides her see that Adams was a snake in the grass, that his charitable acts and bravado were false? No, she supposed they couldn't. People got cloudy vision when someone donated a new bell to the church and offered to pay half the new schoolteacher's salary for the year. Adams was making himself awful popular. She wondered why. What did he want in addition to the Gamble Line's contracts? Something—she knew. His true nature was about as benevolent as a badger's. She knew that firsthand.

And if she had any takers she would bet Joe Luther didn't wind up at the Diamond just to get drunk. He had business there, or thought he did. Luther could have told plenty if he'd been brought to trial. Plenty. But he wouldn't be talking now.

She got up and went out, when the stage pulled to a halt in front of the office. Strong Bill was back on shotgun and he had ridden this run. She was waiting when he jumped down from the driver's box.

"Any trouble?" she asked.

"We had an easy run," he said, shaking the dust off his long railroad coat. "And there's been no problem with the wagons coming down from the mines either," he added. "Things are goin' so good we ought to—"

"Worry," Teddy said then wished she'd held her tongue. Her pessimistic reply meant she didn't believe this streak would last. The trouble had only quieted down. With Adams after her contracts, bandits after her payloads, and the Frenchman after her money, she was destined for more problems. She had the uneasy feeling that all her adversaries had merely dropped back to regroup and that soon they would be moving in for another assault.

She wondered if she could survive another one.

"I was going to say 'rejoice.' " Strong Bill was never off duty. His Winchester rested in his arms and his eyes were alert for any person or movement out of the ordinary. He wouldn't relax his watch until the payload the coach carried was safely in the Wells Fargo vault in Yuma. "That Frenchman did us a good turn, Teddy," he said. "We owe him."

"I reckon you and Rope would hand the company to him out of gratitude," Teddy snapped. "Me, I'm glad not to have seen hide nor hair of him for a while."

Strong Bill ignored Teddy's grumpiness. Like Rope he was endlessly patient with her. "I been wonderin' where he is. You don't reckon anything's happened to him?" He stepped aside to make room for the spent team to be led off. The horses snorted and stomped, impatient to get to the grain and hay in the Gamble stable. "Mind you, we don't know what Luther did before he showed up at the Diamond," Strong Bill continued. "He might have wanted to settle a score with Delmar."

"I'm not that lucky," Teddy retorted.

The new team was hitched and Strong Bill had a leg up climbing to the box. The driver was in place and adjusting the lengths of rein in his gloved hands. "He could be more trouble to you dead than alive," Strong Bill called down to her. "If you know what I mean."

Teddy swore softly. "All right," she said. "I'll find out where he is."

"Good."

"Now you be careful out there," she implored

Strong Bill with the same words she said nearly every time he rode messenger. "Don't let anybody shoot you."

"Aww, don't you worry about me." Strong Bill winked and gave his trusty rifle a pat. "The only way they'll kill me is to cut my head off and hide it where I can't find it. Now get on and do what you said you would."

"All right," Teddy said. She did not have to look far for Rhys Delmar. He was walking up the sidewalk when the stage rolled out. His black, flat-brimmed hat was pulled low on his forehead. His shoulders were squared.

"Speak of the devil," she said.

"Teddy!" He stepped up close.

He had a savage look in his eye. She saw a dark bruise beneath a pronounced cheekbone and a not-quite-healed cut on his lower lip. She thought of Strong Bill's warning about Joe Luther. She wondered if the outlaw had hunted Delmar down before he got himself shot. A pang of guilt hit her because if that was the case, all other differences aside, Rhys had come to harm as a result of being a passenger on the Gamble Line. The pang lasted only until another emotion came into play. His cocky walk, the perfect fit of his clothes, the way his gaze was leveled on her—all triggered desire. She felt it but didn't recognize it for what it was. "Been tangling with that hussy again?" she asked.

He snarled at her. He'd spent five days practically a prisoner of Mae Sprayberry's. The landlady had taken a motherly interest in him while he was recovering from the beating he'd been given. He was still sore, tired of being cooped up, and guilty of spending too much time deliberating on who was responsible. "I think," he said bluntly, "I am victim to a conniving she-cat who's too underhanded to fight her own battles."

Teddy didn't like the implication, which—as near as she could tell—was that she was somehow responsible for his getting in a fistfight. "What are you hinting at, Delmar?" she asked hotly. "If you mean me, I'd say whoever punched you rattled some spokes loose."

He stepped so close the lapels of his jacket brushed against the fringe of her shirt. People on the street paused to stare before going on about their business. Neither Teddy nor Rhys noticed. Teddy was only conscious of his fiery breath on her face. Rhys was convinced she was the most exasperating woman he'd ever known.

Beneath the bruises, his face flushed with anger. "Are you saying you know nothing about the three men who five days ago ambushed me and warned me to leave town?"

"You're here, aren't you?" she shot back.

"No thanks to you."

Teddy doubled her fist and waved it at him. "Mister, I do my own fighting and shooting and it's face to face. So don't blame me for a scrape you got in on your own. Sure I wish you weren't here but I'm not low enough to hire thugs because of that. You and I have business together whether we like it or not and that business will be settled fair. Understand?"

"I understand. But if I find out that you were in any way responsible—"

"You ought to soak your head," she said scornfully. "By the way, where *have* you been since you got that licking?"

"At Madame Sprayberry's," he replied, beginning to concede that Teddy might not have arranged the assault, but indignant that she assumed he had not given as good as he got. "It might surprise you to know there are some people in this town who treat a stranger with kindness."

"It might surprise you to know there are some strangers who deserve it," she spat back.

Rhys drew himself up taller and stared harshly down at her. "Madame Sprayberry is a fine, charitable lady."

"That old hen." Teddy reared back and laughed so hard her hat fell off. It dangled on her back, held there by the thin leather lanyard tied beneath her chin. "She'll coddle you to death if you don't watch out. But I reckon that's the kind of looking-after a tenderfoot needs."

Teddy's eyes glittered with her poorly concealed contempt. Rhys's mouth compressed into a tight and unpleasant line. Teddy's mockery had come too close to the truth. Mae Sprayberry had nearly smothered him with kindness. And when she wasn't sitting at his bedside or pouring hot broth down him, Justine had been there dutifully watching and working her embroidery. Today he'd had to slip out while they were both in the kitchen. Women liked an invalid, he supposed— except Teddy, who more likely preferred making one.

"I can take care of myself," he said stiffly. "I think I've proven that."

"Ha!" Teddy jeered, her voice cold, her tone condescending. "Any boy in knee britches can make a lucky throw with a rock. Around here you've got to shoot straight and ride hard to prove yourself." Her next words cut like a rusty razor. "And the rule is, a man's not a man unless he's still standing after a fight."

His body went rigid, his nostrils flared, and, for a moment the muscles convulsed in his cheeks. He wanted to shake her, but that wouldn't have been a safe thing to do—not with his temper raging—not when he wasn't sure whether or not he would break her neck. He might regret it if he did. It was a pretty neck, long and slender. He needed to do something about that mouth, though. She talked like a saddle tramp and she always went too far.

For an instant he toyed with the idea of grabbing her there on the street and kissing her so soundly she would regret her caustic words and beg his forgiveness for saying them. He'd make her swoon like any of the dozens of other women he had held in his arms. But then none of them had been wearing a gun—and liable to use it should he be wrong this once about his powers of seduction. Damn her! She had begun to make him question what he had always taken for granted, his manhood.

He did swear, loudly. *Sacré bleu!* "You are one heartless—"

Teddy huffed. "Don't say it!"

He didn't. He had noticed the way the sun was lighting streaks of gold in her hair and revealing, now that her hat was off and she was heated up, that it smelled faintly of summer flowers. He nearly, involuntarily, reached out and touched the glistening strands. But he did not. He let her get away with one more affront, contented that he'd found one more dent in Teddy's tough facade. She might shout and swear, wear leather and spurs and case her legs in trousers. But she used a sweetly scented soap—this spitfire who brooked no recognition that she was a woman.

The facade held on another front, though. Teddy lacked even a shred of sympathy. She had obviously felt no concern for his apparent disappearance. She had, in fact, counted his absence a blessing if her behavior today was any indication. She would like it ever so much if he went away and was never seen or heard from again. Oh yes, she would like to make him a "silent" partner. If she had not been responsible for the mishap which had left him battered and bruised and, admittedly, embarrassed, she certainly wasn't respectably displeased it had happened.

He had endured all the taunts and all the temptation he could stand for one day. "Step aside!" he demanded.

Teddy braced herself. "Not for you."

It was the final straw. Rhys gripped her stiffly set shoulders, lifted her and set her out of his way, surprised by her lightness. He'd half expected she'd be made of lead. Angrily, briskly, he walked off.

"Where are you going?" she shouted after him.

"For a drink." He didn't glance back. "Lots of them."

"Oh hell," Teddy grumbled out the words. "Now

I've sold my saddle for sure. He's heading to the Diamond."

In his cozy back office, Parrish Adams sat like a monarch in his leather chair. He drank a blended whiskey, not the gut-burning redeye he served at the bar. His thin mustache was waxed to perfection. He was basking in the glow of a favorable editorial written about him in the *Wishbone Gazette*. He commended himself on the wisdom of ordering from a foundry a bell cast for the empty tower that had sat atop Wishbone's only church.

"See this, Norine," he said. "See how they praise my generosity." He pushed the paper toward her, leaned back and drank of the expensive whiskey. "Money will buy anything," he extolled. "Friends, respect, anything."

She drummed her long nails on the soft newsprint. "I knew that. I've always had a fondness for money—and you."

"You mean anybody with money."

A knock interrupted them. "Adams," Len Blalock's baritone came from the bar side of the door.

"Get upstairs," he said. "See if those girls are earning their keep."

Norine, resplendent in a form-fitting gown of black, blew him a kiss and silently eased out the back door. Adams invited the sheriff inside when she was gone.

Blalock had his hat in his hand. "Wanted to tell you Delmar is up and about today."

"It's past time," Adams said. "What's it been? Nigh

on a week?" He shook his head. "You disappoint me, Sheriff. I thought you were smarter than Boyd and Pete. That's why I sent you along. I wanted Delmar roughed up and scared, not beaten senseless."

"Wasn't my doin'. Your boys got carried away."

With both hands on the edge of his desk, Adams leaned hard against it. "And a lot of time got by. Time I didn't want to wait." Adams eased back in his chair, shrugged, then stood and took a handkerchief from his pocket. As if the sheriff were not there he folded the white cloth and took a moment to polish the two-carat diamond in his gold stickpin. "Now am I going to have to hunt for Delmar or are you going to see he pays me a visit?"

"I set that up already," Blalock said, uneasily shifting his weight from one foot to the other. He'd looked in on Delmar after Justine told him about the assault. It hadn't been one of his finer moments, pretending outrage and concern to his daughter for an act he was responsible for. But he had done it and Justine, mercifully, had not suspected his duplicity. "I told him you heard of his—misfortune and sent your regards and that you would stand him a drink when he was well enough to visit the Diamond." He stared at Adams's face looking for a sign of approval. "If he's like most men he won't waste much time getting here."

"If so, you've done one thing right, but I suggest you get out on the street and make sure he doesn't forget where that free drink is waiting."

"Yes, sir." The words slipped out. Blalock felt some of his lifeblood drain out with them. They lumped him in the same category as the Smith brothers and, where the unfortunate Joe Luther had been.

He was now one of Adams's boys.

Nineteen

Rhys had one stop to make before he cooled down with a drink. He'd used his time of forced rest to pen an overdue letter to Alain Perrault. He wanted to get it in the day's post. Mae Sprayberry had told him that the place to take care of that was at Penrod's Mercantile. Milt Penrod, besides running the town's general store also served as Wishbone's postmaster. Mae had offered to take care of the chore for him, but Rhys had endured enough of the woman's probing questions.

For a man trying to keep his past a secret, Mae Sprayberry was a trial. He did appreciate her kindness, though. Without her care he'd have suffered much more than he did, and doubted he would be up even yet. Teddy could take lessons from Mae. By all of hell, Teddy could take lessons on politeness from anybody.

He'd reached Penrod's, and walked past the barrels and benches in front of the store, when a tall, thin man in pinstripe trousers and crisp white shirt stepped from the doorway. The man pulled a broom straw from the corner of his mouth. "Mornin'," he said.

"Bonjour." Rhys tipped his hat. "I was told I could post a letter here."

"Delmar, isn't it?" The man stuck the straw between his lips and looked Rhys over from head to foot. " 'Course you are. Couldn't be anybody else. I'd know. Reckon the postmaster gets to know 'bout everybody in town."

"I am Rhys Delmar." Rhys extended a hand.

"Milt Penrod." The thin man shook Rhys's hand. "Postmaster, storekeeper." The straw in the corner of his mouth wiggled up and down as he talked. "Come on in. I'll take care of that letter for you." He gave Rhys a friendly pat on the back as they walked inside the store. "Saw you talkin' to Teddy. Reckon she's right grateful to you for catchin' that holdup man." Penrod wove through the intricately stacked goods with practiced ease. Rhys followed. "Too bad about him gettin' shot before the trial."

Penrod had walked behind a small counter with a wall of pigeonholes behind it.

"A shame, yes," Rhys replied. "Sheriff Blalock was greatly distressed that his prisoner escaped and endangered the life of Mr. Adams."

"That saddle bum was short on smarts to stay around once he was free," Penrod said. "Reckon he wanted to fill his pockets and his gullet before he headed for the border." The storekeeper shrugged and looked around as if he didn't already know there was no other customer in the store. He motioned Rhys in closer to the counter. "Tell you somethin' though, I see things around here nobody else sees." He made a wide sweeping gesture with his arm, one that encompassed the whole of the storefront. "All day I'm lookin' out that big window glass at who rides in and who rides out.

Sometimes I'm here late, workin' my books. Between you and me I've seen that Luther fellow goin' in the Diamond at all hours, sometimes after it's closed." A knowing smile slid onto Penrod's face. "So I'd say that Luther was expectin' to get somethin' besides food and drink over there."

Rhys smiled too. "Ahh, you mean a woman." He pulled the letter from his coat pocket and laid it on the counter.

"That or somethin' else," Penrod suggested as he rather absently took the letter and glanced at the address. "Anyhow Luther sure picked the wrong place this time. 'Course it didn't do Parrish Adams any harm bein' the one to gun him down. Made folks take notice—those that hadn't already. Wouldn't be surprised if Adams ran for mayor next election." Rhys's letter waved in Penrod's hands punctuating each word he uttered. "Heck," he went on, "way he's been buyin' up land around here he'll soon own everything anyway." Pausing, he took a closer look at the letter then glanced up at Rhys. "London," he said. "Friend or family?"

"Friend," Rhys replied, fearing Milt Penrod was about to prove as nosy as Mae Sprayberry. "How much is the postage?"

Sensing Rhys was in a hurry, Penrod quickly calculated the postage, took the money Rhys produced and handed back the change. "You expectin' a reply?"

Rhys was silent for a long moment, wondering just how Alain would respond to his tardy letter. Surely Jenny's son would not believe he *was* responsible for her death. Surely not. And yet the inner turmoil, which had never settled since that event, roiled more strongly within him as he considered the great risk he took in writing to Alain. Jenny's son could alert London authorities and soon, though he was thousands of miles away, he could expect that he would be hunted down. But he had to do it. He had to tell Alain what he knew of Jenny's death and he had to trust that Alain would be his ally in spite of the charges made against him.

"Perhaps," he said quietly, then nodded a curt goodbye to Milt Penrod and wended his way out of the store in what was akin to a sleepwalker's daze. He never consciously noticed the curious assortment of goods lining his path, those tall stacks of denim trousers, rows of sturdy leather boots and hatboxes labeled Stetson. Only one thing actually caught his eye, a long, framed-glass counter housing a selection of pistols, but even so, he did not stop to look.

Outside, he stood a moment on the sidewalk's parched boards, breathed heavily of the fresh air then set a course for the Diamond. He needed a drink more than ever now, even though it was midmorning.

He found the Diamond quiet. The girls had not begun their workday, for which he was glad. He wanted a few moments of solitude to clear his mind before he looked for a game and an opportunity to replenish his empty purse. He thought, too, once he had done so, he might return to Penrod's and purchase a pistol. The men who had assaulted him had taken the derringer he carried. And if he were going to be in Wishbone for a time, as it appeared he would, he wished to be armed.

He ordered whiskey and took the bottle to a table.

Mae did not allow drinking in her house. Despite his insistence that a good whiskey had medicinal qualities, she had refused him even a drop during his convalescence.

He slowly took the first swallow. The taste was sharp, the quality below grade, but it was the effect he was after. With the glass at his lips, he leaned his head back and allowed the raw heat of the whiskey to trickle down his throat. He felt his unsettled nerves calm as the heat penetrated.

"I can offer you better," Parrish Adams announced matter-of-factly. He had come out into the saloon at once after Harley stepped from behind the bar and advised him that the Frenchman he'd been watching for had come in. "I keep a private stock of fine blended whiskey in my office and do enjoy sharing it with the few people in Wishbone who can appreciate the difference," Adams added. As he talked he hooked his thumbs into the small vest pockets that held a hand-scrolled gold watch in addition to a heavy gold chain which stood out smartly against black silk. "If I am not off the mark, you are a man who appreciates fine things."

"I've no aversion to them," Rhys replied. "So if the offer is genuine, I accept." He corked the bottle he had brought to the table and pushed it aside. "Adams, isn't it?"

"Parrish Adams," the other man said. "The Diamond is mine," he explained as they walked off, "although saloonkeeping isn't my mainstay." He stopped at the threshold of his office and ushered Rhys inside. "Ranching's the primary thing for now," he explained.

"I'm building one of the biggest spreads in these parts and building the finest cattle herd in the territory. Out here that takes a lot of land."

Rhys nodded. He would have settled for the good whiskey without the conversation. He still had Teddy on his mind. No woman had ever made him feel more useless. He considered the irony of it. She disdained all the qualities he'd spent a lifetime trying to acquire and admired those he'd left behind. Courtly demeanor and clever conversation were lost on her. She expected a man to prove his worth with hard work and sweat. If it didn't have him in such a pinch it would all be laughable. Here he was in the wrong world with a longing for the wrong woman and a desperate need to figure out what he was going to do about it.

Inside Adams's retreat, Rhys sat in a chair of scarlet velvet that had a soft and comfortable biscuit-tufted back. Adams felt relaxed inside his private quarters. He stood at a cabinet and poured whiskey into short crystal glasses, served his guest, then stood back as Rhys drank his portion.

"Superb," Rhys said, deciding one swallow of the excellent, mellow whiskey was reward enough for listening to Adams. "Is your ranch near Wishbone?" he asked strictly out of politeness, sure Adams had invited him in so that he might have someone new to impress with talk of his grand plans and holdings.

"It's north of here and growing," Adams said. He'd drawn up to his desk and, glass in hand, leaned a hip against the corner of it. "Two thousand acres and I've another five hundred closer in. One day it will all be one big spread." Adams, pausing to allow the size and scope of what he owned and planned to own sink in. Then he reached an arm back and flipped open the humidor on his desk and offered Rhys one of the cigars inside. "The finest," he said.

"I thank you." Having felt a recent lack of luxuries, Rhys gladly accepted, gave the cigar an appreciative sniff and searched his pocket for a match.

"Try this." Adams had a silver object in his hand, a palm-sized case which he stroked across the top with his thumb. A small flame leaped out and Adams leaned down to light Rhys's cigar. "Better than a match," he said of the pocket lighter. "Just had it sent from back East."

Adams snapped the lighter shut and handed it to Rhys. He experimented with it a few moments. After satisfying his curiosity about the gadget, he handed it back. Already Rhys had observed that the office decor, with its fine cherry paneling and furnishings and softly hued Oriental rug, was a cut above the Diamond's main room and a testament that Adams did indeed like fine things.

"I might wonder," Rhys said between draws on the cigar, "why a man of your tastes isn't back East."

"Opportunity," Adams said with no hesitancy. "It's as abundant as the desert out here. A smart man in this territory could—" He'd been about to say "build an empire the like of which has never been seen," but he heeled in his enthusiasm. "Well there's no limit to what a man can do," he said instead. Eyes gleaming, he took a drink, waited a moment and added, "I'm a man who likes living where there are no limits."

"A gambler's philosophy as well," Rhys said. "No

limits at the table, no limits at life." He ended the comparison there. He wasn't in the mood to get into a philosophical discussion, he had too much emotional sorting-out to do privately.

Rhys finished the whiskey shortly, probably too quickly but Adams's braggadocio bothered him and he was anxious to find a game. He thanked Adams for the drink and stood, noticing then, for the first time, a small glass case near a wall of bookcases. The figurine inside, the sole object on display in the case, was exquisite, quite exceeding anything he expected to see in Wishbone. He walked over to the case confirming that the work was similar to others he'd seen in Paris museums. "Remarkable," he said. "Chinese, isn't it?"

Adams nodded affirmatively. "Jade," he said with enough aplomb to express his pride in the piece. "Extraordinarily fine." Smiling proudly, he, too, walked over to the case. "I bought it in San Francisco," he said. "The owner was reluctant to sell but eventually I convinced him to part with it." At that he gave an indifferent shrug, remembering the payment had been a bullet in the ancient Chinaman's back. "But you would not know how the Chinese like to hold on to these old pieces and anyway—" Turning, he walked off, picked up Rhys's glass, took it to the liquor cabinet and refilled it. "Sit down," Adams said firmly. "Finish your cigar. Have another drink and allow me to tell you about something else I am anxious to acquire."

Not about to turn down what was possibly the only good whiskey in Wishbone, Rhys did precisely what Adams was urging, even though it meant listening to another round of the man's boasting of his possessions. "You are kind," Rhys said smoothly, "to a stranger. I must think of a way to reciprocate."

"Hear me out then," Adams said. "Maybe we can be of service to each other."

"Perhaps," Rhys said. Recalling that Adams had complimented his card playing the last time he had been at the Diamond, Rhys assumed the man was about to offer him a deal running a game in the saloon. Or maybe he wanted to bankroll him in a high-stakes game. He was willing to consider either. He had learned early on that a man without money was also a man without power. He did not like the feeling. So, resolved to put aside what was troubling him a few minutes longer, Rhys settled in the soft velvet chair and listened intently as Adams explained what was on his mind.

"In addition to ranching and my other business enterprises I have a stage line in the north country," he said. "A feeder line. Adams Overland. I am anxious to expand the limited routes so that my line serves the territory from border to border." His lean fingers traced the curve of one side of his dark waxed mustache. "The hindrance to that is the existence of another line in this region."

"The Gamble Line," Rhys supplied. He looked up at Adams with rising curiosity but true to his vocation did not give away his emotion as he took a slow draw on the cigar, emitted a cloud of smoke and said levelly, "Surely this region could support more than one line."

Adams shook his head vigorously. "No line runs for long without a mail contract," he said. "And the Gamble Line has a deal with Wells Fargo that amounts to a five-year agreement for this region. My line, though it's better by far, can't compete as long as that is the case. And as you must understand, five years is a long time to wait, and the Gamble Line could succeed in renewing when the present contract is done." Rhys was anxious to appear unemotional. Adams drank down the whiskey in his glass and set it aside. "What I have in mind," he said, "is combining the two companies, a deal I think any sensible person would agree is good for both lines, as both will be bigger and stronger than before."

Rhys was beginning to see that he had not been invited for a drink because of his cosmopolitan ways or his gambling skills. He could also see that Adams was suggesting that Teddy Gamble was not a sensible person. With that he had to concur. Possibly Adams had put the question of a merger to her and been flatly, vehemently, refused. And somehow, in all likelihood, Adams had learned he was Teddy's unwilling partner.

Feeling the kind of rush he felt when a game got interesting, when he knew the cards were about to fall his way, Rhys drew down again on the cigar.

"That sounds sensible," he said, realizing that Adams thought he would immediately reveal his hand and suggest that his shares, in Adams's possession, could achieve exactly what the other man wanted. But he did not make the suggestion or even confirm that he had the shares which Adams evidently wanted. Never one to flinch, no matter what cards he held, he nonchalantly sipped his drink and proceeded carefully and skillfully to calculate just what Parrish Adams had that he, Rhys Delmar, might want.

"Money," Adams said. "You would think it would be as simple as that, but no, not for the Gamble family. They have some notion that a family business is not to be tampered with, not even in the face of greater efficiency and higher profits. I made an offer to buy out Theodor Gamble but he refused. When he died I made the same offer to his daughter thinking she would be grateful for a chance to cash in a business a woman's got no place running. But—well, you've met her. Talking to Teddy Gamble is like talking to a post."

Giving Rhys time to think on what he'd said, Adams moved around his desk and sat in his leather chair where, framed by the rich trappings of his office, he waited for Rhys to comment.

"She has a stubborn nature," Rhys agreed, "but as for running the stage line she seems quite capable."

"Capable?" Adams laughed. "She's holding on by a thread and staying in business by sheer luck. Her line's had a series of holdups," he said bluntly. "The one on your run was not the first and will not be the last. A line run by a woman looks like and is easy prey to every highwayman in the territory," he added. "What does a woman know about protecting lives? Believe me, I'd be doing her a favor by buying into her business or buying her out. She knows it too. She's just too mule-headed to admit she's close to losing all."

Now he had aroused concern. Rhys, uncharacteristically, almost broke his stony, poker face and revealed that Adams's words alarmed him. And well they did. If the Gamble Line was in danger of going under, then his shares, on which so much of his life hinged, might be valueless. Fortunately he remembered that in gaming a man often overstated his hand. "If the Gamble Line is in distress, why not wait out its demise and buy cheap?" Rhys queried.

"Because," Adams said grittily, "I for one do not find patience a virtue. I am ready to expand the routes of Adams Overland. Now." He had his palms flat on the surface of his desk. His face was tight. "Just as I am ready to end this parleying. Both of us know what this talk is about." He leaned toward Rhys. His face was bland, although his pupils had widened. "You have Zack Gamble's shares of the Gamble Line. I am prepared to offer you ten thousand dollars for them. Immediately. Before you leave this office. It's better than Teddy can pay you now or later. So—" He pushed himself up and stood staring down at Rhys. "Take my advice and sell."

Rhys gulped the last of his drink then coolly smiled up at Adams getting a measure of satisfaction that the saloonkeeper had shown his hand first. "Your offer tempts me," he said, knowing that Adams's yielding so quickly indicated a level of desperation that could be worth far more than ten thousand dollars. "But as it is unexpected and bears thought, you must allow me time." Unperturbed by Adams's sudden sour look, he continued. "I came here today to play cards and, I fear, I've not the presence of mind to negotiate on a matter of such importance."

Adams looked briefly dumbfounded—an expression Rhys did not miss and which he found mildly gratifying. Adams would offer considerably more later. In the meantime he could use the present offer to persuade Teddy to be more malleable. Yes. He smiled broadly. This was turning into a grand day.

He had but one ill thought. It was that his faculties were not up to snuff. In all the time he'd been in Wishbone, it had not occurred to him that someone outside the Gamble Line might be interested in buying his shares. But he bet it had occurred to Teddy. She was the smooth one, bluffing him all the way. Tonight he was going to call her bluff. He didn't think he would have sold out to Adams had the offer been twice the ten thousand offered, not until he'd gotten some enjoyment from tormenting Teddy as much as she had him.

Rhys excused himself, leaving Adams baffled and angry that he had been turned down though he carefully concealed his disappointment with a smile and flippant parting words.

"Take your time," he said. "The Gamble Line is worth less every day. I could get it for nothing."

"I'll keep that in mind," Rhys said, feeling as pleased with himself as he'd been since arriving in the frontier town. Adams had made a poor bluff and Rhys didn't believe a word of it.

As he engaged in a game of poker a few minutes later, Rhys felt that his wits were sharp as a razor. He thanked Adams for that. Rhys was so enthusiastic about his new state of affairs that he was oblivious to Harley leaving the bar and once again going to the boss's office.

"You wanted me?" the big man wiped his hands on the apron stretched across his middle.

Adams had a cold look in his eye that made the burly bartender flinch. He hoped he was not responsible for putting it there. "Harley." The voice was ice. The obvious menace in his tone put Harley even more on guard. "Let Delmar play out the game he's in, then pass the word to the regulars that he's poison."

"You want to shut him out?"

"Completely," Adams snarled, causing the short hairs on the back of Harley's neck to rise.

"Shouldn't be no trouble," Harley returned. "The boys ain't gonna mind backin' off somebody that cleans 'em out every time he sits down. I'll make sure I tell 'em what's what soon as Delmar leaves," he said, pleasantly satisfied that it was the Frenchman who had drawn Adams's ire. Harley knew the depth of his boss's temper. He had no wish ever to feel it directed at him. Which was not to say he did not enjoy seeing someone else suffer under that dark wrath. He wondered how Delmar had gotten on the wrong side of Adams so fast. "What's that foreigner done?" he erred in asking. "Tried to cheat you?"

Adams's sneering smile unnerved Harley and the bartender immediately regretted his inquiry.

"Not that's it's any of your business, Harley, but the son of a bitch has something I want and he just turned down my offer for it." His voice was low. His face was the color of a white-hot coal. Adams swore. "But mark my words and mark them good. Before I'm done with Delmar he'll want to give it to me."

Reprieved, Harley was suddenly anxious to please Adams. "You want me to see he doesn't come back in the Diamond after today?" he asked. Of all Adams's men Harley had been with him the longest. The bartender was loyal to a fault and felt no compunction about giving a customer the boot should Adams say the word.

"No," Adams stated. "Let him come in at will. I want to watch him so I'll know when to make my next offer."

Understanding, Harley laughed.

Twenty

Rhys had won every hand. Nevertheless, he left his gaming partners smiling with a victor's round of drinks in their bellies. He did not recall when he had played better—a testament that a man's mood was the key to success. Admittedly, the low stakes had not added up to make him rich, but he was no longer a pauper and, in the greater game, the one he played with Teddy, he felt assured of winning.

Not ready for a return to Mae's he stopped off at a cafe and ordered the highest-priced meal plus a bottle of wine for his own private celebration of his change of fortune.

When he had finished his repast he stepped out into the deepening dusk in time to see the magnificence of a desert sunset. The sky was fused with amber and coral and the craggy mountains in the distance transformed to gold as the fading light fell over them. He strolled along the street, watching the shadows grow into total darkness that was again transformed by the lighting of lanterns inside windows. He was as happy as he'd been in months. And he had nowhere to go and nobody to share his happiness with.

He thought of Honor but there was really nothing he could tell her and she wasn't the one who could satisfy the other yearning he had. That would be Teddy, but she was probably already at the ranch. Even if she was around, he had about as much chance of cozying up to her as safely hugging a cactus. On top of that he wanted to let her stew a few days, let her worry and wonder if he was making a deal with Adams.

The little she-cat had put him through it and he wanted to return the favor. He smiled as he thought of her rousing him out of Honor's room at the Diamond. Teddy must have been tied in knots wondering if Adams had included the girl as part payment in a deal for the shares. She was something, Teddy Gamble, hard as granite but she had to have a soft side. He wondered . . .

His rambling had brought him to the Gamble stable. Half expecting a challenge, he opened a door and walked in, but found only the horses inside. Someone had left a lantern lit. Casting a wide spray of golden light, it softly illuminated the big barn. Careless, or else someone was coming back. Bullet, he reasoned. If that mare he had seen earlier was ready to drop her foal she was sure to need someone with her.

The animal nickered as he approached her stall. She was still standing, but her head was down and there were signs that she was in labor. Making sure he didn't spook her he carefully and quietly entered the stall and gave the mare a few comforting pats. She snorted but didn't even try to get her head up. A few moments later she dropped down on the straw and began thrashing her legs, obviously in more distress than a healthy animal giving birth ought to be.

"Sacré bleu!" Rhys swore softly. The way she was blowing and kicking meant something was seriously wrong and, he feared, that without help she was never going to deliver the foal.

Reluctantly, after calling out to be sure there was no one else around, Rhys slipped out of his coat and hung it over the stall gate. While talking soothingly to the mare he rolled his sleeves, pushed them over his elbows and untied the blue cravat at his throat. With the cravat tucked away in a coat pocket he loosened his collar. Resigned to the job of delivering the foal, he knelt beside the mare.

An hour passed with the animal alternately calmed and struggling to rise. Knowing she would do herself harm if he left her, Rhys stayed on his knees at her side, humming a French lullaby and stroking her sweat-dampened neck each time she got restless.

He did not hear the soft sound of footsteps behind him or even suspect that someone stood back and listened to his calming song until a shadow fell over his shoulder and a slightly sarcastic voice muttered, "Mighty purty."

In trying to jump up without stepping on the mare, Rhys banged the back of his head on the side of the stall. Rubbing his head he stood. "Where is Bullet?" he demanded, his voice falling a note when he saw that in the soft light, with her scowl half hidden, she was prettier than ever. His mind took that thought and created a flashing image of her in satin and lace. Irresistibly beautiful.

Teddy, decked out in dusty buckskins and a pair of old boots, carried a bucket filled with foul-smelling bottles and clean rags. She set it down and leaned on the gate. "Out at the first station tending a couple of horses that got in a kicking match in the corral." Her worried look swept over the downed mare then turned to indifference when she raised her cool green eyes to him. "This one isn't supposed to foal until next week."

"Birth makes its own time, Teddy," he said with conviction. "The foal is on its way."

Teddy leaned in and bent her head over the inside of the stall, to make her own assessment of what he said. He was right, that was plain. But she didn't like it in the least that he had found one of her animals needing help that wasn't handy. She directed her annoyance at herself for not having been there earlier. Then she gave him a dark look. "That's why I rode in," she remarked. "So get your fancy self out of there and I'll take care of her."

Rhys stood firm. Damn her! That dismissive tone again. Once more she had assumed he was incapable of anything worthwhile. Or maybe she was still miffed because he had not her taken her offer to work for her while he waited for proof of his claim. He wondered what she would say when he told her he didn't have to wait anymore, that Parrish Adams had made him an offer that didn't require any wait for verification from London. She wouldn't be high and mighty then. In fact, he thought she would get immensely more congenial the minute he told her. He was going to do so as soon as the mare was taken care of. Meanwhile he would prove to her he wasn't a fancy fool who was in the way. "Oh," he said, his pale eyes drilling her. "Are you experienced enough to turn a foal before it's born?" He raised his brows in challenge. "Because this one is positioned badly and the mare is in for a bad time unless she has expert help."

He watched her sublimely confident look falter, heard her feet shuffle in the scattered straw outside the stall. "Well, I've never actually . . ."

He leaned heavily on the gate from the other side, getting face to face with her. "Well, I have. And unless you're willing to risk this animal's life I suggest we both remain and do what we can to make the ordeal bearable and to end up with mother and foal alive."

"Move over," Teddy said, frowning. Grabbing the bucket, she eased into the stall and to a spot where she could get a good look at the mare's progress. "But you'd better be more than talk on this. You'd better know plenty about delivering a foal or—"

The mare kicked and Rhys roughly shoved Teddy aside, knocking her off her feet and onto her backside. "More than I know about splinting a leg," he said. "So stay clear of her hooves. She's going to get wilder before this is over." Very softly he added, "From experience I can tell you one mad female is all I can handle."

Teddy gave him a scathing look as she hurriedly scooted up and positioned herself behind the mare's head. That way, the animal could see and hear her when Rhys was ready to reach into the birth canal to turn the foal. "I'm sure you like them sugar-coated and agreeable," she quipped.

Rhys was bent over the mare's belly feeling her distended abdomen attempting to confirm what he feared about the way she was carrying the foal. He lifted up and flashed a smile at Teddy. "Sugar-coated, salty, spicy. Anything but sour," he said.

Teddy huffed out a hot breath. "Don't you have something to do besides clue me in on your love life? I'm not interested, especially not in a horny French—"

A tremor shook the mare and once again Teddy had to get clear, this time to avoid being hit by the animal's big head as the mare flung it back and forth.

"Hold her if you can," Rhys ordered. "If you can't, get out of the way. That was a contraction and she's presented—*Sacré bleu,*" he said softly. "A hindquarter." He was all business then, his face grim. The mare was trying to deliver too fast and with the foal turned backwards neither of them was going to make it.

Hurriedly he stripped off his waistcoat and shirt and tossed them out of the stall.

"What can I do?" Teddy's query ended in a gulp when she saw Rhys half-naked. Her imagination had drawn him leaner and much less imposing. That broad chest was anything but lean. It was banded with muscles that rippled and tensed as he toiled with the mare. The sight of him hard at work, with his overlong black hair waving down his neck, clinging in damp curls to his sculpted cheekbones, captivated her so that she stood and stared dumbly, with her face flushed and hot.

"Keep her head down," Rhys said, breaking her trance, reminding her there was work to do that would not wait while she gaped to her heart's content.

She dropped down quickly and gripped the mare's halter, pitting her strength against the horse's power and fear. Fortunately the animal sensed that she needed this human help. She offered minimal resistance, trembling but not fighting when the foal moved within her. Still it was slow, tedious work turning the foal, since a too-sudden or too-forceful move could result in a rupture and hemorrhage and cause the death of the mare even if the foal could be saved.

The mare's nostrils were wide and her heavy outflow of breath made a sound like a bellows in the silence of the stable. Her heaving sides and neck were foam-flecked and wet. Sweat streamed from Rhys's brow nearly blinding him with the sting of salt in his eyes. He was bloody to his elbows, still struggling with the mare half an hour after he'd begun.

Teddy, seeing him blink and grimace, snatched a clean cloth from the bucket and mopped his face. Inadvertently her fingertips grazed his heated skin and brushed against the bristly growth of late-day beard on his chin. A jolt shot up her arm. Her heartbeat quickened and a lump formed in her tight, dry throat. She put the cloth aside and moved away, puzzling over the reaction this man had wrought in her, knowing what she felt was the beginning of desire. *Desire.* She had no room in her life for it, no room for entanglements and no room for a man whom she had never even wanted to meet. But she had met him and he was a part of her life, a large part for now. And she was both repelled and attracted to him, which was a predicament she didn't need and, dammit, wouldn't have.

"Is it going to work?" she asked abruptly, wanting to change the worrisome direction of her thoughts.

"I almost have it in place," he said softly. Shortly he drew his blood-stained arms free and rocked back on his heels. "They ought to make it now, both of them."

Teddy smiled and nodded, admiring—in spite of her misgivings—the effort he had made, noting, gratefully, that the mare's breathing had eased and a tiny pair of hooves had emerged. It would not be long before the rest of the foal followed. Sensing that his relief was as great as hers she slid down closer to him to watch, fascinated as she always was by such marvels, laughing gleefully when, not long afterwards, the youngster was out, strong and whole in spite of the ordeal.

"A little stallion," Teddy said, the wonder still in her voice as she wiped down the small, struggling animal doing the job the exhausted mare was unable to do. The foal was soon on his feet, stamping and shaking and wobbling his way around the stall. The mare shuddered once, then gathered the strength to stand. Upright, she whinnied to her offspring and began nuzzling his still damp coat. Teddy stepped back for a good look at the two of them, silently acknowledging that without Rhys, neither animal would have been likely to live. Alone, she could never have been as much help to the mare. She had no doubt of it.

She wanted to thank him as she would have done any other man. But then, she had so many points of difference with him that she couldn't quite do it. This was the man who could ruin everything her family had worked long and hard for. This was the man who made her feel giddy and uncertain in a way no other man ever had. So, doing her best not to show too much gratitude she cocked her head to one side, took a long pensive look at the newborn then at Rhys. "I reckon in light of your being responsible for getting him here we ought to call him—"

"Delmar," Rhys suggested.

Teddy had a mischievous grin as she opened the stall door. "Frenchy," she said, and motioned to Rhys. "Come on. I'll get some soap and water so you can wash up."

Arms akimbo, wondering if she ever gave an inch, Rhys followed her out back where she pumped water into a bucket and handed him a cake of strong hard soap that smelled of pine. He scrubbed for several minutes cleaning skin and nails. When Teddy had refilled the bucket with fresh water, he rinsed his face and splashed the dried sweat from his chest and shoulders. When he was clean and smelling more of pine than horseflesh, he ran damp fingers through his tousled hair. The gesture, a habitual part of his grooming, showed to perfection every sinewy inch of his well-formed torso. Her sense of desire returned. Teddy had hoped it had been but a momentary foolish reaction to the sight of bare male flesh.

Rhys sensed her eyes on him and turned around. If he'd had any idea of the effect he was having on her he'd have pushed on. But with the darkness partly shielding her face, he could detect only the start of the scowl she usually wore in his presence.

"Frenchy," he said, with some amusement grasping

that even a compliment from Teddy had barbs, "will be fine. The mare needs watching."

"Oh," Teddy said, afraid he'd seen the untoward interest in her eyes.

He hadn't and he went on innocently flexing his powerful muscles as he used one of Teddy's cloths to dry his skin. "I believe I did her no harm," he said. "But I cannot be entirely sure of what I could not see. Since I am responsible in either case, I will stay the night." He glanced up at the sky and the bright silver disc of the moon high in the blue-blackness. "What is left of it in any case. Should the mare go down, there is the foal to see to—"

"I'll stay."

They had begun walking toward the stable. Rhys was a few steps behind Teddy but close enough that when she stopped abruptly at the stable door to tell him he need not remain with the mare, he pinned her against it, not intentionally, but solidly, the arm he'd stretched out to catch the door resting above her left shoulder.

For Rhys it was like catching a rainbow or, unexpectedly, a quicksilver nymph. His blood roared in his ears, his loins tightened. He forgot entirely what he had intended to tell her about Adams. Fate had gifted him with this moment. He wanted to make the best of it. He wanted Teddy. He wanted to hold onto her, however ill-advised that notion was.

"We could both stay," he suggested softly, his warm breath wafting gently over her face which was tilted up, temptingly gilded by the moonlight.

What she had seen at a distance was even more

appealing up close, a flash of white in his smile, a hard, flat belly, a sinewy chest that was, in any critical assessment, magnificent. Her tongue flicked out over dry lips. His nearness, the warmth and bareness of him, intoxicated Teddy, deprived her of her sanity or she would have shoved him into the dirt and aimed her gun at his head.

But curiosity and desire, wild and reckless, prevented that. They urged her to wait a moment and see if what she felt madly surging inside her was real, or merely misplaced gratitude for what he had done on her behalf. Quietly she raised her eyes and stared up at his alluringly handsome face.

Astonished that she had held still even a few precious seconds, Rhys was beset with suspicion that she was drawing him into a trap, setting him up for a rebuff he would never forget. And yet, in the seductive darkness, with Teddy almost in his arms, so close he could smell her woman's scent and, faintly, the lingering essence of desert flowers in her hair, he was rashly willing to pay any price to see the test out.

His arms encircled her, gently, soft as light he brought her against him. He felt no resistance in her body, only soft lush curves pressing into him and setting his need for her loose like a thief in the night. Logic and caution vanished. He no longer cared that at any moment she was apt to draw her gun or resort to any of the hundred ways a woman such as Teddy must know how to use to defend herself. He wanted her at any cost. His lips came swiftly down on hers, found them soft and parted, sweet and willing. His tongue swept past them testing her further, finding her mouth delectable as a honeycomb. Wild, sweet honey. "Teddy." He whispered her name.

She moaned against him, caught up in the incredible sensation of his body melding into hers, of his mouth hotly pressed to her lips. And yet it was as if she had left her physical self and in some mystical way observed what she felt, seeing *that* Teddy in Rhys Delmar's arms responding, wantonly raking her hands down his naked back in a way she would never, could never, do.

She felt hot and restless. He felt hard as steel against her. His hands went sliding down her sides to mold tightly around her buttocks. Her back nudged against the desert-dried boards of the stable as he came hard against her, his corded thighs pinning her to the unyielding wall. She felt his need for her, urgently, unabashedly straining his tight trousers. Where he touched she burned, hot and silky wet between her thighs.

"Damn you . . . Rhys . . . Delmar," she murmured. Her skin was aflame, she could not think, did not wish to. His hand was at her breast and the laces which held her buckskin shirt snugly in place had somehow loosened opening up soft, sensitive flesh to his marauding mouth. "Ohhh . . ." The feel of him there, his face buried in the soft, fragrant valley between her breasts took her breath away.

Rhys was ready to sweep her inside and find a soft stack of hay where he could make love to her until the sun rose. He lifted his head, and brought his mouth near hers again. "Teddy." His voice was raw and strained. "Both of us. Together."

Wish You Were Here?

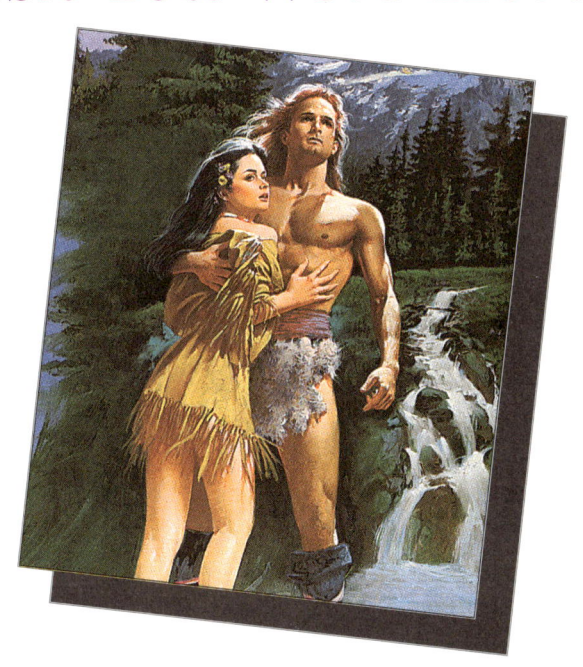

You can be, every month, with Zebra Historical Romance Novels.

AND TO GET YOU STARTED, ALLOW US TO SEND YOU

4 Historical Romances Free

AN $18.00 VALUE!
With absolutely no obligation to buy anything.

YOU ARE CORDIALLY INVITED TO GET SWEPT AWAY INTO NEW WORLDS OF PASSION AND ADVENTURE.

AND IT WON'T COST YOU A PENNY!

Receive 4 Zebra Historical Romances, Absolutely <u>Free!</u>

(An $18.00 value)

Now you can have your pick of handsome, noble adventurers with romance in their hearts and you on their minds. Zebra publishes Historical Romances That Burn With The Fire Of History by the world's finest romance authors.

This very special FREE offer entitles you to 4 Zebra novels at absolutely no cost, with no obligation to buy anything, ever. It's an offer designed to excite your most vivid dreams and desires...and save you $18!

And that's not all you get...

Your Home Subscription Saves You Money Every Month.

After you've enjoyed your initial FREE package of 4 books, you'll begin to receive monthly shipments of new Zebra titles. These novels are delivered direct to your home as soon as they are published...sometimes even before the bookstores get them! Each monthly shipment of 4 books will be yours to examine for 10 days. Then if you decide to keep the books, you'll pay the preferred subscriber's price of just $3.75 per title. That's $15 for all 4 books...a savings of $3 off the publisher's price! What's more, $15 is your <u>total</u> price...there is no additional charge for the convenience of home delivery.

There Is No Minimum Purchase. And Your Continued Satisfaction Is Guaranteed

We're so sure that you'll appreciate the money-saving convenience of home delivery that we guarantee your complete satisfaction. You may return any shipment...for any reason...within 10 days and pay nothing that month. And if you want us to stop sending books, just say the word. There is no minimum number of books you must buy.

It's a no-lose proposition, so send for your 4 FREE books today!

YOU'RE GOING TO LOVE GETTING
4 FREE BOOKS

These books worth $18, are yours without cost or obligation when you fill out and mail this certificate.
(If the certificate is missing below, write to: Zebra Home Subscription Service, Inc., 120 Brighton Road, P.O. Box 5214, Clifton, New Jersey 07015-5214

Complete and mail this card to receive 4 Free books!

Yes! Please send me 4 Zebra Historical Romances without cost or obligation. I understand that each month thereafter I will be able to preview 4 new Zebra Historical Romances FREE for 10 days. Then, if I should decide to keep them, I will pay the money-saving preferred publisher's price of just $3.75 each...a total of $15. That's $3 less than the publisher's price, and there is no additional charge for shipping and handling. I may return any shipment within 10 days and owe nothing, and I may cancel this subscription at any time. The 4 FREE books will be mine to keep in any case.

Name _____

Address _____ Apt. _____

City _____ State _____ Zip _____

Telephone ( ) _____

Signature _____
(If under 18, parent or guardian must sign.)

LF1194

Terms, offer and prices subject to change without notice. Subscription subject to acceptance by Zebra Books. Zebra Books reserves the right to reject any order or cancel any subscription.

TREAT YOURSELF TO 4 FREE BOOKS.

*An $18 value.
FREE!*

*No obligation
to buy
anything, ever.*

ZEBRA HOME SUBSCRIPTION SERVICE, INC.

120 BRIGHTON ROAD

P.O. BOX 5214

CLIFTON, NEW JERSEY 07015-5214

AFFIX
STAMP
HERE

The mare's frantic whinnying decided for her. Rhys backed away at the first shrill cry yet neither of them dashed into the barn. Teddy was too weak-legged to move and needed to press a palm against the stable wall to balance herself. Rhys was short of breath and too drunk with desire to comprehend that he ought to see why the animal sounded an alarm. Finally, he shook his head to clear it, growled out a curse, and rushed inside. Teddy followed a few seconds later, eyes dazed and face flushed to berry red.

Rhys had the foal in his arms. One of them had left the stall door unlocked, and the small creature had pushed through and gotten separated from his mother. He put the foal inside, secured the gate and turned to Teddy with every intention of taking up where he had left off.

She had other ideas. Looking as if the devil himself had whispered a plan to her, she drew her gun, twirled it around her finger twice and brought it to rest pointing low but at him. "You stay," she said acidly. Her eyes were resting where the gun pointed. "And if you value your life and your lady-pleaser, don't ever try anything like that again."

Twenty-one

The last place Boyd Smith wanted to be at dark was the hideaway of Taviz and his men. But there he was at sunset, two days after he'd left Wishbone, riding into the derelict mining camp that Taviz's gang occupied.

Skull, the place was called, a name that added to Boyd's apprehension as he spotted a tin roof and a chimney of smoke rising from it. Skull was one of those towns that had sprouted out of the ground overnight with word of a promising gold strike a few years back. The strike had proved disappointing and the mine had petered out faster than a desert rain. The buildings that had not been cannibalized for the next short-lived town, now housed the cutthroats Taviz rode with.

Boyd shouted out a friendly greeting when he was close enough for the lookout to see him. He heard the click of a safety on a rifle somewhere nearby and felt sweat pop out on his forehead. "Boyd Smith," he yelled. "Adams sent me." He waved a white handkerchief high in the air but didn't breathe easy until a raspy voice from the dark responded.

"Ride in," the man said. "But keep them hands on the saddle horn or get them shot off."

Boyd nudged his horse along with his spurred heels, not daring even to move the reins before he rode into a circle of light cast from lanterns strung from the sagging eaves of rooftops. One of the men gathered around a popping fire got up and walked over to him. The women—three or more interspersed with the half-dozen men—didn't look back at him. He hoped their lack of interest didn't bode ill for him.

"Leave that gun on your saddle and get down!" The man giving that order was Taviz himself. Pete could see his harsh face and the long jagged line of a scar that ran from one cheek clear down to his collarbone. The scar didn't ruin the man's looks. Pete assumed he would have to be female to understand just how it added to his dangerous Latin countenance. He didn't know, either, how Taviz had gotten that scar, but he was certain the man that gave it to him was no longer alive.

To any who knew men from the underbelly of life, Taviz was the worst of them. His cruelty shocked even the vicious men who rode with him. It was made all the worse because Taviz was no lackwit who turned to thievery and murder because he had failed at an honest living. He killed and robbed because he liked it. He relished the power he held over life and death, and it thrilled him to outsmart those who'd worked hard to make a fortune only to lose it to the likes of him.

It was rumored that at times when Taviz tired of the company of his coarse men he dressed himself up in finery and rode to places where he'd never been heard of. There he passed himself off as a well-to-do rancher. He was said to appreciate a night in the theater after which he would buy his companions a round of White Seal champagne. It was said, too, that he had danced with ladies from the finest families in Phoenix. Boyd doubted none of it. Taviz was savvy and intelligent and completely without conscience.

"Adams must want me bad to send you up here at night," Taviz said. Standing in the shadows, dressed all in black but for the red silk scarf knotted around his neck, he appeared strangely disembodied.

"He does," Boyd answered, feeling a shiver run down his spine. "He's got a job for you."

"One you couldn't do?" Taviz grinned.

"That's right," Boyd admitted and looked down at the ground. A grin was misplaced on Taviz's diabolical face and it gave Boyd an eerie feeling. He jumped like a skittish horse when a woman's scream tore out of the night and after it the faint, reedy cry of a newborn.

Taviz kicked the door of the cabin the scream had come from. "Tell that woman to shut up!" he yelled. "I've heard enough of her moaning." Cursing those within, he gave the weathered door another kick. "And bring a bottle of mescal out here. I've got company." Over his shoulder he called for one of the men to take Boyd's horse to the corral then urged Boyd over the bright, crackling fire. "Go on! Get out of here," he told the men. "I'm tired of you, too."

Those men who would have killed another for looking at them wrong got up and drifted off, some grumbling but none challenging Taviz for sending them away from the warm fire. The women went with them, disappearing with their men into the dark or into the tumble-down cabins in the camp. A few minutes later, a woman who had not been among those at the fire came out of the largest cabin. It was the most brightly lit—the one from which Taviz had demanded silence. She had a gray woolen shawl draped over her head and wrapped loosely around her shoulders. She was not young, not pretty, and she looked tired and frightened. In her hands was the mescal and a plate of beans for Boyd.

She handed Taviz the mescal, gave the stranger the food, then stood with them a moment, biding her time until Taviz spared her a look. "You have a son," she said quietly. "My sister has given you a boy but she—she is not well. She wants to see you. She begs—"

He shot her a cold look that shut her off. "Bring the boy out here," he said. "And tell the woman I'll see her when I'm done drinking."

The woman who had served them backed away then turned and ran into the cabin. Boyd heard voices from within, a harried chattering in Spanish, an argument, a cry of anguish, then silence. He felt uneasy, sensed that something was wrong and feared trouble, but beside him Taviz was calmly drinking the mescal. Boyd had no appetite for the beans but ate a few mouthfuls anyway then remembered that Adams had sent a gift for Taviz. Setting the tin plate and spoon aside, he reached into his pocket and brought out a dozen of Adams's best cigars carefully wrapped in brown paper and tied with string.

"Adams sent them," he said.

Taviz handed him the mescal and took the package, tore off the wrapping and smiled. While Boyd stared into the fire Taviz stuffed eleven of the cigars into his breast pocket. He lit the twelfth with an ember from the campfire. While Boyd fidgeted and hoped for an opening to deliver all of Adams's message, Taviz smoked, amusing himself making stacks of smoke rings until he tired of it and started gazing at the stars. Boyd thought he had been forgotten until the toe of Taviz's boot struck him hard on the thigh. "Tell me what Adams wants." His black-capped head was still bent toward the stars. "Maybe I'll do it."

Boyd, bolstered by a few swigs of mescal, told Taviz what Adams wanted. Boyd first explained that he and his brother had been causing havoc for the Gamble Line until one of their band got caught and then killed.

"He wanted to put a scare in Teddy Gamble so she would sell out. But now he's ready to do more than scare her out of business."

"She." Taviz spat a mouthful of mescal into the fire and watched the flames leap high. "Adams cannot stop a woman?" Laughing loudly he slapped Boyd on the back. *"Sí,* he does need Taviz if a woman stands in his way and he cannot make her do what he wants. Taviz, my friend, knows what to do to—"

A weak cry and quiet footsteps interrupted. The woman in the shawl was carrying an infant wrapped in a bright Mexican blanket. Only a bit of the baby's tiny face was revealed and this she showed to Taviz. "Your son," she said.

With the cigar dangling from his large white teeth

Taviz got to his feet. He gave Boyd, still seated by the fire, a light kick. "A son, gringo," he said proudly. "Taviz sires only sons, ehh. This one will grow up smart and strong like his papa. *Sí.*" The woman holding the infant began trembling and this seemed to infuriate Taviz. Distrustful by nature, he glared at her and roared, "Show me the boy!"

The woman could not meet his eye but she shook her head and hugged the wiggling bundle to her. "It is a cold night," she said. "He is small."

"Show me!" This time the command and the anger evident in Taviz's contorted face struck fear in the woman.

Slowly, hesitantly she unwrapped the blanket. The baby screamed when the cold night air hit him. His small red, wrinkled body began to jerk and twitch. Boyd saw the infant clearly and even his inexperienced eyes could tell that the baby was undersized and ill-formed, and that his tiny legs, twisted and stunted as they were, would never be right. Taviz's son would grow up lame or, more likely, never walk at all.

Uttering a curse, Taviz threw his cigar off into the night and grabbed the howling baby in one big hand. Teeth clenched, he held the infant before him, his dark face set so fierce the woman trembled and dropped the child's wrapping at her feet. Taviz shook the helpless baby. "This is not my son!" he roared. "I did not beget this misfit! This bastard brat!" Cursing anew, he shoved the squalling infant into the woman's arms. "Get him out of my sight! Get him out of my camp! Take the whore too! She's crawled to some other man's blanket and tried to foist her brat on me. Get her out of here! Tonight!"

"Señor Taviz," the woman, quaking so she could hardly speak, dropped to her knees in the dirt before him and pleaded. "Please. He *is* your child. You know it. Let her stay. Please. She is not well enough—"

He shoved her away with his boot. She nearly tripped on the hem of her skirt as she scrambled to her feet balancing the baby in her trembling arms. Realizing too late that she had done the unthinkable in balking at Taviz's orders, she broke into a frantic run to the cabin. No one defied Taviz and lived, least of all a woman.

But this once he seemed to have shown mercy. Already he had signaled his men to bring up a horse. They held it outside the cabin door and soon the women came out, both crying, one, the baby's mother, barely able to stand. Whimpering with fear, her sister helped her on the horse and handed up the child. Neither of them looked at Taviz or even dared to look back as the woman in the gray shawl led the horse in a brisk trot along the trail Boyd had ridden upon.

The way was steep and they would have the devil of a time getting down the mountain in the dark but they could not have feared the journey more than they feared Taviz's rage. The mescal bottle tipped to his lips, he watched them depart. When they were well out of sight, he called one of his men and spoke to him in a low, rough voice. The bandido nodded, and with his rifle in hand mounted a horse and rode out after the women.

Taviz was done with the matter then and sat down

at the fire to talk about the job Parrish Adams offered. "How much will Adams pay?" he demanded.

Boyd named an amount and gave Taviz the five hundred in gold that was the first of it. Adams had told him to bargain for the balance but he disregarded that instruction and named the top sum to start.

Taviz nodded, satisfied with what would surely be easy money and certain he would not be cheated. He never was. "What is this woman like?" He looked hard at Boyd. The flames from the campfire were flickering in his black eyes like the fires of hell. "This Teddy Gamble? Pretty? *Sí?*"

"Some might think so." Boyd's voice croaked and his throat felt like it had a fist inside it. "But she shore ain't the frilly type and I shore wouldn't want her in my bed."

Taviz's bawdy laughter echoed off the canyon walls. "My friend, that is the only place for a woman," he said.

A while later and after Taviz had left him, Boyd heard, far in the distance, the report of a rifle firing three times. He knew he would not sleep that night.

Rhys slept well in his soft bed of straw. It was there that Bullet found him at sunup. The mare and her offspring had fared well too. The mare was stronger, proud and protective of her baby and hesitant to allow Bullet near the stall until she had sniffed his shirtsleeve and hand and confirmed that he was trustworthy.

"I rode by the ranch on the way in." Bullet wore a

white pullover shirt and the silver and turquoise belt that was apparently a part of him. He nudged Rhys awake. "Teddy said you brought in this little 'un."

"With her help." Rhys sat up and stretched, then searched beneath the straw for his boots. "And the mare did her part as well."

He slid his boots on, got up and rubbed his shadowed chin. Mae Sprayberry would think he'd spent the night with a floozy since he'd failed to return to his rented room. He did not care too much if she did, not if it would keep Mae from constantly knocking on his door when he wanted to be alone.

Bullet, moving soundlessly on his moccasin-clad feet, slipped inside the stall and examined first-hand the latest addition to the Gamble remuda. Bullet valued the horses that were in his care and treated them better than many people did their families. He'd have blamed himself if the two he was looking at had not survived the night. So it was with great satisfaction that he pronounced the leggy colt and his mother sound.

"You are a better man than I thought, Delmar," Bullet admitted. "Reckon that just proves everything ain't the way it looks at first glance. Anyhow I say a man that's got a feel for horses ain't half bad. An' listen," he added, "if you change your mind about givin' Teddy a hand while—while things are gettin' settled, you're welcome to work with me."

Rhys realized that Bullet's effusive speech was more than most had ever heard him say at one time. Rhys thanked the half-breed, but declined. Given a choice he'd rather have spent the night in the cozy feather bed at the boarding house. That was where he was headed as soon as he could pick all the straw off his wrinkled clothes. He wanted a shave and a wash-up and some of Mae's coffee and biscuits—then a few hours napping in that feather bed before he headed over to the Diamond and got to work doing what he did best.

Everything went according to plan until he got to the Diamond early that afternoon. He had a hard time getting into a game though finally he put together one that ran late into the night. The next day was a repeat of the one before and each day afterwards he had more and more difficulty finding players willing to allow him at their table. Even the faro dealer shut down when he showed an interest in the game he was running. By the end of the week Rhys found himself alone with a deck of cards except for the few occasions when Honor pulled herself away from her cowboy admirers and came and sat with him.

He shared a few drinks with the girl but since he was disinclined to go up to her room and pay for her services, her visits at his table were short. With too much time on his hands Rhys grew restless. He kept thinking of Teddy, remembering the sweetness of her mouth—the depth of his longing for her that night at the stable—the way it had come on him like a fever. He wondered what would have happened if Frenchy hadn't squeezed out of the stall door and upset his mother.

Most of all he wondered how Teddy had turned off her passion and turned on him so fast. Even a black widow spider waited until after the mating to turn mean. But Teddy was more devious than that treacherous creature. She apparently had a penchant for toying with her prey before she did him in. An ugly thought occurred to him all at once. He had begun to suspect that, as had once happened in London, he had been shut out of gambling circles in Wishbone.

Why that should be had seemed a mystery. Maybe it was not. Maybe Teddy's devious hand was in that, too. He recalled from his conversations in the Diamond that almost everyone in town knew Teddy and most of them, for reasons he wasn't entirely sure of, seemed to be fond of the bad-tempered spitfire of a woman. He wouldn't put it past Teddy to be vindictive enough to enlist her friends in a scheme to make him go bust. On the other hand she had to know that kind of spite would only drive him to accept Adams's offer.

He planned to tell her that, as soon as he saw her again. She'd been avoiding him, he thought. Every time he'd dropped by the stage office she'd been out. He suspected some of those "outs" had been the result of a convenient dash behind the boxes and crates in the back room of the office, and had lasted only until he left the premises. Undoubtedly she felt safe tormenting him as long as Adams was out of town. Harley had told him that the Diamond's boss was up north for a time taking care of interests he had there. Harley had volunteered this information when Rhys had asked the man's opinion on why he was *persona non grata* at the tables. Harley had offered little insight into Rhys's problem.

He'd shrugged his wide shoulders and said, "Nobody likes to lose. Get my meanin'?"

Rhys didn't.

Twenty-two

The next morning, with one of Mae's hearty breakfasts in his stomach, Rhys made up his mind he was going to see Teddy and have it out with her no matter what. This he decided as he stood on Mae's front porch looking up at a silvery moon which still hung in the brilliant blue sky long after sunrise. That moon didn't belong up there, not in the bright light of day. And he didn't belong in Arizona, no matter that he liked the clear air and bare, red mountains and the spare desert floors that stretched endlessly toward the ragged, high peaks of distant ranges.

It was a beautiful land but it made a man too introspective. It made him spend too much time wondering who he was and what he was about and if he couldn't answer those questions then it proved a hard place to be. And that's how he found it, because he definitely couldn't answer all the questions spinning through his mind. And he was definitely thinking too much about Teddy. That was campaigning for trouble.

Teddy was a rose in a sea of brambles, sweet-looking but dangerous. He wanted her even though getting near her was a risk to his hide and, more significantly for a man, his pride. The enigmatic Teddy cared nothing about pleasing a man, yet thoughts of her kept him awake at night. Visions of her haunted his days. Logic told him he ought to sell out to Adams so he could get away from her. Deep in his mind he feared that it was too late for that. He was helplessly drawn to her, bent on proving to himself that Teddy Gamble was, at the core, like any other woman, conquerable, compliant, leavable.

Angry that she had taken control of his thoughts, suspicious that she was responsible for his trouble in Wishbone, he marched out of the boarding house with the intention of telling her he was done with her. Rhys Delmar was leaving Wishbone, and he hoped she liked her new partner, Parrish Adams, better.

He never told her that. He arrived at the office long after the stage should have come in. Through the office window he got a glimpse of Teddy's face before she saw him. He was touched in a way he could not have expected. She sat behind a paper-strewn desk, her head in her hands. The corners of her mouth quivered like those of a child on the verge of tears. Her lovely eyes were half-closed and sad. She looked vulnerable—the rose without the thorns. Her anguish was palatable and appealed to an inherent protective quality Rhys did not even know he had.

He stepped through the open door. "Something is wrong?"

As if a gate had swung shut between them, Teddy's expression changed. The face that had, a moment before, shown such need was now a mask of defiance.

"Could be," she said, getting to her feet and coming briskly around the desk. "The nine o'clock's two hours overdue and—"

"And what?"

Teddy made no attempt to hide her hesitancy. Only at his insistence did she make a reply. "Both Rope and Strong Bill made that run. It's carrying a payload out of the mines. They wouldn't be late unless there was—somebody to stop them."

"Another holdup," Rhys surmised. "You must alert the sheriff—"

Teddy crossed her arms over her chest and swore. "What you don't know would fill a canyon. Len Blalock won't help. Leastaways not me. He belongs to Adams."

"Adams?" Rhys asked, recalling with some remorse that it was Adams's offer that had prompted him to come to her today. But that could wait. This wasn't the time to tell her that Adams had sounded like a shrewd but sensible man to him and that maybe she wouldn't be so bad off if someone with a good supply of capital did buy into the Gamble Line.

"Aww hell!" she said. "Don't act like you don't know who he is and what he's after. You've been living in that den of iniquity he owns. I wouldn't put a lizard's tooth on the odds that you've come over here to tell me you've sold out to him too."

Her accusation cut to the quick. He pretended indignation. "Are you always so quick to conclusions,

Teddy Gamble? Are you so sure you are the only person with principles? And honor?"

"Let's just say it's quicker to count those that haven't sold out than those that have." She glanced back at the clock behind the desk. Another five minutes had ticked by while she talked with Rhys. "Why did you come over here?" she demanded.

"You seem to have forgotten I have business with you. I thought, perhaps, you had heard from your inquiry to London and hadn't had the time to notify me."

"The deuce!" she said accusingly. "You know as well as I do there hasn't been time." While she berated him, she grabbed her hat from a wall peg and slung it on her head. "But don't worry yourself, when I find out you'll be the first to know. Now git! I've got things to do."

She was backing him out the door as she talked. He stopped in the doorway, stubbornly blocking her exit. "You are leaving? I thought you were worried about the stage."

"I am." She paused and inhaled sharply. "That's why I'm riding out to look for it."

And into danger, Rhys thought, remembering the three road agents he had encountered. He slowly shook his head. She had to be a little crazy to even consider riding out alone.

"No," he said. "Send some of your men."

"I don't have any men to spare. Now get out of my way." Her hand went to the handle of the gun holstered at her side.

He stepped aside, not because of the threat but because he'd made an instant decision. "I am going with you."

She pushed past him. "Oh no!" she proclaimed and bounded out onto the sidewalk. "You I don't need."

"No argument, Teddy," he said. "I am going."

She stalked off down the street. "Got a gun?"

"I'll buy one."

"Got a horse?"

"You'll loan me one?"

She opened her mouth to rebut the assumption but instead quickened her pace toward the stable. "I'm not waiting while you get a gun," she said.

Wondering how any one woman could have so much obstinacy, Rhys watched her head into the stable then hopped off the sidewalk and trotted up the street toward Penrod's to make a selection from the case of guns in the store.

"I got all kinds," Penrod said. "And I can sell you what you want." He displayed a .44 army-pattern Colt with an ornately engraved barrel and a silver-plated handle. "Fancy if you want to impress the ladies."

"No," Rhys said, certain the lady in question would scoff at the weapon.

"Well, if it's tried and true you want this Colt Peacemaker is hard to beat."

Rhys tried the walnut grip and checked the sighting on the blued-metal casing of the second revolver Penrod showed him. The feel was right, the gun was unpretentious and dependable which was all he wanted. He knew how to use the weapon, and declined Penrod's offer for a demonstration. As a youth he had learned to shoot with custom-made weapons from his master's gun room. Rhys knew he could hold his own against any man should he have to.

"This one," he said and quickly selected a holster. Penrod added a box of shells to the order and tallied up a total.

"I'll buy it back if you decide you don't need it." The storekeeper dogged Rhys's tracks all the way outside. " 'Course I'll have to knock off some. It being used—Well, durn!" he said as Rhys, ignoring him, sprinted off toward the Gamble stable.

Teddy was gone.

Two youths Rhys had not met were in the stable. One was tossing hay down from the loft, the other was unenthusiastically cleaning stalls. Both paused at their work when Rhys burst in. "I need a saddle horse," he said.

The boy shoveling manure looked up at the lad in the loft. The boy above gave a consenting nod. "That's him, can't you tell?" He eyed the neat black suit Rhys wore, the rose-silk vest, silver-gray cravat and the nattily polished boots. "Teddy said he'd look like a dandy."

The youngster below leaned on his shovel. "Don't look so dandified to me. Got a gun."

Rhys put a stop to the time-wasting conjecture. "Did Teddy say which horse to take?"

"You Delmar?" the lad demanded.

"Yes. Which horse?"

"That bay in the corral out back," the boy said. "I slung a saddle and bridle on the fence and," he smiled suspiciously wide, "you can catch him yourself."

Cursing Teddy for not waiting and, at the least, for not having one of those boys saddle his horse, Rhys hurried out back. He saw at once why they hadn't volunteered. The bay was a big spirited stallion who began tossing his head and pawing the ground when he saw Rhys approach. He was a fine animal and took a bridle surprisingly well, but the saddle was another matter. One look at it and the stallion hopped and bucked around the corral with Rhys attempting to hold onto him and the heavy saddle.

Not until Rhys threw the saddle down and looped his fine silk cravat over the stallion's eyes did he get him to stand still. By then more precious minutes had passed and Teddy, he knew, would be harder to catch. Shortly, though, he had his mount saddled and out of the corral. He rode through the stable fostering two looks of disbelief.

"Which way?" Rhys shouted.

"West." One of the boys tossed him a canteen as he rode through. "An' Demon there can catch that paint of Teddy's if any horse can."

Demon's hooves thundered through Wishbone. Rhys had a moment of doubt as he took the road west. If Teddy didn't want him along she could have told the boys to send him on a false trail, but then he remembered the mines were northwest of Wishbone and rode on.

He pushed his mount. The stallion felt strong beneath him and eager to run. The day's heat hadn't yet come down. Until it did he would ride hard. He didn't like the idea of Teddy running up on road agents alone.

On the other hand, God help the men who got in her way.

Twenty-three

Teddy spared her horse. The big paint pony Bullet had caught and broken for her two years before was a frisky mare who would have liked testing the wind, but Teddy purposely kept to a trot on the horse she called Dune.

She wasn't slowing the pace because she wanted Rhys to catch up. She didn't care if he did or not. Preferred that he didn't, she swore as she slowed Dune a little more. The Frenchman would be more trouble than he was worth. Probably couldn't shoot either. And he didn't care what happened to the Gamble Line as long as he got his money.

Wending past the scattered sentries of saguaro and the legions of cholla cactus lining the roadbed, Teddy pulled her hat low on her forehead and rode on. She had been dreading the day one of the big Concord coaches would fail to roll in. All she could do now was hope the trouble was a busted wheel or at worst an axle, because if there had been a bona fide holdup and a payroll was lost, it was only a matter of time before she would lose the whole business. Wells Fargo wouldn't stay with her after that. Cabe Northrop had been plain as day about her standing with the company.

She was up to her hatband in debt and trouble, and close to ruin. She felt akin to the prey a white-rumped shrike had just plucked from the desert floor. Shortly the airborne shrike would swoop low again and impale its unlucky victim on a cactus thorn. She watched the bird dive for the kill and somehow, miraculously, the tiny animal in its grasp wrenched free and fell the short distance to the ground—spared, this once, from destruction.

Teddy hoped she would be as lucky—that nothing disastrous had happened to Rope or Strong Bill or the stage, that she and the stage line were not, as it appeared, only a swoop away from devastation.

Without thinking about it she twisted in the saddle and looked down the guttered road for Rhys. No rider was in sight against a backdrop of barren, scattered hills. She wondered if he'd had a change of heart or, more likely, had been unable to ride the stallion she had told the Ansley boys to saddle for him. Teddy sighed wearily and rode on. She hadn't actually expected more of Rhys Delmar than that he would fall by the wayside at the first obstacle.

The first change station was fifteen miles out of Wishbone on a stretch where there was no water except from the station's well. Porter Landau, a lean and desert-baked stock-tender, manned that station alone. Porter had been a prospector, but he had given up the uncertainty of picking and panning, and now had a regular forty-dollar-a-month draw from the Gamble Line. He worked alone because he was closest in to town. Most other stations along the line had two keepers.

Bullet rode out and gave Porter a hand about twice a week and did the same for the first station east of Wishbone. Teddy was about halfway to Porter's when she heard the rapid beat of hooves behind her. She reined Dune in and, involuntarily holding her breath, stared back at a rider galloping her way. She recognized Demon and presumed the rider to be Rhys. Only someone unaccustomed to the desert would be punishing a mount like that.

He pulled Demon to a stop once he was abreast of her.

"You trying to kill that horse?" she shouted.

Rhys shot Teddy an amused glance. The day's heat was still mild and the stallion was pulling at the bit. He'd enjoyed the run and wanted to keep going. Both Teddy and Rhys could see that Demon wasn't spent in the least. "I am trying to catch a fool," Rhys said.

"You had him before you left," Teddy came back. "That horse needs a breather. We'll ride slow on to the station and let's hope we find the stage made it that far. If it didn't, the horses can drink and rest a few minutes before we head out." She held her jaw tight as she gave him a censorious look, and tried hard not to let show that she was glad to see him. "Did you think to bring a canteen?"

"There's one on the saddle." Rhys held the canteen high, smiled, and patted the rolled blanket behind him. "And a bedroll, too," he said.

"You might need it," she said indifferently, giving the paint a gentle nudge with her heels. "I see you got yourself a gun. What can you do with it?"

Rhys moved the bay alongside her horse and looked

over at Teddy. "The usual things a man can do with his gun." His grin was one-sided, infuriating.

Teddy's face flushed and her eyes flashed. "Not a damned thing worth getting excited about then," she said, and urged the paint a length ahead of his mount.

Rhys caught up to her again. "You sound as if you do not like men so much and yet it is with men you choose to spend your time," he said.

"I like men fine," she replied, "as long as they stick to business instead of skirt chasing."

"A little *amour* is good for the heart, Teddy."

The horses were close. He reached over and softly stroked her arm. She snatched it away from him.

"Now that's what I mean," she said angrily. "Some men don't know what to do with their hands."

"I do, I assure you," he said silkily.

"You can save the assurances and the pawing for that saloon sweetie. Or for Justine Blalock. I hear she's gone soft on you."

"Mademoiselle Justine is lovely but a bit young for me. I prefer a woman with—"

"I do not care to hear about your taste in women." Scowling at him she reached into one of her breast pockets, couldn't find what she expected and cursed. Switching the reins to the other hand, she fumbled about in the other pocket.

"If you need help—"

She looked sourly into his eyes as she lit up a long slender cheroot and began smoking. "I don't need your help or your pawing or your kisses. Thank you."

"You liked my kisses well enough when we were kissing," he insisted. "But afterwards, well, Teddy, don't you think you overplayed the offended virgin part?"

Teddy threw the newly lit cheroot away. She had promised Felicity long ago to give up the habit and until lately hadn't been bothered by the urge to resume smoking them. She thought she could blame Rhys Delmar for that too. She glared at him hotly. "What in holy hell makes you think I'm a virgin?"

"Aren't you?"

She gave her head a toss. "No. I had a lover once."

He eyed her surreptitiously. "Once?"

"Once was enough," she said flatly.

"That I do not believe. Making love is like tasting a superb wine. One swallow is never enough."

"It was for me."

"Then you had the wrong lover. He was, perhaps, too young, too inexperienced."

"He wasn't young and he wasn't inexperienced. In fact, he was like you in a lot of ways," Teddy said and scowled at him. "Not that he looked much like you. Jace was fair-haired and had big brown eyes, pretty eyes. What I meant about him being like you was that he was good-looking, too. He had women, like flies to honey, chasing after him—he'd had plenty."

"Of flies?"

"Of women, dammit!" She stared furiously at him. "But in Wishbone he only had eyes for me."

"In that we are alike," Rhys teased.

"Like hell," Teddy responded. "Anyway, I was impressionable and downright silly at nineteen. He'd been courting me on the sly and I'd been thinking I was the luckiest girl in town. Well, like I said I was silly back then. Anyway, one spring night I slipped out and met him down at the river thinking I was about to experience paradise, sublime ecstasy."

"What happened?"

She huffed. "Nothing. Ecstasy turned out to be a lot of hard breathing, smelly sweat and sand in my hair."

"You are saying you did not make love."

"I am saying he was mighty quick on the draw. It was all over faster than a sneeze and I said if that's all there is to it I can live without it."

"There is more to it, Teddy."

"You say so. He did too, but I learned fast that men are mostly talk and disappointment."

With effort Rhys let the comment slide. "You did not see this lover again? This Jace?"

"No. He was a gunfighter. He went and got himself shot down in Tombstone about a month later. So," she said flatly, "I reckon he *wasn't* always quick on the draw."

Rhys had a peculiar mix of emotions. He felt a fierce, burning swell of anger that another man had made love to Teddy, though he had never been particular about a woman's past before. He also felt a groundswell of relief that it had not been Teddy who had shot the inept fellow. There was one other emotion, too, suspicion that she had made up the whole story just to annoy him.

And she had annoyed him.

"This happened long ago," he said. "Surely since there has been a man who made you feel a special stirring in your heart, whose embrace you desired."

A hint of color spread over Teddy's face. "Nope," she said.

"The truth, Teddy," Rhys insisted, recalling unquestionably that she had responded to his kisses, had yielded to his touch. "When I held you, kissed you, you desired me. Is it not true?"

She gritted her teeth and stiffened and decided on the spot that she wouldn't admit what he had said was true even though it was. "It is not. I never wanted to kiss you. I think I made that plain afterwards," she said. "So don't go thinking there was anything to it but you acting the stud. I felt nothing but disgust."

Disgust? He thought not. But he was willing to concede the point at the moment. The time would come when she would admit he was right.

The horses tied outside the corral wore harness. Not a good sign. The stage was nowhere to be seen.

"Port!" Teddy called loudly as they approached the adobe station.

Porter Landau, white-haired and wearing denim pants tucked into knee-high black boots, stepped from behind the station house with his rifle ready.

"That you Teddy?" He put up a hand to shade his eyes and stared at the approaching pair. "Who's that with you?"

"It's me!" Teddy confirmed. "And the Frenchman Bullet told you about. You seen the stage?"

Porter lowered his rifle. "I'm plumb worried," he said. "It ain't never been this late. And with Rope and Strong Bill on the run—Well, it don't bode no good."

"You could be right." Teddy rode up close to the well and dismounted. Not wanting either of the men to see how upset she was, she pulled her hat low and led her horse over to a trough by the well and let the animal drink from the water that had been drawn for the stage team. "I'm worried, too," she said after a minute. "That's why I'm out here."

Rhys dismounted next to Teddy. He stuck out a hand to Porter, who by then had walked over to the well. He introduced himself.

"You helpin' Teddy?" the station keeper asked.

"I am attempting to," Rhys responded. "Although she seems convinced she does not need me."

"Well keep an eye on her anyway," Porter admonished. "She's the type to leap before she looks and I ain't so certain what you two are goin' to find to leap into out there."

Teddy gave Porter a sharp look but let him speak his mind. "What can you spare from the larder, Port?" she asked. "We might need more victuals than I brought along."

"Got plenty of jerky and you're welcome to it," the old man responded. "An' there's beans and coffee and a slab of bacon. Help yourself."

Teddy got the supplies while Rhys filled extra canteens. Ten minutes later they had mounted and were riding off. Teddy remained pensive. Rhys respected her need for quiet. They were an hour's ride out of the station when the stallion's ears flicked back and the big muscles on his withers quivered. The mare snorted uneasily as Teddy guided her along the stage road where it cut through an outcropping of boulders higher than the rooftops in Wishbone. Rhys's keen eyes searched the wayside but could discern nothing that should alarm the horses. A scaly gila lizard lay motionless on a flat, sun-heated rock to his left. Off to his right a speckle-backed chaparral cock searched among the stones for a meal.

Neither should have upset the horses, but something had. Their keen senses detected a threat that Rhys's more civilized ones could not find.

"Can you see anything out there?" he asked Teddy.

She had stiffened in her seat and looked as skittish as the horses. Rhys saw her hand start to slide slowly toward her gun. "Could be a snake, or a coyote, or a man," she said softly. "Anything could hide in those rocks. And you'd best be ready for a fast ride once whatever it is shows itself."

Rhys regretted he hadn't had time to test the Colt he'd bought from Penrod. He could only hope it was as dependable as the storekeeper had said—and that, if necessary, it would save his and Teddy's lives.

He drew it a few minutes later when Teddy abruptly stopped her horse and pointed at the ground. In the hardscrabble and sand of the roadbed were a strange assortment of tracks. Horses had stood and stamped and it looked as if a wheeled conveyance had slid to a stop then cut a deep swath in the ground as it turned about. Bootprints littered the ground, too.

Teddy voiced what both of them feared. "Riders

stopped the stage here," she said unevenly. "A hold-up."

Gun in hand she swung off the paint and began examining the ground, dropping to her knees when she came to a spot where the sand bore a dark unnatural stain. Rhys remained mounted, keeping a wary eye on the road and the rocks. He had his gun ready should anything move. But the desert seemed to have grown abnormally quiet and the small creatures which had been ignoring the riders were suddenly out of sight. The sense of dread he felt was like a fist in his midriff.

Teddy tested the damp sand between her thumb and forefinger.

"Blood?" he asked.

"Looks like it," she said, rubbing her hand clean in the loose sand. "But whose? A road agent's or one of my men." Without remounting she began to slowly circle out from where the disturbance had occurred. "And I'm wondering why the stage went back once whatever happened here was over. Porter's station is closest from here. The sensible thing would have been to keep going."

"Mount up," Rhys told her. "If that blood was still damp it hasn't been there long. We cannot be far behind the stage and those who stopped it."

Teddy nodded and started toward her horse, but when she caught the reins and tried to mount, the paint began backing off. "We're too damned close," she said, stretching out a hand to stroke and soothe the nervous horse. "Dune's caught a scent and it's spooked her." She looked around anxiously, seeing nothing but rocks, stretches of sand and clumps of spiky ocotillo. "But whether it's man or beast—"

"Man," Rhys said quietly. "About thirty yards back in the rocks."

"Armed?"

Teddy swung into the saddle and tried to spot the hombre, but either Rhys had imagined seeing him or the man had ducked out of sight. Skeptical that any of the bandits would have hung around after robbing the stage, Teddy, nevertheless, looked everywhere, even across the road where the landscape was nearly identical. Rhys, who had kept his eyes on the spot where he'd first seen a man poke his head above a rock, now saw a glint as the sun reflected off metal.

"He is armed." Swiftly sliding off the stallion, Rhys pulled Teddy from her mount and into the cover of the rocks. At the same moment a rifle shot whizzed past and cut the crown off the upraised arm of a saguaro. A second shot chipped rock off the small boulder that shielded them. A spray of shots followed, chiseling the boulder on both sides and peppering Rhys and Teddy with chips of stone.

"Over there." Teddy nodded toward a monstrous rock cut through the center by a narrow fissure. "He can't see us in there."

In unison they dove across the exposed ground. Rhys pushed Teddy into the crevice, then plunged in after her. They wound up face to face, thigh to thigh. Both were breathless and excited, in a space scarcely big enough for one body. Teddy was backed against the wall of rock where the fissure ended, squirming so wildly that Rhys nearly forgot what had driven them to cover. In that moment he smiled maddeningly down at Teddy. "Cozy," he said.

Teddy, already tingling where he touched her, reacted with fury and gave him a violent shove that sent him reeling out into the line of fire. A bullet immediately tore through the brim of his hat and sent it flying like a flushed quail. Teddy's outrage died in the face of nearly getting Rhys killed. Hurriedly rectifying the situation, she grabbed him by the shirt front and jerked him back into the crevice. "In, dammit! In!" she cried.

She pulled until he was plastered against her and both of them were wedged like driven pegs into the vein of the rock. They were crushed together as if they were engaged in an intimate act. Rhys felt the fiery heat in Teddy's flesh, the rapid, anxious beat of her heart, the sharp rise and fall of her shapely breasts.

"Any further in, Teddy my sweet," he said softly, insolently, not quite forgetting—in spite of his body's fast and fierce response to her—that she had nearly gotten him killed, "and I'll have to marry you."

The tumescent male part of him, hard as the stone at her back, pressed hotly against her and made his meaning all too clear. An inconceivable heat sped through her. For an instant she forgot the danger, her awareness solely, insanely concentrated on the pressure of his body against hers, on the thrill of knowing he desired her. But that instant passed and lucidity returned quickly.

Cursing like a muledriver, Teddy bucked like a bronco to back away but all that exertion only wedged them closer together. Finally she stopped, her breath coming in irregular, agitated pants. "Damned randy—French bastard!" She gasped. "If I could get this gun—clear. I'd shoot you myself."

"I would die happy," he whispered and, catching her tightly by the shoulders, bent down and kissed the top of her head. "Now hold still," he ordered, "while I get turned around or else people will spend the next century staring at our bones and speculating on what we were doing in this fissure when we got ourselves shot to death."

The turning was an exercise in sensuality. Each carnal part of Rhys's aroused body was rubbing against a quivering part of Teddy's. What enraged her most about the ordeal was that her body had made a liar of her. Only hours before, she had been telling Rhys he'd be wasting his time trying to bed her. But here she was erotically tantalized by the feel of him, and appalled that there was no way to keep him from being aware of her body's instant ardent reaction. Her nipples, pressed into his back, were hard as pebbles and ached from the pleasurable contact. Her breath rasped out like steam against his neck.

"Don't get any idea I like being stuck to you," she hissed. "I don't." A telltale quiver ran through her as the lie passed her lips. "You make me want to retch."

"I can tell," he retorted. "But restrain yourself, my sweet. We are in danger if you have forgotten. I can see the gunman if he approaches and he must, to get a clear shot, but I am not so sure we were wise to choose this hiding place, pleasant as it's been," he added.

"Ohh, you bas—" Teddy pounded his back with her fists.

"Whoa! Stop that!"

"Not until I break something," she came back.

He could not stop her furious pummeling and so, dodging blows he chanced to look up and see that the fissure widened above their heads. With a bit of bracing and a boost he could climb up high and surprise their attacker. If she let him.

Having gotten her legs tangled with his, which only heightened her agony, Teddy stopped striking him.

"Merci," Rhys said gratefully. "With your help I see a way to outsmart the gunman."

"How?" she asked sheepishly, remembering their predicament and now, too late, ashamed of her outburst. "What do you want me to do?"

Pressing one leg and one arm against each side of the fissure Rhys began slowly edging his way up. "Give me a hand." He looked back at her when no boost was forthcoming. "Or would you rather stay the night here?"

Teddy swore at him and, placing her hands on his firm buttocks, gave him a rough shove up. "Move," she said. "Maybe he'll blast your head off."

He did not.

The gunman had been firing lucky but blind. Sometime earlier he had acquired a wound to the head that had poured blood over his face and made his vision fuzzy. His features were indistinguishable. The man was feeling his way along the rocks guided by the low hum of voices. He did not see Rhys perched on the boulder. He did put up as much fight as any man Rhys had ever encountered.

Rhys was upon the gunman with one leap, fortunately knocking his weapon from his hand, but it was as if he had landed on the shoulders of an enraged bull. The gunman swore and roared like a madman and, if his injuries had impaired his strength, it was hard for Rhys to tell.

"Murderin' bastard!" the man shouted. "You won't finish me off easy!" Spinning around, cursing, he clawed at Rhys and when he failed to shake him off, flung himself hard against a rock.

Rhys had to jump clear or be crushed. The gunman swung around again as Rhys landed and lunged in for the fight. He was quick with his elbows and with his fists and had pelted Rhys with hard blows before Rhys got a good hit in. Rhys felt no remorse at kicking the man's feet from beneath him, not until the man spotted his lost weapon in the dust.

The gunman rolled over and fired two shots. One whizzed by Rhys's head. A second thudded into the ground. Rhys flung himself at the man before he could fire again. The whole of Rhys's weight went into a blow to his opponent's jaw. The blow split the skin over Rhys's knuckles and racked his shoulder with pain, but only brought a grunt of outrage from his desperate adversary.

By then Teddy was out in the open, her gun drawn and aimed, her angry eyes on Rhys as he savagely kicked the man's gun from his hand. His own gun hung in the holster at his side.

"If you're not going to use that Peacemaker why did you get it?" Teddy demanded. Cursing a streak, she advanced on the gunman Rhys held, committed to shooting him or scaring him to death. Before she did either, a jolt ran through her body and all the color drained from her face.

"Teddy? *Sacré bleu!* What—" Rhys feared she had been shot, but there had been no sound of gunfire.

"Good God!" Teddy cried. She was inches from firing at the struggling gunman when she saw through the blood and filth. "It's Rope!"

Twenty-four

Teddy holstered her gun and dropped to her knees. Most of the fight had gone out of Rope but he hadn't given up the struggle.

"Godamighty, Rope!" she cried. "What in blazes happened? How'd you get left out here alone?"

Rope stilled. Rhys let him go.

"Teddy?" The bloodied man said uncertainly.

Teddy put her arms around her shaken friend, though in truth she was more shaken than he. His injuries looked severe and only a moment ago she had been berating Rhys for not shooting him. Thanks to Rhys's restraint and no thanks to her, Rope was alive.

"It's me," she said softly, her voice trembling. "And Rhys Delmar." She glanced up at Rhys who was testing his bruised and bleeding hand. He saw anguish in Teddy's eyes but there was condemnation in her voice and he had to assume it was for him. "Round up those horses and get the canteens," she demanded. "He needs water. Jeeze, do I have to think for you?" Her labored sigh shook her whole body. "Dammit!" she cried, spotting the newest contusion on Rope's battered face. "Look at his jaw. What were you trying to do, split it?"

"Ease off, Teddy," Rope said weakly. "He was doin' what he had to do when somebody starts shootin'. An', dang it, I didn't recognize you either. Tarnation I would have shot both of you, out of the saddle if I could have seen straight to do it." His hand jerked up to his hairline, which was crusted with blood and dirt. "Danged road agents held up the stage," he explained. "One of them nicked me and I was out cold a while. Reckon they left me for dead cause when I came to, the coach and everybody was gone." He winced when his fingers found the spot where the bullet had creased his temple. "Gettin' shot kinda fuzzed up my head and my eyesight, too," he said. "Right now I'm powerful glad I couldn't half see."

"So am I," Rhys responded, glad that Rope bore him no ill will for what was an honest mistake. As for Teddy, who could explain the illogical workings of her mind? Expect gratitude and she bit like a crocodile. And be damned if the tart-tongued, she-devil did not come close to making him want to get bit.

With fire in her eyes and her shoulders squared she was a woman to behold. And to be tamed. He relished the thought, though how the taming was to be accomplished bore a great deal of reflection. And now was not the time for it. He nodded compliantly, and, as Teddy had requested, Rhys set off to chase down the horses. He was not gone long. The well-trained animals had strayed only a short distance. Although they were wary, they seemed as glad to see him as he was to find them. As a precaution, however, he put hobbles on both mare and stallion after leading them to the road and nearer Teddy and Rope. No use chancing having to walk to the stage station should the animals get another fright.

Teddy had Rope propped and resting against a rock when Rhys got back to her. She had removed the cotton bandana that had been knotted around her neck. She was waiting for water to soak it in so she could clear the blood and dirt from Rope's face. Upending one of the canteens, she wet the cloth while Rope swigged water from the other. She started mopping at the grime before he finished drinking.

"Dang it, Teddy, you got a heavy hand." Flinching, he pulled the canteen from his lips and complained when she rubbed lightly over his bruised chin. "Give me that bandana. I'll do it myself." Gingerly, he started mopping but winced again as soon as he'd begun. "Owww! Reckon it's too sore for air to hit," he said, abandoning the effort and instead raising the canteen and pouring a stream of water over his face. Much refreshed, and with his pallid face brightening afterwards, he said, "Teddy, that Frenchman of yours throws a strong punch."

"He's not my Frenchman." Teddy took the canteen from Rope's hands. As she capped it, her snapping eyes were on Rhys, whose mocking grin annoyed her as much as Rope's errant comment. "If he was, I'd crate him up and ship him back to France."

"And I would go," Rhys said, shrugging. "But let us now concern ourselves with what happened to Rope and to Strong Bill and the others. It may be that they too have been abandoned on the desert and if so we must attempt to find them."

Rope hung his head. "Guess I didn't want to remember," he said grimly. "Strong Bill's dead. He was shot through the heart before I got hit and fell off the box. We weren't carrying no passengers but, well, Teddy, they got the shipment and the mail."

Teddy swore and hoped neither Rhys nor Rope noticed the tears welling in her blue-green eyes. "I'll see them hung for killing Strong Bill," she swore.

Rope nodded that his sentiments were the same.

"Did you get a look at them?" Teddy queried. "Were they the same no-good crooks that have been hounding us all along?"

"That's the peculiar thing, Teddy." Rope exhaled slowly. "This was a new bunch an' a more connivin' threesome I ain't never met. One of them was standin' in the road with his saddle. Flagged us down like he needed a ride. When we slowed the team, them other two came ridin' in shootin'," he said tersely, pausing to rub sand from his eyes. "They meant to kill me an' Strong Bill."

"We should look for Strong Bill," Rhys said, noticing that nightfall was near. He had learned already that at night the desert was like a black sea with danger lurking beneath every wave.

"And get him buried," Teddy said. She thought of Strong Bill's body cast out on the desert for prowling scavengers to find and ravage. The image cut like a blade in her heart. She choked on a lump in her throat and looked away from the men. "Where did they—throw him?"

"Somewhere down the road," Rope said. "They turned the coach around and—"

"We'll find it too," Teddy cut in, her voice wavering but determined. "Minus the strongbox."

"That's another strange thing, Teddy," Rope said. "I heard them talkin' when they was turnin' the stage around."

"About what?" Teddy asked, hopeful that Rope's slowly returning memory of the event would yield a clue to the identity of the holdup men.

"About the coach," Rope replied thoughtfully. "I swear I heard the big fella that was in charge say they were keepin' it."

"You must have heard wrong," Teddy responded, urging the injured Rope to his feet, fearing the nick on the head had rattled him more than she'd first believed. "What would be the sense in it? I can't think why any holdup men would want a stagecoach. Where could they hide it?" She gave Rope an encouraging pat on the back as he took a first unsteady step. "You must have heard wrong. We'll find that coach, maybe without the team, somewhere between here and the next stop."

"Maybe," Rope mumbled.

Rhys loosened the hobbles from the horses' legs and led the paint mare around for mounting. "Take Teddy's horse," he said to Rope. "She can double up with me. The stallion is plenty strong enough to carry two."

She opened her mouth to angrily tell him he was deluded. But then she recalled that the three had only two horses. Since she and Rhys were the lightest load for the stallion, he had suggested a logical arrangement. "All right," she said reluctantly. "Mount up. I'll ride behind you."

They had ridden almost a mile in the fading light when Rhys spied Strong Bill's body a few yards off the roadbed. He heard Teddy sob twice before she slid from the stallion's back and went running over to the dead man. She knelt over him while Rhys and Rope thoughtfully hung back for a few moments.

"Damn them!" she cried, lifting her face to the darkening heavens. "Damn them to hell! He was a good man. A fine friend. Why? Rope—" She walked off by herself when the men came up.

Rhys saw her sitting cross-legged on a rock as he and Rope scraped out an indentation on the desert floor, laid Strong Bill's body in it and covered him with a mound of rocks. The moon was well into the sky when they finished and gathered around to recite a prayer over the dead man.

They made a camp nearby afterwards. Rope and Teddy skillfully collected enough debris to build a small fire. They were able to have warm food for supper. Rope settled into a bedroll and fell asleep shortly afterwards. Rhys and Teddy sat near the dying fire and watched the glowing embers dwindle away to darkness. Teddy sat stiffly, saying nothing, staring out into the night.

"I am sorry about Strong Bill getting killed," Rhys told her.

"Why?" Her head snapped around. "You didn't care about him," she said bitterly.

"I care that any man would be shot down as he was."

"You say."

Rhys sighed. Her haunted face told more of her anguish than she wanted to reveal. Strong Bill's death added another grief to the layers of sadness in Teddy. Rhys remembered what Rope had told him about her brother, how she blamed herself. He suspected, rightly, that she was blaming herself for Strong Bill's death, too. He knew the feeling, lived with it. Because he understood how self-placed guilt ripped and tore at a person's heart he wanted to give Teddy comfort, but could see he was not getting past the hard, brittle shell she had closed around herself.

Determined to make her feel a little better, he persisted. "I know the feeling of losing a beloved friend, Teddy," he said gently. "I know the pain and the anger and the frustration of wondering why it had to happen. I know how it feels to wish you could change what happened in a single day so the person you cared for would still be alive. I know how it feels to think you are responsible for what happened."

"I am responsible." Teddy got up and turned away from Rhys. "Strong Bill worked for me and that got him killed."

Head down, she walked away from the camp. Rhys got up and followed. His footsteps were silent, but his words echoed from the big boulders strung out across the desert. "You couldn't have known there would be another holdup," he said.

She spun around. Her expression was as anguished as a hurt child's. Her eyes were burning brightly in the pale moonlight as she stared in dismay at him. "I knew," she said. "Bill knew, too. Somebody wants to put me out of business. Including you, I reckon."

He stepped up close. Her hands were balled at her sides and she was trembling as if she were about to cry. "Wrong," he said. "You're entirely wrong about me, Teddy." Gently he placed his hands on her shoulders and lifted her quivering chin with his thumbs. "I want the Gamble Line to flourish until you get your verification from London and I get my money. Beyond that I wish only that we could be friends." Gently his thumbs stroked her jawbones, feeling the tension in her, the jolt of stifled sobs. "You need a friend."

"I had a friend," she said bitterly. "He's dead."

Rhys wrapped his arms around her. She would not permit herself to open up and cry. But now and then her body shuddered softly against him. Her held-back sobs knocked at his heart, making him forget that she was an intemperate, willful woman. He sensed he was seeing the other side of Teddy, finding the softness in her, the woman, an experience as uncommon as glimpsing the hidden side of the moon. She allowed him to hold her for a long while—not, he regretted to think, because he was Rhys Delmar but because he was there in a rare, vulnerable moment.

He did not plan to do more than merely offer Teddy solace. But in time the slow-burning heat of her, the soft sounds she made, the enthralling feel of her ripe breasts pressed into him, proved more than he could withstand. Desire, hot as an inferno, surged within him, quickening his loins, stirring his passion. His arms involuntarily tightened around her, his lips strayed to her temple and rained soft kisses on silky skin rendered pale as silver in the moonlight.

"I could hold you through the night, Teddy," he whispered hoarsely. "Make the pain go away, if you let me. You would not be sad in my arms."

His mouth moved over her face, a soft, tempting breeze that made her quiver and moan. His hands plucked away the plaited leather cord that held her hair in a long, tight braid. His agile fingers combed through the sun-lightened strands until her hair hung loose and free and shimmered around her like quicksilver loosed from a bottle. He wove his fingers into the flowing tresses, amazed at the fluid, silky feel of them. Lavender. A trace of the heady scent abided since the last washing—enough to make him imagine her naked lying in a bed of the fragrant blue flowers, her arms outstretched. Teddy. Loving him. Wanting him.

Teddy burrowed into him. She was hurt through—fraught with guilt that it was her stubbornness, her determination not to let go of her father's dream, which had cost Strong Bill his life. Part of her wanted to throw up her hands and say, *enough*. Enough dying. Another part of her could not give up, could not let her father's dream be forgotten or Bill's death be in vain. Still another part remembered a truth she had been unwilling to admit. She had, despite her protestations, once felt brief but overwhelming pleasure in Rhys's arms.

That part of her wanted to forget all the painful happenings of the day. That part, so long denied, so secretive, so unfamiliar, wanted to cling to Rhys Delmar, to seek a woman's solace in his arms, to leave behind sadness and sorrow for a time, however short. That budding part, seizing upon the weakness that brought it forth, would not be denied, would not be shut out. It demanded to be heard, to be satisfied.

With a soft, throaty moan she gave in to it, so easy when he held her, when his kisses offered comfort and refuge. Slowly, she wrapped her arms around him, and plied her fingers into the rippling muscles in his back. He felt strong as the mountains, sure as the wind, warm as the heat of a roaring fire on a chill night.

Whispering his name, she lifted her face to his. "Hold me," she said.

"Ahh, Teddy." Her eyes shone out of the darkness, sparkling blue-green as a mountain pool. Her face reflected the iridescence of the stars—showcasing her finely etched features, her long shadowy lashes that brushed her cheeks, her lips as full and inviting as ripe red berries that begged to be tasted. Again.

He took the bounty offered, relishing what had been forbidden fruit—the sweetness of her, the nectar of her mouth—as his tongue stabbed past her lips and drank her in. He could not get enough of her, though he tried, his mouth plundering, assaulting, stealing what she was not quick enough to give.

He took her breath, left her giddy, reeling, anxious for more of his devouring kisses. Euphoric kisses. How they intoxicated. How they made her forget that she had wanted only to be held and comforted enough to dull the pain of loss. But she did not understand that emotions denied so long, so completely, once aroused would not be hers to command.

It was as if he had taken possession of them, whipping up a fierce, intense yearning that ran through her like a gale, a tempest in her veins.

She felt herself swept up in the storm. The earth was falling away beneath her feet. She saw the stars spinning brightly in the inky sky above. In a moment she was stretched out on a shadowed mountain peak, Rhys was alongside her, his hands cradling, caressing as the wind tugged at her clothes and fire lapped at her skin.

Incredible sensations sped through her. She felt weightless as a bird in flight, soaring too high, too fast. Terrified, tantalized, she wound her hands around his neck—holding on, guiding his mouth to her bared breasts, crying out as his lips brushed across her nipples, inflaming them. What was this power he had, this magic that awakened a woman she did not know, could not understand, a woman she feared would yield all to him?

"You will not be sorry, *chérie,* I promise you that," he whispered, his breath warm and soft on her skin.

Chérie. Chérie. The word lashed like a whip. He had called that whore *chérie* and now he would make a whore of her. She cried out, a sudden, violent sound as if she had been awakened abruptly from a runaway dream that had been too real and terrible.

"Back off! Back off!"

Teddy drew her gun and swung the butt of it at him but he was not as passion-dazed as she. He ducked the blow and let her go, watched her scurry off from where he had lain her on the desert floor.

Cursing him, calling into question his ancestry, she punched her arms into the shirt he had stripped from her moments before, and viciously pulled the garment over her head.

Hair flying around her, she bounded back another step and kicked a cloud of dust toward him. Haloed in moonlight, she stood above him, an angry vengeful goddess with a hand clenched on the handle of her pistol.

"One day," she said, threateningly.

Wanting her still, he lay where she had left him, counting himself a doomed man. He would have her or die. But he did not tell her so.

"One day, Teddy," he said, taunting, "you will not have that gun."

Twenty-five

Taviz, with a cigar gripped in his teeth, sat on the plush leather seat of the Gamble stage reading letters from a ripped canvas bag containing U.S. mail.

"Ehh, listen to this one, Juan," he said, tossing away an envelope postmarked Philadelphia:

Dearest Thomas,
The twenty dollars you sent were sorely needed. Young Thomas had been ill and the doctor has carried us on credit for months. I trust your prospecting will yield greater rewards in the future than it has thus far. We miss you dearest. You have been gone so long. The children ask for you daily.

Your loving wife,
Martha

Laughing, Taviz threw the letter out the window of the stage. "This Thomas, I bet he spends his gold dust on whiskey and easy women while his wife scrapes by at home. Ehh, what do you think, Juan?"

DEVIL MOON

"*Sí*, that is what I would do." Juan, short and bow-legged and spiteful as a snake when angered, agreed.

"Noo," Taviz said solemnly. "You would have your woman dig for gold while you waited at home."

"*Sí! Sí!*" Guffawing, Juan grabbed a handful of the stolen letters and thrust them at Taviz. "These make me laugh. Read more to me, *señor*."

Taviz pitched the entire bunch away. "No more," he said, then bellowed out the window. "Ehh, Rennie! Stop the coach! I am tired of this seesaw ride. I want my horse."

Rennie was the most heartless of Taviz's gang and the second of the men Taviz had brought with him. Rennie pulled the team to a halt long enough for Taviz to climb out and mount the showy black stallion with white stockings. He had been tied by a lead to the stage's boot. Juan climbed out after Taviz, bringing with him the iron-bound green treasure box. Taviz had shot the lock off shortly after taking possession of the stage. With Boyd Smith looking over his shoulder he had counted the loot it held. Taviz had agreed to a fifty-fifty split of any booty. In return for his half Adams had promised to keep the sheriff off the trail of the outlaws.

The box taken in this first holdup contained four thousand dollars in eight bags of gold nuggets being sent down to the Wells Fargo office in Yuma.

On Taviz's orders Juan transferred the contents of four of the bags into the saddle packs of Taviz and his men. The other four went to Boyd Smith who had ridden along with Taviz and the stage after the holdup.

"This ought to make Adams feel good." Boyd tied

down the flaps on his saddle packs and made ready to mount and ride to Wishbone with the booty. He looked forward to getting his share, thought he might buy himself a new saddle or some of those hand-tooled boots over at Penrod's.

Taviz grinned. "You tell Adams I send him another, better present soon."

"Yeah?" Boyd was never sure what to say to Taviz. "What's it gonna be?"

"The Gamble Line," Taviz said proudly. "I give it to him soon." He caught the reins of Boyd's horse before the other man could mount and ride away. Though it was the hot part of the day, the look on Taviz's fiendish face raised goose bumps on Boyd's skin. "You wait a little while," Taviz said, "so you can tell Adams what I do."

"Sure," Boyd answered, wanting more than anything to get away from the half-breed and his men. "I'm in no hurry."

Motioning for Boyd to follow, Taviz spurred his horse to a gallop across a rocky stretch of ground that ended at the top of a high canyon wall. The stallion's hooves grated and slid in the rocks when Taviz turned him. They were only inches from the steep drop to the dry valley below. Much more slowly, Boyd rode up a few minutes later and leaned out of the saddle to look over the edge. The ground fell away to the big rocks two hundred feet below. The view gave him a sick feeling deep in pit of his stomach. He didn't like high places. He told Taviz so and backed his horse away a few yards.

"The high place scares you?" Taviz laughed and

pointed to his man perched on the driver's seat of the stage which still sat a quarter mile away. "Watch Rennie," he said. "He will show you how to be brave, ehh."

Taviz raised one arm above his head, held it there a moment and let it fall. At the signal Rennie took the whip to the tired stage horses forcing them into a furious run toward the cliff. Across the plateau they came, lifting a tumultuous cloud of dust that swirled and twisted in their wake. Boyd's heart pounded as furiously as the racing hooves, faster, faster.

Behind the coach Juan rode at a gallop, with Rennie's saddle horse trailing him. Why Taviz and his men wanted to play a fool's game was beyond Boyd Smith's imagination. One thing he knew, though, Rennie hadn't left himself room to stop that stage.

Rennie did not even try. When the lead horses were six feet from the edge he jumped from the driver's box and rolled across the hard ground. The doomed horses tried to turn at the last moment but it was too late to stop the momentum of the coach. The entire outfit went thundering over the edge.

Boyd, grimacing, couldn't make himself look down at the wreckage. Taviz and his men looked and laughed and did a wild victory dance on the rim of the cliff.

"We could have made some money sellin' them horses," Boyd pointed out.

"Now we make stew, ehh?" The half-breed slapped Boyd's horse hard on the rump sending him bolting across the plateau. Boyd let the animal run unchecked. He could not get away from the trio of outlaws fast enough. "You tell Adams how Taviz does business, my friend!" Taviz roared after him.

Hundreds of miles away the roar of train wheels went rolling over a lonely stretch of track, and kept Derby Seward awake. He was tired, and thirsty for a whiskey. His skin blackened by the coal dust blowing in the open windows of the train car, an irritable Seward picked up a discarded newspaper left behind by a former rail passenger.

His trip had been hard. He'd left London with little preparation. Avery Knox was anxious beyond reason for Seward to find and dispose of Rhys Delmar. In the frenzied weeks of travel, Seward had met with bad food, too little sleep and inferior whiskey. He was ready for the end of the line though he did not look forward to leaving the uncomfortable train car for the even less comfortable stage ride to Wishbone, Arizona.

He hoped Delmar had not left Wishbone. As if in answer to a prayer, though in Seward's case it was more likely the favoring hand of the devil, the Englishman chanced to glance at a single story in the weeks-old newspaper, his eye drawn by the word *Wishbone,* the very location he sought.

The subject of the short article was a stage robbery foiled by a rock-wielding Frenchman, one Rhys Delmar. Seward's flagging spirit leaped and a smile played on his wide lips as he silently applauded his detective work. Knox would be elated with a quick end to his problem.

The smile got away from Seward as he thought of the disgusting, would-be earl. He had to consider that he might have trouble collecting his due from Knox once the deed was done. Knox was unstable and growing more so by the day. Suppose he killed Delmar then got back to London and found that Knox had lost what was already a loose hold on his sanity. Then what would he, Seward, have for his trouble? Better think on that, he decided.

He needed safeguards for himself, ways to assure that he got his due whatever happened to Knox, and that he did not come under suspicion the moment he arrived in Wishbone. He was not foolish. He knew a portly, red-haired Englishman would stand out in the small territorial town, unless he had a convincing reason for being there. What was his reason to be? He could not very well present himself in Wishbone as an assassin come to murder Rhys Delmar.

With the discarded paper resting in his lap, Seward closed his eyes and massaged his temples and forced himself to think of all the obstacles he might encounter. Outside, the sun glared down on the roof of the racing train. The hills slipped by in the distance. After a time the sought-after safeguards began to occur to Derby Seward. Maybe, just maybe, he should not be too quick to kill Delmar. Maybe he should consider advising the Frenchman that a fortune was his for the claiming in London. Rhys Delmar might offer extremely generous compensation to the man who gave him that news. Especially if that man could also clear him of a charge of murder.

He might be more generous than Knox. On the other hand perhaps his best chance was to stick with Knox. Seward licked his dry lips and pondered the matter. Delmar or Knox. What a quandary.

"Excuse me," a soft voice said. "Have you any objection to my taking this seat?"

Seward opened his weary eyes in time to see an expensively dressed but homely woman gesturing to the empty seat facing his.

"Please do," he said, smiling warmly. "You'll improve the view immensely."

The woman's cheeks reddened with delight as she slid onto the seat. "I'm sure that's not at all true," she said. "But watching the ground go by does get monotonous. I thought switching sides of the car would help break the boredom."

"Perhaps," Seward said. "Or perhaps this paper would offer a bit of respite." He neatly refolded the paper he had been reading and passed it into the woman's gloved hand. "It's old but you might find enough of interest to pass the time more pleasantly."

The woman slipped off her cream-colored kid gloves and opened the paper for a glimpse at the headlines on the front page. Seward's eyes were drawn to the large, sparkling ruby brooch the woman wore at her collar.

"Thank you, Mr.—"

"Seward. Derby Seward."

"And I am Ada Penrod," the woman said. "I'm making this trip to visit my brother in Wishbone, Arizona."

"Wishbone?" Seward smiled. "How fortunate for me."

"Oh?"

"Wishbone is on my list of destinations as well," Seward explained.

"Have you family there?" Ada asked.

"No, no relations there. I'll be a stranger in town," he said, instantly concocting a plausible reason for his being in Wishbone and for asking questions about Rhys Delmar should the man prove difficult to locate. "I'm a reporter, you see. I've come West to do a series of stories for my London paper."

Ada leaned forward. "How exciting."

"Yes, it is rather," Seward continued, elaborating on his lie. "My topic is outlaws and lawmen of the territory and, most certainly, any person who stands out from the ordinary."

"That would be most everyone in Wishbone," Ada Penrod declared. "Of course, I contend there is no civilized person west of St. Louis." Her deep-set hazel eyes grew bright for an instant. "I should be delighted to speak with you again after a few weeks to learn if you agree."

Seward stroked his beard. "An intriguing suggestion," he said.

"Perhaps I could—No." Ada's narrow face spotted with red. A spinster and anxious to rectify the condition, she did not often meet a truly interesting man. "That would be presumptuous of me."

"Please do go on as you began," Seward pleaded.

"Well—that is—My brother has a mercantile business in Wishbone. For a time—before I moved back to our family home—I helped him in the store. So, of course, he and I know almost everyone in town. Perhaps we could introduce you to some of the more colorful residents.

"Splendid," Seward beamed a smile at Ada Penrod. He could not have been more pleased. Having someone of prominence, someone trusted, to vouch for him would make his job in Wishbone a breeze. "We could, perhaps, lunch together or take tea—" When he broke off and gave her an apologetic smile, his imperfect teeth shone out of his bright red beard. "Now I am the one who is presumptuous."

"Not at all," Ada Penrod insisted. "I would be delighted to lunch with you, and take tea. As often as is necessary to aid you in your undertaking," she added.

"You, dear lady, will be the first highlighted in my column. Your hospitality is extraordinary."

One compliment was all Ada needed to launch into a much-embellished version of her life history. An hour later, with a little encouragement, she followed up by telling the flatteringly attentive Derby Seward every anecdote that crossed her mind regarding those she knew in Wishbone. Seward, having quickly assembled props for his new occupation, scribbled notes in a leather-bound tablet he had taken from his valise.

As Ada rambled on and on, he jotted down the names of persons he thought might prove useful to his cause: Sheriff Len Blalock, Parrish Adams, owner of the elegant Diamond Saloon, and Teddy Gamble—in Ada's words "a misguided young woman trying to run her father's stage line." Not so ironically, the same stage line on which Rhys Delmar had foiled a robbery attempt.

Twenty-six

Teddy awoke to find the dawning sky streaked with crimson. She thought of blood and death and felt such an ache in her heart that it seemed the weight of the heavens had descended on her. Her first thought was that she wanted to pull her bedroll blanket over her head and stay where she was until the hurt eased, if it ever did.

In short order, though, curiosity overcame Teddy's misery. She heard the crackle of a campfire and the sizzle of bacon and smelled the tantalizing aroma of coffee brewing. Briefly she wondered if Rope had recouped enough to be up and preparing breakfast.

But how could he? Rope would be a mass of stiff muscles and aching parts and would probably need assistance getting to his feet. Which meant, she feared, as she slowly eased the blanket off her face, that she was about to be indebted to Rhys for one more thing.

Sure enough it was the handsome Frenchman squatting before the licking flames of the small fire and flipping bacon in a blackened skillet. Somehow in the midst of the desert he had achieved that well-groomed look that seemed a part of him. He was as cleanly shaved as if his valet had steamed and attended his face. His dark hair was as sleekly combed as if he'd spent half an hour brushing it into place. His crisp white linen shirt was half open down his chest and his sleeves were rolled to the elbows. There was a casual elegance to his appearance. She could hear him humming a soft melody as he tended the meal he was preparing.

An unwarranted warmth stole over Teddy. She remembered how good his arms had felt, how his demanding kisses had swept away her senses, how being locked in his embrace had made her feel that nothing mattered. How easy it would be to lose herself in those stirringly sensual feelings, and forget she had a mountain of cares and responsibilities.

Rhys Delmar was polish and style, the kind of man she used to daydream about when she was a silly young girl who believed dashing princes rode in on chargers and rescued damsels in distress. Teddy gave a troubled sigh and rubbed the backs of her hands over her eyes. Something had gone wrong with the fairy tale. Instead of Prince Charming she had gotten the prince of mayhem. Rhys Delmar hadn't ridden in to rescue her. He had come to rob her of the things she held most dear. Just her luck. And damn him to everlasting hell for making her wish he was the other kind of prince.

Slowly, irritably, she rolled clear of her bedroll and got up. "Anything worth eating in that pan?" she asked.

Rhys twisted around to look at Teddy as she stretched her long limbs. *Mon Dieu.* She was beautiful in the morning, her hair in silky tangles, her eyes lazy with sleep. Heat struck him, flying straight to his loins as he recalled the wonder of holding her, the sweetness of her mouth, the softness and warmth of her flesh. The unattainable Teddy. For now.

"To be sure," he said. "Bacon, an omelet seasoned—"

"A what?"

"Omelet," he said the word slowly. "Eggs whipped frothy and cooked slowly."

"I know what an omelet is." Teddy, hopping from one foot to the other, pulled on her tight fitting boots. "Where did you get eggs?"

"Birds of the field," he said cheerfully, and turned back to his cooking.

Her feet softly striking the ground she came up behind him and suspiciously looked over his bent back at what he'd prepared. Eggs indeed. He'd robbed a nest somewhere and made a sunny omelet that was sprinkled with herbs plucked from a few carefully selected shrubs. She usually managed to scorch bacon but he had obviously taken his time, slicing the rasher into thick strips then cooking them to crisp perfection. Her stomach tightened, reminding her she was hungry.

"Looks passable," she said, ever-stingy with praise for the Frenchman. "I'll take coffee to Rope. See how he's feeling."

"He's got coffee and he's eaten," Rhys told her. "And he is feeling better."

"I'll ask him that myself," she retorted, annoyed that he was up ahead of her, already had the day in hand and was cheerful to boot.

"Not now." Rhys shook his head. "He's—ahh—"

Teddy spotted Rope's empty bedroll. Quickly comprehending that Rope had sought a few minutes of privacy and wouldn't appreciate being disturbed, she dropped down cross-legged beside the curling flames of the fire and poured steaming coffee in a tin cup. She took a sip of the hot brew as Rhys dished out a portion of the omelet and a few slices of the bacon. He gave her the plate he'd served then poured coffee and prepared a plate for himself.

"This is good," she admitted after sampling the omelet. "I wouldn't have thought—"

"That much was obvious," Rhys interrupted, his cheerful expression vanishing. "Just what do you think of me, Teddy? I would like to know."

"Well, you're—you're—" Further perturbed, she grappled for an answer. Most of her negative opinions of Rhys Delmar had been dashed down as untrue. She couldn't fault his looks, or his courage, or even his patience. Nettled, she couldn't, at the moment, think of one thing to complain about, she took a bite of the eggs. Not even his cooking was second rate. "You're a bother," she said at last.

Rhys smiled. A bother. That was progress.

Rope joined them before they were done eating. He dragged his weary body over to the fire and slowly eased down by Teddy.

Teddy smiled as warmly as she could and still keep hidden the worry she had for Rope. "How's the head?" she asked.

"Feels like somebody exploded a keg of powder in it," Rope replied. "And that's an improvement over yesterday."

He asked for a refill of coffee. Rhys was quicker than Teddy and poured Rope's chipped tin cup full.

"We aren't far from the second station," Teddy said. "Once we get you there you can rest until today's stage comes through. From there you can take the coach to Wishbone and see the doc and get patched up proper. Me and—" She paused and started on another tack. "I intend to find that lost coach and salvage the mail bag if I can. Bandits wouldn't have cared about the letters that didn't contain money, so maybe most of them are with the coach. I've no hope of recovering the mine shipment right off but, believe me, I won't give up until it's returned either in gold or blood."

"We got to let Cabe Northrop know what's happened," Rope reluctantly pointed out. "We got an obligation to Wells Fargo to let them know a man's been killed and a shipment's been lost." He turned up his cup and took a big swallow. "Cabe ain't gonna like it either."

"Well, hell, who does?" Teddy popped back. "Well, blazes." She looked accusingly at Rhys. "I reckon I can think of a few of your pals who do."

Rhys allowed Teddy to vent her anger without comment. She had lost a friend and she was mad at everybody. And she was entitled.

A few minutes later she thrust her tin plate at him and strode off.

Rope spoke up when she was out of earshot. "You got to overlook a lot with Teddy," he explained. "She's got more spikes than one of them cactuses." He gestured to one of the spiny varieties nearby. "But she's soft-hearted underneath."

"I take your word for that," Rhys said quietly as he watched her square her shoulders and hoist a saddle on one of the horses. While she got the other animal ready to ride, he smothered the fire and packed the utensils.

Within minutes the three of them were mounted and traveling farther away from Wishbone to reach the second Gamble change station. Rope, complaining of a headache, rode silently. Teddy, occasionally bumping against Rhys's back, felt stiff as stove wood.

Her misty eyes were on the ground following the deep-cut track of the missing stage. When they reached a point where the stage had clearly been turned off the road and onto a path that ran due north of the change station, Teddy cursed her luck. Up until that moment she had hoped the horses had taken the empty stage on to the station. Now she knew it had been driven north. She knew, too, that whoever had held up the stage had wanted more than gold. They had wanted to destroy her and the Gamble Line. There was no other explanation for stealing the coach.

Rope muttered a curse. "Teddy, if I was able, we'd go find that coach and who took it," he said. But his voice shook and both Teddy and Rhys could see that his hands trembled on the reins. He was weak from his injuries, and he'd already been too long in the saddle.

"We ought to give the horses a rest," Teddy said.

"I can make the station," Rope said weakly. "Anyways I'd rather stop where I can stay 'cause when I get off this horse I want to stay off."

"You sure?"

He nodded that he was. The trio rode on a few more miles. Rhys was beginning to wonder if there was anything else out in the distance but rock and cactus, when a shack and a corral appeared against the hazy horizon. The penned horses tramped and neighed as the riders approached. To Teddy's relief, Rope seemed to perk up the minute the station was in sight. Color reappeared in his ashen face and his voice had strength again.

"That's Bo Tilton and his brother Jolly you see out by the corral," he said. Rhys's eyes followed the fence line to the pair, one husky, one lean and wiry. "Good men." Rope's voice faltered with the last pronunciation and the reins went slack in his hands. He'd been holding on with sheer determination and it had just run out.

Putting his heels to the stallion Rhys rode up close and stuck out an arm to steady the wavering rider. With Teddy's help they kept him in the saddle until they reached the station grounds. The Tilton brothers had seen them riding in and, recognizing the horses, ran out to meet them.

"Gol' dang, Rope! Looks like you stopped a bullet." Bo Tilton's beefy arms helped lower Rope from the saddle.

"Stopped it with that hard skull of his." Teddy swung off the stallion. "Get him inside and on one of the cots," she said. "We found him late yesterday. Holdup men left him on the road about halfway between here and Porter's. Strong Bill's dead and the coach is missing."

"Dammit!" Bo Tilton shot one quick questioning

look at Rhys, then turned his focus on Rope. With barely a groan of effort he half lifted Rope from the ground as he urged the injured man inside the adobe hut where he and his brother lived. Jolly Tilton threw back the blanket on a cot and Bo lowered Rope to it. Like all the men who worked for Teddy, the Tiltons were loyal and almost as concerned for the survival of the business as she was. "Don't seem like it could be true, Strong Bill dead. All this trouble."

"We got to do something about this killing," Jolly Tilton said. "And these holdups." The smaller Tilton brother filled a dipper with water from a bucket. Shuffling across the floor, he took the drink to Rope. "Me and Bo and some of the other men could ride out and look for those killers. We got to," he said emphatically. "Don't look like we'll get any help from anywhere else."

"We will find them," Teddy said. "I promise you we will. Meanwhile the best thing you and Bo and the other men can do is keep this line running. You leave this station and we're shut down."

"Aww, you're right, Teddy," Jolly said reluctantly. "But I feel like a dog without a tail to wag sittin' around waitin' for another holdup."

"I'm doubling the guards soon as I can get the word through." Teddy pulled off her dusty hat and wiped her brow with the back of her arm. "You tell the boys on today's run to be watching for trouble. And," she added, "see that Rope gets on that stage to Wishbone."

"What about you?" Bo had pulled Rope's boots off and made sure he was resting comfortably as possible. But he had been listening to the exchange between

Teddy and his brother and he kept an eye on the stranger who had ridden in with Teddy. When Rope was settled, Bo stared suspiciously at Rhys. "And who's this fellow?"

Teddy spoke up before Rhys could explain his presence and set Bo at ease. "I'll keep looking for that missing coach," Teddy told Bo. "Or I'd be riding shotgun on today's run." She glanced over at Rope who was well into getting some of the rest he needed. Soft snores came from the sleeping man. "Rope will be feeling better when he wakes up. Even with that nick on his head he can still shoot so he can back up the guard if there is trouble."

"And him?" Bo put his big frame between Teddy and Rhys and insisted on knowing about the stranger. "He with you or—"

"I am with her," Rhys said, his hackles up that the big man had taken a defensive stance toward him.

"He's Delmar," Teddy said.

"Aww." Bo thrust out a big, rough-skinned hand. "I ought to have known. Strong Bill was talkin' about you yesterday. Said you wasn't a half-bad fellow."

"Nor was he." Rhys shook Bo's hand and felt the bone-crushing strength in the big man's grip. Rhys, remembering how Strong Bill had spoken up for him from the first day he'd arrived in Wishbone, meant what he said. "We buried him the best that we could," Rhys said.

Bo nodded solemnly.

"Well, if there's going to be any justice for Strong Bill I had better get going," Teddy said, walking out into the bright sun with Bo. Jolly and Rhys came along directly behind them.

"Now?" Bo asked.

"Now," Teddy replied. She headed for the corral where they had tied up the stallion and the mare. "Our horses are played out. I'm going to need one of your mounts to go on."

"Two mounts," Rhys said. "She is not going on alone."

"I'm danged glad of that," Jolly Tilton spoke up while Teddy stared oddly at Rhys. "But look up there, Teddy." The wiry stock-tender motioned to the ragged line of the mountains far to the north. "Looks like there's a storm in the makin'," he said. "And like it could be movin' this way."

Teddy stood silently for a few moments looking grimly at the darkening clouds above the sharp, bare peaks. To Rhys the clouds looked too far away to be any threat to them.

"We'll have to chance it," Teddy insisted. She began unfastening the mare's saddle girth.

Bo moved her aside and took over the familiar task. Jolly grabbed a couple of bridles from a shed and slipped through the parched rails of the corral. He caught the two saddle horses he and his brother kept penned with the coach animals. They were bay geldings. Neither was as fine a mount as Demon or Dune, but both looked long on stamina. Bo saddled the animals while Jolly got fresh supplies and water for Teddy and Rhys.

Teddy, impatient to be on the trail, swung into the saddle before Jolly was back. Rhys was about to mount, when Bo caught him tightly by the shoulders. "You look out for Teddy," he said, bringing his heavy bass voice down to a whisper. "You see she gets back here safe."

"I guard her with my life," Rhys answered swiftly, softly, surprising himself with the passion and conviction of his reply. He would guard Teddy with his life, but the desire to do so had stolen unforeseen upon him. What had started out as simple desire, a wish to conquer a challenging woman—his lust to take her to bed—had become something more. He wondered where it would lead.

Teddy, saddlebags and canteen full, put her heels to the borrowed gelding. "Get a move on, will you? Those bandits aren't waiting for you to poke around all day."

Rhys mounted his horse and urged the animal to a gallop until he could escape the trail of dust Teddy had left as she rode out. "Teddy, wait," he called to her. She never looked back. Heartless woman. She did nothing but torment and taunt him. But she did look fine bent over the gelding's neck, as her firm derrière bounced up and down in the saddle.

Without warning his loins tightened. She did have a way of setting him afire at the most inappropriate of moments. *"Mon Dieu,"* he whispered to himself. What was wrong with him? He had begun to care very much—too much for that impossible woman. He had completely lost his mind. He had come to this rugged place seeking to right his life, not to bog it down with more complications. And yet he had not tried to deter her nor did he turn his horse back. Instead he spurred the animal to a full thundering gallop to close the gap between him and Teddy.

He rode hard, with the wind and dust stinging his face. His lips curled down as he softly cursed Teddy for the spell she had cast over him. With the next breath he cursed himself and wondered what she was leading him into.

Twenty-seven

The stars glittered above two wearied riders who paused to make camp, high in the rocky hills above the stage road, long after the moon was high in the night sky. Rhys and Teddy did not bother with a fire. Having followed the tracks of the stolen stage until both of them were too tired to see the ground, they had finally stopped and taken refuge for the night beneath the hospitable shelter of an overhang in a small, shallow canyon.

"Since the rain held off, this spot will do us for the night," Teddy said.

Rhys nodded and gladly pulled his horse to a stop.

Teddy dismounted and looked the place over. Given options, she preferred camping on higher ground, but the valley they were in was little more than a hollow and was the best place for the horses if she wanted them ready to ride in the morning. A small ribbon of a stream curled lazily between the hollow's walls. Along its banks grew enough vegetation for the animals to get a good feeding.

As soon as the saddles and bridles were removed and hobbles put in place, the horses waded into the shallow stream and began drinking. Teddy and Rhys trudged upstream from the animals, to refill the canteens and to wash some of the dust and grit from their faces. With little aplomb they prepared a cold and sparse supper for themselves. Both were reflective. Rhys sensed that Teddy had too much on her mind to think of conversation. Later, when they shook out their bedrolls, Teddy spoke up and he learned one thing she had been thinking.

"Don't get it in your head I want company under this blanket." She had her gun in hand and twirled it around her finger several times.

Rhys yawned. "The only company I seek is sleep," he assured her. "Your virtue is safe." Never having considered himself soft, Rhys had not, admittedly, spent an entire day on a horse in several years. He ached in every muscle and though it had crossed his mind he'd like to spread his blanket next to hers, he was willing to save the pleasure for a later time.

"Well, your vitals aren't safe if you come crabbing over here." Teddy was grateful the deepening darkness made it impossible for him to see that she was too tired to put up a fight with a feather. She watched as he eased down on his blankets and methodically pulled off his boots. When she was sure he was settled where he lay, she spread her blankets a few yards away and slowly slid between them. She placed her gun at arm's reach. Halfheartedly she wished he would disregard her warning, for the weapon did not give the comfort she needed. A gun, though it might save her life, had no tenderness, no warmth, no ability to soothe away shock or sorrow. Rhys quietly watching the climbing moon, looked as if he could offer all she longed for, even make her forget she had no use for the kind of closeness a man and woman could have.

She bit down sharply on her lip and told herself that seeking solace with Rhys Delmar was one of the dumbest and most desperate thoughts she'd ever had. He was almost as much her enemy as the men who had attacked the stage. She had no idea why she had let him ride out with her. None at all.

As she looked up at the sky, she felt as if an enormous, heavy ocean of darkness was pressing down on her. She felt terribly alone and terribly confused about what she was doing out on the desert with Rhys Delmar.

She found it easy to blame him directly for most of the confusion. Being around him kept all her feelings so knotted up she couldn't think straight. But that wasn't so bad, maybe. She wasn't sure she wanted to think straight. A clear head meant deliberating on Strong Bill's death and the almost-sure demise of the Gamble Line as soon as word of the holdup reached Cabe Northrop.

Soul weary, saddle weary, Teddy rolled to one side so she wouldn't have to look at Rhys or that endless, leaden sky. But a change of position only brought her to another avenue of worrisome thoughts. She kept picturing the people who had believed in her, Felicity, Rope, Strong Bill, Bullet, most everybody who had stayed on with the stage line after her father died. She had told them all she wouldn't fail them. Worst of all she had believed what she said. She had been so sure she could finish the job her father had started.

Thinking, somberly, that nothing had gone right for

her in a long time, Teddy drifted off. Sleep, however, offered no comfort. She tossed about so much that she had her blankets in a snarl. She moaned and mumbled so loudly that Rhys lay awake long after she had closed her eyes. He was ready to go to her should she cry out for him. If he'd thought his efforts would have been well received he'd have forgone the waiting and awakened her and tried to comfort her as best he could. But guessing what reaction he'd get if he did, he let her continue in unsettled sleep. He was hoping that, even though she was restless and troubled, she would feel better by morning.

She missed the fireworks, the distant blaze of blue-white light splitting the sky. The brilliant spectacle lit the horizon for a full hour but occurred so far away Rhys could barely hear the rumble and crackle of the thunder and lightning. He judged the distance to be dozens of miles off, so it was with no concern for a dousing that he eventually fell asleep.

He was not so troubled as Teddy and slept soundly. Even so, he was awakened after only a few hours by a strange sound. His eyes blinked open to darkness confirming that his rest had been brief. The noise grew louder, humming like a gigantic swarm of bees descending on the valley, roaring like pent-up ocean waves. Lying still, listening a few moments more, he tried to define what he heard but found his sleep-sogged mind reluctant to cooperate.

What was it? Not wind. He'd never heard the wind sound that way. He'd never heard anything that sounded like the ever-nearing roar. Or felt the air quite so still. Or the earth quiver beneath him. One of the horses whinnied nervously. Rhys sat up and jerked on his boots.

"Teddy!" He ran to her and shook her awake. "Something is wrong!"

She came to, sputtering and cursing. "Bastard! Get your hands off—My God!" she cried and came flying to her feet. "Cut the horses loose! Then run! Run like hell! This place is about to be under water."

Rhys sped toward the horses and cut them free. He saw one of the bays go racing down the canyon, the other found a climbable slope on the canyon wall and scrambled up. Teddy grabbed Rhys's hand and ran after the climbing horse. Before they gained the top, an aquatic snare lassoed their legs and dragged them down the slope into the raging flood.

Teddy, screaming, pitched headlong into the torrent. Rhys jumped in after her, managed to maneuver his way to her and shield her from the rocks and limbs the water cast them into. As they were carried around a bend he fought the rising currents and ragged canyon wall, eventually shoving her toward a wind-twisted pine whose roots were locked in a rocky ledge.

She gasped for breath. Her eyes were wild with fear. She caught hold of a spindly bough and saved herself from being swept on. Rhys caught hold too, and would have been as safe as she had not his desperate hold on the pine branch been broken when the rushing of water hurled a piece of debris that hit him squarely in the back. Stunned, he fell into the brutal waters a second time and was carried off down the canyon.

He could hear Teddy scream, "Timmy! Timmy!" as he was swept around another bend in the canyon. *Mon*

Dieu! She was thinking of her brother, thinking he was her brother. As the current latched onto him and carried him away, he got a last fleeting look at her agonized face and saw the absolute terror in her eyes.

He prayed he wouldn't drown. She would need someone after this was over.

Thankfully the powerful wash of the flash flood tossed him near the edge of the canyon. Fighting to stay above water he grabbed for any stationary object clinging to the muddied banks. A hundred yards downstream from Teddy the sturdy root of a single tree offered him a lifeline. Knocked breathless by a hard slam into gnarled wood, he clung on with nothing but determination. A few seconds later, air again began filling his lungs, and he began the arduous climb to safety.

The distance to the flat ground above wasn't far in feet. But the rocks were wet and slippery and his hands had been cut and bruised from grabbing at the craggy bank during his watery ride. Rhys snaked his way up, progressing only an inch at a time, knowing that a misstep could send him back into the deluge of water below. Only once did he look back. That was when a rattling crash came from where he had been moments before. His lifeline was gone by then, ripped from the wet canyon wall by the crushing impact of a small boulder.

When his feet were once more on firm, dry ground he thought of Teddy. Had she managed to get uphill or was she still clinging to the skinny tree branch where he had last seen her? Calling her name, he started to run, hoping she could hear him above the roar of the water.

She did hear him as he neared. His voice, welcome as a song, brought her momentarily out of the shock of reliving the horror she had experienced the day her brother had drowned. She was up to her shoulders in the rising water. Though her tree branch held fast, the tree itself was losing the battle with the water. When it broke loose she would be carried down the canyon with it.

Shouting to Rhys for help, she kicked against the current for a foothold but could not control her legs in the rushing water. She saw Rhys drop to the ground four feet above her, but at that very moment, the tree broke loose. Part of the upended trunk struck her shoulder, to end any chance she had of reaching out for Rhys's help. In an explosive instant she was underwater, swept down deep, as Timmy had been. She would be beaten to pieces against the rocks before she drowned as her twin brother had done.

Teddy surfaced endless moments later and saw Rhys desperately reaching towards her. She shouted to him for help one last time. Then she was sucked down again, as water filled her open mouth and flooded into her lungs. Beneath the torrent, as she was twisted and spun about, she thought she saw Timmy's boyish, terror-stricken face as it had been that last moment before he, too, had been carried under the black waters the day he had drowned.

Timmy. Timmy. She had relived the horror of his death a thousand times in her mind. Now she was following her brother to the same dreadful end, failing him too, failing everyone.

Pain stabbed into her as all at once her head seemed to have been wrenched from her neck. Beneath the dark water she opened her mouth to scream her rage. She had not thought dying would hurt so much.

Twenty-eight

The soggy, tawny braid was the only part of Teddy that Rhys could reach. He hooked it with his fingers, grappling desperately into the long strands of hair until he had a tight, determined grip. He was fighting the current for her, pulling with all his might to hang on and beat the driving waters. He knew he had won when his savage, insistent jerk pulled her above the swirling deluge.

Hoping he hadn't snatched the hair from her head, he hauled her to the bank and got a grip first on her collar, then her arm. Her eyes were closed when he got her clear, but she was sputtering and coughing. He knew she was alive. Taking no chances that the water might leap over the canyon wall he tugged Teddy up a rise some ten feet away and set to work pumping out the water she had swallowed. He welcomed her moans of protest as he rolled her to her stomach and pressed and lifted her back.

With her loose hair plastered to her face, she looked like a dunked tabby cat. She came to, with about as much fury as a bedraggled cat would have had. She began twisting beneath him so that she was face up instead of down. Her greenish eyes flashed like flames. Her scowl was so deep it looked as if it was there to stay. Her battered hands went to her head and gingerly felt it all over.

"Jeeze!" She made a sound that sounded exactly like a growl. "Did you have to scalp me while I was out cold?"

Rhys didn't care if she cursed him. He was too glad to be alive, too glad to have her alive and sound enough to complain. "I am sorry," he said softly. "Your scalp is no doubt sore. I had to pull hard, or lose you to the water."

She found some gratitude then. "You caught me? By the hair?"

"Yes." He reached out and brushed the limp, wet strands off her pale face. "The rest of you was underneath." Her skin was cold, her face lined with scratches from the tree that had betrayed her to the water. His hands tenderly stroked her cheeks as he silently wished away the injuries. "I am sorry I had to hurt you. I would not have done so if there had been any other way. Not for the world."

Teddy groaned softly, just then comprehending fully that Rhys had miraculously pulled her from the water. "You saved my life," she said.

"I suppose."

"No supposing." She coughed, clearing the last remnant of her ordeal from her constricted throat. "If you hadn't caught me I would be dragging along the bottom of that canyon with the rest of the debris that water is carrying. I would be dead."

"I suppose," he said more softly.

She recalled then that he too had been swept away

by the fury of the water. He too had come close to the passageway between life and death and must feel as relieved, as buoyantly alive as she did.

Somehow he had managed to find the path back alone, and to save himself from the wild current and come to her aid. Considering the way she had badgered him, rebuffed him at every encounter, she wondered why he had bothered.

She was glad he had. Troubled as her life was, she wanted to live to know the satisfaction of having long, full decades of life behind her. She had survived her skirmish with death, thanks to Rhys. Quick as it was, the ordeal had changed Teddy, made her see that there is always another way to solve a problem, no matter the issue.

She sure had a new point of view for Rhys. Maybe her brain was waterlogged. Whatever the reason, he did not look like an enemy anymore. Poised above her, he appeared regal and proud as a pagan god who had spared one of his mortals and was waiting to be rewarded for his actions.

His eyes glittered bright as the stars that hung overhead. His taut muscles rippled through the soaked and ragged shirt that hung open from collar to waist. Her clothing had fared no better against branches and current. Her shirt was tattered, ripped away at one shoulder, hanging by a few frayed threads at the other. It covered little of her.

Teddy did not care that she was half-naked or that he was. What mattered was that they had survived a disaster and would live to see the glowing sun bring morning light. Another day.

A rivulet of water, clear and cold, fell from Rhys's dripping hair to Teddy's throat. It traversed the hollow between her collarbones breaking into silver droplets that flowed slowly between her softly rising breasts. Rhys watched the tiny droplets inch along, saw the dark crests of her breasts harden and rise against what remained of her shirt, felt her shudder as if the icy beads had penetrated her skin.

What had been a lifesaving posture, Rhys on his knees and straddle-legged over Teddy, became a prelude to something else in that moment. Electricity fired between them, hot and devastating, forging one strong, highly pitched emotion into another. Teddy felt as if a bolt of fire and light had hit her. Rhys felt as if he were filled with it, and had become uncontrollable heat and flame.

Rhys fought against it, told himself that he was wrong to want her, could not allow himself to do what he feared he would in another moment.

"Mon Dieu. Teddy," he said, his hoarse voice not rising above a whisper, his breath like a flame as he bent close to her face.

The pressure of his strong thighs against her, the gentle stroke of his fingers on her skin sealed her fate. She wanted him—wanted to prove she was alive, wanted to prove she could live forever. Death be damned. She craved him as much as she had craved the clear, fresh air when he had pulled her from beneath the water.

"Oh hell," she whispered, her arms going out to him, sliding up his broad, hard chest to lock like vines around his neck. She brought his mouth to hers, and felt his teeth graze sensuously upon her lips as his tongue shot possessively past them.

The roar of her racing blood pounded in her ears, drowning out the roar of the rushing water. A glimmer of moonlight fell across her face, a rare bedeviling red-gold light that brought her yearning for Rhys Delmar to a fever pitch. She cried out his name, with ragged cries that came in a breathless whisper as his hands tore away the shreds of her shirt exposing more of her to the magical light, more of her to his skillful mouth and hands. His fingers ran rampant and wild over silky flesh, caressing fullness and hollows, stripping away the clothing that had become as binding as chains. His mouth devoured her sweetness, tasting her as if she were luscious summer fruit, a banquet of delicacies laid out for him, him alone.

Beneath him she was soft as a cloud, sweet as a meadow of wildflowers. Her hair made a veil around her, honey and gold spun out like threads of fine silk. Softly, gently he looped his fingers in the damp golden strands, brought a soft handful to his lips, trailed it like a mass of curling ribbon across his chest, down his bare thigh.

The touch of the silken tassels brought a quiver to his hard flesh that Teddy felt beneath her delving fingers as they wove into the inky, wet curls at his nape. Whispering her name over and over, Rhys stretched out beside her as their discarded wet clothing cast aside as they lay upon a smooth dry stone, an altar to their passion, a bed for their mating.

Sweet. She was sweet. Her kisses rained across his face warm as summer, as laden with promise as spring. He pulled her close so that she lay against the length of him, but she would not be still beneath his questing hands.

Hot, then cold, Teddy writhed and twisted beneath Rhys, wanting him, fearing her need for him, yet powerless to turn back what she had begun. His palms cupped her breast, molding, squeezing, shaping, stroking the flushed areolae until the peaks grew tight as rosebuds. Her breath caught in her throat and her skin flushed with heat, then yielded to a sweeping chill as icy as a winter wind. A single touch of his lips, hot as a brand on her throat, melted the cold away, fusing it into a burning ache for more, more.

She moaned helplessly, pleadingly, felt she was drowning again, this time swept beneath the surface of desire and need. Raggedly, softly, Teddy whispered his name, a confirmation to herself and to him that for once, she would allow herself to be carried as deep as her latent, molten passions ran, as many fathoms down as his would take her. For long, dazed moments she twisted and shivered beneath his touch, euphoric, exultant, eyes heavy with the pleasure of lazily watching the one who had brought her to this heady state.

His eyes shimmered like deep blue water. Clear, warm ocean depths intoxicated and carried her deeper, leagues beneath the surface to currents of silver-flamed passion. He moved over her and her hands were upon him, feeling the sinewy muscle in his hips and thighs as he positioned himself between her legs. His body was hard, bronzed in the moonlight, perfect as masterfully hewn statuary.

He was, though, fire and blood, and his thundering need for her was imminent as he poised above her. His eyes sought hers in the instant he came to her, his manhood stabbing hard and deep, bringing a mingled cry of shock and pleasure from her lips. He sank into her again and again, filling her with searing, raging heat. She rose to meet his fierce thrusts. Her nails were savagely scoring his back. She buried her face against his shoulder, while his breath blew hot against her skin. Aflame, consumed by flame, she felt his thrusts grow stronger, faster, and her own body quicken in response. Breathlessly, unexpectedly, shuddering uncontrollably, she plunged headlong into a fiery river of ecstasy, swept along on waves of flame until all feeling was burned away by the searing heat.

Still, locked together, both reluctant to part, they lay cradled in each other's arms until the heat of their lovemaking yielded to the growing chill of the night.

"*Chér*—Teddy," he amended. "Much as I despair of letting you out of my arms, I must. We need a fire to dry our clothes and—"

Slowly, Teddy sat up and hugged her knees as he began to search his soaked clothing in hopes of finding matches dry enough to light a fire. She did not like what had come over her. Watching him, she wanted him back beside her, with his arms around her. Indifference had been her barrier, her protection. Now she had none.

"I guess I ought to have known it would feel like that," she said.

Looking crestfallen, he left off his search and came to her. "You were disappointed? I was, perhaps, too quick on the draw?"

"No. Dammit!" she retorted, resenting his reminding her of that complaint. "I wasn't and you weren't. That's what's bothering me."

A smile stole onto his face like sunshine after a storm. He had felt her response and known she had experienced satisfaction. He had not expected her to admit to it. "I am glad you were pleased."

"I didn't say I was pleased," she spat back. "I don't even know how this happened. Hell! That dunking must have washed all the sense out of my head."

"Or washed some in," he said. "Teddy, what happened between us was a beautiful thing. It happened because it had to happen, was meant to. For no other reason," he said, softly, huskily, realizing she was not alone in feeling surprised by the depth of it, by the lingering pleasure. All along he had thought he wanted her simply to satisfy his lust. Making love to her had not ended his longing for her. Already he wanted her again. Already he feared he always would.

Briefly the look in her eyes seemed to concede that he was speaking from the heart, seemed to acknowledge he was not merely gloating over another conquest. But then her face clouded over and she was the old, combative Teddy. She crossed her arms over her chest. With her head thrown back, she huffed out a breath and said, "It won't happen again. Now, are you going to light a fire or not?"

Twenty-nine

A broken wheel, a shattered axle, a few scraps of leather, the battered carcass of a coach animal, were all that remained of the stolen Gamble stage, once floodwaters had ravaged through the deep canyon into which Taviz had sent team and coach.

Teddy and Rhys stood solemnly on the wind-whipped canyon rim looking down at the wreckage. Teddy's insides tightened painfully. Such destruction was insane. She found it hard to believe even Adams would stoop so low as this. But who else could have been responsible? Common road agents wouldn't have taken the trouble to drive a stage twenty miles into nowhere and run it off a cliff.

"No mail. No coach. Nothing," Teddy said. She had a white-knuckled grip on the reins of the one saddle horse they had chased down after the disastrous night. She had found her saddle pack, too. The sturdy leather pouches had lodged under a rock. Most of the contents had been washed away but she had recovered a sopping wet shirt which she quickly dried in the sun. Though they had lost both canteens and food she had insisted on continuing the search for the stage. Now she felt the effort had been a waste.

"Senseless," Rhys said, his sympathy for her high as he saw the pain in her grim face. Another loss for her. Not a life this time but to her it must feel like one more straw upon the camel's overburdened back. "Will you be able to keep to the schedules without this coach?"

"Don't you worry," she returned sharply. "I'm not beaten. I'll keep the Gamble Line running if I have to drive every run myself." With a quick tug on the reins, she pulled the barebacked animal around, gripped the shaggy black mane at the crest of his withers and swung astride. Eyes stormy she stared hard at Rhys. "You'll get your money's worth if it's due you," she said. "Don't worry about that."

As effortlessly as she had mounted he swung up behind her. "That was not my concern," he said. His warm breath was stirring the tangled hair at her nape.

Teddy shivered and scooted forward on the horse's back. "I'll bet," she said.

She didn't talk to him for the first half of the long journey back to Tilton's station. She was afraid that if she opened her mouth she would say things she would regret later. He didn't need to know the extent of the turmoil her emotions were in. Or to be aware that, with his hard, lean body pressed tightly to hers, her heart was hammering so fast she could hardly breathe. Thoughts of him, the feel of his arms, the way he had kissed her as if he needed her as much as air, the loving invasion of her body. No invasion. She had welcomed him, relished the feel of him, longed for him, even now.

Dammit! She couldn't feel that way about him. Not

him. Not anybody. She had no time and no room in her life for a man who would want to change her into one of those flossy, frilly skirt-wearing women who peek though the curtains at night waiting and watching for their man to ride in. She wasn't that kind of woman. Never could be.

It had been a mistake, a lapse that never would have happened if she hadn't been caught in that flood and come so close to dying. It had been a mistake, a dreadful one, she told herself again, never quite succeeding in clearing away the formidable doubt that her brush with death had simply been the excuse she needed to do what she had wanted all along.

Rhys felt the anger in her and wondered if that was the only emotion he could raise in her. Then he remembered how she had clung to him, moved with him, responded to his kisses, the soft, desperate sounds she had made when he held her. Not anger.

She had wanted him, even needed him then. Now she was either ashamed or afraid of what she had felt. He had regrets, too. Now he felt bound to her, committed. It wasn't what he had wanted or expected. And it wasn't right. He didn't belong in this savage country hungering for a woman who was half savage herself. He preferred caviar and fine champagne to campfire meals and brackish water—an elegantly appointed bedroom to a sand-filled bedroll—unless Teddy was in it.

He sighed heavily. That did it. The woman was getting in his blood. They were a combination that would never work. He had more than enough obstacles in his life. He didn't need Teddy, with her gunpowder temper, needling her way into his heart. Didn't want her there.

The horse started down a low rise. Rhys slid forward on the animal's sweat-slickened back and bumped harder against Teddy. He resisted the impulse to lock his arms around her waist to steady the two of them. Even so, his loins tightened as the horse's swaying walk rocked him against her. Desire, unleashed, surged through him, the power of it jolting his body, telling him he had been lying to himself. He needed Teddy. He wanted her enough to consider giving up returning to his world.

The horse stumbled. Rhys instinctively threw an arm around Teddy's rib cage, holding tightly until the animal had its footing again. He felt her breasts rise and fall against his arm. Fever, hot as a wildfire, swept through him and once again all reason burned out of him. He exhaled roughly and thought of telling her she could have his shares, all of them. But he didn't. The shares were his only link with her. He wasn't ready to break that link—illogical, impossible as it was to think there was anywhere to go with it.

The feel of his gentle hold on her, seemed to permeate her flesh and fill her with fire. And terror. She pushed his arm away. He was driving her loco, changing her, making her forget the things that mattered, making her think of things that didn't. Couldn't. His breath, warm against her neck, sent a shiver down her spine. Desire curled and twisted deep inside her.

Teddy scowled. That was it. She couldn't live with this yearning for him, with the way he leaped into her thoughts a dozen times a minute, with the way his slightest touch turned her to mush. She wished there were a way she could pay him off, send him packing, forget him. And she wondered, if the way was there, if she would do any of the three.

"Jeeze!" she said irritably. "You're wearing this poor horse out rollicking around back there. We better get off and walk him before he drops in his tracks." Quick as a wink she slid her leg over the gelding's neck and jumped to the ground, reins in hand.

"As you wish, Teddy." Rhys slid down behind her, as glad as she was to break the maddening physical contact.

Leading the horse, they walked the remaining miles to the Tilton station, reaching it after sundown, both exhausted and hungry and thirsty. Teddy was glad to learn that the last two days' runs had come through on schedule. Bo gladly reported that Rope had sent news that both had made it safely to Wishbone.

The following morning, rested, Teddy and Rhys mounted the horses they had left in the Tiltons' care. "I'll see you get paid for that horse we lost in the flood," Teddy promised Jolly Tilton. "Meanwhile you boys be careful and keep an eye out for trouble."

"Count on it," the Tiltons said in unison.

Porter Landau, his jaw bulging with a chaw of tobacco, was expecting them when they rode into his station that afternoon. He shaded his eyes as he arched his other arm and waved from the corral. "Rope said you'd be comin' through soon." One of the coach horses, finished with his feed, came ambling by. Porter gave it a sound pat on the rump. "What did you find out there?"

"A busted-up coach at the bottom of a canyon," Teddy told him flatly.

Porter spat tobacco juice in the dust. "Them bandits drove it up there and wrecked it? That's plumb mean."

"It's malicious all right," Teddy said.

"That, too," Porter said. "Any sign of them that done it?"

Teddy shook her head. "We lost a horse in a flash flood and couldn't keep hunting for the bandits." She had dismounted by then and was brushing dust off her shirtsleeves.

"What are we gonna do, Teddy?" Porter lifted the loop of braided leather rope that held the corral gate closed. Waiting for Teddy's answer, he pushed the gate open, walked through, and latched it behind him. "We're a man short without strong Bill and sure as sin them bandits will be back."

"What we're going to do, Port," she said, "is put on more men and double up the guards. Another gun will give those no-good bastards something to think about if they try robbing another of my stages." Hoping her plan wasn't wishful thinking she went on. "All we have to worry about is finding men to take the job." And paying them, she added silently.

"I am an excellent shot," Rhys said. "Until these bandits are stopped I can be second guard on one of the runs."

"You?" Teddy's sloping brows lifted. "Why would you risk your hide?"

"Why wouldn't I?" Rhys responded, though in truth

he wondered the same. "I, too, have an interest in keeping this stage line running. At least until I am paid."

"You're on then," Teddy said against her better judgment. "Provided you can back up that bit about being an excellent shot."

"I got some old bottles," Porter said. "An' a Winchester."

Rhys proved his point by shattering the ten bottles Porter set up back of the station even though Teddy kept varying the distance he fired from.

"All right," Teddy said, pleasantly surprised. "If you can do that from a moving stage and you don't mind shooting at men you'll make a fair guard."

"Fair?" Rhys retorted.

"Fair," she repeated. "And remember you volunteered for this job. Don't go quitting on me the first time somebody shoots at you."

The next trouble didn't come on Rhys's run. Taviz, a marksman himself, winged both guards and the driver as the stage rattled through a narrow pass on the run to Yuma. With the team racing out of control his men had swooped down out of the rocks and lassoed the lead horses, bringing the coach to a teetering, skidding halt. This time they had left the coach and team intact but when they were done, another mail shipment was missing and five bags of gold dust were in the wrong pockets. Just as bad for the Gamble Line, three more men were out of commission.

Adding to Teddy's streak of bad luck was a telegram

from Cabe Northrop advising that he would be in Wishbone the following week to discuss what was happening. If that wasn't enough to rattle anybody, she had continued to be plagued by thoughts of Rhys. At night when she wasn't worrying about holdups and going broke she was thinking of him. She lay awake, tossing in her bed, reliving her night of lovemaking with him.

And damned if he hadn't fitted right in with the men. He'd taken to wearing a long canvas duster on the runs. With his long-barreled rifle slung over his shoulder, his hat pulled low, he looked as rugged and dashing as a cavalry officer. Justine Blalock thought so, too, and made a point of seeing that Rhys had something appetizing from Mae's kitchen whenever he rode out.

Teddy got tired of seeing the calf-eyed girl walk up to the office with a carefully packed cloth-covered basket in her hands. Teddy once tried to discourage her by explaining that the station masters kept grub on hand for the drivers and guards.

"Nothing like this," Justine had replied confidently. "I've got fresh sandwiches and cake." Blushing, she had added, "Mae always says the way to a man's heart is through his stomach."

Something had gotten into Teddy and she had snatched the basket from Justine and said, "I'll give it to him. Now scat!"

But Justine hadn't been discouraged and had come back the next day with another basket. Nor was she the only one smitten. Most of the time when Rhys's run pulled in or out of town she could count a dozen women hanging out of windows begging for a look from those pale blue eyes of his. Most times she wanted one herself.

Parrish Adams, clad in black, stood silhouetted against the red enamel doors of the Diamond Saloon. He had a newly lit cigar in his hand. When he saw the stage pull out with Rhys Delmar riding as guard, he muttered a curse, threw the stogie to the sidewalk and ground it out with his heel.

Looking over the swinging doors, he barked an order to Boyd Smith who stood at the bar, about to enjoy his first beer of the day. At Adams's urgent call Boyd reluctantly put his glass down and headed for the door.

"You want me for something?" he asked.

Adams looked up and down the street making sure they had relative privacy for what he was about to say. "Yes. I want you to ride out and find Taviz. Delmar's taking the Yuma run again. Describe him to Taviz and tell him to make sure nothing happens to that Frenchman," he said irritably. "I want Delmar healthy enough to beg me to buy those shares off him once I've got Teddy Gamble on her knees."

Boyd's mouth watered for the beer he'd left on the bar when he thought of the long, hot, dusty ride he'd have trying to find Taviz. If the crazy half-breed had moved his camp any further west he'd have to spend the night out there with them. And if that thought didn't make a man need a beer nothing would. "I can ride out after him if you like," Boyd said, fishing for a plausible excuse not to go. "But it'll probably be a waste of time. Taviz is not likely to hold up today's stage," he suggested to Adams. "You already told him to space out the raids so them guards have time to get a little slack in between."

Adams's voice was deadly as he turned his black eyes on Boyd Smith. "I don't pay you to second-guess my orders," he said. "Get on your horse and find Taviz."

"Yes sir." Boyd wasn't about to push past Adams to go in and finish the beer. And Pete, who was upstairs trading his pay for a little fun, would just have to figure out where he'd gone. Turning on his heel, Boyd strode quickly down the street to the stable where he kept his horse. He dreaded seeing Taviz again but Adams, when he was riled, wasn't much better. Boyd sent a boy over to Penrod's for a supply of grub and was soon ready to ride out. Damned if he wasn't starting to question the company he kept. But Adams, at least, paid good.

Norine Adams, in a form-defining scarlet and gold dress stepped out on the sidewalk just in time to shock a passing matron and to hear her husband grumbling that nobody was worth a nickel anymore.

"Except me," she said sweetly. "Last night you said I was good as a gold mine."

Adams bit the end off a cigar and spat it into the street. "You are a useful commodity, Norine." Solemn-faced, he struck a match on his bootheel. With the flaring match cupped in his hands and the cigar gripped between his teeth he said, "And it's high time I put you to your best use."

"What's that?"

"Insurance." His smile was predatory. He'd devised a secondary plan for obtaining Delmar's shares. Norine was it. She could turn a man inside out when she took a notion to. He didn't think the Frenchman would be immune to a siren like Norine—or balk because she was much higher priced than the saloon girls.

She hated it when he talked over her head. Her sullen face told him this was one of those times. "Parrish, sometimes you don't make a dab of sense," she said tartly.

"Don't get yourself in a stitch," he replied. "This is a job to your liking." He had her curiosity up and she hung on his arm. Her long nails were raking him. She was listening intently as he went on. "I want you to butter up that Frenchman who drops by for a drink most nights."

"The handsome one?"

"The one Honor's always rubbing on. See if you can do more with him than she can. I want those shares he's holding. If he won't take money for them maybe he'd be willing to trade. For something."

"How much do I do with him?" Norine licked her red lips and eyed her husband suspiciously. The job was to her liking but she knew better than to take anything her husband said at face value.

"Just make him hungry," Adams said. "Don't feed him. Not until I say so."

"Madame. Sir." A red-haired, bushy-bearded Englishman interrupted the discussion. "I'm a stranger

here and I'm looking for the best place to get a shot of good whiskey."

"Look no further." Adams beamed a friendly smile at the well-heeled gentleman with the blustery, out-of-his-element look. He appeared the sort of man who might easily be parted from his money. Stepping aside, Adams pushed the wide doors open for the Diamond's newest customer. "Step up to the bar. Tell the man the first one is on me."

"And to whom do I owe my gratitude?" the Englishman asked.

Adams nodded. "Parrish Adams is the name. I own the Diamond and I try to see that a man can find most any kind of refreshment he wants inside."

"Derby Seward." The red-haired man tipped his hat. "And may I say your hospitality overwhelms me, sir."

Thirty

Derby Seward kept a supper date with Ada Penrod the next evening. She had invited him to her brother's modest house. Just as Seward had expected, his acquaintance with the homely woman was paying immediate dividends. Milt Penrod, a talkative sort, was easily directed to recount the names of recent arrivals in Wishbone. He soon mentioned a Frenchman called Delmar.

Seward was surprised that Delmar had not taken the precaution of assuming a new name, but then, if Delmar had been that clever he might not have needed to flee London.

"Wishbone's a jumping-off place for prospectors," Milt Penrod explained. "We get all kinds here, mostly farmers and ranchers who are looking for an easier way to get money out of the ground, but we also get our share of tradesmen and clerks. There's even one genuine doctor up in the hills. He'd rather set a pick in rock than set bones."

"Plenty of odd fellows here," Seward said. "I should have no trouble writing my articles."

"Almost everyone who comes to Wishbone passes through Milt's store now and then," Ada explained.

"Either buying supplies or sending mail." She had worn her best gown for this evening. It was made of rose-colored silk that played havoc with her florid complexion. But she had been unable to resist it when she had seen it in the window of her favorite dressmaker. "I'm sure Milt wouldn't mind if you dropped in now and again to talk with some of them."

"No trouble if you do," Milt confirmed. "Always a prospector or two trading a little dust for supplies."

"My gratitude," Seward said in the gushing, effusive tone he had adopted for his stay in Wishbone. "I will, you may be sure, avail myself of your hospitality." Pausing a moment, he pulled a snowy linen napkin to his face and gently blotted his mouth and spattered beard. "I wonder though," he queried when he was done, "what becomes of those sojourners who do not become prospectors."

"Ain't many of them," Milt said, missing his sister's grimace at his lapse in grammar. "Can't think of any this year but Rhys Delmar—I mentioned him to you—and that fellow who was his valet." Milt wagged a finger while he munched a bit of biscuit. "Now there's an odd pairing for you. Delmar's as dapper a fellow as you'll ever see, and he winds up riding shotgun on the stage. The valet fellow's left him and is running a faro game over at the Brass Bell."

"Interesting," Seward said and smiled at Ada, sending her heart fluttering. "I may confine my articles here entirely to the aberrant, the eccentric prospector or pilgrim in Wishbone. And may I say I am grateful for the information you've provided." He gave Ada a warm look. "Your sister said you would be helpful." Boldly, he reached across the table and patted her spindly hand.

Later that evening he got an even greater dividend when Ada suggested that since the hotel accommodations in Wishbone were deplorable, he should be their guest during his stay. With a suitable display of gratitude and surprise, he agreed. "This way Milt and I can personally introduce you to many of the people you are interested in," Ada insisted.

Seward again thanked brother and sister for their hospitality. "Of course I shall have to mention your altruism in one of my articles, dear lady," he said.

Ada Penrod preened like a mating bird, completely beside herself with joy at having successfully maneuvered the Englishman into such promising confines.

Seward made a point of visiting the Brass Bell late that evening. He wanted to meet Lucien Bourget, who had been Delmar's valet. If the fellow had been dismissed after loyally following Delmar from London to Arizona, he might not feel too charitable toward his former master. Seward's experience was that disgruntled servants were free with information about those they once served. He wanted to know more about Delmar's plans, and his frame of mind. Then Seward would make a decision on whether to kill the man or sell out Knox to him. He particularly hoped to get an indication as to whether or not Delmar had any suspicion he was being cheated out of an inheritance back in England.

He had to join in the busy faro game to talk to the lame Frenchman. He didn't mind that too much when his luck ran good and he won a small sum. He was glad, though, that half an hour before the saloon was to close, the gamblers deserted the game for another round at the bar, leaving Seward and Lucien alone.

Seward seized the moment to tell Lucien who he was and why he was in Wishbone. "Doing articles for my paper," he said. "Thought I might make you the subject of one."

Lucien shook his head negatively. He was pleased with his fresh start at life and anxious to forget most of the former one. *"Monsieur,"* he said. "You could find a better topic."

"Don't know that I could," Seward persisted. "Heard you came out here as a valet then lost your position. Don't suppose you feel too kindly disposed toward the fellow who let you go."

"Au contraire," Lucien said, wondering why the Englishman seemed vaguely familiar. He decided, at length, there was something about all Englishmen that made them seem one and the same and, preferably, to be avoided. Politely, but reluctantly, in response to the man's probing he said, "He did me the grandest favor. I am forever indebted to Monsieur Delmar."

"Delmar is it?" Seward spoke the name as if he were hearing it for the first time. "Hear the man is working as an armed guard for a stage company. He's come quite a way down the ladder, hasn't he?"

Pride overcame prudence for Lucien. He felt compelled to set Seward straight about Rhys's status with the stage line. "Monsieur Delmar is one of the owners of the stage company," he said.

"That so?" Seward replied.

"That is so." Lucien had the final word as he closed up his game and hobbled across the saloon, leaving Seward at the faro table. He looked forward to the end of the long day and welcomed the pleasurable nights spent with Carmen. The sight of her cheerfully shooing out the last of the straggling customers so that she could close, brought a swell of love to his heart. He remembered as he watched her what he had said to the overly inquisitive Englishman. He *was* indebted to Rhys Delmar, more than he could ever repay. The man had once saved his life, but Lucien was grateful for more than that. Had it not been for Rhys Delmar he'd never have come to Arizona, never entered the Brass Bell, never known Carmen.

Lucien slowly climbed the stairs to the big room he shared with his ladylove. He didn't see enough of his friend anymore. He ought to remedy that.

Rhys had a day off and planned to drop in on Lucien then spend the rest of his free time in a leisurely game of poker if he could find one. He didn't expect to join a game in the Diamond but Honor had sent him a note asking him to drop by next chance he got. Today was it.

He stepped through the Diamond's doors and into

DEVIL MOON

a haze of smoke, and air strongly scented with whiskey and beer. Someone in back was experimentally plunking out chords on the piano. Honor hadn't come down yet. Rather than go up and take a razzing from the girls, Rhys asked the barkeeper to send for her.

He ordered a drink while he waited. He was nearly done with it when someone tapped softly on his shoulder. He turned to look into the face of a stunningly beautiful woman.

"Honor's busy today," she said. "I'm not."

"You're Adams's wife," he said, remembering that Honor had pointed Norine Adams out to him once when she had walked through the saloon.

"I'm Adams's wife when I want to be." Her silky voice was matched by the smooth strokes of her fingers massaging his shoulders. Her potent perfume evoked images of dim lights and satin sheets. "Today I want to be whatever *you* like, Mr. Delmar."

"I see nothing about you to change," Rhys said cautiously, aware that various patrons had grown interested in Norine's attention to him. "Would you join me for a drink?" He rose and offered her a chair, certain she would be less conspicuous merely sitting at his table.

"Glad to." She purred like a cat as she sensuously slid her voluptuous form against him and moved around him. She was dressed to kill—or to get someone killed—in a dress of ebony silk overshot with sheer red lace. The plunging neckline revealed fully half her large, lush breasts. As she lowered herself into the chair Rhys held for her, she made sure he got the full view.

Rhys didn't like it. Intentionally or not she could be setting him up for a scrape he didn't want. Some husbands, he knew, gave their wives free rein to roam, provided they were discreet. Evidently Norine Adams didn't know the meaning of *discreet*. He had no inkling how long a line Parrish Adams gave his spouse. Nor was he especially interested in finding out.

Norine motioned to Harley at the bar and momentarily the big bartender brought over her favorite refreshment. His big, round face showed no reaction to seeing his boss's wife sitting intimately close to another man. That made Rhys marginally calmer at sharing a drink with her. He noted too, that, as he had hoped, the curious patrons who had been staring at Norine had found other interests. Which was exactly what he wanted to do as soon as he could finish his drink and politely excuse himself to Norine.

"To your beauty, *madame*," he said, raising his half-empty glass to the cloying woman, "with apologies that I cannot stay and enjoy it longer."

He started to rise but Norine quickly caught him by the wrist and held on. Her sharp nails were digging into his flesh. "I'm not accustomed to men walking out on me," she said. Her lash-shaded eyes slowly, suggestively, descended from his face to his groin. "Stay a while. Parrish isn't here. We could have another drink—in my private room if you like.

I think you'll find I make a much better deal than he does."

Deal? He was puzzled but too anxious to get away from Norine Adams to search out what she meant. "I am sorry to have to decline," he said and slowly unlatched her fingers from his wrist, briefly held her warm hand and bowed over it, lightly grazing the back of it with his lips. "I only stopped by to visit a friend," he explained, letting go of her. "Honor. One of the girls who works here. Perhaps you'll tell her I couldn't wait."

Norine raised the hand he had kissed to her lips and slowly pressed her lips to the exact spot his had touched. "Nobody ever kissed my hand like that," she said. "It feels good."

He nodded to her. "You will remember my message."

"Oh, forget about that girl," Norine retorted, her full red lips drawing up in a pout. "I'm the one that asked you over here tonight. All the good it's done me."

"Madame," Rhys said, making a slight bow and moving away. "It has been a pleasure."

"It could have been," she said. Not quite ready to be dismissed Norine jumped up and insisted on taking his arm. Hanging on so tightly that their thighs bumped she accompanied him all the way to the street. When he tried to extract his arm from hers, she clandestinely slid her arms around his neck and, in a last attempt to change his mind about staying, pulled his head down, ground her hips against him and hotly, hungrily kissed him. "Anytime you want more," she said. "You come back."

Teddy, winding up a long day of bookkeeping and schedule shuffling saw the whole torrid exchange. And imagined the rest.

Thirty-one

Norine's disappointment heightened as she twisted through the crowded, noisy saloon and through the doors which led to the private quarters she and her husband shared. The big bedroom with the full tester bed was dark except for the light of one candle in a twisted silver sconce. The door to the adjoining dressing room stood open a few inches and it was toward that darkened portal that Norine spoke.

"I'm alone," she said. "He wasn't interested. Tonight."

Parrish Adams, a revolver in his right hand, shoved open the dressing room door and confronted his wife. "How did you know I was here?"

Nonchalantly, she sat at her dressing table and, guided by the scant light of the flickering candle, began plucking pins from her upbound hair. "I know you," she said tartly. "You thought I'd bring Delmar up here and—give him a few nibbles, enough for you to come rushing in playing the wronged husband to the hilt."

Adams slid the revolver into the waistband of his black trousers and walked up behind his wife. His long dark fingers slid around her slim white neck. "And you let me down." He brought his fingers over her windpipe and tightened the pressure of his grip. He'd looked forward to the scene of the Frenchman, distraught, pleading for his life, finally trading his Gamble shares to keep it. Breathing heavily, he squeezed a little tighter and was pleased to see a look of fear flicker onto his wife's expertly painted face. "Losing your touch, Norine?"

Gasping for breath, her hands fell to the dressing table as silently she stared at the vicious reflection Parrish Adams made in the shadowed mirror, behind the helpless woman whose throat his hands encircled. And then she twisted away from him. "No!," she said acidly. "I'm not through with him yet. You'll get what you want."

His hands found their way to her shoulders, making red marks on her pale flesh as he jerked her to her feet and spun her around. "Will you get what you want?" Adams demanded. "From him?"

Norine's head rocked back. A sound of rending cloth filled the room and her expensive gown, torn in two, floated down around her feet. "Ummmm," she said. "From somebody."

A week passed with no raids on the stage and Teddy began to hope the holdups had been enacted by a band of renegades who had moved on to other pickings. Maybe Adams had given up taking over the routes. Maybe she was crazy as a loon. Maybe he hadn't been behind these last attacks like she had thought. The boys who had lived through them described a different set of outlaws than those who had first given the line trouble.

As for Rhys Delmar, she hadn't said two unnecessary words to him since she'd seen him kissing that hussy Norine Adams. Lately she had been wishing that letter from London would hurry up and arrive. She no longer cared whether his claim was legitimate or not. All she wanted was to get him out of her hair. Seeing him nearly every day, being reminded, painfully, of what had occurred between them, was, loaded on the rest of her problems, more than she could bear.

He had betrayed her. How that was so she didn't bother to reason out. She felt betrayed and it was interfering with everything else she had to do. What's more she didn't seem to have the stamina she used to have. By midafternoon most days she was weak as water.

"It's the strain," Felicity Gamble said. Concern for her overwrought granddaughter showed in her face. "Teddy, you've done all anybody could to keep this line running, but maybe it's time to sell out. If you can't stand selling to Adams, find another buyer. We'd still have the ranch if we did that." Fearing she wasn't getting past Teddy's stubborn resistance, Felicity continued. "Nobody who matters is going to think worse of you if you give up now. Your father would understand. You know he would. Why, I don't think even he could keep going in the face of all you have to contend with."

"I'll never quit!" Teddy paced the dining room where she and Felicity met for breakfast. Always. Felicity insisted that the household run as it had when

Theodor Gamble had been alive, that schedules be kept, routines followed. Teddy was grateful for the order and comfort Felicity added to her life. This morning, though, she hadn't touched her breakfast. She had no appetite at all, though she knew she had a hard day ahead and would need the nourishment of a good meal. Felicity, as usual, was a step ahead of her and had already wrapped up two fat biscuits filled with ham. She was tucking them in the saddle pack hanging on the back of Teddy's chair.

By then some of the sting had gone out of Teddy. She stopped her pacing and kissed Felicity's papery cheek. "I'm sorry," she said. "I've got no cause to shout at you but I do mean it. I'll never quit. Cabe Northrop will be here today and I'll tell him the same thing." Looking for tolerance, at least, from Felicity, she threw the saddle pack over her shoulder and continued, "If he wants to cancel my contract I'll fight him all the way. If he wants the shipments coming through safe let him get one of his detectives in here to help instead of threatening to shut me down. Maybe if somebody went looking for those outlaws instead of leaving it up to Len Blalock we'd be through with them by now."

Felicity gave her a maternal pat. "Hard as all this is, Teddy, I'm sure it's going to turn out the way it ought to."

Teddy nodded, wanting to believe what her grandmother said was true, but doubting. In her opinion Wells Fargo had been slow to step in. True, no Wells Fargo shipments had been lost in the first few attacks but in the last two the strongbox had been taken and, as was their policy, Wells Fargo would have to make up the loss. She didn't like costing them money but, dammit, they were quick enough settling up with other companies who suffered losses. Because she was a woman she got treated differently. Cabe might not say so but the results were obvious enough.

Teddy left the ranch before the sun was up, her mood blacker than the early morning sky. The first thing Cabe was going to want to know was when Zack Gamble would be arriving to get the company running right. She would have to 'fess up about Zack's death and tell Cabe there would be no man coming in to straighten things out. And, in spite of all her talk, she was finished the minute he pulled the contracts.

Dune whinnied in protest as Teddy suddenly pulled her saddle horse to a halt. By damn, maybe there was a way. Maybe, if she could stomach it, she could acknowledge Rhys Delmar's part in the company. If she could get him to indicate that he'd come to Arizona with the intention of being an active partner in the line, possibly even hint that he'd had experience with a company in France, maybe that would satisfy Cabe and Wells Fargo and keep the Gamble Line alive. Of course all that was just a shade away from a lie, but, she was desperate.

Scowling at what she had sunk to, she clucked to the horse and rode on, a jittery bundle of nerves in the saddle. Dammit! It was the only way. She would just as soon ask favors from a scorpion—but it was the only way. Unless she presented a new partner, a man, she was done. Shoulders hunched, mood worsening, she rode on. No use in trying to tell Cabe that

Rope was running things. He knew both of them too well and knew Teddy would override any decisions Rope made—and that Rope would let her do so. So, Rhys Delmar, it was. She would find a way to run the low-down Frenchman off later. Right now, hard as it was to take, she needed him.

Telling him was the hardest thing she ever did. She kept seeing him with Norine Adams wrapped around him, their lips fused in passion. Seeing those two together should have gotten the memories of her intimate night with Rhys out of her mind but it hadn't. It had only made them stronger. She hadn't stopped wanting him, even though she suspected he spent his off-time in one of the rooms above the Diamond doing sensuous things to Norine Adams or one of those other chippies.

"Rhys."

"Yes." He turned. Hearing her speak his name without snapping out an order sounded good. It also made him suspicious. Since the night they had made love Teddy had been in the same ill humor as when he'd arrived in town and announced that he was there to collect on Zack Gamble's debt. The last few days had been even worse. She'd had about as much use for him as for a mad dog.

He'd let all that go. Life, at present, was hard for her. He understood that she needed time to sort out her feelings about what had happened between them. He needed great patience. A hundred times he'd wanted to drag her off somewhere alone and demand that she admit something was there, between them. He wanted to tell her it was foolish to pretend nothing had happened or to believe that it wouldn't happen again.

"I need to talk to you," she said. "It's important. I've got a man to replace you as guard today."

Rhys knew a moment of apprehension. He feared that Teddy's cordiality bode ill for him. The mail had come through every day for a week. Possibly yesterday's bag had brought the letter from London that would decide his fate. Very possibly Teddy's contact there had learned of the charges against him and relayed the news to Teddy. He wondered what she was going to do about it.

The stage rumbled out of Wishbone a few minutes later. The driver cracked his long black whip inches above the team's backs. Both guards rode on top. The lone passenger was the local schoolteacher who had gotten a better offer. He was California bound and could be heard above the roar of the wheels shouting a cheerful farewell to everyone the stage passed.

Teddy motioned Rhys into the cramped Gamble Line office as the stage disappeared. She moved around the stacks of boxes and bundles tagged for the eastbound stage and dragged one of the cane-bottomed chairs out in the clear. In one of the most unladylike moves Rhys had ever seen, she sat with her long legs straddling the chair's back.

"I reckon you've been around long enough to know the line's in serious trouble," she began. "And I reckon you're smart enough to know that your shares could wind up being half of nothing soon enough."

"I know there have been setbacks," Rhys said cautiously. Teddy had tried every argument to weasel out of paying off Zack Gamble's debt. He braced for a new one.

"Setbacks?" Teddy returned. "By damn I could be hours away from being out of business. And when I'm out of business you're out of luck."

"Every shipment has gone through since we added the extra messenger to the runs," Rhys reminded.

"That's right," Teddy said, drawing herself up to look as tall as possible. "But because of the ones that didn't, the Wells Fargo agent over this district is coming in this afternoon." Someone walked by the open door and Teddy quietly fumed until the footsteps faded. "It's good as gone," she said. "He aims to cancel our contract. When he does we're busted. Me. And you."

"Busted?" Rhys hadn't heard the term. While he might normally have picked up the meaning from the gist of the conversation, he was too distracted by Teddy's widely spread, buckskin-clad legs. Didn't the woman know she shouldn't sit like that?

"Broke." She got up but it was too late to redirect the line of his thoughts back to money and Wells Fargo agents. He'd been caught by a fever. His belly tightened. The veins in his temples throbbed. He'd have taken her in his arms but she went stalking across the room, kicking bundles out of her way as she went. "Dammit! I've got one chance." She spun around. "I want you to tell Cabe Northrop you're running things." She paused a moment, having to choke out the next words. "I'm not waiting on that letter from London," she said. "I'm acknowledging your ownership of Zack's shares. I'm ready to sign a document to that effect. But if you want it to be worth more than paper, you tell Cabe Northrop you're my partner and that you'll be around as long as it takes to get this line up to snuff." Again she stopped to gather her courage. "He's got to think you know how to run a stage line, got to think you've had some experience somewhere. Understand?"

Rhys slowly nodded.

"Once this line's out of jeopardy," she added, "I can borrow enough to buy you out. Pronto." She stood in the shadows but he saw tears welling in her eyes. He'd never seen her cry, not even in the worst of times. When a tear slid down her cheek it was his undoing. Teddy swabbed her face with the back of her hand. "Dammit! Got a speck in my eye," she said.

He'd have granted her anything—had she but known to ask. As it was, Teddy was giving him exactly what he had come for. She was clearing the way for him to leave Wishbone and get back to the life he preferred—a life which, with all its complications, was beginning to look simpler than the one here. By now Alain Perrault had his letter and should have responded. He trusted that Alain had already begun efforts to clear him of the charges against him. As soon as he had the money Teddy owed him he could afford a defense. He could leave, forget the past, forget Teddy, be a devil-may-care man again.

His lips curved into a half smile, infuriating Teddy, who suspected he was laughing at her evident desperation and spineless show of weakness. She wasn't mollified when he said, "I will do it. Whatever you want."

Thirty-two

Late in the afternoon of that same day Teddy didn't feel much better, even though the meeting with Cabe Northrop was going well.

"This is a surprise but a good one," he said, heartily shaking Rhys's hand after a look at the postdated papers of partnership the two had signed. "Ought to make the superintendent good and happy." He smiled at Teddy. He'd gone out on a limb sticking up for her and now he could say she'd taken his advice and gotten a man in to run the company. Since he'd never expected Teddy to take his advice, or anybody else's, he was overwhelmed with relief when he met the Frenchman.

"Ought to make everybody good and happy, except maybe Parrish Adams," Teddy said curtly. "I noticed you made time to drop by the Diamond for a drink right after you got here."

"Needed one, Teddy." Cabe shifted his bulk in the small chair in the Gamble office. "Had dust in my throat."

Or crow in the craw, Teddy thought. "Well, if your throat needs washing out again tell him the Gamble

Line's solid and he can stop trying to run me out of business."

Cabe shook his head. "Teddy, Adams is a businessman with big plans. Nothing unnatural about him wantin' to buy out a small line and expand his own." He got up. "Take my advice and make friends with Adams. He's gettin' to be important in this area. Heck! He owns most of it. One of these days you'll be needin' his business."

"He'll haul freight out on his back before the Gamble Line carries so much as a letter for him." Teddy swung off the box top she'd been sitting on and paced across the crowded office floor. The fringe on her buckskins went swinging in tempo with her hurried steps. "Looks like somebody besides me should be asking where Adams gets the money to buy up everything between here and Prescott."

Rhys could see Teddy was about to talk her way out of the understanding she had with Cabe and Wells Fargo. He put himself between Teddy and Cabe and gave the big man his warmest smile. "The Gamble Line will accept all customers who can pay for service," he said. "We wish Monsieur Adams the best of luck. His prosperity is our prosperity."

Cabe Northrop laughed and slapped Rhys on the back. "Well, sir," he said. "I can see you've got a good head on your shoulders. You'll be good for the line, good for Teddy. No doubt about that."

Teddy had to bite her tongue until all the handshaking and backslapping was over. But as soon as Cabe was gone—and right to the Diamond like she figured—she lit into Rhys. "I ought to kick you in the caboose," she said, gritting her teeth. "I run this line and let me tell you I wouldn't carry freight for Adams if—"

Rhys cut her off. Smiling that maddening smile he said, "Until you convert my shares to cash, I run things. You told Cabe Northrop that was so." One dark brow lifted sharply, wickedly. "You would not like me to tell him otherwise, would you?"

"You conniving French fool! The only thing you're going to run is out of here!"

Teddy raised a balled fist and swung at him, but Rhys had gotten to know her ways much better and was prepared. He swiftly caught both her arms and twisted them behind her back, pressing her squarely against a wooden crate, molding his thighs hard against hers.

The fever flared in him again. "Partners ought to get along better than that," he said huskily. "Understand?"

She saw his face moving toward hers and struggled to wrest free of his steely grip. "Don't you kiss me, you bastard!" she shouted.

But he did, and in a moment her clenched teeth parted and her clenched muscles relaxed. He released her arms and, like one hypnotized, she slid them around him. When his tongue invaded her mouth, the yearning, the excitement she had denied invaded her body like spring invades the earth. She moaned and fell against him, wildly wanting him. She was breathless when he drew his mouth away, breathless and helpless.

"Understand?"

"Yes," she said, managing only a whisper. "I do."

"Teddy!" Rope, already inside the office, knocked three times on the open door to get her attention.

Teddy's face flamed red as she broke away from Rhys. "We were—discussing what Cabe had to say."

"I could see you had your heads together." A knowing twinkle shone in his eye. "Anyhow, that's what I came to ask about."

"He was satisfied." Teddy cut her eyes at Rhys, giving him a searing look. "He thinks this son of a—Rhys can run the line better than you and I can."

"Maybe so," Rope said, annoyingly unperturbed by what had riled Teddy. "An' you're gonna need all the help you can get right now 'cause I ain't been worth a wooden nickel since I got that nick on the head." His fingers grazed over the angry red whelp on his temple. "Still can't sit the saddle without gettin' lightheaded," he added. "Which is another reason I came by. I got a wagon full of supplies for Porter and the Tiltons an'—Dang it! I ain't up to drivin' them out."

Teddy walked over to the coatrack in the back corner and strapped on her gunbelt. "You sit in here till closing," she said. "I'll drive the supplies out and be back tomorrow late."

"You ain't goin' out alone," Rope insisted.

"Get another messenger to cover my run tomorrow," Rhys said. "I will accompany Teddy." He countered her look of protest by quickly adding, "We have more company business to discuss."

Rope's irksome, understanding smile made Teddy mad enough to spit. When Rhys left to drive the wagon around from the stable, Rope unwittingly added fuel to the fire.

"Kinda nice seein' you pay attention to a man, Teddy," he commented. "It's time too. Time you thought about gettin' hitched and having a passel of children. 'Cause unless you do you're the last of the Gambles. An' I know that ain't what you want."

His words brought a shiver to her, a feeling a goose had walked over her grave. She crossed her arms over her chest. "Last or not I've got no intention of becoming a brood mare," she said tersely. "And let me tell you that Frenchman is too damn high strung to stand good at stud."

Rope chuckled. "You know that for sure?"

"Aw hell!" she said and strode out. "Tell Felicity where I'm going."

Rhys had to drive past the Diamond. Parrish Adams flagged him down. The saloon owner had had a drink and an informative talk with Cabe Northrop. He'd been disappointed in the latter. One more time Teddy Gamble had talked Wells Fargo into continuing her contract. One more time the irksome bitch had foiled his plans. Time was running out for him. He had financed his land purchases by mortgaging one property to buy another, but the numbers were catching up with him. He needed access to the mining shipment schedules in order to safely execute a few key robberies that would put everything straight and make him, in fact, the wealthy businessman he pretended to be.

"Delmar," he said smoothly—neither of them was

noticing that, directly above them, Derby Seward, a customer of one of the saloon girls stood at the open window shielded by the red curtains, while his companion slumbered in the rumpled bed. "I hear from Cabe Northrop that you're running the Gamble Line now," Adams said. "That so?"

Rhys pulled back the brake on the wagon and rested a booted foot on the high wooden brace in front of the seat. "I am," he answered.

Adams offered Rhys a cigar then lit one for himself, too. "Well, now," he said, taking a few slow puffs. "That surprises me. Especially when I've just seen my way clear to offer you twice as much as before for your shares."

"Forty thousand—dollars," Rhys said.

Adams, a gray plume of smoke rising from the cigar clenched in his teeth, glanced down the street and saw Teddy Gamble staring back at him. "Fifty," he said. "Fifty thousand. I'll have it for you by night."

Seward parted the curtains slightly and strained to hear Rhys Delmar's reply.

Rhys swallowed hard. Fifty thousand dollars would hire the best barrister in London and tempt the truth out of a lying witness. Fifty thousand. All he needed, or so he thought until he, too, glanced down the street and saw Teddy standing in front of the stage office looking like she could bite spikes in two. She was one troublesome woman, bad tempered, bad mouthed, insulting, one difficult handful. He thought maybe he was in love with her. He knew he couldn't let her down.

"I made a deal with Teddy. Sorry." Rhys pushed the

brake lever, gave the reins a shake, and drove off leaving Adams mad as hell.

Seward closed the curtains and walked across the room stroking his red whiskers. He was puzzled. He had expected Delmar to jump at the money and the man hadn't. That could mean Delmar was a man of principle and, if so, Seward would be wasting his time trying to make a better bargain than he had with Avery Knox.

Down below, Boyd Smith rode up in front of the Diamond about the time Adams's cigar arched across the street. Dust-caked and bone-tired, Boyd pulled his horse up at the rail. "I'm back," he said, ravenous for a tall glass of beer.

"Don't get off that horse," Adams snapped.

"Why not?" Boyd lightened his foot in the stirrup and settled his sore rump back on the hard leather.

"Because you're going back to Taviz. You're going to tell him to forget what I said before. Tell him I want the Gamble Line hit so hard and so often they won't dare drive a stage out of Wishbone. Tell him to do it any way he wants, to do anything he wants."

Boyd shrugged. His worn saddle felt like it was full of splinters. "You sure?" He didn't need to ask. The malicious look in Adams's eyes reinforced every word. "All right," Boyd said and heaved out a wearied sigh. Thankfully Taviz had brought his cutthroat band closer to town. The ride would take a few hours but if he rode hard he could get there and back before midnight. "I'm goin'," he said. "But I gotta get a good meal before I ride out again and I need a fresh horse."

"See that you don't waste any time," Adams told

him. "And see me again before you leave." He inclined his head toward the Gamble Line office where the supply wagon sat. "I'm going to find out where that wagon's headed and who's going to be with it."

An hour after supper at Porter's station Teddy got around to asking Rhys why he had stopped the supply wagon to talk to Adams. They had walked out by the corral after Port shooed them out so he could get the supper dishes washed and, as Teddy well knew, so he could have his nightly sips from the demijohn of home-brew he kept locked in a cupboard.

"Is that the reason you have had so little to say to me since we left Wishbone," Rhys inquired.

Teddy climbed up on the top rail of the corral fence. The bright silver moon was lighting her face in a way that could lead a man to make foolish promises if he weren't careful. Rhys took a deep breath and swore to himself he'd be careful.

"That's half the reason," Teddy told him. "The other is that you can't seem to get it through your thick skull that I don't like being pawed and kissed and—"

"Made love to?" He smiled.

She frowned. "That's right. I've got no use for it."

He strode up close and rested his hands on the fence rail on either side of her. "What you've got is a bad memory," he said, his voice sliding down low, taking her heart along for the ride.

He stepped closer, brushing against the inside of her knees. She began to shake and knew he could feel it. He knew she was lying, that she wanted to slide into his arms, that if he pressed her she would slip away somewhere in the moonlight and welcome what she had decried.

She was angry at herself and at him and it was the anger that saved her. She quickly swung her long legs over the fence and dropped down behind it, braced against it and faced him with the rails between them. "I remember you never answered my question about Adams," she said.

"He offered me fifty thousand dollars for my shares," he said smoothly.

Teddy lost her breath. "What did you say?" The shares were worth it but she would have a hard time coming up with that much credit even when things settled down.

He propped his elbows on the fence rail and leaned in close. "That you could give me a better deal."

She had no clear idea when or how she could top Adams's offer but she boldly told him she would. Teddy was overwhelmed with gratitude and too choked up to speak for a moment. He could have sold her out, left Wishbone with fifty thousand dollars in his pocket instead of driving a supply wagon across the desert. "I can't tell you how much I appreciate the fact that you're willing to wait. I promise I'll make the wait worth your while."

"I'm counting on that," he replied. "You making it worth my while."

She started to smile then realized what he was hinting. She stared up at him. Her eyes were growing dark with anger, her temper flaring like a geyser. When he reached through the fence rails for her, a move she expected, she cursed him and ducked.

A shot whizzed in front of Rhys's face. *"Sacré bleu*—Teddy—"* He thought he'd finally pushed her too far but then another shot sounded and he realized it was rifle fire. He threw himself on the ground. Teddy was already there, pistol in hand, but both of them knew that handguns couldn't match the rifle's range. Their best chance of survival was getting behind cover.

Like a pair of snakes they slithered across the corral, beneath the nervous, stamping horses and toward the small shed where Port kept tack and feed.

Another shot splintered a fence post and sent the horses bolting to one end of the corral, exposing Rhys and Teddy to the moonlight and the rifleman. A fourth shot blasted the heel off Teddy's boot. She lunged into the shed. Rhys plowed in behind her.

"Son of a bitch!" she said, settling in a crouch and examining her ruined boot. "These were new!"

Thirty-three

From a craggy hilltop overlooking the change station, Rennie raised his rifle to his shoulder and aimed at the window of the shed. No return fire had come from the small building but several reports had rung out from the adobe building where the station master lived.

"I'll keep these two on their knees, Juan." He jumped aside as a shot raised sparks on the bare rock beside him. "You ease around and git that man with the rifle. He ain't a half-bad shot."

"*Sí.* I take care of that," Juan replied. Moving swiftly on his bowed legs he started down the back side of the hill and, keeping to cover, worked his way toward the house.

Alternating the direction of his aim, Rennie pumped shots into the shed and the window of the adobe building, protecting Juan until the short Mexican assassin had made his way to the door of the house. Brandishing a pistol in each hand Juan blasted off the lock, kicked in the door and fired four shots into Porter Landau.

Taking a protected position behind the adobe walls Juan then aimed his pistols at the shed and peppered it with shots at window level. Rennie's rifle shots quickly joined the heavy barrage. Wood chips and harness showered down on Teddy and Rhys, who could only fire back blindly through the walls. Rhys could tell the rifle shots were getting closer, indicating the first gunman was moving down the hill to join his compatriot.

While Teddy kept returning fire, Rhys hurriedly reloaded his empty revolver, filling the chambers with his last round of ammunition. He fired judiciously as the gun battle continued. Taking his lead Teddy slowed down her firing too, but was soon down to her last round as well.

"Got any more bullets?" she mumbled between dodging flying slivers of wood and Rennie and Juan's rapid shots.

"Four," Rhys said. He heard one of the men running toward the shed and fired two more times in the direction the sound had come from.

Teddy emptied her gun. A few more shots tore into the building then silence came. The calm was worse than the gunfire because both knew it was temporary, a foreshadowing of worse things to come. Teddy felt her heart beating hard enough to shake the shed down around them. She heard Rhys's deep breaths reverberating in the small, dark space. "This is one hell of a way to die," she said angrily. "Caught like two rats in a box."

"We are not going to die," Rhys told her. "I—"

The door flew in before he could tell her why not. Rhys saw a man dart away from the door's wreckage. He fired through the wall to his right and heard a scream of fury and pain. "I am hit! Rennie!" Juan yelled.

Rhys listened for an answering voice but Rennie replied with another barrage from the rifle, this time blasting a plate-sized hole in the back of the shed only inches above Rhys's and Teddy's heads. Rhys threw himself over Teddy but held his last shot for a sure target. He got it an instant later when Rennie fired through the window. Rhys fired back, but Rennie's last shot had winged his arm and the bullet he had saved for the rifle-wielding killer went astray.

Shouting at Teddy to stay down, Rhys scrambled to his feet, prepared to make a last defense, but Rennie had already marched into the shed. The rangy gunman never slowed until he was over them. He swung the stock of his rifle up, striking Rhys in midleap, squarely beneath the chin. As Rhys fell Rennie swung down and clubbed him on the back of the head.

"Jeeze!" Teddy, caught beneath Rhys, landed a furious kick on Rennie's shin earning herself an ear-ringing thump on the head with the rifle stock. Stunned, she fell back in all the dirt and litter.

"Kill them!" Juan dragged himself to the door and shouted at Rennie. "Or I shoot him myself." A bloodstained hand covered the wound in his side. A gun dangled loosely in the other hand.

Rennie cursed and took the weapon from Juan. "No, my friend," he said. "Taviz wants these two alive for a time and neither of us wants to make Taviz mad."

None too gently, Rennie caught the dazed Teddy by the collar and dragged her out while Juan, cursing and complaining, shuffled off to get the horses they had left up in the hills. Before Teddy came to enough to put up a fight, Rennie bound her hands and feet and loaded her on one of the horses from the corral. Rhys got the same treatment and no consideration given for his wound. Though he was not conscious, blood ebbed freely from the bullet hole in his biceps as he was bound and thrown over a horse.

Rhys had not regained consciousness when, an hour or so later, he and Teddy were hauled into Taviz's secluded camp. Teddy had come to long before and had put up such a fuss that Rennie had stopped and put a gag in her mouth.

"Where is Taviz?" Juan demanded of the ebony-haired woman who sat alone on a blanket by the campfire. His side hurt and he wanted to see those responsible for his wound get some of Taviz's hospitality.

"Taviz ride into town," the pretty, young Mexican woman replied. Taviz had sent one of the men back to the main camp for her when he got tired of sleeping alone. "He want more whiskey," she said, rising and swinging her hips as she walked over to the riders. All of them knew Adams had ordered the bandidos to stay clear of Wishbone. Juan reminded the woman of this. She tossed back her head. "He don't care who tell him to stay in the hills when he want whiskey," she said.

Juan climbed off his horse and dropped down on the blanket where the woman had been, demanding that she take care of his wound.

"And get us something to eat," Rennie added.

The woman made no immediate move to do either,

having gotten curious about the prisoners. Easing around the horses she looked at Rhys first, catching his black locks in her fist and raising his head, smiling prettily when she saw his handsome face. "This one we keep," she said. "This one we send back." She roughly poked Teddy's leg. "We don't want her."

"Taviz wants her," Juan returned, biting his lip as he pulled the blood-soaked bandage from his side and began searching the woman's belongings for something to replace them with.

"Taviz got me!" The Mexican woman thumped her chest with her fist then hurried back to the blanket and snatched her possessions away from Juan. Among them she found an old scarf and reluctantly gave it to the wounded man. Almost immediately she began tearing a long, homespun skirt into strips. Juan reached for them but, frowning at him, she jerked them away. "These are for him," she said, nodding toward Rhys.

Juan was satisfied after a good look with the aid of the firelight that his wound was not life-threatening, and that the bleeding had at last been stanched. He stretched out to sleep. Rennie dragged Rhys off the horse and pulled him into a shallow cave with a mouth so narrow he had to bend the man double to get him through the door. Teddy, hindered by her bonds, was forced to crawl into the cave. Rennie, who had come out after taking Rhys inside, squeezed in behind her carrying a brightly flaming torch lit from the campfire. He planted the torch in the soft earth of the cave's floor and stood over Teddy, with his legs braced wide apart.

Teddy's eyes blazed at him, relaying all the fury and

hatred she could not shout out with the gag in her mouth.

"I can tell you'd like some live company in here, little spitfire." He knelt down and ran his hand down her shoulder, across her heaving breasts, down her long, buckskin-clad legs, feeling, squeezing until he reached the ropes at her ankles. "But we got a rule that Taviz gets a woman first and I got better sense than to break it." He drew a knife out of his boot, tested the point of it on a callused finger and smiled. "I want you to know I'm looking forward to my turn. Ain't you?"

Teddy squirmed fitfully and mumbled into the gag, then stiffened and got stone still when Rennie walked off and pointed the gleaming knife at Rhys. Her heart started beating again when he cut the bindings on Rhys's hands and feet. A minute later he did the same for Teddy giving her a warning, as the knife sliced through the rope, that anyone who came out of the cave before daylight would be shot. When he was done, Teddy snatched the gag from her mouth, then moaned aloud as blood began to flow freely but painfully into her swollen hands and feet.

Without complaint Rennie let Taviz's woman take the prisoners water and bind Rhys's arm, but when she was done he again demanded food.

Several hours later, long after Teddy had ventured near the mouth of the cave to confirm that Rennie waited there ready to shoot, Rhys regained consciousness. He came to, slowly. His head and jaw were throbbing. His first sight was of Teddy, sad-eyed as a little girl who had lost her favorite doll. She was sitting over him, bathing the lumps on his head with a wrung-out cloth. "It's about time," she whispered when she saw his heavy lids open. "I thought you were going to die on me."

"Not while you owe me," Rhys said hoarsely.

"Ha!" she said. "The way I see it you owe me, for getting us into this." As she spoke she shimmied over closer to him so she could be sure of not being heard by Rennie.

"How did I—" He tried to sit up, but quickly got reminded that he would have to move slowly and favor his left arm.

"You'd try to seduce a duck, I reckon," she said disgustedly. "Anyhow if you hadn't been sweet-talking and turning those blue eyes on me out there by the corral I might have been alert to somebody watching."

Rhys smiled in the darkness, the only thing he could do that didn't hurt. "So you admit you feel something for me?"

She plopped the cold, wet cloth on top of his head. "I feel like killing you myself, for the hundredth time," she ground out. "You got any idea how we're going to get away from here before that Taviz fellow gets back and slits both our throats?"

Rhys caught her hand. "You liked making love to me, too, didn't you Teddy?"

"For all the difference it makes now," she said dispassionately. "It wasn't too bad."

"It was perfect and you know it."

"All right!" She blurted out the words then clamped her hand over her mouth and dropped her voice to a raspy whisper. "It was perfect. Now can you stop crowing like a rooster let loose in the hen yard and help me think of how we can get away."

"I knew it was perfect."

He put his arm around her and caressed her face with his fingers. She was cold and trembling.

"I'm scared," she admitted.

He pulled her close, laid her head against his shoulder, completely forgetting the burning pain in his arm. Her hair had come loose from the braid and spilled over his face and hands. The delectable scent of it, flowers and sunshine, her scent, filled him and made his heart thunder wildly. He kissed her face, then caught the fullness of her lips beneath his and kissed her deeply, passionately, savoring her, drawing strength from her as if he feasted on manna.

"We have long lives to live, Teddy," he whispered. "We'll get away."

Taviz found them locked together and sleeping early the next morning. He pushed them apart with his boot and ordered Teddy up while he rested the barrel of his rifle against Rhys's throat. Half of Rhys's shirt was blood-soaked and judging by the look of his face there was more blood on the shirt than was left inside him. His eyes had rolled back and he moaned weakly, frightening Teddy who feared his wound had started bleeding again in the night.

Taviz cautiously judged him hurt badly enough not to be a serious threat. "You move, I shoot your hands off," he said brusquely. "Then you have to write with your toes, ehhh. Me, I don't care, but Adams he might be disappointed if you can't sign your name to the papers he's got for you?"

"I knew that bastard was behind all this!" Teddy shouted. Scowling like one of hell's furies she was backed against the cave wall where Taviz had shoved her. She was defiant to the last, and stood proudly, hands on her hips, feet apart, head thrown back. "You can tell that sidewinder he won't get me to sign anything."

Taviz turned, getting his first good look at Teddy as the sun crested the nearby hills and flooded into the cave. He was used to dark-haired, dark-eyed women. With her honey-colored tresses and flashing green eyes, she was a tempting change. His gaze slid lewdly over every inch of her. He liked all that he saw, though to his mind he didn't see nearly enough of her.

Taking his gun off Rhys, Taviz stepped closer to Teddy, grabbed a handful of her hair, slid his dirty fingers through it, then gave it a hard tug that jerked her head to one side. "He don't want you to sign nothing," the bandido informed her. "He gives you to me."

Teddy understood at once that Adams intended to force Rhys to hand over his shares. Once he had those he didn't care who owned the others. He'd have enough say in the company to merge the Gamble Line with Adams Overland or see that it went bust. She was expendable already. Rhys would be too, as soon as Adams got his shares.

For a few seconds Teddy forgot the predicament she was in and was overcome by a flurry of murderous thoughts involving Parrish Adams. He'd hated her father for turning down his original offer. Now he was playing out that hatred on her. Well, damn his black soul! He wouldn't get away with it! She swore out loud, though she wasn't aware she was shouting out her defiance until Taviz told her to shut up.

She came to her senses when she saw the barrel of his rifle turn toward her and slowly drop down. All three of them followed the path of it with their eyes. Teddy trembled in astonishment and fear as the cold metal slid between her spread legs, sidled up the inside of one thigh and bumped to a stop against her pubic bone. Taviz licked his thick lips. "You talk too much but I think I like what I got, ehhh?"

Teddy shoved the rifle barrel away and, challenging Taviz with a scathing look, squared her shoulders. "You get nothing!"

Taviz threw his head back and laughed loud enough to start a rock slide. "She's gutsy, this one. I ain't had a gutsy woman in a long while." Licentiously eying her, touching her from head to toe in his mind, Taviz ran his tongue over his lips and imagined what it would be like to have the gutsy, honey-haired woman beneath him squirming and shouting and fighting him. He did not want to wait long to find out. He made a cautious glance over his shoulder at the helpless Frenchman, daring the moaning man to move if he wanted to live any longer. Taviz laughed as Teddy cursed him. He shifted the rifle beneath his left arm, locked his finger on the trigger and reached for the tempting woman with his freed right hand. He caught her by the collar, ripped her shirt open with one swift pull and plunged his dirty fingers deep inside.

"Soft," he said, smacking his wet lips.

Teddy rallied from the shock of being mauled and roughly batted his hand away. "Get your grubby claws off me, you bastard!"

The Mexican liked a little fight in a woman, but not too much. He grabbed Teddy again, heaved her even harder against the stone wall and shoved his forearm against her throat. "You treat Taviz right," he growled. "Or I kill him."

"Adams wouldn't like that," Teddy retorted.

Taviz thrust his weight against her, brought his scarred face right up against hers. "Maybe I don't need Adams for nothing," he growled. "Maybe I rob stages for me. Ehh, what you think now?" He was no fool and made another glance back at the Frenchman, saw that the wounded man had not moved, then turned himself fully to Teddy. "I kill him, or you be good to Taviz?"

"I'll be good," Teddy whispered. "You leave him alone and I'll be good if that's what you want." Heaving in one hard breath after another she stood as still as she could while Taviz eagerly stripped the torn shirt off her. She did no more than cringe when his big rough hand sought her breast and pinched and squeezed. "Ehh. So this is what you hide in a man's clothes, Teddy Gamble," he said. "You been saving this for me, ehhh? Don't you worry, Taviz will teach you what to do with it. Taviz will teach you what a woman is for."

His filthy hands. His putrid breath. She was afraid she was going to blow up like a stick of dynamite. But she tried, tried hard to pretend it wasn't happening, that he wasn't going to rape her right there in the cave with Rhys watching and too weak to help. She tried, never doubting for an instant that he would kill Rhys if she resisted. She tried, but when his wet mouth followed where his hands had been she couldn't hold the bargain and shoved away from him.

Taviz, all roused and ready for her, cursed and grabbed for her again. Fortunately for Teddy, a night of drinking had slowed his reflexes. Laughing, no longer concerned about interference from Rhys, he chased her around the cave, grabbing for her, taunting her with what he would do when he caught her, missing twice as his hand slid across bare flesh.

Teddy kept moving, finding it easy to dodge. She felt a heady optimism that she could keep him distracted from Rhys and stay a step ahead of him all day if necessary. But she couldn't outrun the aim of his rifle and when he pointed it at her head and pulled the trigger halfway back, she obeyed his command to stop.

She called him a mangy, stinking dog. He laughed, called her his bitch, and made another clumsy lunge at her, tired of the chase and ready for the prize. This time he did not miss, his rock-hard arms locked around Teddy nearly cracking her ribs. His bristled face slid across her cheek and he carried her down to the cave floor.

Or so she thought until she saw that Rhys had somehow rallied and launched himself at the bandido's knees and knocked both of them off their feet. Teddy sailed down hard. Her head collided with the rock so heavily that she blacked out. Taviz crashed down on top of her.

Taviz's rifle slid across the cave, out of reach of both men. But Taviz was not the kind of man to rely on only one weapon. He pulled a long-bladed skinning knife from a sheath at the center of his back and, twisting off Teddy and around on the cave floor, swung it at Rhys. The blade sliced through Rhys's shirt but missed his flesh.

Rhys had to temper his attack to avoid the knife. Taviz took the instant of retreat to jump to his feet. Crouching, he swung again at Rhys, scarcely missing opening his opponent's lower belly. Rhys got to his feet, too, and, crouched like Taviz, dodged and reached, jumped and stretched, trying to get past the swinging blade to get a grip on the bandido.

Taviz was shouting for Rennie, but the subordinate who had sat up all night guarding the cave had slipped off to another small cave to make up for lost sleep. The woman had ridden off, unwilling to sit around and watch her man take another woman as Taviz had boasted he would do. Juan could give him no aid either. Pained by his wound, he had drunk himself into a stupor since Taviz returned to camp with a new supply of whiskey.

The duel continued for what seemed to Rhys endless hours. Taviz slashed and jabbed. Rhys danced and dashed out of his way, battling not only the bandido but also Rhys's own dwindling strength. He was weak. He was slowing and he knew that unless he got an advantage soon Taviz would cut him to pieces. Taviz seemed to know he was gaining the advantage and began savagely pressing Rhys, slashing on and on. One well-aimed jab slit the back of Rhys's hand. Another gave him a deeper cut across the chest. Soon Taviz had the weary, weakened Frenchman gasping for breath. But, as the deadly dance continued, the exertion was telling on Taviz, too. He wheezed for air and swung wild with the knife.

Teddy brought the fight to an end. Taviz swung around in a full circle, his sharp blade scored Rhys on the rib cage, causing him to cry out in agony. The quick turn, however, threw the slightly drunk Taviz lumbering back a step to catch his footing. He stumbled over Teddy's outstretched legs and went down. Rhys dove the six feet to the rifle, swung it up and fired just as Taviz regained his footing and threw the knife.

The blade missed. The bullet did not. A black hole pierced the forehead of the big bandido. He toppled to the cave floor. Rhys gasped a few deep breaths of air then grabbed Teddy and hauled her out of the cave. Taviz's saddle horse, a big bald-faced roan, stood a few feet away. With Teddy slung across the saddle, Rhys mounted behind her, kicked the animal into a gallop and thundered off.

Thirty-four

Pushing the horse unmercifully, Rhys rode until he was too weak to sit in the saddle. He had come upon a small, trickling stream by then. He brought Teddy's limp body down with him when he dismounted and, dragging her heels across the hard ground, carried her near the water. He bathed her face with cool water before he tended his wounds.

He was shirtless and splashing water on his myriad cuts and bruises when Teddy's eyes blinked open. She watched him quietly for a few moments until she could focus clearly. He was bleeding in several places but the sight of him out in the open, free, was the best thing she had ever seen.

"Jeeze! You look like a side of beef," she said.

He stopped splashing, turned and smiled at her. "I feel like I've had a couple of steaks sliced out. How is your head? Taviz gave you a big lump."

Teddy lifted a finger to her lips, shushing him. "Don't say that name," she insisted. "Just tell me where the bastard is and how far behind—"

"He's in hell, I suppose." Rhys waded through the gently rushing shallow water and dropped down on the bank beside her.

"You killed him?"

"Not soon enough. I am sorry you had to endure what he did to you."

"Me too," Teddy replied. At that moment she realized that she, like Rhys, was shirtless. She didn't try to cover herself. After what they had been through, being half naked was a minor concern. "I feel like I've been dragged through a cow lot," she said, smiling feebly. "Help me down in that water. I want to wash that bastard's touch off my skin."

Rhys picked her up, which wasn't such a good idea since he was as weak as she. Teetering on the slippery bank with Teddy in his arms he lost his footing and slid headlong into the water, carrying her with him. But this small stream had a soft shallow bottom and both landed easily, getting no more than a good dunking out of the fall. Teddy came above water sputtering and laughing. Rhys was anxious and apologetic.

"Truly I am sorry," he said. "I never—"

"Oh, forget it!" She dipped her head back and washed her long hair from her face and gave the lump on her head a good cooling. For ten minutes more she sat in the stream bed, scrubbing and splashing, eventually feeling satisfied that she had washed every trace of Taviz away.

Rhys waited on the bank. He'd had the foresight to bring along Taviz's rifle and he cradled it in his arms as he kept a watch in the event Rennie had found Taviz's body and decided to follow. When Teddy was ready to come out he laid the rifle aside and tossed her the fringed buckskin vest she'd used to pillow his head in the cave. It didn't cover much of her but it was more decent than nothing.

Teddy slipped her arms through the sleeves and started to come out of the water. Rhys offered her a helping hand but she quickly burst past him and ran into a clump of trees. He saw her bent over and heard her heaving.

"Teddy? Do you need help?"

"No!" she yelled back. Shortly she came staggering out of the copse of trees and flopped down limply beside Rhys. "The bastard made me sick," she said. "And damned if I don't feel too tuckered out to get on that horse again. And you need some bindings on those cuts. You reckon we'd be safe staying here a few hours?"

While he couldn't be sure, Rhys's intuition was that Rennie would head out in the opposite direction. "I'll watch over you," he said softly. His calm voice reassured Teddy that everything would be fine. "You find a place to rest."

At Adams's suggestion Len Blalock had obligingly taken a trip out of town so that when the stage came in and the driver announced Porter Landau was dead, out at the first station, there was no lawman to turn to.

Rope, forgetting he wasn't sound enough to ride, got together all the company men who were available to ride out and make a search for Teddy and Rhys since he had learned, too, that the supply wagon they were driving had been left partially loaded beside Port's house.

Rope was mounted and giving orders to the men, when he saw someone hurrying up the sidewalk toward him, moving as fast as his limping gait would allow.

"Bourget, isn't it?" Rope said to the man.

"Oui," Lucien drew close to the mounted man. His worried eyes scanned the crowd then came to rest on Rope. Lucien had spoken with the English newspaperman again that morning and the meeting had stirred his memory. He thought he knew where he had seen the distinctive red-haired man before. He anxiously wanted to alert Rhys that he was almost certain he had observed Derby Seward across the street from the Countess Clemenceau's house on the morning he had found Jenny Perrault lying outside the door. "I am looking for Monsieur Delmar," he said.

Rope slowly shook his head. "I'm lookin' for him, too. An' I think he's in bad trouble." Rope quickly explained what he feared had happened and asked Lucien if he wanted to join the posse.

Devastated that something might have happened to his friend and benefactor while he stood uselessly by, he sought a way to help. *"Monsieur,* I am the worst of riders," he said. "I would be a hindrance to you, but is there a way I can assist here?"

"Sure is." Rope pulled his hat low on his forehead readying for some hard riding. "Get a buckboard and get out to the Gamble ranch and tell Felicity what's happened. An' tell her not to worry none. We'll bring those two back."

Lucien assured Rope that he would do just that. Hurriedly, he limped off toward the livery stable as Rope and the small search party rode out of town. Shortly before Lucien reached the stable he had the misfortune to pass Derby Seward strolling out of a cafe with Ada Penrod on his arm. Seward tipped his hat and said good-day. Lucien's suspicion of Seward was growing more ominous by the moment. He looked askance and hastened past the couple without responding.

"How utterly rude," Ada Penrod commented loud enough for the retreating Lucien to hear.

"Think nothing of it, my dear." Seward, his whiskers red as a bonfire in the bright sun, patted Ada's thin arm. "There is a running feud between the French and the English." He laughed to mask his concern. But he knew with certainty that it had been fear and not rudeness that had sent Lucien Bourget hurrying past him. He suspected he knew the reason. With his coloring he was a man who stood out. Although he thought he had been hidden in a doorway when Delmar's valet found the Perrault woman, he could not be sure that Lucien Bourget had not gotten a glimpse of him.

Ada Penrod, chattering away about nothing, was briefly distracted by the display in the local millinery shop. Seward took the moment to cast a scurrilous glance after Lucien. He was determined to find out for certain why the lame Frenchman's demeanor toward him had so quickly changed.

* * *

Hours later, at his carefully selected table by the window at the Diamond, Seward enjoyed a drink and a round of affection from his favorite sporting woman. He saw Lucien, in a hired buckboard, being driven into town. The table he had chosen, afforded Seward not only an excellent spy post but also an opportune spot to eavesdrop on Parrish Adams. Gazing out over the Diamond's red doors, he conducted a hushed conversation with his attractive wife.

"I'm afraid you've lost your chance for another go at Delmar." The anger that had gripped Adams earlier burned in his eyes like deeply banked coals. "The man has run me to the end of my patience."

"As if you had any," Norine quipped.

Adams shrugged. Norine's wit was not her best feature. "Patience is a useless virtue," he said. "Results are what count. Remember that, Norine."

"I remember everything," she said. "What changed your mind about Delmar?"

"He refused fifty thousand. Said he made a deal with Teddy."

Norine's ruffled red skirt swished around her ankles as she drew closer to her husband. "She's got no money."

"Money isn't the only currency a man trades in. You ought to know that."

Her hands went stiffly to her flaring hips. "I'd sooner believe he doesn't care a fig for money than that he could prefer Teddy Gamble to me, not that bit of goods. I doubt the woman's ever had her legs around anything but a saddle."

Adams gave his wife a cynical smile. "She does know how to sit a horse."

Norine gave her carefully coiffed head a toss. "Maybe the Frenchman is one of those fellows who's up to his jowls in principles."

Adams spun around slowly. "It no longer matters whether he is or not."

He left her beside the red doors and went to his office. Norine stared out at the street for a few minutes then ambled over to the bar and had Harley pour her a drink.

Derby Seward sent the attentive saloon girl away and sat at his table digesting the bits and pieces of information he'd gathered. Adams had offered Delmar an impressive sum of money and the Frenchman had turned it down. Adams was angry about it. Seward smiled. Another man's anger could be useful.

And Delmar. A man not swayed by money. A fool. Maybe a principled fool. Not a man he could dicker with.

He thought of Lucien Bourget. A man trained to forget everything he sees. Was he starting to remember? He would be a dangerous man if he did.

Seward drained his whiskey glass dry. Maybe Knox would get double for his money.

The moon was red as blood and dark with images when Teddy awoke with a start. She hadn't expected darkness and she hadn't expected to see the crimson-stained moon. Felicity's devil moon. A moon that portends change for those caught gazing at it, and not always change for the better. Sometimes a death followed, sometimes a windfall, always change. Teddy shivered but couldn't take her eyes off the glowing red moon.

"I saw it like that once before," Rhys said. He put an arm beneath his head and stared at the heavens. "The night before I arrived in Wishbone. It was entrancing, red earth, red moon. I felt I was entering another world where things would—"

"Never be the same," Teddy supplied. "You were right." She looked at the moon again. The dark images seemed to change shape before her eyes. Change was coming. Again. But good or bad?

"I meant to stay awake," he told her. "To watch over you."

"You needed rest. You're hurt." She had rinsed his torn shirt and ripped it into strips before they left the stream bank. As best she could, she had bound it around him where Taviz's knife had struck. The blade had not gone deep but even when the cuts healed, Rhys would have scars to remind him of the contest.

"Not so much," came huskily from him. He caught one of her hands, softly kissed the back of it and brought it to rest on his chest. It was good having her there beside him. She was wild and beautiful as the moon overhead. Like no other.

"You sure?"

She rolled to her side, bringing her body in line with his. The laces holding her fringed buckskin vest together had pulled loose as she slept and the smallish garment covered even less of her than it was designed to do. Rhys felt his rage rising anew when he saw the dark bruises Taviz's assault had left on her flesh.

He stretched out a hand and let his fingers graze over a blue mark just below her collarbone, making a soft, feather stroke on her skin. "He hurt you." His voice was low and hoarse.

"Not so much," she said, savoring the soft, tender stroke of his hand. The warmth of it brought a shiver of excitement to her. He'd saved her life. He'd nearly been killed doing it, and all he was concerned about was the angry marks Taviz had put on her. Smiling, feeling her heart melt a little, she clasped her hand over his and brought it to her breast.

He felt her tremble slightly as his hand covered one soft, velvety mound. He forgot that he was wounded and that it had been a terrible day. The best that he was good for was lying on his back and looking at the moon, his need for her surged, rising like a fierce wind, churning through him, stirring his blood.

She touched him, bringing her hand down the center of his chest, down low. His response was instant. "Teddy, don't do that unless . . ." His voice trailed off. She bent over him and her hair tumbled down on his chest, a billowing veil of silk that teased and caressed his skin. Her mouth came down on his, sweet as a berry, the taste of her intoxicating as the strange light of the vermilion moon.

He took her in his arms, buried his face in her hair, found the soft curve of her shoulder and kissed her there. Teddy moaned softly, inflamed, needing him, this time not to prove she was alive but for the simplest of reasons. They were man and woman, and fate had deemed them together at this moment. What would come later did not matter. Nothing mattered but to be held and caressed, to feel the power of him inside her. Nothing mattered more than that.

Her hands were upon him like the moonlight, skimming over him in tender, soft strokes so provocative he forgot the danger that might be a mere step away. He thought only of the enchantment of her body, the burning sweetness of her closing around him. He would die for that if he must. Willingly.

In a moment he thought he had. The world ceased to be around them. The moonlight was their universe, a place with no time, no restraints. He cried out his need for her as he unlaced her buckskin vest and slid it from her arms. He saw the beautiful curves of her body, the way her skin glistened in the moonlight. He held her tightly and then he was above her, bending to her.

His tongue flitted lightly over her tight rosy nipples making her shudder and dig her nails into his shoulders and arch her body to him urging his tantalizing mouth to seek more, more.

She felt his hands at her waist easing her pants from her hips. She helped him shed his garments too and when they were naked they lay together a moment, gilded red-gold by the moon, curious, elated, each by the other. But the calm could not last. In a flash a storm surge brought them together. Teddy beneath him, dazed by her need of him, gripped her hands on his back—her words offering a soft entreaty for him to come to her.

"Please, I need you. I do," she whispered.

"I know," he said. His hands brushed her flesh. His touch was soft as a cloud yet titillating as fire. Tenderly he stroked where the bruises marred her skin, urgently he stroked her thighs seeking the core of her, the heart of her, catching her soft desperate cries with his lips when his fingers plunged deep within.

His kisses followed, spark and flame on her skin, leaving no part of her untouched by his mouth, uncaressed by the licking flame of his tongue. She felt herself consumed by him, burned and renewed, a phoenix rising out of ash, more passion than person in her new form, a strange erotic creature who craved his touch, his kisses, all that he gave.

She closed her eyes, shuddering in what was both aftermath and foretaste of ecstasy, opening to him as a flower unfurls to the sun, welcoming his heat, taking him deep inside her, relishing his groan of pleasure, his violent, savage thrusts. She met him with equal fury, arching her hips to his, clinging, climbing until they reached the crest, the gate of paradise, and began the spiraling, shuddering fall within.

Afterward, with her arms about him, she felt his taut muscles relax. She wondered at the paradox of what was between them. He was her enemy, her lover. She wanted him with deep abandon yet feared every yielding to him. Every coming together brought her perilously closer to the brink of finding her world crumbled to dust. He had adapted with amazing ease to the rough desert life she loved and yet he had retained the elegance, the sophistication she had thought made him ill-fitted to the task. She knew him so well and yet so little. *Marc André Rhys Delmar.*

Dreamily, she stared into his eyes, calm now as a balmy, waveless sea. Then she lifted her gaze to the red-gold moon, the devil moon, and wondered again what change it would bring.

Thirty-five

"We buried Port back of the station."

Rope, Teddy, Rhys and the search party sat gathered around a small fire, heating beans and coffee for a meal. They had met on the trail before noon. Rhys and Teddy had taken to the rocks at the first sound of hoofbeats, fearing Rennie had defied their expectations and followed after all. The tension and dread had flown away like a soaring eagle when they recognized familiar, friendly faces.

"Adams is responsible," Teddy said. "Those bastards admitted they were taking orders from him." She wore Rope's striped cotton shirt. The big loose garment hung well over her hips and she'd needed to make thick rolls on the sleeves to uncover her hands, but it was decent cover and made it possible for her to sit and eat with the men.

"Then we have to press on 'til we find them," Rope said grimly. "Let one of them see a noose swing over his head and he'll tell whoever'll listen that Adams is behind all these holdups and murders."

"I'll go too," Teddy said, and got a chorus of *no* from the entire party, Rhys's voice sounding out the loudest objection of all.

"Take care how you come up on that Rennie," Rhys warned. He put his tin plate aside and cradled a scarred coffee cup in both hands. "He's a sure marksman and he could pick off most of you with the rifle should he see you coming."

"We'll chase him to hell," one of the men spoke out. He'd been a messenger since Teddy's father had started the line. He'd also been a close friend of Port's and took the station manager's death as personally as anyone.

"We left a man at Port's," Rope said, absently stirring a stick in the fire's embers. "He's well armed and he'll stay and run the station as long as he's needed. 'Course all of us bein' out here means we had to pull the extra guards off the runs."

Rhys spoke up again. "I think Rennie is—as you say here—high-tailing. He has a wounded man with him. We can hope, at least, he will not consider holding up a stage soon."

Rope nodded his agreement. "You and Teddy get on into town and see what you can do about Adams. He ain't gonna be expectin' you and seein' you two ride in just might shake a showdown out of him. Mind you it ain't one with any shootin'. He's still got hired guns around him and we got no law on our side until we can get word to Cabe and get help from Wells Fargo."

Teddy reluctantly agreed not to get into any gunplay with Adams. Rhys agreed to the same and, privately to Rope, to keep Teddy from losing her head when she saw the man.

"I don't want to lose any more men," Teddy said

as they cleared the camp and mounted up. "You fellows come back with your boots in the stirrups."

The men galloped off. Rope hung back a moment longer. "Almost forgot," he said, holding his horse steady. "That pal of yours, Bourget, was lookin' for you when we rode out. Acted like he had a bug in his britches about somethin'."

A mile outside of town Rhys and Teddy parted ways. Teddy, on one of the spare horses the search party had brought along, went riding on to the Gamble ranch to let Felicity know she had come to no permanent harm. Rhys rode the "borrowed" roan into Wishbone, knowing he looked a sorry sight with his shredded shirt wrapped around him as a bandage over the worst of the cuts he'd suffered in the fight with Taviz.

His appearance raised a lot of curious stares and several queries about what happened. Rhys told them he was trying to figure that out himself and rode on to Mae's boarding house. If Adams wasn't watching the street he would soon have word that Rhys Delmar, very much alive, had ridden in.

He ought to be thinking more about Adams. He'd misjudged the man. He'd dismissed Teddy's accusation as hot-headed and unfounded. But Teddy consumed his thoughts. He ought to have said something to her after making love. He ought to have told her who he was and why he was there and why she had no business giving herself to a man who was accused of murder, a man who had sworn he would bed her to take her down a notch. It wasn't much consolation to his conscience that now he was the one humbled, taken down a notch. He had to tell her the truth about him. Soon.

"Land sakes! Rhys Delmar! What got after you?" Mae came running from the boarding house. Justine Blalock stood on the porch, twisting her apron in her hands. Her eyes were wide and frightened.

Rhys threw his leg over the roan's haunches and dismounted. "Teddy and I were ambushed out at the first station," he explained. "And we were taken prisoner by the bushwhackers."

"What happened to Teddy?" Mae's voice had a hollow sound. Like most of Wishbone she'd been swayed by Parrish Adams's magnanimous contributions to the town. And, like most, she'd thought Teddy's refusal to sell out to him had been stubborn and foolish, and a detriment to progress.

"Teddy's at the ranch," Rhys told Mae as she led him to her kitchen and began tearing away his makeshift bandages. He recounted most of what had happened but was careful not to mention Adams. "She's fine now," he added.

After hearing what Rhys and Teddy had endured, Mae's sympathy began to swing in the opposite direction. "Where's your pa, Justine?" she demanded. "It's his job to raise a posse and search out these bushwhackers. Where is he?"

"I don't know." Justine's head hung down. There had been a time when her father would have been the first one outraged over any crime. But now he hid in the face of trouble, and he never acted on anything without first paying a visit to the Diamond Saloon.

He wasn't the same man she had loved and been proud of and she was afraid she knew why.

Patched up, cleaned up, Rhys went by the Gamble office to confirm that the runs, if off schedule by a few hours, were getting through. Afterwards he walked over to the Brass Bell, making a point to stroll boldly down the sidewalk past the Diamond, tipping his hat and saying a how-do-you-do to everyone he met.

In the Brass Bell's busy, smoke-clouded bar he was surprised to find Lucien's faro game closed for the night. At the bar he asked for his friend and was told Lucien had been under the weather and was presently upstairs resting.

Had he not anticipated being watched he might have noticed that one man's curiosity was especially great, that of a red-haired, bushy-bearded man who peered from behind a newspaper.

Derby Seward waited until Rhys had climbed the steps then discreetly followed, stepping lightly on the treads so that he would not be heard. Seward had experienced no luck finding Bourget again since the chance meeting on the sidewalk, an outcome he did not take as a good sign. There had been that glint of remembrance in the valet's eyes and it was highly possible that the man was not ill but was staying out of sight to avoid him. He had not worried so much over that while Delmar was out of town. But now the man was back, and, Seward was sure, on his way to talk to Bourget.

Stepping softly on the carpeted floor as he turned into a hallway, Seward saw Rhys at the far end of the dark hall knocking on a door. To avoid being seen, the Englishman hastily backed into an alcove and accidentally thudded his shoe heel softly against the wooden panels of a door within the alcove. He had not thought the sound could be heard by any ears but his, but momentarily the knob turned and the door slowly opened. Lucien Bourget stood within, a look of fear frozen on his face.

Lucien came out of his shock slowly, too slowly to block Seward's entry into the room, too slowly to shove the Englishman out before he had pulled the door to behind him. "You know me," came Seward's soft, menacing voice. "I see it in your eyes. You remember."

"No! I—" Lucien stumbled back, hampered by his lameness and his fear. He did remember, now as clearly as if he were reliving the instant he'd opened the door, seen Jenny slumped at his feet, the red-haired man across the street, a handkerchief in his hand. The man had been cleaning something with the handkerchief.

The stiletto blade slid between Lucien's ribs piercing his heart. When Seward was sure the deadly knife had done its work he released the ebony hilt. Lucien did not live long enough to gasp before he sagged to the floor.

Seward smiled. The killing had been clean and quiet. He felt a sense of power, a heightening of all his senses. He was, as ever, at his best when the risk was highest. And even as he drove the blade into Lucien, he had planned his alibi. Without delay he stepped over Lucien and hurried into the adjoining room to seek his escape. He had the devil's luck that day. The room was a corner one and the door opened into a different hallway. He saw a back stair across the way and eased out, silent as a shadow, in time to hear Rhys Delmar at the door he had entered, calling for Bourget.

"Lucien! Luce!" Rhys had mistaken the room and, after convincing the disappointed female occupant that he was not there for her services, had asked where he might find his friend.

The door wasn't shut completely. Rhys pushed it open a few inches and called for Lucien again, then saw there was no need.

"Sheriff'll be back tomorrow. Maybe." Pavy Tucker, Len Blalock's deputy, sat in with the prisoners whenever duty called the sheriff away. He wasn't qualified or willing to find a killer. He hastily pointed out that with a steady stream of customers up and down the stairs and everyone minding their own business, anyone could have come and gone without raising suspicion.

Rhys was the only one out of the ordinary that any of the girls could remember.

"I'll see he gets a fine burying." Carmen Bell wept into her lace hankie. "He was good to me. Always a gentleman. Treated me like I was a queen. I'm going to miss him." She sobbed then, looked up at Rhys with red-rimmed eyes. "He'd been wanting to see you bad," she said. "Wanted to tell you something." Her sobs grew louder and she began to shake so violently that one of the girls who worked for her led her away to bed. But she called back over her shoulder to Rhys as she left the room. "I think he would want you to have his things."

Rhys told her he would come back for Lucien's valise when she'd had time to pack it. Downstairs, shaken, he stopped for a whiskey but ended up getting a bottle to take to Mae's. Teddy wouldn't be in town before morning. He was going to drink until then, drink and think about Lucien.

Mae was out at a ladies' social and for once he got into his room without giving her an accounting of himself. He let his clothes fall where they dropped and climbed into bed, the bottle in his hand. He did not bother with a glass.

Lucien would have been scandalized. Poor Lucien. He'd gotten Lucien killed. Never should have brought him to Arizona, kept pounding in Rhys's brain. He kept trying to wash the thought away with another drink from the bottle. Gentle, loyal Lucien was dead. Like Jenny. A blade in the heart. Like Jenny.

Unsteadily Rhys placed the half-empty bottle on the stand by the bed. As he slid down on the pillows and into an unconsciousness brought on by fatigue and the quantity of whiskey he'd consumed, he wondered what Lucien had wanted to tell him. Maybe Carmen Bell would have the answer to that. Tomorrow.

* * *

Felicity had rubbed Teddy with a pleasantly scented liniment, fed her an enormous supper and sent her to bed. Teddy lay atop a stack of pillows and looked out the open window at the night sky. The moon had turned a shimmering silver, round and full as a gourd. It hung in a sky of midnight blue, a beautiful, tranquil sky. Not at all the way Teddy was.

She'd been so busy lately. She'd had so many fires to put out she hadn't had time to think of the days and weeks that had passed since Rhys had saved her from the floodwaters. They had made love on the hillside above the raging waters. But she knew the moon had been full at least once since then. And now it was full again.

Her hands slid tentatively down over her abdomen and, as she feared, found it gently rounded between her hipbones where it had once been flat as a frying pan. She'd been around enough stock animals to know the other signs were there, too. She was pregnant, carrying Rhys Delmar's child. As if she didn't have enough problems.

"Dammit. Damn everything," she mumbled into the quiet of her room. She didn't have a maternal bone in her body. Didn't have time for a baby. She'd look ridiculous carrying one. A belly out over her boots. Teats like a milk cow's.

It wasn't fair. Nothing was. Teddy plopped a pillow over her face and smothered an anguished groan. She should have followed her instinct and shot Rhys Delmar the first time he kissed her. That would have been easier to handle than this.

Her hand slid over her belly again and rested there.

A baby. She wondered if she ought to tell him. Why the devil should she? Scowling, she pitched a pillow across the room, saw it hit the wall and split and fill the room with floating goose feathers. Hell no. Why should she? He'd had his fun. Damned fancy Frenchman.

Bemoaning her fate, she rolled over. Well, he was a good-looking son of a bitch. Briefly she remembered how she had felt in his arms, the feverish way they had come together, the hardness of him, the sleekness of his back beneath her hands, the softness of his words in her ear. It had been beautiful. It had been right. And they would have a beautiful baby.

Thirty-six

Derby Seward did not count his drinks that night after he murdered Lucien Bourget. But as he waited in the Diamond for Parrish Adams to find the time to see him, he perfected his plan to fulfill his commission for Avery Knox.

When Adams sent for him he knew exactly how it would all play out. "Sir," he said. "I have a proposition for you."

Five narrow shadows interspersed with bright sunlight fell across Rhys's face and brought him to. His head quaked when he opened his eyes. He thought maybe he was in the midst of a nightmare. He wasn't in Mae's feather bed, wasn't in his room at her boarding house. He was looking at bare adobe walls and bars. Iron bars. He sat up fast. He was in Len Blalock's jail.

"He's the same man." The sheriff's face was haggard and his shoulders were weary from a long night of riding. He sat at his desk. Parrish Adams had sent for him and demanded he be in Wishbone before sunup. And here he was. Across his desk sat a red-haired man wearing a tweed suit and holding a bundle of newspaper clippings in his large hands.

"Don't know why I held on to these," Derby Seward said, spreading out an article from London papers which showed a likeness of Rhys and told of the crime he was accused of committing there. "Took an interest in the case though. My profession, you know. Thought I recognized him when I saw him at the Brass Bell last night. Happened to go up the stairs a few minutes after he did. Saw him push his way into the room where that fellow was killed. You have my statement and if it's necessary I'll stay until the trial. Provided it's not long in coming."

"That's good of you, Mr. Seward," Len Blalock said. "Should be a short trial. It's gettin' the territorial judge in that's gonna take some time. We'll try to schedule an early date if the judge is willin'. Otherwise it's gonna be better than a month before his case comes up on the docket."

Seward pushed for the early trial. Sheriff Blalock had assured him there was no chance of Delmar being turned over to London authorities before he was dealt with in Wishbone. Seward wanted Rhys Delmar hung before he left. When the man was dead he could take copies of the *Wishbone Gazette* back to Knox and show him the pictures and story. Then Knox would have his fortune and Seward would have his share. This was better than killing Delmar with his own hand, and safer. Delmar, he'd learned, was a fine shot and the sort of man who watched his back and would put up a fight at the first hint of danger. Seward might not be lucky in a contest with the Frenchman. And should Seward succeed in outwitting the man in a deadly contest, there was ever the chance Seward himself might come under suspicion should he kill a second man in Wishbone.

Getting the sheriff's word that he would write to the judge, Seward looked back at the holding area where a bewildered Rhys sat on a wooden bunk rubbing his pounding head and trying hard to understand what he was hearing. "I say, the chap's come to," Seward said.

Teddy wasn't long in learning what had happened to Rhys, not with every tongue in Wishbone wagging about the murder of Lucien Bourget and the news that his killer had also stabbed to death a woman in London.

She didn't know what made her madder, that Rhys was locked up or that Len Blalock threatened to put her in the cage with him if she didn't stop making accusations about Parrish Adams.

"I've had about enough of your sass, Teddy," the sheriff warned. "Unless you've got proof, hard proof that Adams had anything to do with what you say happened—"

"What I say?" Contempt flared in Teddy's eyes. "Porter Landau is dead."

"I'm sorry about that but—"

"But not sorry enough to lock up the man who's behind his death."

Blalock stood firm. "Not unless you have proof."

Teddy pointed stiffly at Rhys in the jail cell. "He

was there. He heard that bandido say Adams hired them."

The sheriff sat up straighter and ran his fingers through his hair. "His word don't count for much."

"I don't believe he killed anybody," Teddy said.

Rhys came to his feet. The sheriff had not allowed Teddy to come back to the cell and speak to him. So he had not been sure just what her opinion of him was. He'd pleaded his innocence and demanded to be released until his throat ached from the shouting. Finally he'd resigned himself to waiting for a trial and to trusting there was someone who believed he had not killed Lucien. Or Jenny.

Hearing Teddy say she believed him innocent gave him his first hope that he might get out of the situation he was in. He couldn't quite champion a smile, but he tried to relay his appreciation with a look. He got Teddy's scowl in return just as Len Blalock was telling her she ought to leave because he had work to do.

"I'll be back," she threatened, "when Rope and the boys bring those bandidos in. Then we'll see what kind of song you sing."

With Rhys shouting to her and the sheriff nudging her out the door, Teddy reluctantly left the office.

The following morning Mae Sprayberry came by. Mae sometimes supplied the prisoners with their meals and did not meet the same resistance from Len Blalock that Teddy had received. With her calico-covered basket over her arm she was allowed access to Rhys's cell. She had brought biscuits and honey and ham, enough to keep him fed for a day. She had also brought a change of clothes from the garments he'd left in his rented room at her house. Because of his wounds Mae took pity on Rhys and insisted on entering the cell to change his bandages.

None too pleased that the man who had put a twinkle in her eye and set Justine's heart aflutter had gotten himself in so serious a scrape, she offered him a cool greeting and ordered him to take off his shirt. Not a woman to hold her tongue for long, though, Mae embarked on severely scolding Rhys for his rather serious shortcomings. In the meanwhile she peeled away the bindings he wore on his abdomen and arm and replaced the strips with fresh layers of cloth. "Don't know what the world is coming to when a woman winds up sheltering a murderer in her house," she said.

Mae reminded him a little of Jenny and he was saddened to have broken her trust though it was through no fault of his own. "Lucien was my friend," he said softly. "I didn't kill him."

Mae paused at the task of knotting a bandage that crisscrossed his flat, firm belly. "What about that woman in London?"

"I was falsely accused—just as I am here."

"Hmmm." Mae tugged the ends of the bandage together. She gave a satisfied look to her work and handed Rhys a clean shirt. "Justine's been too upset to leave her room," she said. Her voice was a note softer than it had been before. "You know the girl's sweet on you."

"No," he said, slipping his arms into the sleeves of his shirt. "I never—"

"I know you never did anything to encourage her," Mae acknowledged as she reached in the basket she had brought and doled out more clean bandages and a bottle of ointment for him to use later. "But it's hard on her, especially since it's her father who has you locked up."

Rhys looked uneasily at Mae. The last thing he needed was having Len Blalock even less kindly disposed toward him because he suspected Rhys had misled his daughter. "Please tell Justine I am grateful for her concern," he pleaded. "And tell her—I hope she will find someone who makes her very happy."

Three interminable days passed after Mae's visit. Teddy was turned away at the jail door every time she tried to come in, mainly because she was in a temper and making threats when she came by. On the fifth day that Rhys was in jail, Rope and the search party rode back into Wishbone, empty-handed.

The men, clothes thick with dust, horses worn out, scattered as they rode in. Only Rope headed his horse to the Gamble office where Teddy waited. He was shaking his head when she came flying out hoping against hope he had found Rennie and Juan. He slid off the horse slowly, and handed the reins to one of the stableboys who had come running at first sight of him. Then he went inside the office with Teddy.

"We found Taviz in the cave where you said he would be," Rope explained. "But the others were gone. Must have left right after you and Rhys did and headed north as best we could tell. We tried trackin' them but lost their track in the rocks a day after we set out. Never could pick up the trail again and finally figured we weren't doin' any good out there ridin' in circles." He pushed his hat back off his forehead. The deep creases in his face were filled with dust. "What's happenin' here? You holdin' your own against Adams?"

She felt her throat constrict. "Losing ground," she said. "Oh, the runs are back on schedule and I've sent word to Cabe but I doubt it's of any use. Nobody's willing to take my word the bandidos worked for Adams."

Rope cocked a brow. "What about Rhys's word? He heard them outlaws name Adams, too."

"He's locked up." Teddy's voice cracked but she went on to explain about the murder in Wishbone and that Rhys was accused of committing a similar crime in London, which evidently was true. The *Gazette* had printed a copy of one of the articles from a London paper. *She didn't believe it.* She couldn't. If she did she was admitting the child she carried had been fathered by a murderer. And that couldn't be true.

Three days dragged by for Rhys, and the territorial judge sent word he would schedule a special trial in ten days' time. Rhys got the news shortly before an insistent visitor was shown to his cell. She was Carmen Bell.

Still mourning Lucien, she wore a gown of black silk and a small, tilted hat with a veil that covered her ebony hair and powdered face. "I was too mad to think, when I heard you were the one who killed Lucien," she whispered. "But as time went on and I thought about it I knew it couldn't be. Luce said you were the only good friend he ever had and that you had once saved his life." She glanced back at Len Blalock to see if he was watching and listening. Satisfied that he wasn't, Carmen continued. "I know Luce worked for you but—well—he loved you like a brother."

"As I did him," Rhys said.

"I took his belongings over to Mae's," Carmen continued. "She said she'd keep them for you until—" she broke off. His future was uncertain and she didn't want to remind him he stood a good chance of hanging. "I had to come over here and tell you that I'll do what I can for you," she said. "I'll testify how Lucien felt about you. Maybe that will help. I just wish I'd been upstairs that night. Luce had been worried and he'd been hoping you would get back so he could tell you about the Englishman."

A chill ran through Rhys. "Did he tell you about him?"

Carmen nodded. "Some," she said. "I don't know what it meant or why it upset him as it did. What he said was he thought he'd seen the man before and he thought his being in Wishbone wasn't by chance."

Rhys reached through the bars of his cell and gripped Carmen's silk-clad arm. "Did Luce say where he had seen the Englishman?"

Carmen's brow furrowed as she tried to remember everything Luce had said. At last she nodded. "Yes. He said it had been when he saw—Jenny. It made no sense to me but—" Her hand clamped over her mouth. "She's the one—"

"Yes," Rhys said hoarsely as the truth came to him with awful clarity. Lucien had been killed exactly as Jenny had. And Rhys had been accused of both crimes. But someone else had been there both times, too. Derby Seward, the red-bearded Englishman who was the witness against him. He had killed Lucien. And Jenny. It had to be.

But why? He'd never been able to reason out Jenny's death. Lucien had probably been killed because he recognized Seward, which meant Seward had followed them from London. And not to take him back for trial, but for some foul purpose.

He had to get to Seward. He had to make the Englishman admit what had been done and why. But he could get no farther than the bars of his cell. "Ask Derby Seward what his business was at the Brass Bell!" he demanded. "Ask why Lucien should go in hiding because of him! You've accused the wrong man!" He beat his hands against the bars but saw that his shouted demands for justice fell on deaf ears.

"Stop that hammerin' and bleatin' or I'll gag and chain you," Len Blalock threatened.

Not doubting the sheriff would do as he said, Rhys glumly retreated to his bunk. He had to hope his trial went well and that the truth would come out when he had his day in court. But as yet he had not succeeded in convincing even the attorney appointed him that Derby Seward was the one who should be charged with Lucien's murder. John Douglas, who had twice counseled Rhys to make a confession and be done with it, was more interested in his next drink than in defending a client.

Somehow Rhys slept the night after Carmen had made her visit, but it was a restless sleep fraught with nightmares in which Jenny and Lucien pleaded for their lives while he, impotent to help, stood by and saw them slain. Well into the night, Teddy's voice, caustic and sweet as only she could sound, brought him out of his fitful slumber. "Get up, damn you! We've got about two minutes to ride out of town."

He shot up from the bunk, saw the cell door open and Teddy, clad in her snug buckskins and low-slung gunbelt, was inside the cubicle gesturing like a wild thing. Out in the office Pavy Tucker lay slumped over the sheriff's big paper-strewn desk. "Teddy!" Rhys cried. "What have you done? Don't you know the trouble you're in for this?"

He gave her a shake then wound his arms around her, dragged her to him and kissed her savagely. Hissing like an angry feline, she twisted loose from him. "I might have known you'd be randy as all git out. Now move before someone happens by here and we both get to live in that cell."

They dragged Pavy behind the bars and locked him in then slipped out the back of the jail and down an alley where Teddy had two horses waiting. Soon they were past the last scattered houses in Wishbone and had the horses in a dead run.

Not until Teddy was satisfied that no one was following did they ride off the trail and let the winded animals rest.

They had ridden east, a few miles out of town leaving the road and taking to the hills. Among the rocks they dismounted. Teddy stood holding her horse's reins. He could see her troubled face in the scant moonlight. She was speaking to him softly, telling him he had to keep moving, telling him to avoid the next town. He noticed then that he had tightly packed saddlebags and a bedroll tied behind his saddle and that Teddy did not.

He looked unhappily at her. "I'm not going on," he said. "There's a man in Wishbone I have to see."

Teddy put her hand on his arm. He could feel the tension in her fingers, see it in her eyes. "You can't touch Adams," she said. "Believe me I've tried, since you were in jail. His time is coming but it's not now."

He gritted his teeth. "Adams isn't the man I want. It's Derby Seward."

"Seward!" she said sharply. "He and Adams are thick as thieves. Adams has put him up at the Diamond and given him the run of the place, all the drinks the man wants, on the house. The same for those 'sweethearts' Adams employs. Why, they've tried and hung you every day in the Diamond, just as you'll be tried and hung for real. It's been arranged and the jury's picked and paid. Even that rattlesnake who's defending you works for Adams. What's more, your property, namely your shares of the Gamble Line, will be confiscated by the court and I don't have to tell you who gets first dibs at them." She sighed. "Don't look at me like I'm loco. Justine overheard Adams talking to her father about all of it."

"Justine?" He gripped her shoulders and gave her a hard shake. "Does she know what you've done? Teddy, I can't let you—"

She huffed out a hot breath. "Dammit! There's

nothing you can do about it now. And yes, Justine does know. She helped me."

"*Mon Dieu!* Are you both crazy?"

"Probably. But Justine doesn't think you're guilty either and when she heard what Adams had engineered she couldn't stand by. She came to me and we worked it out that she played sick tonight and made her pa sit with her to be sure Pavy was the one at the jail. She figured Pavy would fall asleep on the job and he did. And—shut your mouth—he didn't see me, so nobody is going to know I broke you out."

"Then it won't matter if I slip back into Wishbone later and see Seward."

"Not if you'd like to get shot. And since I've gone to all the trouble of breaking you out to save your fancy hide I wouldn't like that."

He smiled ruefully. "If that's your way of saying you care, I'm touched."

"The hell it is!" Teddy retorted and broke away from him. The feel of his hands had been playing havoc with her emotions and she had sworn to keep the lid on them tonight. Scowling because restraint was proving extremely hard, she reached into a shirt pocket and pulled out a roll of bills. "A thousand dollars is all I could put together right now." She pushed the bills into his hand. "You take it and keep riding. Ride out of this territory and don't come back. When things settle down some, you can write where you are and I'll send what's due you."

He put the bills in his pocket. He didn't want to fight with her. He wanted to hold her and lie her down and make slow, satisfying love to her until the sun rose over the mountain peaks. "I have to see Seward," he said hoarsely. "You ride back to town now. I'll come later."

"No!" She gripped him by the shirt front. "You can't!"

There was never middle ground with Teddy but he was determined to make her listen. Slowly he slid his hands up her arms and across her back and held her. He could see her eyes clearly at that distance and he read something in them that she didn't want him to see. He pulled her closer and stared her down. "You wouldn't run away from a fight, Teddy. Why should I?"

Anger welled up in her and she stiffened in his arms. She hadn't counted on this mule-headed resistance. Why wouldn't he do what she told him? He was going to get himself killed. "Because it's a fight you can't win," she said hotly. "If you go back you'll get caught and you'll get hung. And I don't want the father of my child hung!"

Thirty-seven

"You never would have told me. You would have let me ride away and never know about the baby."

Teddy sunk down on a rock. She'd always been told her temper would be her undoing and now it was. She'd been determined to keep her secret and now she had blurted it out like an angry cawing crow. Something had taken hold of her and damned if she even knew what she was doing. "I thought it would be better if you didn't." She gritted her teeth, furious at herself for making a mess of one more thing. "I thought you had enough to worry about."

He sat beside her, feeling as if he'd taken a hard blow in the belly. In rare moments he had thought of having children of his own, even pictured them playing at his knee and calling him Papa. There had been a woman, too, a wife who loved and revered him. But in his fancy he had been a man of wealth and property, not an outcast gambler suspected of murdering his friends.

All this imagining he had laid down to being the illegitimate son of a servant, tormented and teased by the spoiled and coddled children of the master his mother had served. His had been a hard beginning that he had spent years trying to forget. He did not like the thought he was about to foster even a semblance of that fate on another, his child.

"Teddy, a man has a right to know," he said softly.

"Maybe."

"No maybes. This matters to me. This baby. Yours and mine. I have to think about this."

She shook her head miserably, still angry at herself for speaking out and wondering, guiltily, if the transgression had not occurred because a part of her wanted him to know, wanted him to care and to share in what was happening. "It's a little late for thinking," she said.

"I mean, I have to think what we are to do about it." He had never known his father, not even the man's name. His mother had been silent to the grave about the matter. He surmised that the incident of his birth had severed her relationship with the man who had sired him. He was sure his mother had carried the grief over the parting all her life—not that she hadn't loved her son. She had. He had been her joy, her only happiness. But he had never known about his father.

Teddy thought he had gone daft. Babies got born and there was only one way about it.

"We must marry," he said, startling her out of her troubled musing.

"Oh, hell!" She threw up her hands. "We've probably got a posse after us and you're talking about a wedding. Well, it won't happen. You're riding away from here and that's how it is."

"I'm staying."

"You're a fool!" she said acidly. "You'll be dead

before you're a father if you don't go. So, please, get on that horse and ride away."

He caught her wrists and gripped them painfully tight. "Hear me out, Teddy. You've called me a bastard and you are right that I am. It is not a status I would willingly give to a child. So, please, for the child's sake, marry me."

Teddy leveled angry eyes on him. "It would be good if you loved me and I loved you," she said, wounded that he had not even tried to disguise his motive with a profession of affection.

"Someday, perhaps, we can talk of love, someday when other things are settled, when I've not got the gallows waiting for me." He let her go, ran his fingers through his hair and looked at her a moment, his eyes pleading with her to understand. "I'm not asking that you take me," he said. "Only that you take my name for the child."

Teddy smiled bitterly. "I don't know," she said.

He felt himself the unworthiest of men. He could give her nothing but a name for the child and even that was tainted. He was an accused murderer, penniless, a man whose word wasn't good enough to convict a true criminal. He couldn't help her stop Adams without making things worse for her. She had said long ago that he wasn't much of a man. She was right.

"You find a man of the cloth to marry us and I'll sign the shares over to you, Teddy," he promised. "That ought to help you hold things together until something can be done about Adams."

She couldn't believe what he was saying. He wanted the child, their child, to have his name. He wanted that enough to give up the only thing of value he had left. But he didn't want her. She looked off across the desert. "If I do will you ride away?"

"Yes." He owed her that, he thought. And maybe he could turn things around from the other end, get back to London and hope he would have Alain's help in clearing him of Jenny's murder. If he did then he would come back. If he didn't then she was better off not knowing what had happened to him there.

With the baking sun on their backs and an uneasy bargain between them, they rode a full day. Teddy would not take Rhys where a stage ran or where the news of his escape could have preceded them. Toward the end of the long ride when the first golden hues of sunset had begun to draw the searing heat from the sky, a cluster of buildings appeared in the distance, a small adobe house, a barn and, in the yard, a well.

Teddy knew the Reverend Jack Cheatam and his wife Bess who ranched the place and ministered to the Indians in the area. Preacher Jack, as he was known by most, was another of her father's old friends, one of those who had come to Wishbone when it was a stop on a dusty two-rut trail. Later he'd moved on to this spread and the work he'd felt called to do.

Preacher Jack could be trusted to perform the simple ceremony that would bind her to Rhys Delmar, in name if not in fact, and to keep his silence about the deed. At times his place was teeming with Indians and wayfarers but today there was no one about to greet them except Preacher Jack himself. With a rifle at his side, he was at the well drawing water for the stock when they rode in.

"Welcome, strangers," he called out. "Well, Teddy!" A cheerful look replaced the wary smile that had first beamed from his face. "You are a surprise!"

She leaped from the horse without using the stirrup and gave the old man a hug so vigorous it knocked his hat from his head exposing a thick thatch of hair bright as polished silver. "How's Bess?"

"Fine and she'll be delighted to see you." He pulled away from her and turned to Rhys who had silently dismounted. "Who's your friend?"

Teddy introduced them but waited until they were all in the house and Bess, too, had recovered from her surprise to tell them why she and Rhys had come.

"I only wish your pa could be here," Bess said. She was white-haired as her husband. Her face, like his, was lined from years of toil in the Arizona sun. But her smile was quicker and deeper than his. "But I'm not in the least shocked that you would ride out here for a wedding." She gently touched Rhys's hands. "No fuss and frills for Teddy, young man. Do you know what kind of bride you're getting?"

"As well as any man can know a woman," he said, smiling guilelessly for Bess but letting Teddy see the two-edged meaning in his eyes.

Teddy's face lit up with color. "We understand each other," she chimed in. "And we are anxious to get it done."

"Of course you are. And we'll get to it as soon as you two wash the trail dust off." Preacher Jack showed them a barrel of water and a cake of soap behind the kitchen and left them to wash while he got his Bible and Bess got together a bouquet of the small, yellow-centered blue asters that grew wild around the barn.

"We do understand each other," Teddy reiterated when Preacher Jack had gone inside. She had cleaned her hands and face and she was drying them on the towel that hung above the bucket. "We get hitched and you ride out of the territory. For good."

He nodded. "I'll write out a contract assigning my shares to you. Preacher Jack and Bess can witness. Mae Sprayberry has my belongings in safekeeping and you'll find the documents you need among them. Teddy—"

She hurried inside, not wanting to hear any more. It wasn't as if any great illusions of a glorious wedding day were being shattered. She hadn't given much thought to marrying, ever. But somehow it seemed there ought to be more shine to the occasion. Still she balked at wearing Bess's wedding veil.

"Over buckskins?" she said.

"I'd be honored if you did." Bess tenderly held in her weathered hands a sheer piece of lace anchored to a coronet of faded silk cornflowers. "I've kept it packed up for forty years and—" Tears misted in her eyes. "A bride ought to have something borrowed. And the flowers in the bouquet are blue and about as new as anything."

Teddy relented. "I'm the one honored, Bess," she said, and kissed Bess's wrinkled cheek and hoped God would forgive her the deception. Teddy took the little bouquet in her hands though the tender stems suffered from the anguish in her grip. She allowed Bess to fasten the coronet and lace over her hastily brushed out hair. She was a reluctant bride and now a laughable one too, though she had made Bess happy. And Rhys, well, there was no accounting for him. He looked cocky as a genuine bridegroom. He smiled at her like an idiot and told her she could not have looked prettier in satin and silk.

She scowled at him, glad there was no mirror to show what a sight she must be with that delicate swath of lace draped above her fringed shirt and britches and high leggings. Maybe it was fitting for what the occasion really was, half desperation, half resignation.

Bess was making a fuss about getting her to stand just so beside Rhys. Trying to muster a smile, Teddy let herself be led around like a sheep going to slaughter. She wanted to scream out her frustration, her disappointment. How the hell had she gotten herself in a fix like this?

She almost did break out into a fit of hysterical laughter but managed to stem it by biting the inside of her jaw. Thank goodness the veil half hid the grimace on her face. Poor Preacher Jack. She hoped she wasn't making too much a mockery of the sanctity of marriage he was talking about.

The other words Preacher Jack was saying came to her like a loud hum but she must have understood, because she answered him something and then Rhys was speaking, too.

"Is there a ring?" Preacher Jack looked at Rhys.

"No. No ring."

The hum started again then it died down and Rhys was turning her, lifting the veil, taking her in his arms.

The pressure of his lips brought her back with a start but not before he plunged his tongue deep in her mouth and kissed her with a ferocity that took her breath. She couldn't hold back a silly little sob. She had done it now. She had married the fool and he was holding onto her like he cared, kissing her again. She felt limp as a rag doll and wound her arms around his neck to keep her legs from buckling and then she was kissing him back, moaning softly as every particle of her trembled and shook and burned for him.

"We should celebrate. All of us," Bess said.

Preacher Jack had a bottle of whiskey that he kept for emergencies and such. He poured each of them a round and made a toast to long life and happiness. Teddy drank her portion down fast hoping it would ease the tightness in her throat and calm her racing heart. But when it was time to sign the documents, the marriage certificate and the contract which Rhys had prepared, her hand was unsteady and she was still in a daze of disbelief that she had married Rhys Delmar.

His head was perfectly clear and when Preacher Jack offered the spare room for the newlyweds, he was quick to accept. The thought of spending his wedding night on a soft bed with Teddy was not an opportunity to pass up. He made damned sure she saw him slide the marriage certificate and contract into his coat pocket before they sat down to supper.

Seething at the audacity of him, Teddy helped Bess repack the treasured wedding veil. Rhys Delmar might think he was getting a wedding night but that had never been part of the bargain. The only thing he would get was a piece of her mind. A big piece. He'd ridden roughshod over her enough. Damn him! She had barely been able to hold her life together before he'd shown up and blasted it into so many pieces she might never get it together again.

He kept smiling at her all through the meal, acting as if there were nothing strange about the whole event, as if she were not an unhappy, unwilling, pregnant bride, and he was not a reluctant father, a man accused of murder and on the run from the law. It was absurd and sad and he didn't seem to care that it was. He kept on talking, charming Preacher Jack and Bess. He kept on smiling, at every chance turning that seductive, maddening half-smile of his on her. She could feel his eyes on her, too, those pale, mercurial eyes that could turn her to butter. Which was what he wanted, no doubt. And wasn't going to get.

Beneath the table, Teddy clenched her fists tight. Rhys was talking to Bess, his voice silvery and mesmerizing. "Teddy has no equals," she heard him say.

Dammit! Why hadn't she shot the scoundrel and saved herself all this trouble? Her temper continued to build, steadily, but she managed to hold it in check throughout the meal. She felt bad enough about rooking Preacher Jack and Bess into thinking she and Rhys were a happy, loving couple. She'd save her heavy guns until she and Rhys Delmar were alone.

Hours later when Preacher Jack and Bess had gone to bed she was ready to fire the first salvo. And fire it she did, behind the closed door of the spare room. Shadowed in the light of a single flickering candle, she waved her fist in his face. "I know your game, you varmint, and I remind you we had a deal!"

Ignoring her threat, Rhys patted the pocket which contained the documents. "These are yours come morning," he said and slipped out of the coat and tossed it on the back of a chair which stood behind him. Teddy thought of grabbing for the coat but was distracted then lulled into fascination as he pulled the tails of his shirt from his trousers and slowly unfastened the row of buttons running down the front. He slid the garment off and cast it on the chair with his coat, smiled warmly and said, "I'd like to enjoy the night."

"Damn you!" She raised her fist to him again. "You said you would ride on. I should have known you wouldn't keep our agreement."

He sighed, turned around and tugged off his boots, treating her to a glimpse of the flexing of bands of muscle in his broad back. She saw, too, that his hard frame still bore the scars of Taviz's knife and she was reminded, painfully, that they had been the price of her rescue, the price of her life. Remorse and regret rose in her, briefly, only to be cut down by the greater weight of her anger.

The heat of it flared in her eyes and they burned critically over him, looking for something to despise and finding only feelings of admiration. The candlelight was no help. It played delightfully on the sinew and muscle of his lean body, rendering him even more appealing than nature already had. Naked to the waist, he bent over the bed and turned back the covers and turned his persuasive eyes on her. Teddy drew a sharp breath and felt the familiar quickening of her pulse.

"Have a heart, Teddy." His voice was low and husky, heavy with desire. She was his wife, for only a night, perhaps, and he wanted to spend it in her arms, more than anything he wanted to spend it in her arms. "I fully intend to keep our deal," he said softly. "But tonight . . ."

The compelling desire in his voice sent a shiver of need sluicing through her, shaking her to her toes. She fought it, bristling at her weakness and his intent. "I won't bed down with you!"

Cursing, she spun around to leave, knowing that if she stayed another second in that room with Rhys, looking at him, at that tempting bed, she'd stay the night.

Rhys caught her shoulders and spun her back to him. "Won't you?"

His mouth came down quickly. His lips twisted across hers in a savage, urgent assault that struck like a bolt of lightning, filling her with fire and steam and such an urgent need for him that she was staggered by the fury of it. She began to struggle, to rail against him, but he clasped her tighter, capturing her like a bird in a net he'd made of his arms.

She thrust her hands against his chest and made a final vain attempt to flee him, but there was no true fight in her and the tension in her limbs fled as she felt the heavy beating of his heart beneath her hands. She sagged against him and her fury ebbed away like a retreating tide, yielding to his strength and warmth.

Her hands slid up and caught his face and she kissed him.

What was the harm, she thought? The damage was done, the seed sown. Let her reap some pleasure before the harvest. In the morning he would be gone and she might never see him again. She could savor the memory, a last sweet memory of him.

A long, whimpering cry came from her as he briefly pulled his mouth away. She was impatient with him now, as filled with need as she had been with anger, anxious for him to tear her clothes away and bend her back upon the bed. In a minute he was by her side, his clothing strewn at his feet.

He touched her face, felt the damp warmth of her breath on his skin. He touched her hair and reveled in the soft feel of it, the fragrance of wildflowers that rose up and wrapped around him. He slipped his hand down the length of her, grazing over her silken skin, stroking gently over the curve of her breast, lightly lingering on her belly. He felt the gentle swell beneath his palm and was filled with yearning, not only to possess her but to possess all the things a man and woman might have together, time, and love—and children. Together.

Some day he would speak to her of love, when things were right, when he was whole and free. Tonight he would take only the physical pleasure she offered—that he had wrested from her. He joyed in it, in the soft responsive sounds she made, the breathless, halting sighs, the silken moans that tore at his heart as he stroked and kissed her flesh. She did not love him, but she desired him as he desired her. Perhaps one day she could love him too.

His hands floated over her and if there was a part he had not touched before he touched it then, marveling at the softness of her, the beauty of her in the wavering candlelight. He rose up though his hands lingered on her thighs, stroking the center of her, weaving through the mossy curls at the apex of her parted legs, seeking the molten core of her, stroking within, bringing a cry of hunger, of wanton desire from her.

He sought her lips as he gripped himself and guided his way into her, plunging swift and deep, his eyes half-closed, his cry of need rough and passion-laden. He felt he was riding the wild wind as she rose to meet him, tossing beneath him like a gale. Her hair shimmered, gilded streaks against clouds of white muslin. Her green eyes glowed, distant lanterns beckoning, driving him as the storm rose in him, a twisting whirlwind unleashed and clamoring through him, thunderous and wild.

His whole body shook as release came. He felt her shuddering beneath him, felt the squeeze of her body around him, heard the ragged cry of his name.

And so it was through the night, hours of endless loving, brief minutes of sleep. No questions, no promises.

In the hour before dawn Teddy became hazily awake to find the welcome weight of Rhys's leg across her thighs, the soft touch of his hand upon her breast. She thought he meant to love her again but saw that his sooty lashes rested on his cheeks and that he slept.

She smiled and softly stroked his shoulder, surprised that after a night with more lovemaking than sleep she should feel this aching pleasure at being near him. She had been rash and angry when she broke him out of jail. She had wanted to save him but she had also wanted him out of her sight and out of her mind. She realized that could never be. He was in her heart, in her blood.

She carried his child. Such a blissful, happy thought. She didn't want him to go. Whatever they had to face, each of them, they would face together. She would tell him that when he awoke.

And she would tell him about the letter that had come for him the day before. She had been too riled, too bewildered, to remember anything that mattered and she had completely forgotten about stashing the letter in his saddle pack. But there was time for that, plenty of time.

Sighing softly, she nestled closer to the warm comfort of his body, expecting him to awaken and take her in his arms at any moment. She would tell him everything then, in the clear light of morning she would bare her heart and soul.

It was not to be. The coziness of his arms and her exertion conspired against Teddy and sleep came and caught her and tumbled her in its darken lair.

When she awoke hours later, Rhys was gone. And her thousand dollars was too.

Thirty-eight

Rhys hoped Teddy would forgive him for the lie. He had intended to honor his word and ride out of the territory, even slipped out to the barn while she was sleeping, and saddled his horse to spare himself the pain of saying good-bye. He'd come across the letter as he checked the supplies in the saddle pack. Alain's letter.

He still had a lump in his throat over the words Alain had written. Jenny Perrault's son had never believed for a moment that Rhys had murdered his mother. What's more he had immediately begun to search out the truth. He had known his mother had a letter and news for Rhys. He had found the letter hidden in his house, an astonishing letter from a solicitor representing the estate of a man called Knox, Lord Andrew Knox. His father.

Not trusting it to the mail, Alain had copied the text of the letter. Rhys read it in disbelief. If it was true he was the son—the legitimate son of an earl. He stood to inherit an estate and a sum, which even now, after hours to think on it, astonished him. On a darker note Alain had learned of a cousin, Avery Knox of London, who stood in line for the whole of Sir Andrew

Knox's estate should Rhys be found to be deceased or, as Sir Andrew had provided, convicted of any crime.

Avery Knox, Alain had learned, had let it be known to his many creditors that he fully expected to inherit his uncle's wealth. It was with the avaricious Avery Knox that Alain's suspicions had come to rest. He had learned of a minion Knox had employed to those ends—a despicable fellow known to be cunningly successful at his craft. Red-haired, red-bearded.

"Seward," Rhys said aloud.

The moon lay upon distant mountain peaks when he rode into Wishbone, darkness as his cover, foolhardiness his companion. He sought out Carmen Bell, counting on her love of Lucien Bourget to make her sympathetic to his cause. He shadowed his face beneath his hat as he bribed a half-drunk drifter to take her a message.

Hoping she would not betray him he waited in the heavy darkness of an alley behind the Brass Bell. Shortly he saw a woman's figure emerge from a doorway and heard the hushed tone of a feminine voice. "I knew it must be you," she whispered. "When he said 'Luce' I knew it must be you." She laid a hand on his arm and drew him back the way she had come, inside the saloon to a small private room. "You're crazy to be here. Len Blalock's had a posse out looking for you since you got away."

"Do they know who—"

"Who busted you out? No. And don't tell me," she

said. Carmen poured him a whiskey and he swallowed it down slowly. "Why have you come back?"

"For Seward," he said. "Lucien's killer."

Carmen sat silent a moment then her head bent low and she sobbed. "I—I'll help you if I can," she said staunchly. "I haven't seen the man for a couple of days but you'll find him at the Diamond if he's about anywhere."

With Carmen acting as lookout, Rhys managed to break in through a window on the back side of the Diamond. His guess was that he had gained entry into Parrish Adams's private quarters. The room he was in had heavy velvet curtains trimmed with thick golden fringe, and walls hung with Japanese silk. Most of the space was taken up by an enormous tester bed of much too fine a quality for the rough patrons of saloon girls.

A softly glowing lamp with a hand-painted shade helped him pick his way across the room. He was celebrating his good luck at getting so far undetected when the big paneled door swung open.

"Norine? You in here?" Adams, getting ready to retire for the night, strode in.

Rhys, pressed against the wall behind a long velvet drape, watched as Adams removed his coat and vest, then unbuckled his gunbelt and laid it on a chest near the bed. A moment later the man was sitting on a round-tufted footstool removing his boots.

Rhys, gun in hand, swung the shielding drape away and stepped before Adams. "Where's Seward?" he demanded.

Hatred and surprise twisted Adams' lean visage in a hideous way. He lunged up but halted almost immediately knowing that too rash a move could cost his life. "I pegged you a smarter man than this, Delmar," he said. "You should have taken my offer. You wouldn't have to worry about Seward."

"And you wouldn't have to worry about me putting a bullet between your eyes," Rhys said tonelessly. "Which is precisely what I am going to do unless you sign a statement admitting you are responsible for the attacks on the Gamble Line." Gun cocked and aimed at the inch of white skin between Adams's dark brows, Rhys took a step toward his target. "As you well know I have nothing to lose. I am twice damned already."

His calm smile gave Adams a chill and the sneer he had worn with confidence disappeared from his face. *Nothing to lose.* The truth sunk in with dreadful slowness. Rhys Delmar had nothing to lose by shooting him and everything to gain by forcing an admission from him. This was the man who had fought Taviz, a madman if ever one lived, and been the one to ride away. He didn't doubt for an instant that unless he was forthcoming with the statement Delmar demanded it would be the Frenchman who rode away again.

Adams growled out a curse that was cut short by the sound of a footstep outside in the hallway. Rhys warned Adams not to make another sound, lest it be his last, and hurried to conceal himself behind the door. Once again it swung open.

Norine Adams started in. Rhys caught her slender arm and jerked her past him, sending her petticoats flying as she stumbled and spun across the room toward her husband. "Ooof," she cried as Rhys hurriedly bolted the door behind her. Adams caught Norine, snatched her to him and, with an arm about her waist, held his trembling spouse close against him.

Norine gasped. Her shocked eyes were taking in but disbelieving what was happening in her bedroom. "Don't you worry, love." Adams smiled a savage smile and hugged his wife closer, his hand, concealed by the fullness of her skirt, sliding down her hip and into the pocket where he knew she kept a knuckle-duster, a one-shot derringer. A miserly woman's weapon but it would do.

He raised the tiny gun and took aim at Rhys.

Rhys laughed. "At this distance you'll give me a sting."

Adams swung his arm around, a bold, exaggerated swing that brought the barrel of the derringer to rest against Norine's temple. "At this distance she'll die."

Norine gasped then shrieked. "Parrish! No! What are you doing?"

Rhys was more stunned than the woman. Adams had drawn Norine directly in front of him, the tip of her head reaching just above the line of his chin. He held her in a punishingly tight grip and she looked genuinely afraid. "She's your wife," Rhys said.

With a snarl Adams bored the barrel of the derringer deeper into Norine's temple, cutting an ugly red circle into her smooth skin. "She's my wife," he jeered. "But I can get another woman. And I've got a feeling that even with nothing to lose you aren't the kind of man who will have someone else's blood on his hands. Now put the gun down or watch her die before you shoot me."

Rhys wasn't convinced and he wasn't ready to concede. He rested his thumb on the hammer spur of his gun, pulled it back and steadied his aim at Adams's forehead.

Norine knew her husband better. In a split second she ducked and wrenched her body around, not escaping Adam's grip but getting away from the threatening barrel of the derringer long enough to grab his arm. The two of them tangled like a pair of fighting cats, Norine spitting and hissing, Adams cursing and shouting, her fury a fair match for his greater strength.

Rhys could not get a clear shot at Adams, not without hitting the woman. By now he was convinced that Adams would have sacrificed her to save his skin. His only hope of stopping the fray before Norine was killed or the noise of it brought someone running was to knock Adams unconscious.

He leaped across the room, gun raised, wondering at the mania of a man like Adams, no longer doubting in any degree that the vile man was responsible for all the ill that had befallen Teddy and the Gamble Line.

A shot sounded before he reached the pair. Norine, arms flailing, slid to the floor, her red dress flowing around her like a gigantic pool of blood. Adams staggered back, teeth bared, a look of abject fury on his dark face. He hovered on his feet a moment before his legs gave way beneath him and he, too, fell to the floor.

"Murdering bastard!" Norine cursed the fallen man and, on hands and knees, scurried away, escaping the fierce spray of blood that spurted from his throat and the artery the derringer's shot had severed. The gurgle of Adams's last breath made a terrible sound. Almost as dreadful were the insistent blows on the bedroom door.

"Mr. Adams!" Pete Smith stood outside pounding his shoulder against the paneled door.

Rhys had a moment of believing it had all been for nothing. He cast a worried glance at Norine who had scrambled to her feet and was quickly regaining her wits.

"It's all right, Pete!" she cried.

"I heard a shot."

Norine motioned to Rhys to step out of sight. Smoothing down her skirts and tidying her hair, she crossed to the door and opened it a mere crack. "Is Len Blalock back in town?" she asked.

"He's back." Pete tried to push the door open but Norine stood fast.

"Get him and bring him here," she demanded. Pete hesitated a few seconds then strode off to do as he'd been told. Norine shut the door behind her, fell against it, and looked gratefully at Rhys. "I'm no prize to this world I know," she said. "But maybe I've got a chance to make some things right. I'm going to begin by telling Len Blalock you didn't kill that man over at the Brass Bell."

"Do you know who did?"

Her hand was flecked with her husband's blood. She looked at it a moment then wiped the stains off on her satin skirt. "Parrish had a way of weaseling things out of people. That Englishman that called himself a newspaperman came here and offered Parrish a deal.

He said it was in both their interest that you get hung and that he was in a position to lay the blame on you for killing that man over at the Brass Bell. He all but admitted to Parrish he did the killing himself." She was still covered with gooseflesh and trembling from the ordeal. Mechanically she opened the doors of a tall armoire and pulled out a silken shawl which she slung around her bare, shaking shoulders. "Parrish took the deal and paid off that crooked lawyer of yours, too. Old Douglas was going to see that those shares you've got could be bought for a song."

"But you never actually heard Seward admit he killed Lucien."

"No," she said.

Rhys remembered Alain's letter. Seward was cunning and he would have been too cautious for an outright admission of his crime. But it stood to reason Seward had killed two of those most dear to Rhys. Seward was the man who could clear him of those murders, the man who had to pay for committing them. "Where is he?" he asked Norine.

"Gone," she said. "He was scared silly when you broke out of jail. I think he knew you'd come looking for him. He sneaked out on the stage the same day you vamoosed. The skunk left word with one of the girls that he was going back to London and that Parrish could send for him if you were ever found."

Len Blalock was too relieved over Parrish Adams's death to make any kind of case against Norine or Rhys. "The best I can do is turn my back," he said.

"I got a sworn statement that's nigh as good in court as a live witness. The territorial judge'll be here next week and he's the only one with the power to drop the charges. With Norine's testimony he might see clear to do it, but—well, her word is only hearsay and—"

Norine supplied what the sheriff was having trouble admitting. "And the judge was in Parrish's pocket, too. There's no predicting what he'll do when you show up in his court."

Len Blalock narrowed his eyes. He'd been in purgatory a long, long time because of bad judgment and Parrish Adams. He thought he could see the way out and he wanted to do what he could to hasten that end, to make his daughter proud of him again. He nodded at Rhys. "Get ridin', son."

Thirty-nine

Seward wasn't hard to follow, just hard to catch up with. Rhys dogged him all the way from Wishbone to New York harbor, always a few days behind the retreating Englishman. Now, weeks after he had ridden out after the red-haired killer, Rhys stood on the docks in a driving rain canvassing the legion of ships, many of which would soon depart for England. A storm had held all vessels in the harbor for the past three days, foul weather to sea-faring men but the first good fortune Rhys had experienced since he'd set out after Seward.

With the chill rain seeping down his collar and the icy wind of a northeaster cutting through his clothes, Rhys vowed he would make the best of his turn of luck. Seward could not have sailed. He was bound to have booked passage on one of the vessels waiting for the waters to calm. He had to find the man. Had to get a confession from him. He had to clear his name. He owed that to Teddy. And to his child.

By midnight he feared he had failed. The weather had begun to break, ships would be sailing from the harbor in a matter of hours, and he had not found

Seward on any passenger list nor had he found a seaman who had seen a man of Seward's description.

In need of a drink and a warming fire, Rhys made his way to a dockside tavern and by chance found himself sharing the hearthside heat of a roaring fire with the captain of a frigate destined for London. "Abner Bale is the name." The gravelly-voiced captain turned up his mug of beer and guzzled it down. He had a face that was worn and battered as an old sail. The lines etched in his leathery skin had been cut by the wind and weather of many crossings of the Atlantic's rough waters. Like many a sea captain, Bale could be treacherous as the barnacles on a ship's hull if need be, but there was the look of an honest man in the depths of his brown eyes. "Aye, I've seen a man like you're tellin' about," the *Gloriana*'s captain reported. "Came to my mate the day before this seeking passage."

Rhys expressed his need to see the man and confirm that it was, indeed, Seward. He hoped the captain knew of the man's whereabouts. "He owes me a debt," Rhys said. "And lives hang on it being paid."

Having gained Bale's ear, Rhys told him a small part of why he sought Seward, carefully omitting the fact that it was his life that rested in the red-haired man's malevolent hands.

Bale shrugged, though he was not indifferent to the story Rhys had told. "I've no place in another man's business," he said. Bale put down his empty mug and rubbed his calloused palms before the fire. "But if you've a just claim you can see this Seward, if that be his name, when he boards the *Gloriana*. You'd best be there before dawn," he added. "We're a week off our sailin' date as is an' if the clouds break we sail at first light." He turned his backside to the fire and, having offered what he thought any fair man would, cast a steely glance at Rhys. "Mind you make no trouble aboard my ship," he warned.

Bale left the tavern a short while later. Rhys stayed by the fire a while longer, getting the chill out of his bones and hoping Seward and the man Bale expected aboard his ship were one and the same.

Surmising he had been right to leave Wishbone, Derby Seward readied his small traveling trunk and had the innkeeper summon a carriage to take him to the docks. He had done all he safely could to rid the world of Rhys Delmar. Knox would have to be content with it. True, Delmar was not dead but he was now branded a murdering criminal on two continents. With good representation, Knox should be able to convince the courts that Delmar had failed to meet the terms of the will and that Knox was the rightful heir to his uncle's fortune.

If not, no one would be sorrier than Derby Seward. But no amount of money was worth his life and the moment he'd heard Delmar was free he'd feared that the Frenchman would come looking for him. He still had the feeling. Sheriff Blalock had taken pains to let him know the Frenchman suspected him of killing his former valet. Seward had no idea what the sheriff's purpose had been, since Blalock and others involved in the case acted in Adams's behalf. But Blalock had relayed every word of Delmar's ranting that his accuser had more to hide than he did.

No dimwit when it came to his own welfare, Seward had fled Wishbone immediately upon learning Delmar was on the loose. As yet he had not slowed down. A dozen times a day, as he'd traveled from the Arizona territory to the New York harbor, he'd felt the hairs rising on the back of his neck. Each time he'd looked around expecting Delmar to be there demanding retribution. Each time he'd found he was reacting to no more than his shadow. But he had kept running and kept looking back.

He would continue to do so until he boarded the *Gloriana* and felt the wind catch her sails. There on the sea, at last, he would not feel the need to look over his shoulder. And so it was, haggard from the journey, that Derby Seward cast his trunk to a waiting seaman, doled out a few coins to the driver of the carriage, and prepared to board the *Gloriana*.

He sighed out in relief as the horses's clopping hooves carried the driver and conveyance away and his own thudding footsteps took him toward the waiting frigate.

Rhys drew his breath in and held it until the air grew stale in his lungs. With the dark clouds banked above and a gathering fog on the docks, he could scarcely make out the shape of the man climbing down from a solitary carriage which had ventured far down the wharf. Cautiously, Rhys leaned out from behind the stack of crates and barrels that had shielded him from the man's view. The late-comer had a beard but he could not determine the color.

Rhys saw but one course. He stepped into the clear. "Seward!" he shouted.

Seward froze then cursed himself for reacting to the name. He'd taken the precaution of assuming another for the journey to London. Now it seemed the safeguard had been in vain.

Above, the clouds parted and the moon broke though, its silver light catching Seward full in the face and showing his thick red beard in all its glory. Rhys broke into a run. Seward did the same, shouting a warning to any of the crew who were about on the ship to halt the man who pursued him. His hat flew to the choppy water below and his coat waved in the wind, as Seward scurried aboard the *Gloriana* with the desperation of a rat seeking safety in the bowels of the ship. He had been aboard before and knew the way across the deck. He made haste for the companion hood and threw himself down the steps, gasping for breath as he descended to the lower decks and raced past cargo and men.

A few sailors, knowing Seward had paid his passage, sought to give him aid but stepped aside as, from the quarterdeck, Captain Bale shouted for them to stay at their posts.

Seward raced on. Near a ladder which led to the deep cargo hold he passed a box where the ship's carpenter had laid his tools. The blade of a small hatchet gleamed out in the lamplight. Seward grabbed the wooden handle and thrust the hatchet beneath his coat. A knife was his weapon of choice but for Rhys Delmar, whom he suspected carried a gun, the hatchet would prove a better defense.

With an angry cry tearing from his throat Rhys bounded after Seward, flying past the seamen he had expected to block his way but who now stood aside as they had for the man he chased. He gained the upper deck and sprinted across it. Already Seward was out of sight but he had seen the path the man took and followed down the companion hood. Below he could hear the clatter of Seward's feet and the heavy, gasping breaths of a man not accustomed to exertion. On he ran, gun drawn, not knowing what he would do with Seward when he caught him but determined he would make the man admit his guilt if he had to beat the life from him to do it.

Rhys paused but once, when he saw that Seward had fled to the hold. There in the tightly packed ship's belly a man could lie in wait. The thought that Seward might climb out by another exit and leave the ship before he caught up spurred Rhys on. In one bound he leaped to the bottom of the hold, landing in a crouch among the stacked bales and barrels.

Seward stood behind the ladder, ready to chop off the legs of his adversary as he climbed down. With that advantage taken from him he gave a cry of rage and flung himself, hatchet swinging, upon Rhys. His first brutal blow struck the weapon from Rhys's hand and sent it careening toward a head-high stack of crates lashed to the ship's sides. The gun landed atop the highest of the wooden boxes just as the ship creaked and listed port side. Rhys's only weapon slithered over the edge of the box and wedged between two heavy crates and out of reach of either man.

Seward, however, was still armed with the hatchet

and raised it for another blow. "You've done me a good turn by following, Rhys Delmar," he cried through clenched teeth. "I'll cut you to pieces right here and no man will fault me for it!"

He swung. Rhys sprung aside and the blow missed, bringing a vicious curse from Seward. "You have it to do yet!" Rhys challenged and leaped aside as yet another blow stirred the hair on his head.

"I'll do it!" Seward taunted and pressed on. "You're worth a bloody fortune to me! Dead!"

With Rhys dancing back and Seward edging forward they moved through the crowded hold. One swing of the hatchet sliced a bag of hemp and sent the fiber spilling to the staves beneath their feet.

Seward plowed through what he had unleashed, wielding his hatchet in ever-widening swings which Rhys continued to duck and dodge. Any one swipe could have rendered him headless had he misjudged by a second the speed of the swing. Needing a moment of respite he dove behind a barrel hoping he could keep up the chase long enough to tire Seward so that he dared go on the offensive against the man.

"What was Jenny Perrault worth to you?" he shouted, scrambling behind yet another barrel.

"Not a farthing." Seward peered into the dark where Rhys had disappeared. Sweat poured from his brow and he had to suck in a breath before he could speak again. "It was what she was about to tell you that got her killed."

"About Andrew Knox? My father?"

Seward pressed on, honing in on Rhys's voice. "So

you know about that, do you? For all the difference it'll make!"

For half a second Rhys sat stunned by Seward's admission that he *had* murdered Jenny. He recovered quickly when Seward shoved aside the barrel that was his protection and came near to slicing off his arm with a desperate swing of the sharp blade.

Relieved to see he'd lost only a sleeve and a layer of skin, Rhys shouted a taunt at Seward and kept moving through the tunnels of goods in the hold. He'd gotten his wind back but he had also learned every moment he took to hide and rest gave Seward a moment to recover his strength, too. He tried another tactic as soon as he put another barrel between Seward and himself. While Seward shoved the barrier away, Rhys sprung from the ship's floor, leaping high in the air where he caught hold of the heavy rope that latticed the cargo to the ship's walls. Climbing ape-fashion, he managed to land a hard kick to Seward's skull before the man realized what had happened.

Groaning and with a blood lust in his eye, Seward lunged to his feet and started up the rigging after Rhys. With the axe in one hand his progress was slow but he was relentless even as his big chest heaved in and out for air and each time he got within striking distance he swung the hatchet at Rhys. Only a few minutes into the overhead chase Seward discovered by accident that if he could not catch Rhys Delmar he might bring him down by hacking through the rope Rhys clung to.

On the first occurrence Rhys came tumbling down clinging to the severed rope, landing only a few feet from Seward and the razor-sharp hatchet. He had lost the advantage of distance but he still had his endurance. Rather than leap to the floor and have Seward plummet on top of him and hack him to shreds, Rhys emitted a cry of determination and scurried hand over hand away from his pursuer. Seward, however, had given up the game of chase. He severed another rope and once again Rhys came tumbling to him this time landing with a dazing thump against a huge wooden keg and directly in the path of Seward's weapon.

The darkness in the hold went blacker before Rhys's eyes. He blinked and groaned and tried to clear his head and amass enough strength to dodge a death blow.

Seward laughed. "Got you now you bloody devil!" He drew back his arm and swung.

Rhys never quite knew how he managed to hoist himself out of the way of that blow, but it missed him by a hair's-breadth. Seward's hatchet split the chime hoop of the giant keg releasing the entire top of the wooden barrel and bringing a blast of thick molasses spewing from the container. The gush washed Seward from his perch and he came plunging down into the pile of hemp he had unleashed before.

Choking and coughing and cursing Rhys Delmar, Seward scooted around on all fours in the knee-deep mess looking for his hatchet.

Above him Rhys swung on a dangling rope. He'd have laughed at the spectacle had not he known how deadly that molasses-sopped and hemp-strewn man could be should he find the lost hatchet. He couldn't wait for that to happen. Positioning himself over Seward Rhys dropped directly on the crawling man's back, knocking him face down into the thick, oozing molasses.

Filled with rage, Rhys latched his fingers into Seward's sticky hair and beard and thrust the Englishman's head deeper into the thick black syrup. "You killed Lucien! You killed Jenny! I ought to drown you in it!"

Seward swallowed a mouthful of molasses and when Rhys relented and let him up for air he was clawing it from his mouth to let in the breath he needed. "Aye!" he shouted as soon as he'd filled his lungs. "I killed them both! The Perrault woman and the bloody cripple Bourget. Stabbed them in the heart. Liked the feel of it too. Aye!" He turned his hate-filled eyes on Rhys. "I killed them but you'll hang for it! Not me, you bloody bastard!"

Nearly as crazed as Seward, Rhys slammed the Englishman's head into the syrup again, holding it down a long moment, caring little if he did or did not drown the man. "Then I might as well let you choke to death!" he railed. "It's of no consequence if you do!"

Seward kicked and grabbed but could not wrest the Frenchman off his back or tear his steel-like fingers from his hair. He had begun to give up the fight when Rhys realized a light shone over his shoulder and had been there for some time.

He rose up and looked anxiously back. Abner Bale and a score of his men stood about the ladder in the hold.

"I see you've not kept your promise regarding my ship," the captain said. His steady voice brought a return of reason to Rhys, but he still held Seward's head submerged. "Let him go," Bale said. "My men and I have heard his confession and you'll have our word where you need it. Now let him go. Don't let him make of you what he's claimed you are."

Rhys jerked Seward's head from the molasses. It was as if the Englishman had no face. He'd turned black where the syrup clung and was covered with hemp in hundreds of stringy fibers which stuck as if glued wherever they touched. His body was the same, a mound of molasses dotted with bits of hemp that stood out like tentacles. The only bit of Seward that showed he was not some bizarre creature dragged from the deep was the long pink tongue that lolled from his mouth as he gasped from air.

Rhys had not fared much better in the deluge of syrup but his head was clear of it and he could stand without help. "You're a good man, Captain," he said wearily. "Now if you'll help me get this man ashore and to the authorities here we—"

The captain ordered his men to take Seward above and wash him clean. "Sorry, lad," he said to Rhys. "The *Gloriana* has set sail and the next port we see will be an English harbor."

Forty

August 1876

The moon rose high and shone blood red above the Gamble ranch. Teddy peered out of her bedroom window at the bright sphere. She had not seen a moon like that since—

"Dammit!" she said and pulled the curtains tight over the open portal. It was another of those damned devil moons, Felicity's devil moon, a ball of crimson with dark dancing shadows, fraught with change. She hadn't seen a moon like that since the night after she and Rhys had escaped from Taviz and the bandidos, shortly before she had learned she was carrying his baby. Babies.

She looked over at the twin cradles where tiny, dark-haired Zachary Gamble Delmar and his golden-haired sister Theodora Gamble Delmar slept. Well. Teddy smiled contentedly and felt the wonderful warming in her heart that came every time she looked at them. They were worth it all.

But that bastard father of theirs—Teddy's countenance changed like the shadows on the moon, from a loving smile to a simmering scowl. Well, no he wasn't a bastard. Word had come from Felicity's London correspondent that Marc André Rhys Delmar hadn't been born on the wrong side of the blanket after all. He was the legitimate son of a cantankerous old earl who had not seen fit to acknowledge his heir while he lived.

Additionally Rhys had been the victim of a plot by a rapscallion nephew of Knox's, a degenerate, if Felicity's friend was to be believed. Avery Knox had engineered the plots to have Rhys falsely accused of murder. And hanged. Knox was getting what was coming to him now. As was the unprincipled Derby Seward.

Rhys wasn't on the wrong side of the law any longer either. After months of legal finagling he had been cleared of the murder charge in London and subsequently, through his new attorney in the Arizona territory, of the charge in Wishbone. All this had evidently been fodder for the London papers for Felicity's correspondent, who had been tardy in replying to their original request about Rhys, now took delight in posting clipping after clipping to keep them informed of the events. The last letter and batch of clippings had declared Rhys Delmar sole heir to the sizable fortune of Sir Andrew Knox. An earl.

Teddy didn't care if Rhys was an earl or an eel. He had left her. Left her and the babies. And there hadn't been a word from him since. After all that high and mighty talk about wanting his child to have a name he hadn't even written to ask if he had a son or a daughter.

She supposed she was indebted to him. He'd saved the Gamble Line for her. With Adams gone the holdups had ceased and the company had flourished. She was nearly out of debt and the contracts she depended on were secure. What's more, Cabe Northrop had been beside himself for not believing what she had told him about Adams. Cabe had a lot to make up to her and he was doing his damndest to see she got Wells Fargo's full cooperation on every endeavor.

Yes. She owed Rhys for all that. She wasn't forgetting, either, that he'd saved her life a time or two. And he'd given her his shares free and clear before he left. Except for the thousand dollars he'd taken. But then that wouldn't have bought a good team of horses.

One of the babies stirred and made a sweet little sound that brought the smile back to Teddy's lips. Rhys had given her little Zack and Dora, too. Much as she wanted to, she couldn't hate the man who had given her the most precious of gifts.

When the baby quieted, Teddy rose and walked to the window once more. She was restless and she blamed the moon. Yes. She admitted it all. She owed Rhys Delmar.

But if she ever saw him again he'd best have a good fast horse to get out of her way.

Alain Perrault had brought order to Andrew Knox's neglected estate, purchasing stock for the empty stables, hiring good men to get the fields cleared for the next planting. Even the massive old manor house had begun to shake off the look of an overgrown ruin.

Everything was coming to top-notch shape except the lord of the manor.

"You've no head for being an earl." Alain, broad-shouldered and lean-hipped and as handsome of feature as Rhys Delmar, spoke to his childhood friend.

"Luck is mine that you have served as overseer on an estate nearly as large as this one," Rhys replied. "I doubt I could manage it any better than did Andrew Knox in his final years."

"Not when your mind is ever on the wilderness and that hellion bride you left behind."

"Teddy Gamble didn't want a husband." He turned away from Alain and strode across the marble floor of a room with an arched ceiling that rose thirty feet above his head. He didn't want Alain to see the disappointment in his eyes. Any other man in his place would be happy beyond measure. As he should be. All his life he had dreamed of being master of an estate such as now was his. One who has been a servant has such dreams. But now that all the wealth he could aspire to was his, he'd trade it all for what he'd left behind in Arizona. Teddy. And his babies.

Mae Sprayberry had written about the babies. A boy and a girl. His and Teddy's. Fine and feisty. Like their mother. Not a word from Teddy. But he'd understood. She'd made her one and only concession to him when she'd agreed to take his name.

"She might have changed her mind," Alain suggested.

Rhys shook his head. He'd never meant to stay

away, but at first he had not been free to leave, not until the magistrates had taken their merry time to clear his name. Then there had been the matter of the inheritance to be settled. Another month had passed. Then another. And he'd been afraid of going back and finding all he'd get from Teddy would be a quick invitation to leave Wishbone.

Restless, Rhys walked out into one of the gardens Alain was in the process of restoring. The night was clear and overhead the moon was red as blood. He hadn't seen a moon like that since the night after he and Teddy had gotten away from Taviz.

It was the night he had known with certainty she would always have his heart. Damn her!

The stage rumbled into Wishbone throwing up a wake of dust that hovered in the still, hot air what seemed an unnaturally long time.

Teddy Gamble, in fringed buckskins and wearing a silver and turquoise band around her throat, came out to meet it. "How was the run, Curly?" she called to the new driver.

"Smooth as glass, Teddy," he said and tipped his white Stetson to her. "Got a passenger for you. Says he's been real anxious to get here."

Smiling, Teddy swung open the door of the coach. "Welcome, strang—"

Rhys bounded out, looking fit and fancy as she'd ever seen him in a finely tailored black coat and trousers. As his feet hit the ground he gave a tug to a vest of leaf green brocade and turned that nettling half-smile of his on Teddy.

She found her heart up in her throat and her temper ablaze as she stared at him in surprise and open suspicion. "What in all of hell brings you back?" she said.

He raised his brows. The pale blue eyes beneath them shone brightly and seemed to touch her everywhere. "Why, Teddy. I thought you'd be happy to see me."

"In a pig's eye," she retorted. "Now spill it out. What brings you back?"

"I've a few reasons for being here," he said. "There's the matter of our marriage to be dealt with. And there's the matter of our babies." Aware that, squared off on the street, they had begun to draw the whole town's attention, Rhys caught her by the arm and tugged her toward the office.

"It's about time you remembered," she told him.

Her besieged heart slammed back into her chest where it belonged as she and Rhys slipped through the doors of the stage office, but now it beat so fast she felt lightheaded. Her arm tingled as if burned where his fingers lay against it. The tingling sensation slowly spread, not ceasing when he let her go. It flowed over her body like a warm wash of rain. She felt her resistance to him, which she had been stoking and building all the months he had been gone, washing away like fallen leaves before a flood.

She felt the old yearning for him sliding in. Whether she wanted to or not, she remembered how his touch had moved her, how his hands had slid with gentle determination over her skin, how even the lightest kiss from his lips could rouse her, how he filled her. And, dammit! She wanted him. With all her heart she wanted him and had since the day he had gone away.

None of it was supposed to be like this. She had thought she would want to shoot him on sight but that wasn't at all what she wanted.

He didn't love her, she reminded herself bitterly. And she didn't know why he had come back.

They were inside the small office. Rhys noted that it had changed little in the months he'd been gone. The floor was crowded with crates and boxes, the desk littered with tickets and papers. A new schedule hung tacked to the wall, an indication not quite everything was the same. She had added another run out of the mines which meant business was good. He was glad.

"I never forgot about you, Teddy," he said. "I never forgot about anything." His voice had lost the taunting edge. "You may have heard my circumstances have changed since I left."

Teddy braced herself and scowled. "I heard you got yourself a title and enough money to salt down a gold mine. And I can see you spent a pretty penny on those dandy duds. Anything I'm leaving out?"

He nodded. She wasn't making this reunion easy in the least and he was finding it awfully hard to sit and be civil when what he wanted was to sweep her in his arms and tell her that she was his wife and that he loved her from the depths of his heart. He needed to hold and touch and taste her, feel the provocative warmth of her body around him. He needed her. Always.

DEVIL MOON

"I got myself cleared of murder," he said. "So you can add a good name to the list."

Teddy rested her hands on her hips. "About that name. Knox, isn't it? Am I expected to change my name and that of the babies to Knox?" She cocked her head to one side. "Teddy Knox," she spoke the name thoughtfully. "Can't say I like the sound of it."

"You plan to keep my name then?"

"Knox?"

"Delmar."

She smiled and nodded. Her world was changing again and she was heartily glad of the direction it was going. "Seeing that you paid so much for me to take it, seems only fair I keep it."

"And me?" Hope surged inside him.

Her hands slid off her hips and she gave him a shove that rocked him back on his heels. All his hope evaporated until, in the next instant, she grabbed him and wrapped her arms around his waist.

Teddy felt a shudder rake through him as her arms closed about him. She was trembling too as, eyes darkening, she raised her face to his and answered softly. "I could use a fancy man around. If he's good with his hands." She brought her mouth against his. "And with his lips. And—"

"And?"

"And if he loves me."

"He does, Teddy. And he'd very much like to see his son and daughter. And he'd like to show their mother what else he's good at . . . if she's willing."

"She is."

Rhys bound Teddy to him with his arms and kissed

her with all the fullness of his love, drinking her in like sweet, cool wine, slowly, deeply. He had all the time in the world. And this was a beginning.

Taylor—made Romance From Zebra Books

WHISPERED KISSES (3830, $4.99/5.99)
Beautiful Texas heiress Laura Leigh Webster never imagined that her biggest worry on her African safari would be the handsome Jace Elliot, her tour guide. Laura's guardian, Lord Chadwick Hamilton, warns her of Jace's dangerous past; she simply cannot resist the lure of his strong arms and the passion of his *Whispered Kisses*.

KISS OF THE NIGHT WIND (3831, $4.99/$5.99)
Carrie Sue Strover thought she was leaving trouble behind her when she deserted her brother's outlaw gang to live her life as schoolmarm Carolyn Starns. On her journey, her stagecoach was attacked and she was rescued by handsome T.J. Rogue. T.J. plots to have Carrie lead him to her brother's cohorts who murdered his family. T.J., however, soon succumbs to the beautiful runaway's charms and loving caresses.

FORTUNE'S FLAMES (3825, $4.99/$5.99)
Impatient to begin her journey back home to New Orleans, beautiful Maren James was furious when Captain Hawk delayed the voyage by searching for stowaways. Impatience gave way to uncontrollable desire once the handsome captain searched *her* cabin. He was looking for illegal passengers; what he found was wild passion with a woman he knew was unlike all those he had known before!

PASSIONS WILD AND FREE (3828, $4.99/$5.99)
After seeing her family and home destroyed by the cruel and hateful Epson gang, Randee Hollis swore revenge. She knew she found the perfect man to help her—gunslinger Marsh Logan. Not only strong and brave, Marsh had the ebony hair and light blue eyes to make Randee forget her hate and seek the love and passion that only he could give her.

Available wherever paperbacks are sold, or order direct from the Publisher. Send cover price plus 50¢ per copy for mailing and handling to Penguin USA, P.O. Box 999, c/o Dept. 17109, Bergenfield, NJ 07621. Residents of New York and Tennessee must include sales tax. DO NOT SEND CASH.

PENELOPE NERI'S STORIES WILL WARM YOU THROUGH THE LONGEST, COLDEST NIGHT!

BELOVED SCOUNDREL	(1799, $3.95/$4.95)
CHERISH THE NIGHT	(3654, $5.99/$6.99)
CRIMSON ANGEL	(3359, $4.50/$5.50)
DESERT CAPTIVE	(2447, $3.95/$4.95)
FOREVER AND BEYOND	(3115, $4.95/$5.95)
FOREVER IN HIS ARMS	(3385, $4.95/$5.95)
JASMINE PARADISE	(3062, $4.50/$5.50)
MIDNIGHT CAPTIVE	(2593, $3.95/$4.95)
NO SWEETER PARADISE	(4024, $5.99/$6.99)
PASSION'S BETRAYAL	(3291, $4.50/$5.50)
SEA JEWEL	(3013, $4.50/$5.50)

Available wherever paperbacks are sold, or order direct from the Publisher. Send cover price plus 50¢ per copy for mailing and handling to Penguin USA, P.O. Box 999, c/o Dept. 17109, Bergenfield, NJ 07621. Residents of New York and Tennessee must include sales tax. DO NOT SEND CASH.

WHAT'S LOVE GOT TO DO WITH IT?

Everything . . . Just ask Kathleen Drymon . . . and Zebra Books

CASTAWAY ANGEL	(3569-1, $4.50/$5.50)
GENTLE SAVAGE	(3888-7, $4.50/$5.50)
MIDNIGHT BRIDE	(3265-X, $4.50/$5.50)
VELVET SAVAGE	(3886-0, $4.50/$5.50)
TEXAS BLOSSOM	(3887-9, $4.50/$5.50)
WARRIOR OF THE SUN	(3924-7, $4.99/$5.99)

Available wherever paperbacks are sold, or order direct from the Publisher. Send cover price plus 50¢ per copy for mailing and handling to Penguin USA, P.O. Box 999, c/o Dept. 17109, Bergenfield, NJ 07621. Residents of New York and Tennessee must include sales tax. DO NOT SEND CASH.

DISCOVER DEANA JAMES!

CAPTIVE ANGEL (2524, $4.50/$5.50)
Abandoned, penniless, and suddenly responsible for the biggest tobacco plantation in Colleton County, distraught Caroline Gillard had no time to dissolve into tears. By day the willowy redhead labored to exhaustion beside her slaves . . . but each night left her restless with longing for her wayward husband. She'd make the sea captain regret his betrayal until he begged her to take him back!

MASQUE OF SAPPHIRE (2885, $4.50/$5.50)
Judith Talbot-Harrow left England with a heavy heart. She was going to America to join a father she despised and a sister she distrusted. She was certainly in no mood to put up with the insulting actions of the arrogant Yankee privateer who boarded her ship, ransacked her things, then "apologized" with an indecent, brazen kiss! She vowed that someday he'd pay dearly for the liberties he had taken and the desires he had awakened.

SPEAK ONLY LOVE (3439, $4.95/$5.95)
Long ago, the shock of her mother's death had robbed Vivian Marleigh of the power of speech. Now she was being forced to marry a bitter man with brandy on his breath. But she could not say what was in her heart. It was up to the viscount to spark the fires that would melt her icy reserve.

WILD TEXAS HEART (3205, $4.95/$5.95)
Fan Breckenridge was terrified when the stranger found her near-naked and shivering beneath the Texas stars. Unable to remember who she was or what had happened, all she had in the world was the deed to a patch of land that might yield oil . . . and the fierce loving of this wildcatter who called himself Irons.

Available wherever paperbacks are sold, or order direct from the Publisher. Send cover price plus 50¢ per copy for mailing and handling to Penguin USA, P.O. Box 999, c/o Dept. 17109, Bergenfield, NJ 07621. Residents of New York and Tennessee must include sales tax. DO NOT SEND CASH.